SAVVY. SEXY. SENSATIONAL.

FANCY PANTS

Francesca Day didn't mean to break so many hearts, but if you're beautiful, rich and spoiled rotten, these things happen. When fate leaves her flat broke, she packs her Louis Vuitton bags to cash in on the American dream. Only no one tells her that first she has to find herself—and real life is a road map Francesca can't figure out. Without her wealthy props, she's just a willful, lost little girl who's got to become a woman real fast . . .

Dallas Beaudine, the Lone Star State's last genuine Grade-A male, takes a wrong turn on one of life's back roads and runs smack into Francesca. Hollywood handsome and a lot smarter than he lets on, Dallie is pursued by his own devils. He damn sure doesn't need another one—especially not a saucy little spitfire who rakes up too many long-lost dreams . . .

Scarlett and Rhett . . .   Tracy and Hepburn . . .   And now, Francesca and Dallie, two marvelous lovers who will capture America's heart!

"Pure unadulterated fun! An entertaining, provocative, sexy, witty riches-to-rags-to-riches story."

—*Rave Reviews*

"Stylish, sophisticated, written with panache, *FANCY PANTS* is absorbing and entertaining and certain to win Susan Elizabeth Phillips a multitude of new admirers."

—Jennifer Wilde

Books by Susan Elizabeth Phillips

Fancy Pants*
Glitter Baby
Hot Shot*
Risen Glory

*Published by POCKET BOOKS

FANCY PANTS

SUSAN ELIZABETH PHILLIPS

POCKET BOOKS

New York   London   Toronto   Sydney   Tokyo   Singapore

Blouse courtesy of Della Roufogali
Russian lynx coat courtesy of Sol Feldman Furs, NY
Diamond necklace courtesy of Kenneth Jay Lane

An *Original* Publication of POCKET BOOKS

POCKET BOOKS, a division of Simon & Schuster Inc.
1230 Avenue of the Americas, New York, NY 10020

ISBN: 0-671-74715-0

First Pocket Books printing October 1989

10 9 8 7 6 5 4 3 2

POCKET and colophon are registered trademarks of Simon & Schuster Inc.

Printed in the U.S.A.

To my parents,
with all my love

ACKNOWLEDGMENTS

My special thanks to the following people and organizations:

Bill Phillips—who plays a terrific eighteen holes and steered me away from the bunkers. I love you.

Steve Axelrod—the best there is.

Claire Zion—a good editor is a necessity; one who also has a sense of humor is a blessing.

The Professional Golfers' Association—for so patiently answering my questions.

The Statue of Liberty–Ellis Island Foundation—keepers of the flame.

The management and staff of WBRW, Bridgewater, New Jersey—a small radio station with a 50,000-watt heart.

Dr. Lois Lee and Children of the Night—God bless.

Charlotte Smith, Dr. Robert Pallay, Glen Winger, Steve Adams.

Rita Hallbright at the Kenya Safari Company.

Linda Barlow—for her continued friendship and many helpful suggestions.

Ty and Zachary Phillips—who truly do light up my life.

Lydia Kihm—my favorite sister.

Susan Elizabeth Phillips

Send these, the homeless, tempest-tossed, to me . . .

—Emma Lazarus,
    "The New Colossus"

FANCY PANTS

Prologue

Sable sucks," Francesca Serritella Day muttered under her breath as a series of strobes flashed in her face. She ducked her head deeper into the high collar of her Russian fur and wished it were daytime so she could slip on her dark glasses.

"That's not exactly a popularly held opinion, darling," Prince Stefan Marko Brancuzi said as he gripped her arm and guided her through the crowd of paparazzi that had stationed themselves outside New York City's La Côte Basque to photograph the celebrities as they emerged from the private party inside. Stefan Brancuzi was the sole monarch of a tiny Balkan principality that was rapidly replacing overcrowded Monaco as the new refuge for the tax-burdened wealthy, but he wasn't the one in whom the photographers were most interested. It was the beautiful Englishwoman at his side who had attracted their attention, along with the attention of much of the American public.

As Stefan led her toward his waiting limousine, Francesca lifted her gloved hand in a futile gesture that did nothing at all to stop the barrage of questions still being hurled at her—questions about her job, her relationship with Stefan, even a question about her friendship with the star of the hit television series, "China Colt."

When she and Stefan were finally settled into the plush leather seats and the limo had pulled out into the late night

1

traffic on East Fifty-fifth Street, she groaned. "That media circus happened because of this coat. The press hardly ever bothers you. It's me. If I'd worn my old raincoat, we could have slipped right through without attracting any attention." Stefan regarded her with amusement. She frowned reproachfully at him. "There's an important moral lesson to be learned here, Stefan."

"What's that, darling?"

"In the face of world famine, women who wear sable deserve what they get."

He laughed. "You would have been recognized no matter what you'd worn. I've seen you stop traffic in a sweat suit."

"I can't help it," she replied glumly. "It's in my blood. The curse of the Serritellas."

"Really, Francesca, I never knew a woman who hated being beautiful as much as you do."

She muttered something he couldn't hear, which was probably just as well, and shoved her hands deep into the pockets of her coat, unimpressed, as always, with any reference to her incandescent physical beauty. After a long wait, she broke the silence. "From the day I was born, my face has brought me nothing but trouble."

Not to mention that marvelous little body of yours, Stefan thought, but he wisely kept that comment to himself. As Francesca gazed absently out the tinted glass window, he took advantage of her distraction to study the incredible features that had captivated so many people.

He still remembered the words of a well-known fashion editor who, determined to avoid all the Vivien Leigh clichés that had been applied to Francesca over the years, had written, "Francesca Day, with her chestnut hair, oval face, and sage green eyes, looks like a fairy-tale princess who spends her afternoons spinning flax into gold in the gardens outside her own storybook castle." Privately, the fashion editor had been less fanciful. "I know in my heart that Francesca Day absolutely never has to go to the bathroom. . . ."

Stefan gestured toward the walnut and brass bar tucked discreetly into the side of the limo. "Do you want a drink?"

"No, thanks. I don't think I can tolerate any more alcohol." She hadn't been sleeping well and her British accent was more pronounced than usual. Her coat slipped open and she glanced down at her beaded Armani gown. Armani gown . . . Fendi fur . . . Mario Valentino shoes. She closed her eyes, suddenly remembering an earlier time, a hot autumn afternoon when she'd been lying in the dirt in the middle of a Texas road wearing a pair of dirty blue jeans with twenty-five cents tucked in the back pocket. That day had been the beginning for her. The beginning and the end.

The limo turned south on Fifth Avenue, and her memories slipped further back to those childhood years in England before she had even known that places like Texas existed. What a spoiled little monster she had been— pampered and petted as her mother Chloe swept her from one European playground to another, one party to the next. Even as a child she'd been perfectly arrogant—so absolutely confident that the famous Serritella beauty would crack open the world for her and make all the pieces fall back together into any new configuration she wished. Little Francesca—a vain, feckless creature, completely unprepared for what life was going to hand her.

She had been twenty-one years old that day in 1976 when she lay in the dust on the Texas road. Twenty-one years old, unmarried, alone, and pregnant.

Now she was nearly thirty-two, and although she owned every possession she had ever dreamed about, she felt just as alone now as she had been on that hot autumn afternoon. She squeezed her eyes shut, trying to imagine what course her life would have taken if she'd stayed in England. But America had changed her so utterly that she couldn't even envision it.

She smiled to herself. When Emma Lazarus had written the poem about huddled masses yearning to breathe free, she certainly couldn't have been thinking of a vain young English girl arriving in this country wearing a cashmere sweater and carrying a Louis Vuitton suitcase. But poor little rich girls had to dream, too, and the dream of America had proven grand enough to encompass even her.

Stefan knew something was bothering Francesca. She had been unusually quiet all evening, not at all like herself. He had planned to ask her to marry him tonight, but now he wondered if he wouldn't do better to wait. She was so different from the other women he knew that he could never predict exactly how she would react to anything. He suspected the dozens of other men who had been in love with her had experienced something of the same problem.

If rumor could be believed, Francesca's first important conquest had occurred at age nine on board the yacht *Christina* when she had smitten Aristotle Onassis.

Rumors . . . There were so many of them surrounding Francesca, most of which couldn't possibly be true . . . except, considering the kind of life she had led, Stefan thought that perhaps they were. She had once told him quite casually that Winston Churchill had taught her how to play gin rummy, and everyone knew the Prince of Wales had courted her. One evening not long after they had met, they had been sipping champagne and exchanging anecdotes about their childhoods.

"Most babies are conceived in love," she had informed him, "but I was conceived on a display platform in the center of Harrods' fur salon."

As the limousine swept past Cartier, Stefan smiled to himself. An amusing story, but he didn't believe a word of it.

The Old World

Chapter
1

When Francesca was first placed in her mother's arms, Chloe Serritella Day burst into tears and insisted that the sisters at the private London hospital where she had given birth had lost her baby. Any imbecile could see that this ugly little creature with its mashed head and swollen eyelids could not possibly have come from her own exquisite body.

Since no husband was present to comfort the hysterical Chloe, it was left to the sisters to assure her that most newborns weren't at their best for several days. Chloe ordered them to take away the ugly little imposter and not come back until they had found her own dear baby. She then reapplied her makeup and greeted her visitors—among them a French film star, the secretary of the British Home Office, and Salvador Dali—with a tearful account of the terrible tragedy that had been perpetrated upon her. The visitors, long accustomed to the beautiful Chloe's dramatics, merely patted her hand and promised to look into the matter. Dali, in a burst of magnanimity, announced he would paint a surrealistic version of the infant in question as a christening gift, but mercifully lost interest in the project and sent a set of vermeil goblets instead.

A week passed. On the day she was to be released from the hospital, the sisters helped Chloe dress in a loose-fitting black Balmain sheath with a wide organdy collar and cuffs.

Afterward, they guided her into a wheelchair and deposited the rejected infant in her arms. The intervening time had done little to improve the baby's appearance, but in the moment she gazed down at the bundle in her arms, Chloe experienced one of her lightning-swift mood changes. Peering into the mottled face, she announced to one and all that the third generation of Serritella beauty was now assured. No one had the bad manners to disagree, which, as it turned out, was just as well, for within a matter of months, Chloe had been proved correct.

Chloe's sensitivity on the subject of female beauty had its roots in her own childhood. As a girl she had been plump, with an extra fold of fat squaring off her waist and small fleshy pads obscuring the delicate bones of her face. She was not heavy enough to be considered obese in the eyes of the world, but was merely plump enough to feel ugly inside, especially in comparison to her sleek and stylish mother, the great Italian-born couturiere, Nita Serritella. It was not until 1947, the summer when Chloe was twelve years old, that anyone told her she was beautiful.

Home on a brief holiday from one of the Swiss boarding schools where she spent too much of her childhood, she was sitting as inconspicuously as possible with her full hips perched on a gilt chair in the corner of her mother's elegant salon on the rue de la Paix. She watched with both resentment and envy as Nita, pencil slim in a severely cut black suit with oversize raspberry satin lapels, conferred with an elegantly dressed customer. Her mother wore her blue-black hair cut short and straight, so that it fell forward over the pale skin of her left cheek in a great comma-shaped curl, and her Modigliani neck supported ropes of perfectly matched black pearls. The pearls, along with the contents of a small wall safe in her bedroom, were gifts from Nita's admirers, internationally prosperous men who were only too happy to buy jewels for a woman successful enough to buy her own. One of those men had been Chloe's father, although Nita professed not to remember which one, and she had certainly never for a moment considered marrying him.

The attractive blonde who was receiving Nita's attention

in the salon that afternoon spoke Spanish, her accent surprisingly common for one who held so much of the world's attention that particular summer of 1947. Chloe followed the conversation with half her attention and devoted the other half to studying the reed-thin mannequins who were parading through the center of the salon modeling Nita's latest designs. Why couldn't she be thin and self-assured like those mannequins? Chloe wondered. Why couldn't she look exactly like her mother, especially since they had the same black hair, the same green eyes? If only she were beautiful, Chloe thought, maybe her mother would stop looking at her with such disgust. For the hundredth time she resolved to give up pastries so that she could win her mother's approval—and for the hundredth time, she felt that uncomfortable sinking sensation in her stomach that told her she didn't have the willpower. Next to Nita's all-consuming strength of purpose, Chloe felt like a swans-down powder puff.

The blonde suddenly looked up from a drawing she had been studying and, without warning, let her liquid brown eyes come to rest on Chloe. In her curiously harsh Spanish, she remarked, "That little one will be a great beauty someday. She looks very much like you."

Nita glanced over at Chloe with ill-concealed disdain. "I see no resemblance at all, *señora*. And she will never be a beauty until she learns to push away her fork."

Nita's customer lifted a hand weighted down with several garish rings and gestured toward Chloe. "Come over here, *querida*. Come give Evita a kiss."

For a moment Chloe didn't move as she tried to absorb what the woman had said. Then she rose hesitantly from her chair and crossed the salon, embarrassingly aware of the pudgy calves showing beneath the hem of her cotton summer skirt. When she reached the woman, she leaned down and deposited a self-conscious but nonetheless grateful kiss on the softly fragrant cheek of Eva Perón.

"Fascist bitch!" Nita Serritella hissed later, as the First Lady of Argentina departed through the salon's front doors. She slipped an ebony cigarette holder between her lips only to withdraw it abruptly, leaving a scarlet smear on the end.

"It makes my flesh crawl to touch her! Everyone knows there wasn't a Nazi in Europe who couldn't find shelter with Perón and his cronies in Argentina."

The memories of the German occupation of Paris were still fresh in Nita's mind, and she held nothing but contempt for Nazi sympathizers. Still, she was a practical woman, and Chloe knew that her mother saw no sense in sending Eva Perón's money, no matter how ill-gained, from the rue de la Paix to the avenue Montaigne, where the house of Dior reigned supreme.

After that, Chloe clipped photographs of Eva Perón from the newspapers and pasted them in a scrapbook with a red cover. Whenever Nita's criticisms became especially biting, Chloe looked at the pictures, leaving an occasional chocolate smudge on the pages as she remembered how Eva Perón had said she would be a great beauty someday.

The winter she was fourteen her fat miraculously disappeared along with her sweet tooth, and the legendary Serritella bones were finally brought into definition. She began spending hours gazing into the mirror, entranced by the reed-slim image before her. Now, she told herself, everything would be different. For as long as she could remember, she had felt like an outcast at school, but suddenly she found herself part of the inner circle. She didn't understand that the other girls were more attracted to her newfound air of self-confidence than to her twenty-two-inch waist. For Chloe Serritella, beauty meant acceptance.

Nita seemed pleased with her weight loss, so when Chloe went home to Paris for her summer holiday, she found the courage to show her mother sketches of some dresses she'd designed with the hope of someday becoming a couturiere herself. Nita laid out the sketches on her worktable, lit a cigarette, and dissected each one with the critical eye that had made her a great designer.

"This line is ridiculous. And the proportion is all wrong here. See how you ruined this one with too much detail? Where is your eye, Chloe? Where is your eye?"

Chloe snatched the sketches from the table and never tried to design again.

When she returned to school, Chloe dedicated herself to becoming prettier, wittier, and more popular than any of her classmates, determined that no one would ever suspect that an awkward fat girl still lived inside her. She learned to dramatize the most trivial events of her day with grand gestures and extravagant sighs until everything she did seemed more important than anything the others could possibly do. Gradually even the most mundane occurrence in Chloe Serritella's life became fraught with high drama.

At sixteen, she gave her virginity to the brother of a friend in a gazebo facing Lake Lucerne. The experience was awkward and uncomfortable, but sex made Chloe feel slim. She quickly made up her mind to try the whole thing again with someone more experienced.

In the spring of 1953, when Chloe was eighteen, Nita died unexpectedly from a ruptured appendix. Chloe sat stunned and silent through her mother's funeral, too numb to understand that the intensity of her grief sprang not so much from her mother's death as from the feeling that she'd never had a mother at all. Afraid to be alone, she stumbled into the bed of a wealthy Polish count many years her senior. He provided her with a temporary refuge from her fears and six months later helped her sell Nita's salon for a staggering amount of money.

The count eventually returned to his wife and Chloe set about living on her inheritance. Being young, rich, and without family, she quickly attracted the indolent young men who wove themselves like gilded threads through the fabric of international society. She became something of a collector, dabbling with one after another as she searched for the man who would give her the unconditional love she'd never received from her mother, the man who would make her stop feeling like an unhappy fat girl.

Jonathan "Black Jack" Day entered her life on the opposite side of a roulette wheel in a Berkeley Square gambling club. Black Jack Day had received his name not from his looks but from his penchant for games of risk. At twenty-five, he had already destroyed three high-performance sports cars and a significantly larger number of women. A wickedly handsome American playboy from Chicago, he had chestnut hair that fell in an unruly lock over his forehead, a roguish mustache, and a seven-goal handicap in polo. In many ways he was no different from the other young

11

hedonists who had become so much a part of Chloe's life; he drank gin, wore exquisitely tailored suits, and changed playgrounds with the seasons. But the other men lacked Jack Day's reckless streak, his ability to risk everything—even the fortune he had inherited in American railroads—on a single spin of the wheel.

Fully conscious of his eyes upon her over the spinning roulette wheel, Chloe watched the small ivory ball jostle from *rouge* to *noir* and back again before finally coming to rest on black 17. She permitted herself to look up and found Jack Day gazing at her over the table. He smiled, crinkling his mustache. She smiled back, confident that she looked her very best in a silver-gray Jacques Fath confection of satin and tulle that emphasized the highlights in her dark hair, the paleness of her skin, and the green depths in her eyes. "You can't seem to lose tonight," she said. "Are you always this lucky?"

"Not always," he replied. "Are you?"

"Me?" She emitted one of her long, dramatic sighs. "I've lost at everything tonight. *Je suis misérable.* I'm never lucky."

He withdrew a cigarette from a silver case while his eyes trailed a reckless path down her body. "Of course you're lucky. You've just met me, haven't you? And I'm going to take you home tonight."

Chloe was both intrigued and aroused by his boldness, and her hand closed instinctively around the edge of the table for support. She felt as if his tarnished silver eyes were melting through her gown and burning into the deepest recesses of her body. Without being able to define exactly what it was that set Black Jack apart from the rest, she sensed that only the most exceptional woman could win the heart of this supremely self-confident man, and if she was that woman, she could forever stop worrying about the fat girl inside.

But as much as she wanted him, Chloe held herself back. In the year since her mother's death, she had grown more perceptive about men than about herself. She had observed the reckless glitter in his eyes as the ivory ball clattered through the compartments of the spinning roulette wheel, and she suspected that he would not highly value what he could obtain too easily. "I'm sorry," she replied coolly. "I have other plans." Before he could respond, she picked up her evening bag and left the room.

He telephoned the next day, but she gave her maid orders to say she was out. She spotted him at a different gambling club a week later and after giving him a tantalizing glimpse of herself, she slipped out the back before he could approach. The days passed, and she found she could think of nothing else but the handsome young playboy from Chicago. Once again he telephoned; once again she refused the call. Later that same night she saw him at the theater and gave him a casual nod, a hint of a smile, before she moved away to her box.

The third time he telephoned, she took the call but pretended not to remember who he was. He chuckled dryly and told her, "I'm coming for you in half an hour, Chloe Serritella. If you're not ready, I'll never see you again."

"Half an hour? I can't possibly—" But he had already hung up.

Her hand began to tremble as she replaced the receiver on the cradle. In her mind she saw a spinning roulette wheel, the ivory ball skipping from *rouge* to *noir, noir* to *rouge,* in this game they were playing. With trembling hands, she dressed in a white wool sheath with ocelot cuffs, then added a small hat topped by an illusion veil. She answered the door chimes herself exactly half an hour later.

He led her down the walk to a sporty red Isotta-Fraschini, which he proceeded to drive through the streets of Knightsbridge at breathtaking speed using only the fingers of his right hand on the steering wheel. She gazed at him out of the corner of her eye, adoring the lock of chestnut hair that fell so carelessly over his forehead as much as the fact that he was a hot-blooded American instead of someone predictably European.

Eventually he stopped at an out-of-the-way restaurant where he brushed his hand against hers whenever she reached for her wineglass. She felt herself aching with desire for him. Under the intensity of those restless silver eyes, she felt wildly beautiful and as thin inside as she was outside. Everything about him stirred her senses—the way he walked, the sound of his voice, the scent of tobacco on his breath. Jack Day was the ultimate trophy, the final affirmation of her own beauty.

As they left the restaurant, he pressed her against the trunk of a sycamore tree and gave her a dark, seductive kiss. Slipping his hands behind her, he cupped her buttocks. "I want you," he murmured into her open mouth.

Her body was so replete with desire that it caused her actual pain to let him go. "You're too fast for me, Jack. I need time."

He laughed and tweaked her chin, as if he were especially pleased with how well she played his game; then he squeezed her breasts just as an elderly couple came out of the restaurant and looked their way. On the drive home, he kept her amused with lively anecdotes and said nothing about seeing her again.

Two days later when her maid announced he was on the telephone, Chloe shook her head, refusing to take the call. Then she ran to her room and indulged in a passionate fit of weeping, fearing she was pushing him too far but afraid to risk losing his interest by doing anything else. The next time she saw him at a gallery opening, he wore a henna-haired showgirl on his arm. Chloe pretended not to notice.

He showed up on her doorstep the following afternoon and took her for a drive in the country. She said she had a previous engagement and couldn't dine with him that evening.

The game of chance went on, and Chloe could think of nothing else. When Jack wasn't with her, she conjured him in her imagination—the restless movements, the careless lock of hair, the roguish mustache. She could barely think beyond the thick, wet tension that suffused her body, but still she refused his sexual overtures.

He spoke cruelly while he traced the shape of her ear with his lips. "I don't think you're woman enough for me."

She curled her hand over the back of his neck. "I don't think you're rich enough for me."

The ivory ball clattered around the contours of the roulette wheel, *rouge* to *noir*, *noir* to *rouge*. . . . Chloe knew that it would make its final drop soon.

"Tonight," Jack said when she answered the telephone. "Be ready for me at midnight."

"Midnight? Don't be ridiculous, darling. That's impossible."

"Midnight or never, Chloe. The game's over."

That night she slipped a black velvet suit with rhinestone buttons over a champagne-colored crepe de chine blouse. Her eyes shone brightly back at her from the mirror as she brushed her dark hair into a soft pageboy. Black Jack Day, clad in a tuxedo, appeared at her door exactly at the stroke of midnight. At the sight of him, her insides felt as liquid as the scented lotion she had stroked over her flushed skin. Instead of the Isotta-Fraschini, he led her to a chauffeured Daimler and announced that he was taking her to Harrods.

She laughed. "Isn't midnight a little late to go on a shopping expedition?"

He said nothing, merely smiling as he settled back into the soft leather seats and began chatting about a polo pony he thought he might buy from the Aga Khan. Before long, the Daimler pulled up to Harrods' green and gold awning. Chloe looked at the dim lighting glowing through the doors of the deserted department store. "Harrods doesn't seem to have stayed open, Jack, not even for you."

"We'll see about that, won't we, pet?" The chauffeur opened the rear door for them, and Jack helped her out.

To her astonishment, a liveried doorman appeared from behind Harrods' glass door and after a surreptitious look to see if anyone on the street was watching, unlocked the door and held it open for them. "Welcome to Harrods, Mr. Day."

She looked at the open door in astonishment. Surely even Black Jack Day couldn't simply walk into the most famous department store in the world long after closing hours with no salespeople present. When she didn't move, Jack urged her forward with a firm pressure on the small of her back. As soon as they were inside the department store, the doorman did the most astonishing thing—he tipped his hat, walked out onto the street, and locked the door behind him. She couldn't believe what she'd seen, and she looked toward Jack for some explanation.

"The roulette wheel has been especially kind to me since I met you, pet. I thought you might enjoy a private shopping spree."

"But the store is closed. I don't see any clerks."

"All the better."

She pressed him for an explanation, but he would say little beyond the fact that he'd made a private—and she was certain quite illegal—arrangement with several of Harrods' newer and less scrupulous employees.

"But aren't there people who work here at night? Cleaning staff? Night security?"

"You ask too many questions, pet. What good is money if it can't buy pleasure? Let's see what catches your fancy this evening." He picked out a silver and gold scarf from a display and draped it over the velvet collar of her jacket.

"Jack, I can't just take this!"

"Relax, pet. The store will be well compensated. Now, are you going to bore me with your worries or can we enjoy ourselves?"

Chloe could barely believe what was happening. There were no salespeople in sight, no custodians or guards. Was this great department store really hers? She glanced down at the scarf draping her neck and uttered a breathless exclamation. He gestured toward the cornucopia of elegant merchandise. "Go ahead. Pick something."

With a reckless giggle, she reached out and pulled a sequined handbag from a display, then looped the braided cord over her shoulder. "Very nice," he said.

She threw her arms around his neck. "You are absolutely the most exciting man in the world, Jack Day! How I adore you!"

His palms crept down from her waist to curve around her buttocks and pull her hips tight against his own. "And you're the most exciting woman. I couldn't allow our love affair to be consummated in any place ordinary, could I?"

Noir to *rouge . . . rouge* to *noir . . .* The hardness pressed against her belly kept her from mistaking his meaning, and she felt herself growing hot and cold at the same time. The game would end here . . . in Harrods. Only Jack Day could carry off something so outrageous. The thought of it made her head spin like a red and black wheel.

He pulled the purse from her shoulder, removed her velvet jacket, and draped them both over a display of silk umbrellas with rosewood handles. Then he took off his tuxedo coat and placed it with hers so that he stood before her in a white shirt with black jet studs securing the pleated front, his narrow waist wrapped with a dark cummerbund. "We'll get these later," he announced, resettling the scarf over her shoulders. "Let's explore."

He took her to Harrods' famous food hall with its great marble counters and frescoed ceiling. "Are you hungry?" he inquired, lifting a silver box of chocolates from a display.

"For you," she replied.

His mouth curved beneath his mustache. Removing the lid from the box, he pulled out a dark chocolate confection and bit into one side, opening the shell so that the center oozed a drizzle of creamy cherry liqueur. He quickly pressed it to her lips, sliding the candy back and forth so that some of the rich filling was transferred to her. Then he put the chocolate back into his own mouth and lowered his head to kiss her. As her lips opened, sweet and sticky with cherry liqueur, he pushed the chocolate shell forward with his tongue. Chloe received the candy with a moan, and her body became as liquid and formless as the fluid center.

When he finally drew away, he selected a bottle of champagne, uncorked it, and tilted it first to her lips and then to his own. "To the most outrageous woman in London," he said, leaning forward and licking off a last speck of chocolate that clung to the corner of her mouth.

They wandered through the first floor, picking up a pair of gloves, a nosegay of silk violets, a hand-painted jewelry box, and placing them in a pile to be reclaimed later. Finally, they arrived at the perfume hall, and the heady mixture of the finest scents in the world washed over her, their fragrances undisturbed by the herds of people who thronged along the carpeted aisles during the day.

When they reached the center, he dropped her arm and turned her to face him. He began unbuttoning her blouse, and she felt a strange mixture of excitement and embarrassment. Regardless of the fact that the store was deserted, they *were* standing in the center of Harrods. "Jack, I—"

"Don't be a child, Chloe," he said. "Follow my lead."

A thrill shot through her as he pushed aside the satin material of her blouse to reveal the eggshell lacework on her bra. He pulled a cellophane-covered box of Joy from an open glass case and unwrapped it.

"Lean against the counter," he said, his voice as silky as the crepe de chine of her blouse. "Lay your arms along the edge."

She did as he asked, weak from the intensity in his silver eyes. Extracting the glass stopper from the neck of the bottle, he slipped it inside the lace edge of her bra. She drew in her breath as he rubbed its cold tip against her nipple.

"That feels good, doesn't it?" he murmured, his voice low and husky.

She nodded her head, incapable of speech. He inserted the stopper back inside the bottle, picked up another drop of Joy, and slid it beneath the other side of her bra to touch the opposite nipple. She could feel her flesh puckering beneath the slow, circling movement of the glass, and as the heat welled up inside her, Jack's handsome, reckless features seemed to swim before her.

He lowered the stopper and she felt his hand reach beneath the hem of her skirt and slowly move upward along her stocking. "Open your legs," he whispered. Clasping the edge of the counter beneath her hands, she did as he asked. He trailed the stopper up along the inside of one thigh, over the top of her stocking and onto the bare skin, moving it in slow circles to the very edge of her panties. She moaned and eased her legs open wider.

He laughed wickedly and withdrew his hand from beneath her skirt. "Not yet, pet. Not quite yet."

They moved through the silent store, going from one department to another, talking very little. He caressed her breasts as he fastened an antique Georgian pin to the collar of her blouse, rubbed her buttocks through her skirt while he slid a brush with a filigreed sterling handle down the back of her hair. She tried on a crocodile belt and a pair of kid shoes with needle-pointed toes. In the jewelry department, he removed her pearl earrings and replaced them with gold clips encircled with dozens of tiny diamonds. When she protested the expense, he laughed at her. "One spin of the roulette wheel, pet. Just one spin."

He found a white maribou boa and, pushing her against a marble column, slid the blouse from her shoulders. "You look too much like a schoolgirl," he declared, reaching behind her to remove her bra. The silky fabric slipped from his fingers to the carpeted floor, and she stood before him naked from the waist up.

She had large, full breasts capped by flat nipples the size of half-dollars, now hard and puckered from her excitement. He lifted each breast in his hand. She delighted in showing herself to him and stood perfectly still, the chill of the column decidedly welcome against the heat of her back. He tweaked her nipples, and she gasped. With a laugh, he picked up the soft white boa and draped it over her bare shoulders so that it covered her. Then he slowly moved the feathered ends back and forth.

"Jack—" She wanted him to take her there. She wanted to slide down the length of the column, open her legs, and take him inside her.

"I've developed a sudden craving for the taste of Joy," he whispered. Pushing the boa away on one side, he covered her large nipple with his mouth and began an insistent sucking.

She shivered as heat filled every part of her, burning her internal organs, searing her skin. "Please . . ." she murmured. "Oh, please . . . don't torture me any longer."

He pulled away from her, his restless eyes teasing. "A little longer, pet. I haven't finished playing yet. I think we should look at furs." And then, with a half-smile that told her he knew exactly how far he had pushed her, he rearranged the boa over her breasts, lightly scraping one nipple with his fingernail as he settled the ends in place.

"I don't want to look at furs," she said. "I want . . ."

But he led her to the elevator where he operated the levers as if he did it every day. As she rode upward with him, only the white feather boa covered her naked breasts.

When they reached the fur salon, Jack seemed to forget her. He moved along the racks, inspecting all the coats and stoles on display before selecting a full-length Russian lynx. The pelts were long and thick, the color silvery white. He studied the coat for a moment and then turned to her.

"Slip off your skirt."

Her fingers fumbled with the side zipper and for a moment she thought she would have to ask for help. But then the catch gave and she slid the skirt, along with the half-slip beneath, down over her hips and stepped out of them both. The ends of the boa brushed against the very top of her lacy white garter belt.

"The panties. Take the panties off for me."

Her breath was coming in short, soft gasps as she did as he asked, leaving only her garter belt and stockings in place. Without waiting to be told, she pulled the boa away from her breasts and dropped it to the floor, pushing her shoulders slightly back so he could feast on the sight of her breasts, ripe and outthrust, and her *mons* with its silky covering of dark hair framed by the lacy white straps of her garter belt.

He walked toward her, the magnificent coat outstretched in his hands, his eyes glittering like the jet studs in his snowy shirtfront. "To choose the right fur, you have to feel the pelts against your skin . . . against your breasts. . . ." His voice was as soft as the lynx pelts as he slid the fur along her body, using its texture to excite her. "Your breasts . . . your stomach and buttocks . . . the insides of your thighs. . . ."

She reached for the coat and clasped its fur to her skin. "Please. . . . You're torturing me. Please stop. . . ."

Once again he drew away, but this time only to slip the jet studs from the front of his shirt. Chloe watched him undress, her heart pounding and her throat tight with desire. When he stood naked before her, he took the coat from her arms and laid it with the pelts turned upward on a low display platform in the center of the room. Then he stepped up and drew her along to stand next to him.

The touch of his naked flesh against hers fired her excitement until she could barely remember to breathe. He ran his hands down along her sides, then turned her so that she faced out toward the display floor. Moving slightly behind her, he began stroking her breasts as if he were arousing her for an invisible audience watching silently in the dark salon. His hand trailed down over her stomach, along her thighs. She felt his penis jutting hard into the side of her hip. His hand moved between her legs, and the heat welled up from his touch, a yearning for release from a myriad of pounding pulses inside her.

He pushed her down into the soft, thick fur. It brushed the backs of her thighs as he opened them and positioned himself between her outspread knees. Turning her cheek into the soft pelts, she tilted up her hips, giving herself to him in the center of the fur salon, on a platform designed to display the very best that Harrods had to offer.

He glanced at his watch. "The guards should be coming back on duty right now. I wonder how long it will take them to follow our trail here." Then he thrust himself inside her.

It took a moment for his words to sink in. She let out a hoarse exclamation as she realized what he had done. "My God! You planned it like this, didn't you?"

He crushed her breasts in his hands and drove himself hard. "Of course."

The fire in her body and the terror of discovery joined together in a shattering explosion of feeling. As her orgasm crashed over her, she bit into the flesh of his shoulder. "Bastard . . ."

He laughed and then found his own release with a great, noisy groan.

They barely escaped the guards. Drawing on a minimum of his own clothing, Jack threw the lynx coat over Chloe's nakedness and dragged her to the stairway. As her bare feet flew down the steps, his reckless laughter rang in her ears. Before he left the store, he tossed her panties on top of a glass display case along with his engraved calling card.

The next day she received a note saying that his mother had been taken ill and he needed to return temporarily to Chicago. While she waited for him, Chloe lived in an agony of jumbled emotions—anger at the risk to which he had exposed her, excitement at the thrill he had given her, and a wrenching fear that he wouldn't come back. Four weeks passed, and then five. She tried to call him, but the connection was so bad she couldn't make herself understood. Two months slipped by. She was convinced he didn't love her. He was an adventurer, a thrill seeker. He had seen the fat girl inside and wanted nothing more to do with her.

Ten weeks after the night at Harrods, he reappeared as abruptly as he'd left. "Hello, pet," he said, standing in the doorway of her house with his cashmere suit coat carelessly hooked over his shoulder. "I've missed you."

She fell into his arms, sobbing out her relief at seeing him again. "Jack . . . Jack, my darling . . ."

He ran his thumb across her bottom lip, then kissed her. She drew back her hand and slapped him hard across the face. "I'm pregnant, you bastard!"

To her surprise, he immediately agreed to marry her, and they were wed three days later at the country home of one of her friends. As she stood next to her handsome bridegroom at the makeshift garden altar, Chloe knew that she was the happiest woman in the world. Black Jack Day could have married anyone, but he had chosen her. As the weeks passed, she determinedly ignored a rumor that his family had disinherited him when he was in Chicago. Instead, she daydreamed about her baby. How exquisite it would be to have the undivided love of two people, husband and child.

A month later, Jack disappeared, along with ten thousand pounds that had been resting in one of Chloe's bank accounts. When he reappeared six weeks later, Chloe shot him in the shoulder with a German Luger. A brief reconciliation followed, until Jack enjoyed another turn of good fortune at the gambling clubs and was off again.

On Valentine's Day 1955, Lady Luck permanently deserted Black Jack Day on the treacherous rain-slicked road between Nice and Monte Carlo. The ivory ball dropped for the last time into its compartment and the roulette wheel jerked to a final stop.

Chapter

2

One of the widowed Chloe's former lovers sent his Silver Cloud Rolls to take her home from the hospital after she'd given birth to her daughter. Comfortably ensconced in its plush leather seats, Chloe gazed down at the tiny flannel-wrapped baby who had been so spectacularly conceived in the center of Harrods' fur salon and ran her finger along the child's soft cheek. "My beautiful little Francesca," she murmured. "You won't need a father or a grandmother. You won't need anyone but me . . . because I'm going to give you everything in the world."

Unfortunately for Black Jack's daughter, Chloe proceeded to do exactly that.

In 1961, when Francesca was six years old and Chloe twenty-six, the two of them posed for a fashion spread in British *Vogue*. On the left side of the page was the often reproduced black-and-white Karsh photograph of Nita wearing a dress from her Gypsy collection, and on the right, Chloe and Francesca. Mother and daughter stood in a sea of crumpled white backdrop paper, both of them dressed in black. The white paper, their pale white skin, and their black velvet cloaks with flowing hoods made the photograph a study in contrasts. The only real color came from four jolts of piercing green—the unforgettable Serritella eyes leaping out from the page, shimmering like imperial jewels.

After the shock of the photograph had worn off, more critical readers noted that the glamorous Chloe's features were, perhaps, not quite as exotic as her mother's. But even the most critical could find no fault with the child. She looked like a fantasy of a perfect little girl, with a beatific smile and an angel's unearthly beauty shining in the oval of her tiny face. Only the photographer who had taken the picture viewed the child differently. He had two small scars, like twin white dashes, on the back of his hand where her sharp little front teeth had bitten through his skin.

"No, no, pet," Chloe had admonished the afternoon Francesca had bitten the photographer. "We mustn't bite the nice man." She wagged a long fingernail polished a shiny ebony at her daughter.

Francesca glared mutinously at her mother. She wanted to be home playing with her new puppet theater, not having her picture taken by an ugly man who kept telling her not to wiggle. She stubbed the toe of one shiny black patent leather shoe into the crumpled sheets of white backdrop paper and shook loose her chestnut curls from the confines of the black velvet hood. Mummy had promised her a special trip to Madame Tussaud's if she cooperated, and Francesca loved Madame Tussaud's. Even so, she wasn't absolutely certain she'd driven the best bargain possible. She loved Saint-Tropez, too.

After consoling the photographer over his injured hand, Chloe reached out to straighten her daughter's hair and then pulled back with a sudden yelp when she received the same treatment as the photographer. "Naughty girl!" she wailed, lifting her hand to her mouth and sucking on her wound.

Francesca's eyes immediately clouded with tears, and Chloe was furious with herself for having spoken so sharply. Quickly, she pulled her daughter close in a hug. "Never mind," she crooned. "Chloe isn't angry, darling. Bad Mummy. We'll buy you a pretty new dolly on our way home."

Francesca snuggled securely into her adoring mother's arms and peeked up at the photographer through the thick fringe of her lashes. Then she stuck out her tongue.

That afternoon marked the first but not the last time Chloe felt the sting of Francesca's tiny, sharp teeth. But even after three nannies had resigned, Chloe refused to admit that her daughter's biting was a problem. Francesca was merely high-spirited, and Chloe certainly had no intention of earning her daughter's hatred by making an issue out of something so trivial. Francesca's reign of terror might have continued unabated if a strange child had not bitten her back after a tussle over a swing in the park. When Francesca discovered that the experience was painful, the biting stopped. She wasn't a deliberately cruel child; she just wanted to get her way.

Chloe purchased a Queen Anne house on Upper Grosvenor Street not far from the American embassy and the eastern edge of Hyde Park. Four stories high, but less than thirty feet wide, the narrow structure had been restored in the 1930s by Syrie Maugham, the wife of Somerset Maugham and one of the most celebrated decorators of her time. A winding staircase led from the ground floor to the drawing room, sweeping past a Cecil Beaton portrait of Chloe and Francesca. Coral *faux marbre* columns framed the entrance to the drawing room, which held a stylish mix of French and Italian pieces as well as several Adam chairs and a collection of Venetian mirrors. On the next floor Francesca's bedroom was decorated like Sleeping Beauty's castle. Against a backdrop of lace curtains swagged with pink silk rosettes and a bed topped by a gilded wooden crown draped with thirty yards of filmy white tulle, Francesca reigned as a princess over all she surveyed.

Occasionally she held court in her fairy-tale room, pouring sweetened tea from a Dresden china pot for the daughter of one of Chloe's friends. "I am Princess Aurora," she announced to the Honorable Clara Millingford on one particular visit, prettily tossing the chestnut curls she had inherited, along with her reckless nature, from Black Jack Day. "You are one of the good women from the village who has come to visit me."

Clara, the only daughter of Viscount Allsworth, had no intention of being a good woman from the village while snooty Francesca Day acted like royalty. She set down her third lemon biscuit and exclaimed, "I want to be Princess Aurora!"

The suggestion astonished Francesca so much that she laughed, a delicate little peal of silvery sound. "Don't be silly, darling Clara. You have those great big freckles. Not that freckles aren't perfectly nice, of course, but certainly not for Princess Aurora, who was the most famous beauty in the land. I'll be Princess Aurora, and you can be the queen."

Francesca thought her compromise was eminently fair and she was heartbroken when Clara, like so many other little girls who had come to play with her, refused to return. Their abandonment baffled her. Hadn't she shared all her pretty toys with them? Hadn't she let them play in her beautiful bedroom?

Chloe ignored any hints that her child was becoming dreadfully spoiled. Francesca was her baby, her angel, her perfect little girl. She hired the most liberal tutors, bought the newest dolls, the latest games, fussed over her, petted her, and let her do everything she wanted as long as it could not possibly endanger her. Unexpected death had already reared its ugly head twice in Chloe's life, and the thought of something happening to her precious child made her blood run cold. Francesca was her anchor, the only emotional attachment she had been able to maintain in her aimless life. Sometimes she lay sleepless in her bed, her skin clammy, as she envisioned the horrors that could befall a little girl cursed with her father's reckless nature. She saw Francesca jumping into a swimming pool never to come up again, tumbling from a ski lift, tearing the muscles in her legs while practicing ballet, scarring her face in an accident on a bicycle. She couldn't shake the awful fear that something terrible lurked just beyond her vision ready to snatch up her daughter, and she wanted to wrap Francesca in cotton and lock her away in a beautiful silken place where nothing could ever hurt her.

"No!" she shrieked as Francesca dashed from her side and ran down the sidewalk after a pigeon. "Come back here! Don't run away like that!"

"But I like to run," Francesca protested. "The wind makes whistles in my ears."

Chloe knelt down and held out her arms. "Running musses your hair and makes your face all red. People won't love you if you're not pretty." She clasped Francesca tightly in her arms while she uttered this most terrible threat, using it the way other mothers might offer up the horrors of the boogey man.

Sometimes Francesca rebelled, practicing cartwheels in secret or swinging from a tree limb when her nanny's attention was distracted. But her activities were always discovered, and her pleasure-loving mother, who never denied her anything, who never reprimanded her for even the most outrageous misbehavior, became so distraught that she frightened Francesca.

"You could have been killed!" she would shriek, pointing to a grass stain on Francesca's yellow linen frock or a dirty smear on her cheek. "See how ugly you look! How awful! Nobody loves ugly little girls!" And then Chloe would begin to cry in such a heartbroken fashion that Francesca would grow frightened. After several of these disturbing episodes, she learned her lesson: anything in life was permissible . . . as long as she looked pretty doing it.

The two of them lived an elegant vagabond life on the proceeds of Chloe's legacy as well as the largess of the stream of men who passed through her life in much the same way their fathers had once passed through Nita's. Chloe's outrageous sense of style and spendthrift ways contributed to her reputation on the international social circuit as an amusing companion and highly entertaining houseguest, someone who could always be counted upon to enliven even the most tedious occasion. It was Chloe who dictated that the last two weeks of February must always be spent on the crescent-shaped beaches of Rio de Janeiro; Chloe who enlivened the leaden hours at Deauville, when everyone had grown bored with polo, by staging elaborate treasure hunts that sent all of them out racing through the French countryside in small sleek cars searching for bald-headed priests, uncut emeralds, or a perfectly chilled bottle of Cheval Blanc '19; Chloe who insisted one Christmas that they abandon Saint-Moritz for a Moorish villa in the Algarve where they were entertained by a group of amusing-ly dissolute rock stars and a bottomless supply of hashish.

More frequently than not, Chloe brought her daughter

with her, along with a nanny and whatever tutor was currently in charge of Francesca's slipshod education. These caretakers generally kept Francesca separated from the adults during the daytime, but at night Chloe sometimes offered her up to the jaded jet-setters as if the child were a particularly clever card trick.

"Here she is, everyone!" Chloe announced on one particular occasion as she led Francesca onto the afterdeck of Aristotle Onassis's yacht *Christina,* which was anchored for the night off the coast of Trinidad. A green canopy covered the spacious lounge at the stern, and the guests reclined in comfortable chairs at the edge of a mosaic reproduction of the Cretan Bull of Minos set into the teak deck. The mosaic had served as a dance floor barely an hour before and later would be lowered nine feet and filled with water for those who wished to take a swim before retiring.

"Come here, my pretty princess," Onassis said, holding out his arms. "Come give Uncle Ari a kiss."

Francesca rubbed the sleep from her eyes and stepped forward, an exquisite baby doll of a little girl. Her perfect little mouth formed a gentle Cupid's bow, and her green eyes opened and closed as if the lids were delicately weighted. Froths of Belgian lace at the throat of her long white nightgown fluttered in the night breeze, and her bare feet peeked out from beneath the hem, revealing toenails polished the same delicate shade of pink as the inside of a rabbit's ear. Despite the fact that she was only nine years old and had been awakened at two o'clock in the morning, her senses gradually grew alert. All day she had been abandoned to the care of servants, and now she was eager for a chance to garner the attention of the grown-ups. Maybe if she was especially good tonight, they would let her sit on the afterdeck with them tomorrow.

Onassis, with his beaklike nose and narrow eyes, covered even at night with sinister wraparound sunglasses, frightened her, but she obediently stepped into his embrace. He had given her a pretty necklace shaped like a starfish the night before, and she didn't want to risk sacrificing any other presents that might come her way.

As he lifted her onto his lap, she glanced over at Chloe,

who had cuddled next to her current lover, Giancarlo Morandi, the Italian Formula One driver. Francesca knew all about lovers because Chloe had explained them to her. Lovers were fascinating men who took care of women and made them feel beautiful. Francesca couldn't wait to be grown up enough to have a lover of her own. Not Giancarlo, though. Sometimes he went off with other women and made her mummy cry. Instead, Francesca wanted a lover who would read books to her and take her to the circus and smoke a pipe like some of the men she had seen walking with their little girls along the Serpentine.

"Attention everyone!" Chloe sat up and clapped her hands in the air above her head, like one of the flamenco dancers Francesca had seen perform the last time they were in Torremolinos. "My beautiful daughter will now illustrate what abysmally ignorant peasants all of you are." Derisive hoots greeted this announcement, and Francesca heard Onassis chuckle in her ear.

Chloe snuggled close to Giancarlo again, rubbing one leg of her white Courrèges hip-huggers against his calf while she tilted her head in Francesca's direction. "Pay no attention to them, my sweet," she declared loftily. "They're riffraff of the very worst sort. I can't think why I bother with them." The couturier giggled. As Chloe pointed to a low mahogany table, the wedge-shaped front of her new Sassoon haircut swept forward over her cheek, forming a hard, straight edge. "Educate them, will you, Francesca? No one except your uncle Ari is the slightest bit discriminating."

Francesca slid off Onassis's knee and walked toward the table. She could feel everyone's eyes on her and she deliberately prolonged the moment, taking slow steps, keeping her shoulders back, pretending she was a tiny princess on the way to her throne. As she reached the table and saw the six small gold-rimmed porcelain bowls, she smiled and flipped her hair away from her face. Kneeling on the rug in front of the table, she regarded the bowls thoughtfully.

The contents shone against the white porcelain of the bowls, six mounds of glistening wet caviar in various shades of red, gray, and beige. Her hand touched the end bowl, which held a generous heap of pearly red eggs. "Salmon roe," she said, pushing it away. "Not worth considering. True caviar comes only from the sturgeon of the Caspian Sea."

Onassis laughed and one of the movie stars applauded. Francesca quickly disposed of two other bowls. "These are both lumpfish caviar, so we can't consider them either."

The decorator leaned toward Chloe. "Information gleaned at the breast," he inquired, "or through osmosis?"

Chloe gave him a wicked leer. "At the breast, of course."

"And what glorious ones they are, *cara.*" Giancarlo ran his hand over the front of Chloe's bare-midriff top.

"This is beluga," Francesca announced, not pleased at having the attention slip from herself, especially after she'd spent the entire day with a governess who kept muttering terrible things just because Francesca refused to do her boring multiplication tables. She placed the tip of her finger on the edge of the center bowl. "You'll notice that beluga has the largest grains." Shifting her hand to the next bowl, she declared, "This is sevruga. The color is the same, but the grains are smaller. And this is osetra, my very favorite. The eggs are almost as large as the beluga, but the color is more golden."

She heard a satisfying chorus of laughter mixed with applause, and then everyone began congratulating Chloe on her clever child. At first Francesca smiled at the compliments, but then her happiness began to fade as she realized that everyone was looking at Chloe instead of at her. Why was her mother getting all the attention when she wasn't the one who'd done the trick? Clearly, the grown-ups would never let her sit on the afterdeck with them tomorrow. Angry and frustrated, Francesca jumped to her feet and swept her arm across the table, sending the porcelain bowls flying and smearing caviar all over Aristotle Onassis's polished teak deck.

"Francesca!" Chloe exclaimed. "What's wrong, my darling?"

Onassis scowled and muttered something in Greek that sounded vaguely threatening to Francesca. She puffed out her bottom lip and tried to think how to recover from her mistake. Her small problem with temper tantrums was supposed to be a secret—something that, under no circumstances, could ever be displayed in front of Chloe's friends. "I'm sorry, Mummy," she said. "It was an accident."

"Of course it was, pet," Chloe replied. "Everyone knows that."

Onassis's expression of displeasure did not ease, however, and Francesca knew stronger action was called for. With a dramatic cry of anguish, she fled across the deck to his side and flung herself in his lap. "I'm sorry, Uncle Ari," she sobbed, her eyes instantly filling with tears—one of her very best tricks. "It was an accident, really it was!" The tears leaked over her bottom lids and trickled down her cheeks as she concentrated very hard on not flinching from the gaze of those black wraparound sunglasses.

"I love you, Uncle Ari," she sighed, turning the full force of her pitiful tear-streaked face upward in an expression she had gleaned from an old Shirley Temple movie. "I love you, and I wish you were my very own daddy."

Onassis chuckled and said he hoped he never had to face her over a bargaining table.

After Francesca was dismissed, she returned to her suite, passing by the children's room where she took her lessons during the day at a bright yellow table positioned directly in front of a Parisian mural painted by Ludwig Bemelmans. The mural made her feel as if she'd stepped into one of his Madeline books—except better dressed, of course. The room had been designed for Onassis's two children, but since neither was on board, Francesca had it all to herself. Although it was a pretty place, she actually preferred the bar, where once a day she was permitted to enjoy ginger ale served in a champagne glass along with a paper parasol and a maraschino cherry.

Whenever she sat at the bar, she took tiny sips from her drink to make it last while she gazed down through the glass top at a lighted replica of the sea complete with little ships she could move with magnets. The footrests of the bar stools were polished whales' teeth, which she could just touch with the toes of her tiny handmade Italian sandals, and the upholstery of the seats felt silky soft on the backs of her thighs. She remembered one time when her mother had screamed with laughter because Uncle Ari had told her they were all sitting on the foreskin of a whale's penis. Francesca had laughed, too, and told Uncle Ari that he was silly—didn't he mean an elephant's peanuts?

The *Christina* held nine suites, each with its own elaborately decorated living and bedroom areas as well as a pink marble bath that Chloe pronounced "so opulent it borders on the tacky." The suites were all named after different Greek islands, the shapes of which were outlined in gold leaf on a medallion fastened to the door. Sir Winston Churchill and his wife Clementine, frequent visitors on board the *Christina,* had already retired for the night in their suite, Corfu. Francesca passed it, then looked for the outline of her particular island—Lesbos. Chloe had laughed when they were put in Lesbos, telling Francesca that several dozen men would most definitely disagree with the choice. When Francesca had asked why, Chloe had said she was too young to understand.

Francesca hated it when Chloe answered her questions like that, so she had hidden the blue plastic case containing her mother's diaphragm, an object Chloe had once told her was her most precious possession, although Francesca couldn't really see why. She hadn't given it back, either—at least not until Giancarlo Morandi had pulled her from her lessons when Chloe wasn't watching and threatened to throw her overboard and let the sharks eat out her eyeballs unless she told him what she'd done with it. Francesca hated Giancarlo Morandi now and tried to stay far away from him.

Just as she reached Lesbos, Francesca heard the door of Rhodes opening. She looked up to see Evan Varian walk out into the corridor, and she smiled in his direction, letting him see her pretty, straight teeth and the matching pair of dimples that indented her cheeks.

"Hello, princess," he said, speaking in the full, liquid tones he used whether playing the rogue counterintelligence officer John Bullett in the recently released and phenomenally successful Bullett spy film, or appearing as Hamlet at the Old Vic. Despite his background as the son of an Irish schoolteacher and a Welsh bricklayer, Varian had the sharp features of an English aristocrat and the casually long haircut of an Oxford don. He wore a lavender polo shirt with a paisley ascot and white duck trousers. But most important to Francesca, he carried a pipe—a wonderful brown daddy's pipe with a marbled wooden bowl. "Aren't you up a little late?" he inquired.

"I stay up this late *all* the time," she replied, with a small shake of her curls and all the self-importance she could muster. "Only babies go to bed early."

"Oh, I see. And you most definitely aren't a baby. Are you sneaking out to meet a gentleman admirer, perhaps?"

"No, silly. Mummy woke me up to do the caviar trick."

"Ah, yes, the caviar trick." He tamped the tobacco in the bowl of his pipe with his thumb. "Did she blindfold you for the taste test this time, or was it a simple sight identification?"

"Just by sight. She doesn't ask me to do the blindfold trick anymore because the last time we did it, I started to gag." She saw that he was getting ready to move on, and she acted quickly. "Don't you think Mummy's looking awfully pretty tonight?"

"Your mummy always looks pretty." He cupped a match in his palm and held it over the bowl.

"Cecil Beaton says that she's one of the most beautiful women in Europe. Her figure's nearly perfect, and of course she's a wonderful hostess." Francesca cast about for an example that would impress him. "Do you know that Mummy did curry before absolutely anyone else thought of it?"

"A legendary coup, princess, but before you exert yourself any further in extolling your mother's virtues, don't forget that the two of us despise each other."

"Pooh, she'll like you if I tell her to. Mummy does everything I want."

"I've noticed," he observed dryly. "However, even if you managed to change your mummy's opinion, which I think highly unlikely, you won't change mine, so I'm afraid you're going to have to cast your net elsewhere for a father. I must tell you that even the thought of being permanently shackled with Chloe's neuroses makes me shudder."

Nothing was going right for Francesca that evening, and she spoke pettishly. "But I'm afraid she's going to marry

Giancarlo, and if she does, it'll all be your fault! He's a terrible shit, and I hate him."

"God, Francesca, you use the most awful language for a child. Chloe should spank you."

The storm clouds gathered in her eyes. "What a beastly thing to say! I think you're a shit, too!"

Varian tugged on the legs of his trousers so he wouldn't crease them as he knelt down beside her. "Francesca, my cherub, you should consider yourself lucky that I'm not your daddy, because if I *were,* I'd lock you up in the back of a dark closet and leave you there until you mummified."

Genuine tears stung Francesca's eyes. "I hate you," she cried as she kicked him hard in the shin. Varian jumped up with a yelp.

The door of Corfu swung open. "Is it too much to request that an old man be allowed to sleep in peace!" Sir Winston Churchill's growl filled the passageway. "Could you conduct your business elsewhere, Mr. Varian? And you, missy, get to bed at once or our card game is off for tomorrow!"

Francesca scampered into Lesbos without a word of protest. If she couldn't have a daddy, at least she could have a granddaddy.

As the years passed, Chloe's romantic entanglements grew so complex that even Francesca accepted the fact that her mother would never settle on one man long enough to marry him. She forced herself to look upon her lack of a father as an advantage. She had enough adults to cope with in her life, she reasoned, and she certainly didn't need any more of them telling her what she should or shouldn't do, especially as she began to catch the attention of a bevy of adolescent boys. They stumbled over their feet whenever she was near, and their voices cracked when they tried to talk to her. She gave them soft, wicked smiles just so she could watch them blush, and she practiced all the flirtatious tricks she had seen Chloe use—the generous laughter, the graceful tilt of the head, the sidelong glances. Every one of them worked.

The Age of Aquarius had found its princess. Francesca's little-girl clothes gave way to peasant dresses with fringed paisley shawls and multicolored love beads strung on silken thread. She frizzed her hair, pierced her ears, and expertly applied makeup to enlarge her eyes until they seemed to fill her face. The top of her head had barely passed her mother's eyebrows when, much to her disappointment, she stopped growing. But unlike Chloe, who still held the remnants of a pudgy child deep inside her, Francesca never had any reason to doubt her own beauty. It simply *existed,* that was all—just like air and light and water. Just like Mary Quant, for goodness' sake! By the time she was seventeen, Black Jack Day's daughter had become a legend.

Evan Varian reentered her life in the disco at Annabel's. She and her date were leaving to go to the White Tower for baklava, and they had just walked past the glass partition that separated the disco from Annabel's dining room. Even in the determinedly fashionable atmosphere of London's most popular club, Francesca's scarlet velvet trouser suit with its padded shoulders gathered more than its share of attention, especially since she had neglected to wear a blouse beneath the deep open V of the wasp-waisted jacket, and the insides of her seventeen-year-old breasts curved enticingly above the spot where the lapels joined. The effect became all the more alluring because of her short Twiggy hairstyle, which made her look rather like London's most erotic schoolboy.

"Well, if it isn't my little princess." The sonorous voice rang out in perfect pear-shaped tones designed to be heard in the far reaches of the National Theatre. "It appears she's all grown up and ready to take on the world."

Except for watching him in the Bullett spy films, she had not seen Evan Varian for years. Now, as she spun around to face him, she felt as if she were confronting his on-screen presence. He wore the same immaculately fitted Savile Row suit, the same pale blue silk shirt and handmade Italian shoes. Silver had threaded his temples since their last encounter on board the *Christina,* but now his hair lay conservatively tamed to his head by an expert razor cut.

Her date for the evening, a baronet home on holiday from Eton, suddenly seemed as young as milk-fed veal. "Hello, Evan," she said, giving Varian a smile that managed to be both haughty and bewitching.

He ignored the obvious impatience of the blond fashion model draped over his arm as he surveyed Francesca's scarlet velvet trouser suit. "Little Francesca. The last time I saw you, you didn't have so many clothes on. As I remember, you were wearing a nightgown."

Other girls might have blushed, but other girls didn't have Francesca's bottomless self-confidence. "Really? I've forgotten. Amusing of you to remember." And then, because she had quite made up her mind to catch the grown-up interest of this most sophisticated Evan Varian, she nodded at her escort and permitted him to lead her away.

Varian called her the next day and invited her to dine with him. "Certainly not," Chloe shrieked, jumping up from her lotus position in the center of the drawing room carpet where she dabbled at meditation twice a day, except on alternate Mondays when she had her legs waxed. "Evan is more than twenty years older than you, and he's a notorious playboy. My God, he's already had four wives! I absolutely won't have you involved with him."

Francesca sighed and stretched. "Sorry, Mummy, but it's rather a fait accompli. I'm smitten."

"Be reasonable, darling. He's old enough to be your father."

"Was he ever your lover?"

"Of course not. You know the two of us never got on."

"Then I don't see what possible objection you could have."

Chloe begged and pleaded, but Francesca paid no attention. She had grown tired of being treated like a child. She was ready for adult adventure—sexual adventure.

A few months before, she had made a great show out of insisting that Chloe take her to the doctor for birth control pills. At first Chloe had protested, but she had quickly changed her mind when she had stumbled upon Francesca in a heated embrace with a young man who was pushing his hand under her skirt. Ever since, one of those pills appeared on Francesca's breakfast tray each morning to be swallowed with great ceremony.

Francesca had told no one that the pills had so far proven unnecessary, nor had she let anyone see how her continued virginity upset her. All of her friends spoke so glibly about their sexual experiences that she was terrified they would find out she was lying about her own. If anyone discovered what an absolute *infant* she was, she was absolutely certain she would lose her standing as the most fashionable member of London's trendy younger set.

With stubborn determination, she reduced her youthful sexuality to a simple matter of social position. It was easier for her that way, since social position was something she understood, while the loneliness produced by her abnormal childhood, the aching need for some deep connection with another human being, only bewildered her.

However, despite her determination to lose her virginity, she had hit upon an unexpected stumbling block. So much of her life had been spent with adults that she didn't feel entirely comfortable with her peers, even those worshiping boys who followed her around like well-trained lapdogs. She understood that having sex would involve placing a certain amount of trust in her partner, and she couldn't imagine trusting those callow young boys. She had immediately seen an answer to her dilemma when she set eyes on Evan Varian at Annabel's. Who better than an experienced man of the world to escort her through those fragile final portals into womanhood? She saw no connection at all between her choice of Evan to be her first lover and her choice of him, years earlier, to be her father.

So, ignoring Chloe's protests, Francesca accepted Evan's invitation to dine at Mirabelle the following weekend. They sat at a table next to one of the small hothouses where the restaurant's fresh flowers were grown and dined on rack of lamb stuffed with veal and truffles. He touched her fingers, angled his head attentively whenever she spoke, and told her she was the most beautiful woman in the room. Francesca privately considered that rather a foregone conclusion, but the compliment pleased her nonetheless, especially since the exotic Bianca Jagger was nibbling at a lobster soufflé in front of one of the tapestried walls on the opposite side of the room. After dinner, they went to Leith's for a tangy lemon mousse and glacé strawberries, and then on to Varian's Kensington home where he played a Chopin mazurka for her on the grand piano in the sitting room and gave her a memorable kiss. Yet when he tried to lead her upstairs to his bedroom, she balked.

"Another time, perhaps," she said breezily. "I'm not in the mood." It didn't occur to her to tell him that she would like it very much if he would just hold her for a while or simply stroke her hair and let her cuddle up against him. Varian didn't like her rejection, but she restored his good mood with a saucy smile that promised future pleasures.

Two weeks later, she forced herself to make the long trek at his side up the curving Adam staircase, past the Constable landscape and recamier bench, through the arched entryway, and into his lavishly decorated Louis XIV bedroom suite.

"You're luscious," he said, coming out of his dressing room in a maroon and navy silk dressing robe with J.B. monogrammed in elaborate script on the pocket, obviously a costume he'd appropriated from his last film. He approached her, his hand going out to stroke her breast above the towel she'd wrapped around herself after she'd taken off her clothes in the bathroom. " 'Beauty like the breast of a dove—soft as down and sweet as mother's milk,' " he quoted.

"Is that from Shakespeare?" she asked nervously. She wished he weren't wearing such heavy cologne.

Evan shook his head. "It's from *Dead Men's Tears,* right before I pushed the stiletto through the Russian spy's heart." He ran his fingers along the curve of her neck. "Perhaps you'd go over to the bed now."

Francesca didn't want to do any such thing—she wasn't even certain she liked Evan Varian—but she'd come too far to turn back without humiliating herself, so she did as he asked. The mattress squeaked as she lay down upon it. Why did his mattress have to squeak? Why was the room so cold? Without warning, Evan fell on top of her. Alarmed, she tried to push him away, but he was muttering something in her ear while he fumbled with her towel. "Oh . . . stop! Evan—"

"Please, darling," he said. "Do as I ask. . . ."

"Get off me!" Panic pounded at her chest. She began shoving at his shoulders as the towel gave way.

Again he muttered something, but in her distress she caught just the last part of it. ". . . make me excited," he whispered, pulling open his dressing gown.

"You beast! Get away! Get off me." As she screamed, she curled her hands into fists and began beating at his back.

He pried her legs open with his knees. ". . . just once and then I'll stop. Just once call me by name."

"Evan!"

"No!" An awful hardness probed at her. "Call me— Bullett."

"Bullett?"

The instant the word left her lips, he thrust inside her. She screamed as she felt herself being consumed by a hot stab of pain, and then, before she could release the second scream, he began to shudder.

"You swine," she sobbed hysterically, beating at his back and trying to kick at him with her pinioned legs. "You awful, filthy beast." Using strength she hadn't known she possessed, she finally pushed his weight off her and jumped from the bed, taking the coverlet with her and holding it over her naked, invaded body. "I'll have you arrested," she cried, tears rushing down her cheeks. "I'll see you punished for this, you bloody pervert."

"Pervert?" He pulled his dressing gown closed and got up from the bed, his chest still heaving. "I wouldn't be so quick to call me a pervert, Francesca," he said coolly. "If you weren't such an inept lover, none of this would have happened."

"Inept!" The accusation startled her so much that she nearly forgot the throbbing pain between her legs and the ugly stickiness leaking onto her thighs. "Inept? You attacked me!"

He knotted the sash and looked at her with hostile eyes. "How amused everyone will be when I tell them the beautiful Francesca Day is frigid."

"I'm not frigid!"

"Of course you're frigid. I've made love to hundreds of women, and you're the first one who's ever complained." He walked over to a gilded commode and picked up his pipe. "God, Francesca, if I'd known you were such a dreadful fuck, I wouldn't have bothered with you."

Francesca fled into the bathroom, shoved herself into her clothes, and raced from the house. She forced herself to suppress the realization that she had been violated. It had been a dreadful misunderstanding, and she would simply make herself forget about it. After all, she was Francesca Serritella Day. Nothing truly horrible could ever happen to her.

The New World

Chapter
3

Dallas Fremont Beaudine once told a reporter from *Sports Illustrated* that the difference between pro golfers and other big-time athletes was mainly that golfers didn't spit. Not unless they were from Texas, anyway, in which case they pretty much did any damn-fool thing they pleased.

Golf Texas-style was one of Dallie Beaudine's favorite topics. Whenever the subject came up, he would shove one hand through his blond hair, stick a wad of Double Bubble in his mouth, and say, "We're talking real Texas golf, you understand . . . not this fancy PGA shit. Real down and dirty, punch that sucker ball upwind through a cyclone and nail it six inches from the pin on a burned-out public course built right next to the interstate. And it doesn't count unless you do it with a beat-up five iron you dug out of the junkyard when you were a kid and keep around just 'cause it makes you feel good to look at it."

By the fall of 1974 Dallie Beaudine had made a name for himself with sportswriters as the athlete who was going to introduce a welcome breath of fresh air into the stuffy world of professional golf. His quotes were colorful, and his extraordinary Texan good looks spruced up their magazine covers. Unfortunately, Dallie had a bad habit of getting himself suspended for cussing out officials or placing side bets with undesirables, so he wasn't always around when things got slow in the press tent. Still, all a reporter had to do to find him was ask the locals for the name of the seediest country-western bar in the county, and nine times out of ten Dallie would be there along with his caddy, Clarence "Skeet" Cooper, and three or four former prom queens who'd managed to slip away from their husbands for the evening.

"Sonny and Cher's marriage is in trouble for sure," Skeet Cooper said, studying a copy of *People* magazine in the light spilling from the open glove compartment. He looked over at Dallie, who was driving with one hand on the steering wheel of his Buick Riviera and the other cradling a Styrofoam coffee cup. "Yessirree," Skeet went on. "You ask me, little Chastity Bono's gonna have herself a stepdaddy soon."

"How you figure?" Dallie wasn't really interested, but the flickering of the occasional pair of oncoming headlights and the hypnotic rhythm of I-95's broken white line were putting him to sleep, and they still weren't all that close to the Florida state line. Glancing at the illuminated dial of the clock on the dashboard of the Buick, he saw that it was almost four-thirty. He had three hours before he had to tee off for the qualifying round of the Orange Blossom Open. That would barely give him time to take a shower and pop a couple of pills to wake himself up. He thought of the Bear, who was probably already in Jacksonville, sound asleep in the best suite Mr. Marriott had to offer.

Skeet tossed *People* in the back seat and picked up a copy of the *National Enquirer*. "Cher's startin' to talk about how much she respects Sonny in her interviews—that's how I figure they'll be splittin' up soon. You know as well as I do, whenever a woman starts talkin' about 'respect,' a man better get hisself a good lawyer."

Dallie laughed and then yawned.

"Shoot, Dallie," Skeet protested, as he watched the speedometer inch its way from seventy-five to eighty. "Why don't you crawl in the back and get some sleep? Let me drive for a while."

"If I fall asleep now, I won't wake up till next Sunday, and I have to qualify for this sucker, especially after today."

They had just come from the final round of the Southern Open, where Dallie had shot a disastrous 79, which was seven strokes over his scoring average and a number he had no intention of duplicating. "I don't suppose you got a copy of *Golf Digest* mixed in with all that crap," he asked.

"You know I never read that stuff." Skeet turned to page two of the *Enquirer*. "You want to hear about Jackie Kennedy or Burt Reynolds?"

Dallie groaned, then fumbled with the dial of the radio. Although he was a rock-and-roll man himself, for Skeet's benefit he tried to pick up a country-western station that was still on the air. The best he could get was Kris Kristofferson, who'd sold himself out to Hollywood, so he put on the news instead.

". . . Sixties radical leader, Gerry Jaffe, was acquitted today of all charges after having been involved in a demonstration at Nevada's Nellis Air Force Base. According to federal authorities, Jaffe, who first gained notoriety during the riots at the 1968 Democratic Convention in Chicago, has recently turned his attention to anti-nuclear activities. One of a dwindling group of sixties radicals still involved in activist causes . . ."

Dallie had no interest in old hippies, and he flipped off the knob in disgust. Then he yawned again. "Do you think if you try real hard you could sound out the words in that book I got shoved under the seat?"

Skeet reached over and pulled out a paperback copy of Joseph Heller's *Catch-22*, then set it aside. "I looked at this one a couple of days ago when you was out with that little brunette, the one who kept calling you Mister Beaudine. Damn book don't make sense." Skeet flipped the *Enquirer* closed. "Just out of curiosity. Did she call you Mister Beaudine once you was back at the motel?"

Dallie popped a piece of Double Bubble in his mouth. "As soon as she got her dress off, she mostly kept quiet."

Skeet chuckled, but the change of expression didn't do much to improve his appearance. Depending on your viewpoint, Clarence "Skeet" Cooper had been blessed or cursed with a face that made him pretty much a dead ringer for Jack Palance. He had the same menacing, ugly-handsome features, the same pressed-over nose and small, slit eyes. His hair was dark, prematurely threaded with gray, and worn so long he had to tie it in a ponytail with a rubber band when he caddied for Dallie. At other times he just let it hang to his shoulders, keeping it away from his face with a red bandanna headband like his real idol who wasn't Palance at all but Willie Nelson, the greatest outlaw in Austin, Texas.

At thirty-five, Skeet was ten years older than Dallie. He was an ex-con who'd served time for armed robbery and come out of the experience determined not to repeat it. Quiet around those he didn't know, wary of anyone who wore a business suit, he was immensely loyal to the people he loved, and the person he loved most was Dallas Beaudine.

Dallie had found Skeet passed out on the bathroom floor in a run-down Texaco station on U.S. 180 outside Caddo, Texas. Dallie was fifteen years old at the time, a gangly six-footer dressed in a torn T-shirt and a pair of dirty jeans that showed too much ankle. He also displayed a black eye, skinned knuckles, and a jaw swollen twice its normal size from a brutal altercation that would prove to be the final one with his daddy, Jaycee Beaudine.

Skeet still remembered peering up at Dallie from the dirty bathroom floor and trying hard to focus. Despite his battered face, the boy standing inside the bathroom door was just about the best-looking kid he'd ever seen. He had a shock of dishwater blond hair, bright blue eyes surrounded by thick, paintbrush lashes, and a mouth that looked like it belonged on a two-hundred-dollar whore. As Skeet's head cleared, he also noticed the tear streaks etched in the dirt on the boy's young cheeks as well as the surly, belligerent expression on the kid's face that dared him to make something of it.

Stumbling to his feet, Skeet splashed some water in his own face. "This bathroom's already occupied, sonny."

The kid stuck a thumb in the ragged pocket of his jeans and thrust out his swollen jaw. "Yeah, it's occupied all right. By a stinkin' piece of no-good dog shit."

Skeet, with his slitted eyes and Jack Palance face, wasn't

used to having a grown man challenge him, much less a kid not old enough to have much more than a weekly date with a razor. "You lookin' for trouble, boy?"

"I already found trouble, so I guess a little more won't much hurt me."

Skeet rinsed out his mouth then spit into the basin. "You're about the stupidest kid I ever seen in my life," he muttered.

"Yeah, well you don't look like you're too smart, either, Dog Shit."

Skeet didn't lose his temper easily, but he'd been on a bender that had lasted nearly two weeks, and he wasn't in the best of moods. Straightening up, he pulled back his fist and took two unsteady steps forward, determined to add to the damage already done by Jaycee Beaudine. The kid braced himself, but before Skeet could strike, the rotgut whiskey he'd been drinking got the best of him and he felt the dirty concrete floor give way beneath his wobbly knees.

When he woke up, he found himself in the back seat of a '56 Studebaker with a bad muffler. The kid was at the wheel, heading west on U.S. 180, driving with one hand on the wheel and the other hanging from the window, beating out the rhythm of "Surf City" on the side of the car with his palm.

"You kidnappin' me, boy?" he growled, pulling himself up on the back of the seat.

"The guy pumpin' super at the Texaco was getting ready to call the cops on you. Since you didn't seem to have a legitimate means of transportation, I couldn't do much else but bring you along."

Skeet thought about that for a few minutes and then said, "Name's Cooper. Skeet Cooper."

"Dallas Beaudine. Folks call me Dallie."

"You old enough to be drivin' this car legal?"

Dallie shrugged. "I stole the car from my old man and I'm fifteen. You want me to let you out?"

Skeet thought about his parole officer, who was guaranteed certain to frown on just exactly this kind of thing, and then looked at the feisty kid driving down the sun-baked Texas road like he owned the mineral rights underneath it.

Making up his mind, Skeet leaned back against the seat and closed his eyes. "Guess I might stick around for a few more miles," he said.

Ten years later, he was still around.

Skeet looked over at Dallie sitting behind the wheel of the '73 Buick he now drove and wondered how all those years had flown by so quickly. They'd played a lot of golf courses since the day they'd met at the Texaco station. He chuckled softly to himself as he remembered the first golf course.

The two of them hadn't traveled for more than a few hours that first day when it became evident that they didn't have much more than the price of a full tank of gas between them. However, fleeing the wrath of Jaycee Beaudine hadn't made Dallie forget to toss a few battered clubs into the trunk before he hotfooted it out of Houston, so he began looking around for signs that would lead them to the next country club.

As he turned into a tree-lined drive, Skeet glanced over at him. "Does it occur to you that we don't exactly look like country club material, what with this stolen Studebaker and your busted-up face?"

Dallie's swollen mouth twisted in a cocky grin. "That kind of stuff don't count for shit when you can hit a five-iron two hundred twenty yards into the wind and land the ball on a nickel."

He made Skeet empty out his pockets, took their total assets of twelve dollars and sixty-four cents, walked up to three charter members, and suggested they play a friendly little game at ten dollars a hole. The charter members, Dallie declared magnanimously, could take their electric carts and their oversize leather bags stuffed full of Wilson irons and MacGregor woods. Dallie announced that he'd be happy as a clam walking along with only his five-iron and his second-best Titleist ball.

The members looked at the scruffy-handsome kid who had three inches of bony ankle showing above his sneaker tops and shook their heads.

Dallie grinned, told them they were yellow-bellied, shit-stompin', worthless excuses for women and suggested they raise the stakes to twenty dollars a hole, exactly seven dollars and thirty-six cents more than he had in his back pocket.

The members pushed him toward the first tee and told him they'd stomp his smart ass right across the border into Oklahoma.

Dallie and Skeet ate T-bones that night and slept at the Holiday Inn.

They reached Jacksonville with thirty minutes to spare before Dallie had to tee off for the qualifying round of the 1974 Orange Blossom Open. That same afternoon, a Jacksonville sportswriter out to make a name for himself unearthed the staggering fact that Dallas Beaudine, with his country-boy grammar and redneck politics, held a bachelor's degree in English literature. Two evenings later the sportswriter finally managed to track Dallie to Luella's, a dirty concrete structure with peeling pink paint and plastic flamingos located not far from the Gator Bowl, and confronted him with the information as if he'd just uncovered political graft.

Dallie looked up from his glass of Stroh's, shrugged, and said that since his degree came from Texas A&M, he guessed it didn't really count for much.

It was exactly this kind of irreverence that had kept sports reporters coming back for more ever since Dallie had begun to play on the pro tour two years before. Dallie could keep them entertained for hours with generally unquotable quotes about the state of the Union, athletes who sold out to Hollywood, and women's "ass-stompin'" liberation. He was a new generation of good ol' boy—movie star handsome, self-deprecating, and a lot smarter than he wanted to let on. Dallie Beaudine was about as close as you could get to perfect magazine copy, except for one thing.

He blew the big ones.

After having been declared the pro tour's new golden boy, he had committed the nearly unpardonable sin of not winning a single important tournament. If he played a two-bit tournament on the outskirts of Apopka, Florida, or Irving, Texas, he would win it at eighteen under par, but at the Bob Hope or the Kemper Open, he might not even make the cut. The sportswriters kept asking their readers the same question: When was Dallas Beaudine going to live up to his potential as a pro golfer?

Dallie had made up his mind to win the Orange Blossom Open this year and put an end to his string of bad luck. For one thing, he liked Jacksonville—it was the only Florida city in his opinion that hadn't tried to turn itself into a theme park—and he liked the course where the Orange Blossom was being played. Despite his lack of sleep, he'd made a solid showing in Monday's qualifying round and then, fully rested, he'd played brilliantly in the Wednesday Pro-Am. Success had bolstered his self-confidence—success and the fact that the Golden Bear, from Columbus, Ohio, had come down with a bad case of the flu and been forced to withdraw.

Charlie Conner, the Jacksonville sportswriter, took a sip from his own glass of Stroh's and tried to slouch back in his chair with the same easy grace he observed in Dallie Beaudine. "Do you think Jack Nicklaus's withdrawal will affect the Orange Blossom this week?" he asked.

In Dallie's mind that was one of the world's stupidest questions, right up there with "Was it as good for you as it was for me?" but he pretended to think it over anyway. "Well, now, Charlie, when you take into consideration the fact that Jack Nicklaus is on his way to becoming the greatest player in the history of golf, I'd say there's a pretty fair chance we'll notice he's gone."

The sportswriter looked at Dallie skeptically. "The *greatest* player? Aren't you forgetting a few people like Ben Hogan and Arnold Palmer?" He paused reverentially before he uttered the next name, the holiest name in golf. "Aren't you forgetting Bobby Jones?"

"Nobody's ever played the game like Jack Nicklaus," Dallie said firmly. "Not even Bobby Jones."

Skeet had been talking to Luella, the bar's owner, but when he heard Nicklaus's name mentioned he frowned and asked the sportswriter about the Cowboys' chances to make it all the way to the Super Bowl. Skeet didn't like Dallie talking about Nicklaus, so he had gotten into the habit of interrupting any conversation that shifted in that direction. Skeet said talking about Nicklaus made Dallie's game go straight to hell. Dallie wouldn't admit it, but Skeet was pretty much right.

As Skeet and the sportswriter talked about the Cowboys, Dallie tried to shake off the depression that settled over him every fall like clockwork by indulging in some positive thinking. The '74 season was nearly over, and he hadn't done all that bad for himself. He'd won a few thousand in prize money and double that in crazy betting games— playing best ball left-handed, betting on hitting the middle zero on the 200-yard sign at a driving range, playing an improvised course through a dried-out gully and a forty-foot concrete sewer pipe. He'd even tried Trevino's trick of playing a few holes by throwing the ball in the air and hitting it with a thirty-two-ounce Dr Pepper bottle, but the bottle glass wasn't as thick now as it had been when the Super Mex had invented that particular wrinkle in the bottomless grab bag of golf betting games, so Dallie'd given it up after they'd had to take five stitches in his right hand. Despite his injury, he'd earned enough money to pay for gas and keep Skeet and him comfortable. It wasn't a fortune, but it was a hell of a lot more than old Jaycee Beaudine had ever made hanging around the wharves along Buffalo Bayou in Houston.

Jaycee had been dead for a year now, his life washed away by alcohol and a mean temper. Dallie hadn't found out about his father's death until a few months after it had happened when he'd run into one of Jaycee's old drinking buddies in a Nacogdoches saloon. Dallie wished he had known at the time so he could have stood next to Jaycee's coffin, looked down at his father's corpse, and spit right between the old man's closed eyes. One glob of spit for all the bruises he'd earned from Jaycee's fists, all the abuse he'd taken throughout his childhood, all the times he'd listened to Jaycee call him worthless . . . a pretty boy . . . a no-account . . . until he hadn't been able to stand it anymore and had run away at fifteen.

From what he'd been able to see in a few old photos, Dallie got most of his good looks from his mother. She, too, had run off. She had fled from Jaycee not long after Dallie was born, and she hadn't bothered to leave a forwarding address. Jaycee once said he heard she'd gone to Alaska, but he had never tried to find her. "Too much trouble," Jaycee had told Dallie. "No woman's worth that much trouble, especially when there are so many others around."

With his thick auburn hair and heavy-lidded eyes, Jaycee had attracted more women than he knew what to do with. Over the years at least a dozen had spent varying amounts of time living with them, a few even bringing children along. Some of the women had taken good care of Dallie, others had abused him. As he grew older, he noticed that the ones who abused him seemed to last longer than the others, probably because it took a certain amount of ill temper to survive Jaycee for more than a few months.

"He was born mean," one of the nicer women had told Dallie while she packed her suitcase. "Some people are just like that. You don't realize it at first about Jaycee because he's smart, and he can talk so nice that he makes you feel like the most beautiful woman in the world. But there's something twisted inside him that makes him mean right through to his blood. Don't listen to all that stuff he says about you, Dallie. You're a good kid. He's just afraid you'll grow up and make something of your life, which is more than he's ever been able to do."

Dallie had stayed out of the way of Jaycee's fists as much as he could. The classroom became his safest haven, and unlike his friends he never cut school—unless he had a particularly bad set of bruises on his face, in which case he would hang out with the caddies who worked at the country club down the road. They taught him golf, and by the time he was twelve he had found an even safer haven than school.

Dallie shook off his old memories and told Skeet it was time to call it a night. They went back to the motel, but even though he was tired, Dallie had been thinking about the past too much to fall asleep easily.

With the qualifying round completed and the Pro-Am out of the way, the real tournament began the next day. Like all major professional golf tournaments, the Orange Blossom Open held its first two rounds on Thursday and Friday. The players who survived the cut after Friday went on to the final two rounds. Not only did Dallie survive Friday's cut, but he was leading the tournament by four strokes when he walked past the network television tower onto the first tee on Sunday morning for the final round.

"Now, you just hold steady today, Dallie," Skeet said. He tapped the heel of his hand against the top of Dallie's golf bag and looked nervously over at the leader board, which had Dallie's name prominently displayed at the top. "Remember that you're playing your own game today, not anybody else's. Put those television cameras out of your mind and concentrate on making one shot at a time."

Dallie didn't even nod in acknowledgment of Skeet's words. Instead, he grinned at a spectacular brunette standing near the ropes that held back the gallery of fans. She smiled back, so he wandered over to crack a few jokes with her, acting like he didn't have a care in the world, like winning this tournament wasn't the most important thing in his life, like this year there wouldn't be any Halloween at all.

Dallie was playing in the final foursome along with Johnny Miller, the leading money winner on the tour that season. When it was Dallie's turn to tee up, Skeet handed him a three-wood and gave his final words of advice. "Remember that you're the best young golfer on the tour today, Dallie. You know it and I know it. How about we let the rest of the world figure it out?" Dallie nodded, took his stance, and hit the kind of golf shot that makes history.

At the end of fourteen holes, Dallie was still in the lead at sixteen under par. With only four holes to go, Johnny Miller was coming up fast, but he was still four strokes behind. Dallie put Miller out of his mind and concentrated on his own game. As he sank a five-foot putt, he told himself that he was born to play golf. Some champions are made, but others are created at the moment of conception. He was finally going to live up to the reputation the magazines had created for him. With his name sitting at the top of the leader board of the Orange Blossom Open, Dallie felt as if he'd come out of the womb with a brand-new Titleist ball clenched in his hand.

His strides grew longer as he walked down the fifteenth fairway. The network cameras followed his every move, and confidence surged through him. Those final-round defeats of the past two years were all behind him now. They were flukes, nothing but flukes. This Texas boy was about to set the golf world on fire.

The sun hit his blond hair and warmed his shirt. In the gallery, a shapely female fan blew him a kiss. He laughed and made a play out of catching the kiss in midair and slipping it into his pocket.

Skeet held out an eight-iron for an easy approach shot to the fifteenth green. Dallie gripped the club, assessed the lie, and took his stance. He felt strong and in control. His lead was solid, his game was on, nothing could snatch away this victory.

Nothing except the Bear.

You don't really think you can win this thing, do you, Beaudine?

The Bear's voice popped into Dallie's head sounding just as clear as if Jack Nicklaus were standing beside him.

Champions like me win golf tournaments, not failures like you.

Go away, Dallie's brain screamed. *Don't show up now!* Sweat began to break out on his forehead. He adjusted his grip, tried to loosen himself up again, tried not to listen to that voice.

What have you got to show for yourself? What have you done with your life except screw things up?

Leave me alone! Dallie stepped away from the ball, rechecked the line, and settled in again. He drew back the club and hit. The crowd let out a collective groan as the ball drifted to the left and landed in high rough. In Dallie's mind, the Bear shook his big blond head.

That's exactly what I'm talking about, Beaudine. You just don't have the stuff it takes to make a champion.

Skeet, his expression clearly worried, came up next to Dallie. "Where in hell did that shot come from? Now you're going to have to scramble to make par."

"I just lost my balance," Dallie snapped, stalking off toward the green.

You just lost your guts, the Bear whispered back.

The Bear had begun to appear in Dallie's head not long

after Dallie had started playing on the pro tour. Before that, it had only been Jaycee's voice he had heard in his head. Logically, Dallie understood that he'd created the Bear himself, and he knew there was a big difference between the soft-spoken, well-mannered Jack Nicklaus of real life and this creature from hell who spoke like Nicklaus, and looked like Nicklaus, and knew all Dallie's deepest secrets.

But logic didn't have much to do with private devils, and it wasn't accidental that Dallie's private devil had taken the form of Jack Nicklaus, a man he admired just about more than anyone else—a man with a beautiful family, the respect of his peers, and the greatest game of golf the world had ever seen. A man who wouldn't know how to fail if he tried.

You're a kid from the wrong side of the tracks, the Bear whispered as Dallie lined up a short putt on the sixteenth green. It lipped the edge of the cup and scooted off to the side.

Johnny Miller gave Dallie a sympathetic look, then sank his own putt for a par. Two holes later when Dallie hit his drive on eighteen, his four-shot lead had been reduced to a tie with Miller.

Your old man told you you'd never amount to much, the Bear said as Dallie's drive sliced viciously to the right. *Why didn't you listen?*

The worse Dallie played, the more he joked with the crowd. "Now, where did that miserable golf shot come from?" he called over to them, scratching his head in mock bewilderment. And then he pointed to a plump, matronly woman standing near the ropes. "Ma'am, maybe you'd better put down your purse and come on over here so you can hit the next one for me."

He bogeyed the final hole and Johnny Miller birdied it. After the players had signed their scorecards, the tournament chairman presented Miller with the first-place trophy and a check for thirty thousand dollars. Dallie shook his hand, gave Miller a few congratulatory pats on the shoulder, and then went over to joke with the crowd some more.

"This is what I get for letting Skeet hold my jaws open last night and pour all that beer down my throat. My old grandmother could have played better out there today with a garden rake and roller skates."

Dallie Beaudine had spent a childhood dodging his father's fists, and he knew better than to let anybody see when he was hurting.

Chapter
4

Francesca stood in the center of a pool of discarded evening gowns and studied her reflection in the wall of mirrors built into one end of her bedroom, now decorated with pastel-striped silk walls, matching Louis XV chairs, and an early Matisse. Like an architect engrossed in a blueprint, she searched her twenty-year-old face for gremlin-induced imperfections that might have mischievously appeared since she last looked in the mirror. Her small straight nose was dusted with a translucent powder priced at twelve pounds a box, her eyelids frosted with smoky shadow, and her lashes, individually separated with a tiny tortoiseshell comb, had been coated with exactly four applications of imported German mascara. She lowered her critical gaze down over her tiny frame to the graceful curve of her breasts, then inspected the neat indentation of her waist before moving on to her legs, beautifully clad in a pair of lacquer green suede slacks complemented perfectly by an ivory silk blouse from Piero De Monzi. She had just been named one of the ten most beautiful women in Great Britain for 1975. Although she would never have been so crass as to say it aloud, she secretly wondered why the magazine had bothered with nine others.

Francesca's delicate features were more classically beautiful than either her mother's or grandmother's, and much more changeable. Her slanted green eyes could grow as chill and distant as a cat's when she was displeased, or as saucy as a Soho barmaid's if her mood shifted. When she realized how much attention it brought her, she began to emphasize her resemblance to Vivien Leigh and let her chestnut hair grow into a curly, shoulder-length cloud, occasionally even pulling it back from her small face with hair slides to make the likeness more pronounced.

As she contemplated her reflection, it didn't occur to her that she was shallow and vain, that many of the people she considered her friends could barely tolerate her. Men loved her, and that was all that mattered. She was so outrageously beautiful, so utterly charming when she put her energy to it, that only the most self-protective of males could resist her. Men found being with Francesca rather like taking an addictive drug, and even after the relationship had ended, many discovered themselves coming back for a damaging second hit.

Like her mother, she spoke in hyperbole and put her words into invisible italics, making even the most mundane occurrence sound like a grand adventure. She was rumored to be a sorceress in bed, although the specifics of who had actually penetrated the lovely Francesca's enchanting vagina had grown a bit muddy over time. She kissed wonderfully, that was for certain, leaning into a man's chest, curling up in his arms like a sensuous kitten, sometimes licking at his mouth with the very tip of her small pink tongue.

Francesca never stopped to consider that men adored her because she was generally at her best with them. They didn't have to suffer her attacks of thoughtlessness, her perpetual tardiness, or her piques when she didn't get her way. Men made her bloom. At least for a while . . . until she grew bored. Then she became impossible.

As she applied a slick of coral gloss to her lips, she couldn't help but smile at the memory of her most spectacular conquest, although she was absolutely distraught that he hadn't taken their parting better. Still, what could she have done? Several months of playing second fiddle to all his official responsibilities had brought the chill light of reality to those deliciously warm visions of royal immortality she'd been entertaining—glass-enclosed carriages, cathedral doors flinging open, trumpets playing—visions not entirely unthinkable for a girl who'd been raised in the bedroom of a princess.

When she'd finally come to her senses about their relationship and realized she didn't want to live her life at the beck and call of the British Empire, she'd tried to make her break with him as clean as possible. But he'd still taken it rather badly. She could see him now as he'd looked that night—immaculately tailored, exquisitely barbered, expensively shod. How on earth could she have known that a man who bore no wrinkles on the outside might bear a few insecurities on the inside? She remembered the evening two months earlier when she had ended her relationship with the most eligible bachelor in Great Britain.

They had just finished dinner in the privacy of his apartments, and his face had seemed young and curiously vulnerable as the candlelight softened its aristocratic planes. She gazed at him across the damask tablecloth set with sterling two hundred years old and china rimmed in twenty-four-karat gold, trying to let him understand by the earnestness of her expression that this was all much more difficult for her than it could possibly be for him.

"I see," he said, after she'd given her reasons, as kindly as possible, for not continuing their friendship. And then, once more, "I see."

"You do understand?" She tilted her head to one side so that her hair fell away from her face, letting the light catch the twin rhinestone slivers that dangled from her earlobes, flickering like a chain of stars against a chestnut sky.

His blunt response shocked her. "Actually, no." Pushing himself back from the table, he stood abruptly. "I don't understand at all." He looked down at the floor and then up again at her. "I must confess I've rather fallen for you, Francesca, and you gave me every reason to believe that you cared for me."

"I *do,*" she replied earnestly. "Of *course* I do."

"But not enough to put up with all that goes along with me."

The combination of stubborn pride and hurt she heard in his voice made her feel horribly guilty. Weren't the royals supposed to hide their emotions, no matter how trying the circumstances? "It *is* rather a lot," she reminded him.

"Yes, it is, isn't it?" There was a trace of bitterness in his laugh. "Foolish of me to have believed you cared enough to put up with it."

Now, in the privacy of her bedroom, Francesca frowned briefly at her reflection in the mirror. Since her own heart had never been affected by anyone, it always came as something of a surprise to her when one of the men with whom she was involved reacted so strongly when they parted.

Still, there was nothing to be done about it now. She recapped her pot of lip gloss and tried to restore her spirits by humming a British dance hall tune from the 1930s about a man who danced with a girl who had danced with the Prince of Wales.

"I'm leaving now, darling," Chloe said, appearing in the doorway as she adjusted the brim of a cream felt bowler over her dark hair, cut short and curly. "If Helmut calls, tell him I'll be back by one."

"If Helmut calls, I'll tell him you bloody well died." Francesca splayed her hand on her hip, her cinnamon brown fingernails looking like small sculptured almonds as she tapped them impatiently against her green suede slacks.

Chloe fastened the neck clasp of her mink. "Now, darling . . ."

Francesca felt a pang of remorse as she noticed how tired her mother looked, but she repressed it, reminding herself that Chloe's self-destructiveness with men had grown worse in recent months and it was her duty as a daughter to point it out. "He's a gigolo, Mummy. Everyone knows it. A phony German prince who's making an absolute fool of you." She reached past the scented Porthault hangers in her closet to the rack holding the gold fish-scale belt she'd bought at David Webb the last time she was in New York. After securing the clasp at her waist, she returned her attention to Chloe. "I'm worried about you, Mummy. There are circles under your eyes, and you look tired all the time. You've also been impossible to live with. Only yesterday you brought home the beige Givenchy kimono for me instead of the silver one I asked you to get."

Chloe sighed. "I'm sorry, darling. I—I've had things on my mind, and I haven't been sleeping well. I'll pick up the silver kimono for you when I'm out today."

Francesca's pleasure in hearing that she would get the proper kimono didn't quite overshadow her concern for Chloe. As gently as possible, she tried to make Chloe understand how serious all this was. "You're forty, Mummy. You need to start taking better care of yourself. Gracious, you haven't had a facial in weeks."

To her dismay, she saw that she'd hurt Chloe's feelings. Rushing over, she gave her mother a quick conciliatory hug, careful not to smear the delicate taupe shading beneath her cheekbones. "Never mind," she said. "I adore you. And you're still the most beautiful mother in London."

"Which reminds me—one mother in this house is enough. You *are* taking your birth control pills, aren't you, darling?"

Francesca groaned. "Not this again . . ."

Chloe withdrew a pair of gloves from an ostrich-skin Chanel handbag and began tugging them on. "I can't bear the thought of your becoming pregnant when you're still so young. Pregnancy is so dangerous."

Francesca flicked her hair behind her shoulders and turned back to the mirror. "All the more reason not to forget, isn't it," she said lightly.

"Just be careful, darling."

"Have you ever known me to lose control of any situation involving men?"

"Thank God, no." Chloe pushed her thumbs beneath the collar of her mink and lifted the fur until it brushed the bottom of her jaw. "If only I'd been more like you when I was twenty." She gave a wry chuckle. "Who am I fooling? If only I were more like you right now." Blowing a kiss in the air, she waved good-bye with her handbag and disappeared down the hallway.

Francesca wrinkled her nose in the mirror, then jerked out the comb she had just arranged in her hair and stalked over to her window. As she stared down into the garden, the unwelcome memory of her old encounter with Evan Varian came back to her, and she shivered. Although she knew sex couldn't be that dreadful for most women, her experience with Evan three years ago had made her lose much of her desire for further experimentation, even with men who attracted her. Still, Evan's taunt about her frigidity had hung in the dusty corners of her consciousness, leaping out at the strangest times to plague her. Finally, last summer, she'd gathered her courage and permitted a handsome young Swedish sculptor she'd met in Marrakech to take her to bed.

She frowned as she remembered how awful it had been. She knew there had to be more to sex than having someone heaving away over her body, pawing at her most private parts with sweat dripping from his armpits all over her. The only feeling the experience had produced inside her had been a terrible anxiety. She hated the vulnerability, the unnerving sense that she had relinquished control. Where was the mystical closeness the poets wrote about? Why wasn't she able to feel close to anybody?

From watching Chloe's relationships with men, Francesca had learned at an early age that sex was a marketable commodity like any other. She knew that sooner or later she would have to permit a man to make love to her again. But she was determined not to do so until she felt completely in control of the situation and the rewards were high enough to justify the anxiety. Exactly what those rewards might be, she didn't quite know. Not money, certainly. Money was simply *there,* not something one even thought about. Not social position, since that had been very much assured her at birth. But *something* . . . the elusive *something* that was missing from her life.

Still, as a basically optimistic person, she thought her unhappy sexual experiences might have turned out for the best. So many of her acquaintances hopped from bed to bed until they'd lost all sense of dignity. She didn't hop into any beds at all, yet she'd been able to present the illusion of sexual experience—fooling even her own mother—while at the same time, remaining aloof. All in all, it was a powerful combination, which intrigued the most interesting assortment of men.

The ringing of the telephone interrupted her thoughts. Stepping over a pile of discarded clothes, she crossed the carpet to pick up the receiver. "Francesca here," she said, sitting down in one of the Louis XV chairs.

"Francesca. Don't hang up. I have to talk to you."

"Well, if it isn't Saint Nicholas." Crossing her legs, she inspected the tips of her fingernails for flaws.

"Darling, I didn't mean to set you off so last week." Nicholas's tone was placating, and she could see him in her mind, sitting at the desk in his office, his pleasant features grim with determination. Nicky was so sweet and so boring. "I've been miserable without you," he went on. "Sorry if I pushed."

"You should be sorry," she declared. "Really, Nicholas, you acted like such an awful prig. I hate being shouted at, and I don't appreciate being made to feel as if I'm some heartless femme fatale."

"I'm sorry, darling, but I didn't really shout. Actually, you were the one—" He stopped, apparently thinking better of that particular comment.

Francesca found the flaw she'd been looking for, a nearly invisible chip in the nail varnish on her index finger. Without getting up from the chair, she stretched toward her dressing table for her bottle of cinnamon brown.

"Francesca, darling, I thought you might like to go down to Hampshire with me this weekend."

"Sorry, Nicky. I'm busy." The lid on the varnish bottle gave way beneath the tug of her fingers. As she extracted the brush, her eyes flicked to the tabloid newspaper folded open next to the telephone. A glass coaster rested on top, magnifying a circular portion of the print beneath so that her own name leaped out at her, the letters distorted like the reflection in a carnival mirror.

Francesca Day, the beautiful daughter of international socialite Chloe Day and granddaughter of the legendary couturiere Nita Serritella, is breaking hearts again. The tempestuous Francesca's latest victim is her frequent companion of late, handsome Nicholas Gwynwyck, thirty-three-year-old heir to the Gwynwyck brewery fortune. Friends say Gwynwyck was ready to announce a wedding date when Francesca suddenly began appearing in the company of twenty-three-year-old screen newcomer, David Graves. . . .

"Next weekend, then?"

She swiveled her hips in the chair, turning away from the sight of the tabloid to repair her fingernail. "I don't think so, Nicky. Let's not make this difficult."

"Francesca." For a moment Nicholas's voice seemed to break. "You—you told me you loved me. I believed you. . . ."

A frown puckered her forehead. She felt guilty, even though it was hardly her fault he had misinterpreted her words. Suspending the nail varnish brush in midair, she tucked her chin closer to the receiver. "I do love you, Nicky. As a friend. My goodness, you're sweet and dear. . . ." *And boring.* "Who wouldn't love you? We've had such wonderful times together. Remember Gloria Hammersmith's party when Toby jumped into that awful fountain—"

She heard a muffled exclamation from the other end of the telephone. "Francesca, how could you do it?"

She blew on her nail. "Do what?"

"Go out with David Graves. You and I are practically engaged."

"David Graves is none of your business," she retorted. "We're not engaged, and I'll talk to you again when you're ready to converse in a more civilized fashion."

"Francesca—"

The receiver hit the cradle with a bang. Nicholas Gwynwyck had no right to cross-examine her! Blowing on her fingernail, she walked over to her closet. She and Nicky had had fun together, but she didn't love him and she certainly had no intention of living the rest of her life married to a brewer, even a wealthy one.

As soon as her fingernail was dry, she renewed her search for something to wear to Cissy Kavendish's party that evening. She still hadn't found what she wanted when she was distracted by a tapping at the door, and a middle-aged woman with ginger-colored hair and elastic stockings rolled at the ankles entered the bedroom. As the woman began putting away the pile of neatly folded lingerie she had brought with her, she said, "I'll be leavin' for a few hours if it's all right with you, Miss Francesca."

Francesca held up a honey-colored chiffon Yves Saint Laurent evening dress with brown and white ostrich feathers encircling the hem. The dress actually belonged to Chloe, but when Francesca first saw it she had fallen in love with it, so she'd had the skirt shortened and the bust taken in before transferring it to her own closet. "What do you think of the chiffon for tomorrow night, Hedda?" she asked. "Too plain?"

Hedda put away the last of Francesca's lingerie and slid the drawer shut. "Everything looks grand on you, miss."

Francesca turned slowly in front of the mirror and then wrinkled her nose. The Saint Laurent was too conservative, not her style after all. Dropping the gown to the floor, she stepped over the pile of discarded clothes and began digging in her closet again. Her velvet knickers would be perfect, but she needed a blouse to wear with them.

"Would you be wantin' anything else, Miss Francesca?"

"No, nothing," Francesca answered absently.

"I'll be back by tea, then," the housekeeper announced as she headed toward the door.

Francesca turned to ask her about supper and noticed for the first time that the housekeeper was stooped forward farther than normal. "Is your back bothering you again? I thought you told me it was better?"

"It was for a bit," the housekeeper replied, resting her hand heavily on the doorknob, "but it's been aching so these last few days I can hardly bend over. That's why I need to leave for a few hours—to go to the clinic."

Francesca thought how terrible it would be to live like poor Hedda, with stockings rolled at the ankles and a back that ached whenever you moved. "Let me get my keys," she offered impulsively. "I'll drive you to Chloe's physician on Harley Street and have him send me the bill."

"No need, miss. I can go to the clinic."

But Francesca wouldn't hear of it. She hated seeing people suffer and couldn't bear the thought of poor Hedda not having the best medical care. Instructing the housekeeper to wait in the car, she traded in her silk blouse for a cashmere sweater, added a gold and ivory bangle to her wrist, made a telephone call, spritzed herself with the peach and apricot scent of Femme, and left her room—giving no thought at all to the litter of clothes and accessories she had left behind for Hedda to bend over and pick up when she returned.

Her hair swirled around her shoulders as she tripped down the stairs, a tortoiseshell cross fox jacket dangling from her fingers, soft leather boots sinking into the carpet. Stepping down into the foyer, she passed a pair of double-ball topiaries set in majolica pots. Little sunlight penetrated the foyer, so the plants never flourished and had to be replaced every six weeks, an extravagance that neither Chloe nor Francesca bothered to question. The door chimes rang.

"Bother," Francesca muttered, glancing at her watch. If she didn't hurry, she'd never be able to get Hedda to the doctor and still have time to dress for Cissy Kavendish's party. Impatiently, she swung open the front door.

A uniformed police constable stood on the other side consulting a small notebook he was holding in his hand. "I'm looking for Francesca Day," he said, coloring slightly as he lifted his head and took in her breathtaking appearance.

A picture sprang into her mind of the assortment of unpaid traffic tickets scattered in her desk drawer upstairs, and she gave him her best smile. "You've found her. Am I going to be sorry?"

He regarded her solemnly. "Miss Day, I'm afraid I have some upsetting news."

For the first time she noticed that he was holding something at his side. A sudden chill of apprehension swept over her as she recognized Chloe's ostrich-skin Chanel handbag.

He swallowed uncomfortably. "It seems there's been a rather serious accident involving your mother. . . ."

Chapter
5

Dallie and Skeet sped along U.S. 49 headed toward Hattiesburg, Mississippi. Dallie had caught a couple of hours' sleep in the back seat while Skeet drove, but now he was behind the wheel again, glad that he didn't have to tee off until 8:48 in the morning, so he would have time to hit a few balls first. He hated these all-night drives from the final round of one tournament to the qualifying round of the next about as much as he hated anything. If the PGA fat cats had to make a few overnight runs across three state lines and past a few hundred Stuckey's signs, he figured they'd change the rules pretty damned quick.

On the golf course, Dallie didn't care how he dressed—as long as his shirts didn't have animals on them and nothing was pink—but he was particular about his clothes off the course. He preferred faded skin-tight Levi's worn with hand-tooled leather boots run over at the heels and a T-shirt old enough so that he could whip it off if the mood struck him and use it to polish the hood of his Buick Riviera without worrying about scratching the finish. A few of his female fans sent him cowboy hats, but he never wore them, favoring billed caps instead, like the one he was wearing now. He said that the Stetson had been ruined forever being worn by too many potbellied insurance agents in polyester leisure suits. Not that Dallie had anything against polyester —as long as it was American made.

"Here's a story for you," Skeet said.

Dallie yawned and wondered whether he was going to be able to hit his two-iron worth a damn. He'd been off the day before, but he couldn't figure out why. Since last year's disaster at the Orange Blossom Open, he'd been playing better, but he still hadn't managed to finish higher than fourth place in any big tournament this season.

Skeet held the tabloid closer to the glove compartment light. "You remember I showed you a picture a while back of that little British girl, the one who was goin' around with that prince fella and those movie stars?"

Maybe he was shifting his weight too fast, Dallie thought. That might be why he was having trouble with his two-iron. Or it could be his backswing.

Skeet went on. "You said she looked like one of those women who wouldn't shake your hand unless you was wearin' a diamond pinky ring. Remember now?"

Dallie grunted.

"Anyway, seems her mama got hit by a taxicab last week. They got a picture here of her comin' out of the funeral carryin' on something terrible. 'Bereft Francesca Day Mourns Socialite Mom,' that's what it says. Now where do you think they come up with stuff like that?"

"Like what?"

"*Bereft.* Word like that."

Dallie shifted his weight onto one hip and dug into the back pocket of his jeans. "She's rich. If she was poor, they'd just say she was 'sad.' You got any more gum?"

"Pack of Juicy Fruit."

Dallie shook his head. "There's a truck stop coming up in a few miles. Let's stretch our legs."

They stopped and drank some coffee, then climbed back into the car. They made it to Hattiesburg in plenty of time for Dallie to tee off, and he easily qualified for the tournament. On his way to the motel later that afternoon, the two of them stopped off at the city post office to check General Delivery. They found a pile of bills waiting for them, along with a few letters—one of which started an argument that lasted all the way to the motel.

"I'm not selling out, and I don't want to hear any more about it," Dallie snapped as he ripped his cap off and threw it down on the motel-room bed, then jerked his T-shirt over his head.

Skeet was already late for an appointment he'd made with a curly-haired cocktail waitress, but he looked up from the letter he held in his hand and studied Dallie's chest with its broad shoulders and well-defined muscles. "You're just about the stubbornest sumbitch I ever knew in my life," he declared. "That pretty face of yours along with those overdeveloped chest muscles could make us more money right now than you and your rusted-up five-iron have earned this entire season."

"I'm not posing for any faggot calendar."

"O. J. Simpson's agreed to do it," Skeet pointed out, "along with Joe Namath and that French ski bum. Hell, Dallie, you were the only golfer they even thought to ask."

"I'm not doing it!" Dallie yelled. "I'm not selling out."

"You did those magazine ads for Foot-Joy."

"That's different and you know it." Dallie stalked into the bathroom and slammed the door, then yelled from the other side. "Foot-Joy makes a damn fine golf shoe!"

The shower went on and Skeet shook his head. Muttering under his breath, he crossed the hallway to his own room. For a long time it had been obvious to a lot of people that Dallie's looks could have given him a one-way ticket to Hollywood, but the fool wouldn't take advantage of it. Talent agents had been placing long-distance calls to him since his first year on the tour, but all Dallie did was tell them they were bloodsuckers and then make generally disparaging remarks about their mothers, which wouldn't have been so bad by itself, except he pretty much did it to their faces. What was so terrible, Skeet wanted to know, about earning some easy money on the side? Until Dallie started winning the big ones, he was never going to pick up the six-figure commercial endorsements that guys like Trevino could get, let alone the sweetheart deals Nicklaus and Palmer made.

Skeet combed his hair and exchanged one flannel shirt for another. He didn't see what was so damned wrong with posing for a calendar, even if it did mean sharing space with pretty boys like J. W. Namath. Dallie had what the talent agents called sexual magnetism. Hell, even somebody who was half blind could see that. No matter how far down in the pack he was, he always had a full gallery following him, and eighty percent of that gallery seemed to be wearing lipstick. The minute he stepped off the course, those women surrounded him like flies after honey. Holly Grace said women loved Dallie because they knew he didn't own any color-coordinated underwear or Wayne Newton records. What we have with Dallas Beaudine, Holly Grace had insisted more than once, is the Lone Star State's last genuine All-American he-man.

Skeet grabbed the room key and chuckled to himself. The last time he'd talked to Holly Grace on the telephone, she'd said that if Dallie didn't win a big tournament pretty soon, Skeet should just go ahead and shoot him to put him out of his misery.

Miranda Gwynwyck's annual party, always held the last week of September, was in full swing, and the hostess surveyed the platters of Mediterranean red prawns, baby artichokes, and lobster in phyllo with satisfaction. Miranda, author of the well-known feminist work *Woman as Warrior*, loved to entertain well, if for no other reason than to prove to the world that feminism and gracious living weren't mutually exclusive. Her personal politics would not permit her to wear frocks or makeup, but entertaining gave her an opportunity to exercise what she referred to in *Woman as Warrior* as the "domestica"—the more civilized side of human nature, whether male or female.

Her eyes swept over the distinguished group of guests she had gathered between the stippled walls of her living room, newly redecorated that August as a birthday present from Miranda's brother. Musicians and intellectuals, several members of the peerage, a sprinkling of well-known writers and actors, a few charlatans to lend spice—exactly the kind of stimulating people she loved to bring together. And then she frowned as her gaze fell on the proverbial fly in the ointment of her satisfaction—tiny Francesca Serritella Day, spectacularly dressed as always and, as always, the center of male attention.

She watched Francesca flit from one conversation to another, looking outrageously beautiful in a turquoise silk jumpsuit. She tossed her cloud of shining chestnut hair as if the world were her personal pearl-filled oyster when everyone in London knew she was down to her last farthing. What a surprise it must have been for her to discover how deeply in debt Chloe had been.

Over the polite noise of the party, Miranda heard Francesca's generous laughter and listened as she greeted several men in that breathless, wait-until-you-hear-this voice, carelessly emphasizing the most unimportant words in a manner that drove Miranda wild. But one by one the stupid bastards all melted into warm little puddles at her feet. Unfortunately, one of those stupid bastards was her own beloved brother Nicky.

Miranda frowned and picked up a macadamia nut from an opalescent Lalique bowl printed with dragonflies. Nicholas was the most important person in the world to her, a wonderfully sensitive man with an enlightened soul. Nicky had encouraged her to write *Woman as Warrior*. He had helped her refine her thoughts, brought her coffee late at night, and most important, he had shielded her from their mother's criticism over why her daughter, with a yearly income of one hundred thousand pounds, had to meddle with such nonsense. Miranda couldn't bear the idea of standing idly by while Francesca Day broke his heart. For months she had watched Francesca flit from one man to another, running back to Nicky whenever she found herself between admirers. Each time he welcomed her return—a little more battle-scarred, perhaps, a little less eagerly—but he welcomed her just the same.

"When we're together," he had explained to Miranda, "she makes me feel as if I'm the wittiest, brightest, most perceptive man in the world." And then he added dryly, "Unless she's in a bad mood, of course, in which case she makes me feel like a complete shit."

How did she do it? Miranda wondered. How did someone so intellectually and spiritually barren command so much attention? Most of it, Miranda felt certain, was her extraordinary beauty. But part of it was her vitality, the way the very air around her seemed to crackle with life. A cheap parlor trick, Miranda thought with disgust, since Francesca Day certainly didn't have an original thought in her head. Just look at her! She was both penniless and unemployed, yet she acted as if she hadn't a care in the world. And maybe she didn't have a care, Miranda thought uneasily—not with Nicky Gwynwyck and all his millions waiting patiently in the wings.

Although Miranda didn't know it, she wasn't the only person brooding at her party that evening. Despite her outward show of gaiety, Francesca was miserable. Just the day before, she had gone to see Steward Bessett, the head of London's most prestigious modeling agency, and asked him for a job. Although she had no desire for a career, modeling was an acceptable way to earn money in her social circle, and she had decided that it would provide at least a temporary answer to her bewildering financial problems.

But to her dismay, Steward had told her she was too short. "No matter how beautiful a model is, she simply has to be five feet eight inches if she's to do fashion," he had said. "You're barely five feet two. Of course, I might be able to get you some beauty work—close-ups, you know, but you'll need some test shots done first."

That was when she had lost her temper, shouting at him that she had been photographed for some of the most important magazines in the world and that she hardly needed to do test shots like some rank amateur. Now she realized that it had been foolish of her to become so upset, but at the time she simply hadn't been able to help herself.

Although it had been a year since Chloe's death, Francesca still found it difficult to accept the loss of her mother. Sometimes her grief seemed to be alive, a tangible object that had twisted itself around her. At first her friends had been sympathetic, but after a few months, they seemed to believe that she should set her sadness aside like last year's hem length. She was afraid they would stop issuing invitations if she didn't become a more cheerful companion, and she hated being alone, so she had finally learned to tuck her grief away. When she was in public, she laughed and flirted as if nothing were wrong.

Surprisingly, the laughter had begun to help, and in the last few months she had felt that she was finally healing.

Sometimes she even experienced vague stirrings of anger against Chloe. How could her mother have deserted her like this, with an army of creditors waiting like a plague of locusts to snatch up everything they owned? But the anger never lasted for long. Now that it was too late, Francesca understood why Chloe had seemed so tired and distracted in those months before she had been hit by the taxi.

Within weeks of Chloe's death, men in three-piece suits had begun to appear at the door with legal documents and greedy eyes. First Chloe's jewelry had disappeared, then the Aston Martin and the paintings. Finally the house itself had been sold. That had settled the last of the debts, but it had left Francesca with only a few hundred pounds, most of which was gone now, and temporarily lodged at the home of Cissy Kavendish, one of Chloe's oldest friends. Unfortunately, Francesca and Cissy had never gotten along all that well, and since the beginning of September, Cissy had made it clear that she wanted Francesca to move out. Francesca wasn't certain how much longer she could hold her off with vague promises.

She forced herself to laugh at Talmedge Butler's joke and tried to find comfort in the idea that being without money was a bore, but merely a temporary situation. She caught sight of Nicholas across the room in his navy Gieves and Hawkes blazer and knife-pleated gray trousers. If she married him, she could have all the money she would ever possibly need, but she had only seriously entertained the idea for the absolute briefest of moments one afternoon a few weeks ago after she'd received a telephone call from a perfectly odious man who had threatened her with all sorts of unpleasant things if she didn't make a payment on her credit cards. No, Nicholas Gwynwyck wasn't a solution to her problems. She despised women who were so desperate, so unsure of themselves, that they married for money. She was only twenty-one. Her future was too special, too bright with promise, to ruin because of a temporary upset. Something would happen soon. All she had to do was wait.

". . . is a piece of trash that I shall transform into art." The snag of conversation spoken by an elegant Noel Cowardish man with a short cigarette holder and manicured hair caught Francesca's attention. He broke away from

Miranda Gwynwyck to materialize at her side. "Hello, my dear," he said. "You are incredibly lovely, and I've been waiting all evening to have you to myself. Miranda said I would enjoy you."

She smiled and placed her hand in his outstretched one. "Francesca Day," she said. "I hope I'm worth the wait."

"Lloyd Byron, and you most definitely are. We met earlier, although you probably don't remember."

"On the contrary, I remember very well. You're a friend of Miranda's, a famous film director."

"A hack, I'm afraid, who has once again sold himself out for the Yankee dollar." He tilted his head back dramatically and spoke to the ceiling, releasing a perfect smoke ring. "Miserable thing, money. It makes extraordinary people do all sorts of depraved things."

Francesca's eyes widened mischievously. "Exactly how many depraved things have you done, or is one permitted to inquire?"

"Far, far too many." He took a sip from a tumbler generously filled with what looked like straight scotch. "Everything connected with Hollywood is depraved. I, however, am determined to put my own stamp on even the most crassly commercial product."

"How absolutely courageous of you." She smiled with what she hoped would pass for admiration, but was actually amusement at his almost perfect parody of the world-weary director forced to compromise his art.

Lloyd Byron's eyes traced her cheekbones and then lingered on her mouth, his inspection admiring but dispassionate enough to tell her that he preferred male companionship to female. He pursed his lips and leaned forward as if he were sharing a great secret. "In two days, darling Francesca, I'm leaving for godforsaken Mississippi to begin filming something called *Delta Blood*, a script that I have single-handedly transformed from a wretched piece of garbage into a strong spiritual statement."

"I simply adore spiritual statements," she cooed, lifting a fresh glass of champagne from a passing tray while she covertly inspected Sarah Fargate-Smyth's barber-pole-striped taffeta dress, trying to decide whether it was Adolfo or Valentino.

"I intend to make *Delta Blood* an allegory, a statement of reverence for both life and death." He made a dramatic gesture with his glass without spilling a drop. "The enduring cycle of natural order. Do you understand?"

"Enduring cycles are my particular specialty."

For a moment he seemed to peer through her skin, and then he pressed his eyes shut dramatically. "I can feel your life force beating so strongly in the air that it steals my breath. You send out invisible vibrations with just the smallest movement of your head." He pressed his hand to his cheek. "I'm absolutely never wrong about people. Feel my skin. It's positively clammy."

She laughed. "Perhaps the prawns are a bit off."

He grabbed her hand and kissed her fingertips. "Love. I've fallen in love. I absolutely have to have you in my film. From the moment I saw you, I knew you'd be perfect for the part of Lucinda."

Francesca lifted one eyebrow. "I'm not an actress. Whatever gave you that idea?"

He frowned. "I never put labels on people. You are what I perceive you to be. I'm going to tell my producer I simply refuse to do the film without you."

"Don't you think that's a little extreme?" she said with a smile. "You've known me less than five minutes."

"I've known you my entire life, and I always trust my instincts; that's what separates me from the others." His lips formed a perfect oval and emitted a second smoke ring. "The role is small but memorable. I'm experimenting with the concept of physical as well as spiritual time travel—a southern plantation at the height of its nineteenth-century prosperity and then the plantation today, fallen to decay. I want to use you in the beginning in several short but infinitely memorable scenes, playing the part of a young English virgin who comes to the plantation. She never speaks, yet her presence absolutely consumes the screen. The part could become a showcase for you if you're interested in a serious career."

For a fraction of a moment, Francesca actually felt a wild, madly irrational stab of temptation. A film career would be the perfect answer to all her financial difficulties, and the drama of performing had always appealed to her. She thought of her friend Marisa Berenson, who seemed to be having a perfectly wonderful time with her film career, and then she nearly laughed aloud at her own naiveté. Legitimate directors hardly walked up to strange women at cocktail parties and offered them film roles.

Byron had whipped a small leather-bound notebook from his breast pocket and was scribbling something inside with a gold pen. "I have to leave London tomorrow for the States, so ring me at my hotel before noon. This is where I'm staying. Don't disappoint me, Francesca. My entire future is riding on your decision. You absolutely can't pass up the chance to appear in a major American film."

As she took the paper from him and slid it into her pocket, she restrained herself from commenting that *Delta Blood* hardly sounded like a major American film. "It's been lovely meeting you, Lloyd, but I'm afraid I'm not an actress."

He pressed both hands—one containing his drink and the other his cigarette holder—over his ears so that he looked something like a smoke-producing space creature. "No negative thoughts! You are what I say you are. The creative mind absolutely cannot afford negative thoughts. Call me before noon, darling. I simply have to have you!"

With that, he headed back toward Miranda. As she watched him, Francesca felt a hand settle on her shoulder, and a voice whispered in her ear, "He's not the only one who has to have you."

"Nicky Gwynwyck, you're a horrid sex fiend," Francesca said, turning to plant a fleeting kiss on his smoothly shaven jaw. "I just met the most amusing little man. Do you know him?"

Nicholas shook his head. "He's one of Miranda's friends. Come into the dining room, darling. I want to show you the new de Kooning."

Francesca dutifully inspected the painting, then chatted with several of Nicky's friends. She forgot about Lloyd Byron until Miranda Gwynwyck cornered her just as she and Nicholas were getting ready to leave.

"Congratulations, Francesca," Miranda said, "I heard the wonderful news. You seem to have a talent for landing on your feet. Rather like a cat . . ."

Francesca heartily disliked Nicholas's sister. She found

Miranda as dry and brittle as the lean brown twig she resembled, as well as ridiculously overprotective of a brother old enough to take care of himself. The two women had long ago given up the attempt to maintain more than a surface courtesy. "Speaking of cats," she said pleasantly, "you're looking divine, Miranda. How clever of you to combine stripes and plaids like that. But what wonderful news are you talking about?"

"Why, Lloyd's film, of course. Before he left, he told me he was casting you in an important part. Everyone in the room is green with envy."

"You actually believed him?" Francesca quirked one eyebrow.

"Shouldn't I have?"

"Of course not. I've hardly been reduced to appearing in fourth-rate films."

Nicholas's sister tossed back her head and laughed, her eyes gleaming with uncharacteristic brightness. "Poor Francesca. Fourth-rate, indeed. I thought you knew everyone. Obviously you're not as *au courant* as you want people to believe."

Francesca, who considered herself the most *au courant* person she knew, could barely conceal her annoyance. "What do you mean by that?"

"Sorry, dear, I didn't mean to insult you. I'm just surprised you haven't heard of Lloyd. He won the Golden Palm at Cannes four years ago, don't you remember? The critics are simply wild about him—all his films are marvelous allegories—and everyone is certain his new production is going to be a huge success. He works with only the best people."

Francesca felt a tiny thrill of excitement as Miranda went on to list all the famous actors with whom Byron had worked. Despite her politics, Miranda Gwynwyck was a terrible snob, and if she considered Lloyd Byron a respectable director, Francesca decided she needed to give his offer a bit more consideration.

Unfortunately, as soon as they left his sister's home, Nicky took her to a private club that had just opened in Chelsea. They stayed until nearly one, and then he proposed again and they had another terrible row—the absolute final one as far as she was concerned—so she didn't get to sleep until very late. As a result, it was well past noon before she awoke the next day, and even then she only did so because Miranda called her to ask some nonsensical question about a dressmaker.

Leaping out of bed, she cursed Cissy's maid for not having awakened her earlier and then flew across the carpeted floor of the guest bedroom, tugging open the sash on the front of her putty and salmon Natori nightgown as she moved. She bathed quickly, then threw herself into a pair of black wool trousers topped with a crimson and yellow Sonia Rykiel sweater. After applying the bare minimum of blusher, eye makeup, and lip gloss, then tugging on a pair of knee-high zippered boots, she dashed off to Byron's hotel where the clerk informed her the director had already checked out.

"Did he leave a message?" she asked, tapping her fingernails impatiently on the counter.

"I'll check."

The clerk returned a moment later with an envelope. Francesca ripped it open and quickly scanned the message.

Hosannas, Francesca darling!

If you're reading this, you've come to your senses, although it was absolutely inhumane of you not to have called before I left. I must have you in Louisiana by this Friday at the absolute latest. Fly into Gulfport, Mississippi, and hire a driver to take you to the Wentworth plantation according to enclosed directions. My assistant will handle work permit, contract, etc., when you arrive, and will reimburse you for travel expenses as well. Wire your acceptance immediately in care of the plantation address so I can once again draw an easy breath.

Ciao, my beautiful new star!

Francesca tucked the directions into her purse along with Byron's note. She remembered how exquisite Marisa Berenson had looked in both *Cabaret* and *Barry Lyndon* and how jealous she had been when she'd seen the films. What a perfectly wonderful way to make money.

And then she frowned as she recalled Byron's comment about reimbursing her for her travel expenses. If only she'd gotten hold of him earlier so he could have arranged for her ticket. Now she'd have to pay for it herself, and she was almost certain she didn't have enough money left in her account to cover her air fare. This ridiculous nonsense about her credit cards had temporarily closed off that avenue, and after last night she absolutely refused to talk to Nicky. So where was she to get the money for a plane ticket? She glanced at the clock behind the desk and saw that she was late for her appointment with her hairdresser. With a sigh, she tucked her purse under her arm. She'd just have to find a way.

"Excuse me, Mr. Beaudine." The buxom Delta flight attendant stopped next to Dallie's seat. "Would you mind signing an autograph for my nephew? He plays on his high school golf team. His name's Matthew, and he's a big fan of yours."

Dallie flashed her breasts an appreciative smile and then raised his eyes to her face, which wasn't quite as good as the rest of her, but was still mighty fine. "Be happy to," he said, taking the pad and pen she handed him. "Sure hope he plays better than I've been playing lately."

"The co-pilot told me you ran into a little trouble at Firestone a few weeks back."

"Honey, I invented trouble at Firestone."

She laughed appreciatively and then dropped her voice so that only he could hear. "I'll bet you've invented trouble in a lot of places besides golf courses."

"I do my best." He gave her a slow grin.

"Look me up next time you're in L.A., why don't you?" She scribbled something on the pad he handed back to her, ripped it off, and gave it to him right along with another smile.

As she moved away, he shoved the paper in the pocket of his jeans where it rustled against another piece of paper that the girl at the Avis counter had slipped to him when he'd left Los Angeles.

Skeet growled at him from the window seat. "Bet you she

don't even have a nephew, or if she does he's never heard of you."

Dallie opened a paperback copy of Vonnegut's *Breakfast of Champions* and began to read. He hated talking to Skeet on airplanes about as much as he hated anything. Skeet didn't like traveling unless he was doing it on four Goodyear radials and an interstate highway. The few times they'd had to abandon Dallie's newest Riviera to fly cross-country for a tournament—like this trek from Atlanta out to L.A. and back—Skeet's normal temper, prickly at best, turned completely sour.

Now he glowered at Dallie. "When are we getting in to Mobile? I hate these damned planes, and don't you start in on me again 'bout the laws of physics. You know and I know that there's nothing but air between us and the ground, and air can't hardly be expected to hold up something this big."

Dallie closed his eyes and said mildly, "Shut up, Skeet."

"Don't you go to sleep on me. Dammit, Dallie, I mean it! You know how much I hate to fly. Least you could do is stay awake and keep me company."

"I'm tired. Didn't get enough sleep last night."

"No wonder. Carousing till two in the morning and then bringing that mangy dog back with you."

Dallie opened his eyes and gave Skeet a sideways glance. "I don't think Astrid would like being called a mangy dog."

"Not *her!* The *dog,* you fool! Dammit, Dallie, I could hear that mutt whining right through the wall of the motel."

"What was I supposed to do?" Dallie answered, turning to meet Skeet's scowl. "Leave it starving by the freeway?"

"How much did you give 'em at the motel desk before we left this morning?"

Dallie muttered something Skeet couldn't quite hear.

"Whadju say?" Skeet repeated belligerently.

"A hundred, I said! A hundred now and another hundred next year when I come back and find the dog in good shape."

"Damn fool," Skeet muttered. "You and your strays. You got mangy dogs boarded away with motel managers in thirty states. I don't even know how you half keep track. Dogs. Runaway kids . . ."

"Kid. There was only one, and I put him on a Trailways bus the same day."

"You and your damn strays."

Dallie's gaze slowly swept Skeet from head to toe. "Yeah," he said. "Me and my goddamn strays."

That shut Skeet up for a while, which was exactly what Dallie had intended. He opened his book for the second time, and three pieces of blue stationery folded in half slipped out into his lap. He unfolded them, taking in the border of romping Snoopys across the top and the row of X's at the end, and then he began to read.

Dear Dallie,

I'm lying at the side of Rocky Halley's swimming pool with just about an inch and a half of purple bikini between myself and notoriety. Do you remember Sue Louise Jefferson, the little girl who worked at the Dairy Queen and betrayed her parents by going north to Purdue instead of to East Texas Baptist because she wanted to be the Boilermakers' Golden Girl, but then she got knocked up after the Ohio State game by a Buckeye linebacker instead? (Purdue lost, 21–13.) Anyway, I've been thinking about one day a few years back when Sue Louise was still in Wynette and she was feeling like Wynette High and her boyfriend were getting to be too much for her. Sue Louise looked over at me (I'd ordered a vanilla chocolate twist with sprinkles) and said, "I been thinking that life's like a Dairy Queen, Holly Grace. Either it tastes so good it gives you the shivers or it's melting all over your hand."

Life's melting, Dallie.

After coming in at fifty percent over quota for those bloodsuckers at Sports Equipment International, I was pulled into the office last week by the new V.P. who told me they're promoting someone else to southwest regional sales manager. Since that Someone Else happens to be male and barely made quota last year, I hit the roof and told the V.P. he was looking right down the bosom of an Equal Opportunity lawsuit. He said, "Now, now, honey. You women are too sensitive about this sort of thing. I want you to trust me." At which point I told him I wouldn't trust him not to get a hard-on in an old ladies' retirement home. Several more heated exchanges followed, which is why I'm currently lying beside old Number 22's swimming pool instead of living in airports.

News on the brighter side—I Farrah Fawcetted my hair until it looks just short of spectacular, and the Firebird's running great. (It was the carburetor, just like you said.)

Don't buy any bridges, Dallie, and keep making those birdies.

Love,
Holly Grace

P.S. I made up some of that about Sue Louise Jefferson, so if you happen to see her next time you're in Wynette, don't mention anything about the Buckeye linebacker.

Dallie smiled to himself, folded the letter into quarters, and tucked it into his shirt pocket, the closest place he could find to his heart.

Chapter

6

The limousine was a 1971 Chevrolet without air conditioning. This was especially irksome to Francesca because the thick, heavy heat seemed to have formed a cocoon around her. Even though her travels in the United States had until that day been limited to Manhattan and the Hamptons, she was too preoccupied with her own misjudgment to show any interest in the unfamiliar landscape they had passed since leaving Gulfport an hour earlier. How could she have blundered so badly in her choice of wardrobe? She glanced down with disgust at her heavy white woolen trousers and the long-sleeved celery-green cashmere sweater that was sticking so uncomfortably to her skin. It was the first day of October! Who could have imagined it would be so hot?

After nearly twenty-four hours of travel, her eyelids were drooping from weariness and her body was covered with grime. She had flown from Gatwick to JFK, then to Atlanta, and from there to Gulfport where the temperature was ninety-two in the shade and where the only driver she'd been able to hire had a car without air conditioning. Now all she could think about was going to her hotel, ordering a lovely gin and quinine, taking a long, cold shower, and sleeping for the next twenty-four hours. As soon as she

checked in with the film company and found out where she
was being lodged, she'd do exactly that.

Pulling the sweater away from her damp chest, she tried to
think of something to cheer herself up until she reached the
hotel. This was going to be an absolutely smashing adventure, she told herself. Although she had no acting experience, she'd always been a wonderful mimic, and she would
work very hard in the film so that the critics would think she
was marvelous and all the best directors would want to hire
her. She would go to wonderful parties and have a lovely
career and make absolutely scads of money. This was what
had been missing from her life, that elusive "something"
she'd never quite been able to define. Why ever hadn't she
thought of it before?

She pushed her hair back from her temples with the tips of
her fingers and congratulated herself on having so neatly
cleared the hurdle of finding enough money to cover her air
fare. It had been a lark, actually, once she'd gotten over the
initial shock of the idea. Lots of socialites took their clothes
to stores that bought designer labels for resale; she didn't
know why she hadn't done so months before. The money
from the sale had paid for a first-class airline ticket and
settled the most pressing of her bills. People made financial
matters so unnecessarily complex, she now realized, when
all it took to solve one's difficulties was a little initiative. She
abhorred wearing last season's clothes, anyway, and now she
could begin buying an entire new wardrobe as soon as the
film company reimbursed her for her ticket.

The car turned into a long drive lined with live oaks. She
craned her neck as they rounded a bend and she saw a
restored plantation house ahead, a three-story brick and
wooden structure with six fluted columns gracefully set
across the front veranda. As they drew nearer, she noticed
an assortment of twentieth-century trucks and vans parked
next to the antebellum home. The vehicles looked just as out
of place as the members of the crew who wandered about in
shorts with T-shirts, bare chests, and halter tops.

The driver pulled the car to a stop and turned to her. He
had a large round American Bicentennial button affixed to
the collar of his tan work shirt. It read "1776–1976" across

the top, with "AMERICA" and "LAND OF OPPORTUNI-TY" at the center and bottom. Francesca had seen signs of the American Bicentennial everywhere since she'd landed at JFK. The souvenir stands were loaded with commemorative buttons and cheap plastic models of the Statue of Liberty. When they passed through Gulfport, she'd even seen fire hydrants painted to look like Revolutionary War minutemen. To someone who came from a country as old as England, all this celebrating of a mere two hundred years seemed excessive.

"Forty-eight dollar," the taxi driver announced in English so heavily accented that she could barely understand it.

She sifted through the American currency she had purchased with her English pounds when she'd landed at JFK and handed him most of what she had, along with a generous tip and a smile. Then she climbed out of the cab, taking her cosmetic case with her.

"Francesca Day?" A young woman with frizzy hair and dangling earrings came toward her across the side lawn.

"Yes?"

"Hi. I'm Sally Calaverro. Welcome to the end of nowhere. I'm afraid I'm going to need you in wardrobe right away."

The driver set the Vuitton suitcase at Francesca's feet. She took in Sally's rumpled India print cotton skirt and the brown tank top she had unwisely chosen to wear without a bra. "That's impossible, Miss Calaverro," she replied. "As soon as I see Mr. Byron, I'm going to the hotel and then to bed. The only sleep I've had for twenty-four hours was on the plane, and I'm frightfully exhausted."

Sally's expression didn't change. "Well, I'm afraid I'm going to have to hold you up a little longer, although I'll try to make it as fast as possible. Lord Byron moved up the shooting schedule, and we have to have your costume ready by tomorrow morning."

"But that's preposterous. Tomorrow's Saturday. I'm going to need a few days to get settled in. He can hardly expect me to start working the moment I arrive."

Sally's pleasant manner slipped. "That's show biz, honey. Call your agent." She glanced at the Vuitton suitcases and then called to someone behind Francesca's back. "Hey,

Davey, take Miss Day's stuff over to the chicken coop, will ya?"

"Chicken coop!" Francesca exclaimed, beginning to feel genuinely alarmed. "I don't know what all this is about, but I want to go to my hotel immediately."

"Yeah, don't we all." She gave Francesca a smile that bordered on being insolent. "Don't worry, it's not really a chicken coop. The house where we're all staying sits right next to this property. It used to be a convalescent home a few years back; the beds still have cranks on them. We call it the chicken coop because that's what it looks like. If you don't mind a few cockroaches, it's not bad."

Francesca refused to rise to the bait. This was what happened, she realized, when one argued with underlings. "I want to see Mr. Byron at once," she declared.

"He's shooting inside the house right now, but he doesn't like being interrupted." Sally's eyes flicked rudely over her, and Francesca could feel her assessing the mussed clothes and inappropriate winter fabric.

"I'll take my chances," she replied sarcastically, staring at the wardrobe mistress for one long, hard moment before she pushed her hair back and walked away.

Sally Calaverro watched her go. She studied that tiny, slim body, remembering the perfect makeup and the gorgeous mane of hair. How did she manage to flip her hair like that with just a little shrug? Did gorgeous women take hair-flipping lessons or what? Sally tugged on a lock of her own hair, dry and frizzed at the ends from a bad perm. All the straight males in the company would start behaving like twelve-year-olds when they caught sight of that woman, Sally thought. They were accustomed to pretty little starlets, but this one was something else, with that fancy-schmansy British accent and a way of staring at you that reminded you your parents had crossed the ocean in steerage. During countless hours in too many singles bars, Sally had observed that some men ate up that superior, condescending crap.

"Shit," she muttered, feeling like a fat, frumpy giantess firmly entrenched on the wrong side of twenty-five. Miss High-and-Mighty had to be suffocating underneath her two-hundred-dollar cashmere sweater, but she looked as cool and crisp as a magazine ad. Some women, it seemed to

Sally, had been put on earth just for other women to hate, and Francesca Day was definitely one of them.

Dallie could feel the Dread Mondays descending on him, even though it was Saturday and he'd shot a spectacular 64 the day before playing eighteen holes with some good ol' boys outside Tuscaloosa. Dread Mondays was the name he'd given the black moods that seized him more frequently than he wanted to let on, sinking sharp teeth right into him and sucking out all the juice. In general, the Dread Mondays screwed up a hell of a lot more than his long irons.

He hunched over his Howard Johnson's coffee and stared out the front window of the restaurant into the parking lot. The sun wasn't up all the way and other than some sleepy-eyed truckers the restaurant was nearly empty. He tried to reason away his lousy mood. It hadn't been a bad season, he reminded himself. He'd won a few tournaments, and he and PGA Commissioner Deane Beman hadn't chatted more than two or three times on the commissioner's favorite subject—conduct unbecoming to a professional golfer.

"What'll it be?" asked the waitress who came up next to his table, an orange and blue hankie tucked in her pocket. She was one of those squeaky-clean fat women with sprayed hair and good makeup, the kind who took care of herself and made you say that she had a nice face underneath all that fat.

"Steak and home fries," he said, handing her the menu. "Two eggs over easy, and another gallon of coffee."

"You want it in a cup or should I shoot it straight into your veins?"

He chuckled. "You just keep it coming, honey, and I'll figure out where to put it." Damn, he loved waitresses. They were the best women in the world. They were street smart and sassy, and every one of them had a story.

This particular waitress took a few moments to look at him before she moved away, studying his pretty face, he figured. It happened all the time, and he generally didn't mind unless they also gave him that half-hungry look that told him they wanted something from him he damn well couldn't give.

The Dread Mondays came back in full force. Just this morning, right after he had crawled out of bed, he had been standing in the shower trying to get his two bloodshot eyes to stay open when the Bear had come right up next to him and whispered in his ear.

It's almost Halloween, Beaudine. Where are you going to hide yourself this year?

Dallie had turned on the cold water faucet as far as it would go, but the Bear kept at him.

Just what the hell does a worthless no-account like you think you're doing living on the very same planet with me?

Dallie shook away the memory as the food arrived along with Skeet, who slid into the booth. Dallie shoved the breakfast plate across the table and looked away while Skeet picked up his fork and sank it into the bloody steak.

"How you feelin' today, Dallie?"

"Can't complain."

"You were drinkin' pretty heavy last night."

Dallie shrugged. "I ran a few miles this morning. Did some push-ups. Sweated it off."

Skeet looked up, knife and fork poised in his hands. "Uh-huh."

"What the hell's that supposed to mean?"

"Don't mean nothin', Dallie, except I think the Dread Mondays been gettin' to you again."

He took a sip from his coffee cup. "It's natural to feel depressed toward the end of the season—too many motels, too much time on the road."

"Especially when you didn't come within kissin' distance of any of the majors."

"A tournament is a tournament."

"Horse manure." Skeet returned to the steak. A few minutes of silence passed between them.

Dallie finally spoke. "I wonder if Nicklaus ever gets the Dread Mondays?"

Skeet slammed down his fork. "Now, don't start thinkin' about Nicklaus again! Every time you start thinkin' about him, your game goes straight to hell."

Dallie pushed back his coffee cup and picked up the check. "Give me a couple of uppers, will you?"

"Shoot, Dallie, I thought you was going to lay off that stuff."

"You want me to stay in the running today or not?"

"'Course I want you to stay in the runnin', but I don't like the way you been doin' it lately."

"Just lay off, will you, and give me the fucking pills!"

Skeet shook his head and did as he was told, reaching into his pocket and pushing the black capsules across the table. Dallie snatched them up. As he swallowed them, it didn't slip past him that there was a halfway humorous contradiction between the care he took of his athlete's body and the abuse he subjected it to in the form of late nights, drinking, and that street-corner pharmacy he made Skeet carry around in his pockets. Still, it didn't really matter. Dallie stared down at the money he'd thrown on the table. When you were born a Beaudine, it was pretty much predestined that you wouldn't die of old age.

"This dress is hideous!"

Francesca studied her reflection in the long mirror set up at the end of the trailer that was serving as a makeshift costume shop. Her eyes had been enlarged for the screen with amber shadow and a thick set of eyelashes, and her hair was parted at the center, pulled smooth over her temples, and gathered into ringlets that fell over her ears. The period hairstyle was both charming and flattering, so she had no quarrel with the man who had just finished arranging it for her, but the dress was another story. To her fashion-conscious eye, the insipid pink taffeta with its layers of ruffled white lace flounces encircling the skirt looked like an overly sweet strawberry cream puff. The bodice fit so tightly she could barely breathe, and the boning pushed up her breasts until everything except her nipples spilled out over the top. The gown managed to look both saccharine and vulgar, certainly nothing like the costumes Marisa Berenson had worn in *Barry Lyndon*.

"It's not at all what I had in mind, and I can't possibly wear it," she said firmly. "You'll have to do something."

Sally Calaverra bit off a length of pink thread with more

force than necessary. "This is the costume that was designed for the part."

Francesca chided herself for not having paid more attention to the gown yesterday when Sally was fitting her. But she'd been so distracted by her exhaustion and the fact that Lloyd Byron had proved so unreasonably stubborn when she'd complained to him about her awful living arrangements that she'd barely looked at the costume. Now she had less than an hour before she was supposed to report to the set to film the first of her three scenes. At least the men in the company had been helpful, finding a more comfortable room for her with a private bath, bringing her a meal tray along with that lovely gin and quinine she'd been dreaming about. Even though the "chicken coop," with its small windows and blond veneer furniture, was an abomination, she'd slept like the dead and actually felt a small spurt of anticipation when she'd awakened that morning—at least until she'd taken a second look at her costume.

After turning to view the back of the gown, she decided to appeal to Sally's sense of fair play. "Surely you have something else. I absolutely never wear pink."

"This is the costume Lord Byron approved, and there's nothing I can do about it." Sally fastened the last of the hooks that held the back closed, pulling the fabric together more roughly than necessary.

Francesca sucked in her breath at the uncomfortable constriction. "Why do you keep calling him that ridiculous name—Lord Byron?"

"If you have to ask the question, you must not know him very well."

Francesca refused to let either the wardrobe mistress or the costume continue to dampen her spirits. After all, poor Sally had to work in this dreadful trailer all day. That would make anyone cross. Francesca reminded herself that she had been given a role in a prestigious film. Besides, her looks were striking enough to overcome any costume, even this one. Still, she absolutely had to do something about getting a hotel room. She had no intention of spending another night in a place that didn't offer maid service.

The French heels of her slippers crunched in the gravel as she crossed the drive and headed for the plantation house, her great hoopskirt swaying from side to side. This time she wasn't going to make the mistake she had made yesterday of trying to negotiate with lackeys. This time she was going straight to the producer with her list of complaints. Yesterday Lloyd Byron had told her he wanted the cast and crew lodged together to develop a spirit of ensemble, but she suspected he was just being cheap. As far as she was concerned, appearing in a prestigious film didn't make up for having to live like a barbarian.

After several inquiries, she finally located Lew Steiner, the producer of *Delta Blood*. He was standing in the hallway of the Wentworth mansion, just outside the drawing room where her scene was being set up for shooting. His sleazy appearance shocked her. Pudgy and unshaven, with a gold ankh hanging inside the open collar of his Hawaiian shirt, he looked as if he belonged on a Soho street corner selling stolen watches. She stepped over the electrical cables that curled across the hallway carpet and introduced herself. As he looked up from his clipboard, she launched into her litany of complaints while managing to keep a smile in her voice.

". . . So you see, Mr. Steiner, I absolutely can't spend another night in that dreadful place; I'm sure you understand. I need a hotel room before nightfall." She gazed at him winningly. "It's so difficult to sleep when one is worried about being devoured by cockroaches."

He devoted a few moments to ogling her elevated breasts, then pulled a folding chair away from the wall and sat down in it, spreading his legs so wide that the khaki fabric strained over his thighs. "Lord Byron told me you was a real looker, but I didn't believe him. Shows how smart I am." He made an unpleasant clicking noise with the corner of his mouth. "Only the male and female leads have hotel rooms, sweetie, and that's because it's in their contracts. The rest of the peasants have to rough it."

"'Peasants' is the operative word, isn't it?" she snapped, all efforts at being conciliatory forgotten. Were all film people this sordid? She felt a flash of irritation at Miranda Gwynwyck. Had Miranda known how unpleasant the conditions would be here?

"You don't want the job," Lew Steiner said with a shrug,

"I got a dozen bimbos I can have here by this afternoon to take your place. His Lordship was the one who hired you—not me."

Bimbos! Francesca could feel a red haze gathering behind her eyelids, but just as she opened her mouth to explode, a hand cupped her shoulder.

"Francesca!" Lloyd Byron exclaimed, turning her toward him and kissing her cheek, distracting her from her anger. "You look absolutely ravishing! Isn't she wonderful, Lew? Those green cat's eyes! That incredible mouth! Didn't I tell you how perfect she'd be for Lucinda, worth every penny it took to bring her over here."

Francesca started to remind him that she was the one who'd paid those pennies and that she wanted every one of them back, but before she could say anything, Lloyd Byron went on. "The dress is brilliant. Innocently childish, yet sensual. I love your hair. This is Francesca Day, everyone!"

Francesca acknowledged the introduction, and then Byron drew her aside, pulling a pale yellow hankie from the pocket of his tailored vanilla walking shorts and gently pressing it to his forehead. "We'll be shooting your scenes today and tomorrow, and my camera is going to be in absolute raptures. You don't have any lines, so there's no reason to be nervous."

"I'm hardly nervous," she declared. Good gracious, she'd gone out with the Prince of Wales. How could anyone think something like this would make her nervous? "Lloyd, this dress—"

"Scrumptious, isn't it?" He led her toward the drawing room, steering her between two cameras and a forest of lights to the front of the set, which had been furnished with Hepplewhite chairs, a damask-covered settee, and fresh flowers in old silver urns. "You'll be standing in front of those windows in the first shot. I'm going to backlight you, so all you have to do is move forward when I tell you to and let that marvelous face of yours come slowly into focus."

His reference to her marvelous face eased some of the resentment she was feeling over her treatment, and she looked at him more kindly.

"Think 'life force,'" he urged. "You've seen Fellini's work with silent characters. Even though Lucinda never speaks a word, her presence must reach out from the screen and grab the audience by the throat. She's a symbol of the unattainable. Vitality, radiance, magic!" He pursed his lips. "God, I hope this isn't going to be so esoteric that the cretins in the audience will miss the point."

For the next hour Francesca stood still for light readings and then concentrated on a walk-through rehearsal while final adjustments were made. She was introduced to Fletcher Hall, a dark, rather sinister-looking actor in morning coat and trousers who was playing the male lead. Although she kept abreast of movie star gossip, she had never heard of him, and once again she found herself assailed by misgivings. Why didn't she recognize any of these people's names? Maybe she'd made a mistake by not finding out more about the production before she'd jumped so blindly into it. Perhaps she should have asked to see a script. . . . But she'd looked through her contract yesterday, she reminded herself, and everything seemed in order.

Her misgivings gradually faded away as she shot the first setup easily, standing in front of the window and following Lloyd's instructions. "Beautiful!" he kept calling out. "Marvelous! You're a natural, Francesca." The compliments soothed her, and despite the increasingly uncomfortable constriction of the dress, she was able to relax between shots and flirt with some of the male crew members who'd been so attentive to her the night before.

Lloyd shot her walking across the room, making a deep curtsy to Fletcher Hall, and reacting to his dialogue by gazing wistfully into his face. By lunchtime, when she was unlaced from her costume for an hour, she discovered she was actually having fun. After the break, Lloyd positioned her at various points in the drawing room where he shot close-ups from every conceivable angle. "You're beautiful, darling!" he called out. "God, that heart-shaped face and those wonderful eyes are just perfect. Loosen her hair! Beautiful! Beautiful!" When he announced a break, Francesca stretched, rather like a cat who had just had its back well scratched.

By late afternoon her feeling of well-being had succumbed to the stifling heat from the weather and the carbon arc lights. The fans scattered about the set did little to cool the air, especially since they had to be turned off every time the cameras rolled. The heavy corset and multiple layers of petticoats beneath her gown trapped the heat next to her skin until she thought she would faint.

"I absolutely can't do any more today," she finally declared, while the makeup man dabbed at the tiny pearls of perspiration that had begun to form near her hairline in the most disgusting fashion. "I'm simply expiring from the heat, Lloyd."

"Only one more scene, darling. Just one more. Look at the angle of the light through the window. Your skin will positively glow. Please, Francesca, you've been such a princess. My exquisite, flawless princess!"

Put like that, how could she refuse?

Lloyd directed her toward a mark that had been placed on the floor not far from the fireplace. The beginning of the film, she had gathered, centered on the arrival of a young English schoolgirl at a Mississippi plantation where she was to become the bride of its reclusive owner, a man Francesca assumed was intended to resemble Jane Eyre's Rochester, although Fletcher Hall seemed a bit too oily to her to be a romantic hero. Unfortunately for the schoolgirl, but fortunately for Francesca, Lucinda was to die a tragic death the same day. Francesca could already envision a splendid death scene, which she intended to play with the proper amount of restrained passion. She had yet to discover exactly what Lucinda and the plantation owner had to do with the main body of the story, which was set in the present time and seemed to involve a large number of female cast members, but since she wouldn't be appearing in that part of the film, it didn't seem to matter.

Lloyd wiped his brow with a fresh handkerchief and went over to Fletcher Hall. "I want you to come up behind Francesca, put your hands on her shoulders, and then lift up her hair on the side so you can kiss her neck. Francesca, remember that you've been very sheltered all your life. His touch shocks you, but it pleases you, too. Do you understand?"

She felt a trickle of perspiration slide down between her breasts. "Of course I understand," she replied grouchily. A makeup man walked over and powdered her neck. She made him hold up a mirror so she could check his work.

"Remember, Fletcher," Lloyd went on, "I don't want you to actually kiss her neck—just anticipate the kiss. All right, then; let's walk it through."

Francesca took her place, only to suffer through another interminable delay while more lighting adjustments were made. Then someone noticed a damp patch on the back of Fletcher's morning coat where he had sweat through, and Sally had to bring a substitute coat from the costume trailer.

Francesca stamped her foot. "How much longer do you expect to keep me standing here? I won't put up with it! I'll give you exactly five more minutes, Lloyd, and then I'm leaving!"

He gave her a chilly glare. "Now, Francesca, we have to be professional. All these other people are tired, too."

"All these other people aren't wearing ten pounds of costume. I'd like to see how professional they'd be if they were bloody well suffocating to death!"

"Just a few more minutes," he said placatingly, and then he clutched his hands into fists and pulled them dramatically toward his chest. "Use the tension you're feeling, Francesca. Use the tension in your scene. Pass your tension on to Lucinda—a young girl sent to a new land to marry a man who is a stranger. Everyone quiet. Quiet, quiet, quiet. Let Francesca *feel* her tension."

The boom man, who'd been preoccupied with Francesca's cantilevered breasts for the better part of the day, leaned toward the cameraman. "I'd like to feel her tension."

"Stand in line, bro."

Finally the new morning coat arrived and the scene was shot. "Don't move!" Lloyd called out as soon they were done. "All we need is one close-up of Fletcher kissing Francesca's neck and we'll wrap for the day. It'll only take a second. Everybody ready?"

Francesca groaned, but she held her position. She'd suffered this long—a few more minutes wouldn't matter. Fletcher put his hands on her shoulders and picked up her hair. She hated having him touch her. He was definitely common, not her sort of man at all.

"Curve your neck a little more, Francesca," Lloyd instructed. "Makeup, where are you?"

"Right here, Lloyd."

"Come on, then."

The makeup man looked vague. "What do you need?"

"What do I *need?*" Lloyd threw out his hands in a dramatic gesture of frustration.

"Oh, ri-i-ight." The makeup man grimaced apologetically, then called out to Sally, who was standing just behind the camera. "Hey, Calaverro, reach into my box, will you, and toss me over Fletcher's fangs?"

Fletcher's *fangs?*

Francesca felt the bottom drop out of her stomach.

Chapter
7

Fangs!" Francesca screeched. "Why is Fletcher wearing fangs?"

Sally slapped the odious objects into the makeup man's hand. "It's a vampire picture, sweetie. What do you expect him to wear—a G-string?"

Francesca felt as if she'd stumbled into some terrible nightmare. Jerking away from Fletcher Hall, she rounded on Byron. "You lied to me!" she shouted. "Why didn't you tell me this was a vampire picture? Of all the miserable, rotten— My God, I'll sue you for this; I'll sue you to within an inch of your ridiculous life. If you think for one moment I'll let my name appear on—on—" She couldn't say the word again, she absolutely couldn't! A vision of Marisa Berenson flicked into her mind, the exquisite Marisa hearing about what had happened to poor Francesca Day and laughing until rivulets of tears ran down her alabaster cheeks.

Clenching her fists, Francesca cried, "You tell me right this minute exactly what this odious film is about!"

Lloyd sniffed, clearly offended. "It's about life and death, the transfer of blood, the very essence of life passing from one person to another. Metaphysical events of which you apparently know nothing." He stalked away in a huff.

97

Sally stepped forward and crossed her arms, obviously enjoying herself. "The film's about a bunch of stewardesses who rent a mansion that's supposed to be haunted. One by one they get their blood sucked by the former owner—good old Fletcher, who's spent the last century or so pining for his lost love Lucinda. There's a subplot with a female vampire and a male stripper, but that's closer to the end."

Francesca didn't wait to hear any more. Shooting a furious glance at all of them, she swept from the set. Her hoopskirt rocked from side to side and the blood boiled in her veins as she dashed out of the mansion and toward the trailers in search of Lew Steiner. They'd made a fool of her! She had sold her clothes and traveled halfway around the world to play a minor part in a vampire movie!

Quivering with rage, she found Steiner sitting at a metal table under the trees near the food truck. Her hoopskirt tilted up in the back as she came to a sudden stop, banging against the table leg. "I accepted this job because I heard Mr. Byron had a reputation as a quality director!" she declared, stabbing the air with a harsh gesture directed roughly toward the plantation house.

He looked up from a half-eaten ham on rye. "Who told you that?"

An image of Miranda Gwynwyck's face, smug and self-satisfied, swam before her eyes, and everything became blindingly clear. Miranda, who was supposed to be a feminist, had sabotaged another woman in a misguided attempt to protect her brother.

"He told me he was making a spiritual statement!" she exclaimed. "What does any of this have to do with spiritual statements—or life force or Fellini, for God's sake!"

Steiner smirked. "Why do you think we call him Lord Byron? He makes crap sound like poetry. Of course, it's still crap when he's done with it, but we don't tell him that. He's cheap and he works fast."

Francesca searched for some misunderstanding, for the small ray of hope her optimistic soul demanded. "What about the Golden Palm?" she asked stiffly.

"The Golden what?"

"Palm." She felt like a fool. "The Cannes Film Festival."

Lew Steiner stared at her for a moment before he released

a belly laugh that brought with it a small chunk of ham. "Honey, the only 'can' Lord Byron's ever had anything to do with is the kind that flushes. The last picture he did for me was *Co-ed Massacre,* and the one before that was a little number called *Arizona Prison Women.* It did real good at the drive-ins."

Francesca could barely force the words from her mouth. "And he actually expected *me* to appear in a vampire picture?"

"You're here, aren't you?"

She made up her mind immediately. "Not for long! I'll be back with my suitcases in exactly ten minutes, and I expect you to have a draft waiting for me to cover my expenses as well as a driver to take me to the airport. And if you use a single frame of that film you shot today, I'll bloody well sue you to within an inch of your worthless life."

"You signed a contract, so you won't have much luck."

"I signed a contract under false pretenses."

"Bullshit. Nobody lied to you. And you can forget about any money until you're finished shooting."

"I demand to be paid what you owe me!" She felt like some dreadful fishwife bargaining on a street corner. "You have to pay me for my travel. We had an agreement!"

"You're not getting a penny until you're done with your last scene tomorrow." He raked his eyes over her unpleasantly. "That's the one Lloyd wants you to do nude. The deflowering of innocence, he calls it."

"Lloyd will see me nude the same day he wins the Golden Palm!" Turning on her heel, she began to storm away only to have one of the hateful pink flounces on her skirt catch on the corner of the metal table. She jerked it free, tearing it in the process.

Steiner leaped up from the table. "Hey, be careful with that costume! Those things cost me money!"

She yanked the mustard container from the table and squeezed a great glob of it down the front of the skirt. "How dreadful," she scoffed. "It looks as if this one needs to be laundered!"

"You bitch!" he screamed after her as she stalked away. "You'll never work again! I'll see to it that no one hires you to empty out the garbage."

"Super!" she called back. "Because I've had all the garbage I can stand!"

Grabbing two handfuls of ruffle, she hitched her skirts to her knees, cut across the lawn, and headed for the chicken coop. Never, absolutely *never* in her entire life had she been treated so shabbily. She'd make Miranda Gwynwyck pay for this humiliation if it was the last thing she did. She'd bloody well marry Nicholas Gwynwyck the day she got home!

When she reached her room, she was pale with rage, and the sight of the unmade bed fueled her fury. Snatching up an ugly green lamp from the dresser, she hurled it across the room, where it shattered against the wall. The destruction didn't help; she still felt as if someone had hit her in the stomach. Dragging her suitcase to the bed, she wadded in the few clothes she had bothered to unpack the night before, slammed down the lid, and sat on it. By the time she had forced the latches closed, her carefully arranged curls had come loose and her chest was damp with perspiration. Then she remembered she was still wearing the awful pink costume.

She nearly wailed with frustration as she opened the suitcase again. This was all Nicky's fault! When she got back to London, she'd make him take her to the Costa del Sol, and she'd lie on the bloody beach all day and do nothing except think up ways to make him miserable! Reaching behind her, she began struggling with the hooks that held the bodice together, but they had been set in a double row, and the material fit so tightly that she couldn't get a grip to loosen them. She twisted farther around, releasing a particularly foul curse, but the hooks wouldn't budge. Just as she'd reconciled herself to looking for someone to help her, she thought of the expression on Lew Steiner's fat, smug face when she'd squirted mustard on the skirt. She nearly laughed aloud. Let's see how smug he looks when he sees his precious costume disappearing from sight, she thought with a burst of malicious glee.

No one was around to help her, so she had to carry the suitcase herself. Lugging her Vuitton bag in one hand and her cosmetic case in the other, she struggled down the path that led to the vehicles, only to discover when she got there that absolutely no one would drive her into Gulfport.

"Sorry, Miss Day, but they told us they needed all the cars," one of the men muttered, not quite looking her in the eye.

She didn't believe him for a moment. This was Lew Steiner's doing, his last petty attack on her!

Another crew member was more helpful. "There's a gas station not too far down the road." He indicated the direction with a turn of his head. "You could make a phone call from there and get somebody to pick you up."

The thought of walking down the driveway was daunting enough, let alone having to walk all the way to a petrol station. Just as she realized she'd have to swallow her pride and go back to the chicken coop to change her dress, Lew Steiner stepped out of one of the Airstream trailers and gave her a nasty smirk. She decided she'd die before she'd retreat an inch. Glaring back at him, she hitched up her suitcases and headed across the grass toward the driveway.

"Hey! Stop right there!" Steiner yelled, puffing up next to her. "Don't you take another step until I have that costume back!"

She rounded on him. "You so much as touch me, and I'll have you charged with assault!"

"I'll have you charged with theft! That dress belongs to me!"

"And I'm sure you'd look charming in it." She deliberately caught him in the knees with her cosmetic case as she turned to walk away. He yelped with pain, and she smiled to herself, wishing she'd hit him harder.

It would be her last moment of satisfaction for a very long time to come.

"You missed the turnoff," Skeet chastised Dallie from the back seat of the Buick Riviera. "Route ninety-eight, I told you. Ninety-eight to fifty-five, fifty-five to twelve, then set the cruise control straight into Baton Rouge."

"Telling me an hour ago and then falling asleep doesn't help much," Dallie grumbled. He wore a new cap, dark blue with an American flag on the front, but it wasn't doing the trick against the midafternoon sun, so he picked up a pair of mirrored sunglasses from the dashboard and put them on. Scrub pine stretched out on either side of the two-lane road.

He hadn't seen anything but a few rusted junk cars for miles, and his stomach had started rumbling. "Sometimes you're about worthless," he muttered.

"You got any Juicy Fruit?" Skeet asked.

A patch of color in the distance suddenly caught Dallie's attention, a swirl of bright pink wobbling slowly along the side of the road. As they drew closer, the shape gradually became more distinct.

He pulled his sunglasses off. "I don't believe it. Will you just look at that?"

Skeet leaned forward, his forearm resting on the back of the passenger seat, and shaded his eyes. "Now don't that just about beat all?" he chortled.

Francesca pushed herself on, one plodding step at a time, struggling for every breath against the vise of her corset. Dust streaked her cheeks, the tops of her breasts glistened with perspiration, and not fifteen minutes earlier, she had lost a nipple. Just like a cork bobbing to the surface of a wave, it had popped out of the neckline of her dress. She had quickly set down her suitcase and shoved it back in, but the memory made her shudder. If she could take back just one thing in her life, she thought for the hundredth time in as many minutes, she'd take back the moment she had decided to walk away from the Wentworth plantation wearing this dress.

The hoopskirt now looked like a gravy boat, protruding in the front and back and squished in on the sides from the combined pressure of the suitcase in her right hand and the cosmetic case in her left, both of which felt as if they were tearing her arms from their shoulder sockets. With each step, she winced. Her tiny French-heeled shoes had rubbed blisters on her feet, and each wayward puff of hot air sent another wave of dust blowing up into her face.

She wanted to sit down on the side of the road and cry, but she wasn't absolutely certain she would be able to force herself to get back up again. If only she weren't so frightened, her physical discomforts would be easier to endure. How could this have happened to her? She'd walked for miles without coming to the petrol station. Either it didn't exist or she had mistaken the direction, but she had seen nothing except a blistered wooden sign advertising a vegetable stand that had never materialized. Soon it would be dark, she was in a foreign country, and for all she knew a herd of horrid wild beasts lurked in those pines just off the side of the road. She forced herself to look straight ahead. The only thing that kept her from returning to the Wentworth plantation was the absolute certainty that she could never make it back that far.

Surely this road led to something, she told herself. Even in America they wouldn't build roads to nowhere, would they? The thought was so frightening she began playing small games in her head to keep herself moving forward. As she gritted her teeth against the pain in various parts of her body, she envisioned her favorite places, all of them light-years away from the dusty back roads of Mississippi. She envisioned Liberty's on Regent Street with its gnarled beams and wonderful Arabian jewelry, the perfumes at Sephora on the rue de Passy, and everything on Madison Avenue from Adolfo to Yves Saint Laurent. An image sprang into her mind of an icy glass of Perrier with a small sliver of lime. It hung in the hot air in front of her, the picture so vivid she felt as if she could reach out and clasp the cold, wet glass in the palm of her hand. She was beginning to hallucinate, she told herself, but the image was so pleasant she didn't try to make it go away.

The Perrier suddenly vaporized into the hot Mississippi air as she became aware of the sound of an automobile approaching from behind and then the soft squeal of brakes. Before she could balance the weight of the suitcases in her hands to turn toward the noise, a soft drawl drifted toward her from the other side of the road.

"Hey, darlin', didn't anybody tell you that Lee surrendered?"

The suitcase slammed into the front of her knees and her hoop bounced up in the back as she twisted around toward the voice. She balanced her weight and then blinked twice, unable to believe the vision that had materialized directly in front of her eyes.

Across the road, leaning out the window of a dark green automobile with his forearm resting across the top of the door panel, was a man so outrageously good-looking, so devastatingly handsome, that for a moment she thought she might actually have hallucinated him right along with the Perrier and the sliver of lime. As the handle of her suitcase dug into her palm, she took in the classic lines of his face, the molded cheekbones and lean jaw, the straight, perfect nose, and then his eyes, which were a brilliant Paul Newman blue and as thickly lashed as her own. How could a mortal man have eyes like that? How could a man have such an incredibly generous mouth and still look so masculine? Thick, dark blond hair curled up over the edges of a blue billed cap sporting an American flag. She could see the top of a formidable pair of shoulders, the well-formed muscles of his tanned forearm, and for one irrational moment she felt a crazy stab of panic.

She had finally met someone as beautiful as she was.

"You carryin' any Confederate secrets underneath those skirts?" the man said with a grin that revealed the kind of teeth that belonged on magazine pages and made people count back guiltily to the last time they'd flossed.

"I think the Yankees cut out her tongue, Dallie."

For the first time, Francesca became aware of another man, this one leaning out the back window. As she took in his sinister face and ominously slitted eyes, warning bells clanged in her head.

"Either that or she's a spy from the North," he went on. "Never knew a southern woman to keep quiet for so long."

"You a Yankee spy, darlin'?" Mr. Gorgeous asked, flashing those incredible teeth. "Pryin' out Confederate secrets with those pretty green eyes?"

She was suddenly conscious of her vulnerability—the deserted road, the failing sunlight, two strange men, the fact that she was in America, not safe at home in England. In America people packed loaded guns on their way to church, and criminals roamed the streets at will. She glanced nervously at the man in the back seat. He looked like someone who would torture small animals just for fun. What should she do? No one would hear her if she screamed, and she had no way to protect herself.

"Shoot, Skeet, you're scaring her. Pull that ugly head of yours in, will you?"

Skeet's head retracted, and the gorgeous man with the

strange name she hadn't quite caught lifted one perfect eyebrow, waiting for her to say something. She decided to brave it out—to be brisk, matter-of-fact, and under no circumstances let them see how desperate she actually was.

"I'm awfully afraid I've gotten myself into a bit of a muddle," she said, setting down her suitcase. "I seem to have lost my way. Frightful nuisance, of course."

Skeet poked his head back out the window.

Mr. Gorgeous grinned.

She kept going doggedly. "Perhaps you could tell me how far it is to the next petrol station. Or anywhere I might find a telephone, actually."

"You're from England, aren't you?" Skeet asked. "Dallie, do you hear the funny way she talks? She's a English lady, is what she is."

Francesca watched as Mr. Gorgeous—could someone really be named Dallie?—swept his gaze down over the pink and white ruffles of her gown. "I'll bet you got one hell of a story to tell, honey. Come on and hop in. We'll give you a lift to the next telephone."

She hesitated. Getting into a car with two strange men didn't strike her as the absolute wisest course to take, but she couldn't seem to think of an alternative. She stood in the road, ruffles dragging in the dust and suitcases at her feet, while an unfamiliar combination of fear and uncertainty made her feel queasy.

Skeet leaned all the way out the window and tilted his head to look at Dallie. "She's afraid you're rapist scum gettin' ready to ruin her." He turned back to her. "You take a good hard look at Dallie's pretty face, ma'am, and then tell me if you think a man with a face like that has to resort to violatin' unwilling women."

He definitely had a point, but somehow Francesca didn't feel comforted. The man named Dallie wasn't actually the person she was most worried about.

Dallie seemed to read her mind, which, considering the circumstances, probably wasn't all that difficult a thing to do. "Don't worry about Skeet, honey," he said. "Skeet's a dyed-in-the-wool misogynist, is what he is."

That word, coming from the mouth of someone who, despite his incredible good looks, had the accent and manner of a functional illiterate, surprised her. She was still hesitating when the door of the car opened and a pair of dusty cowboy boots hit the road. Dear God . . . She swallowed hard and looked up—way up.

His body was as perfect as his face.

He wore a navy blue T-shirt that skimmed the muscles of his chest, outlining biceps and triceps and all sorts of other incredible things, and a pair of jeans faded almost to white everywhere except at the frayed seams. His stomach was flat, his hips narrow; he was lean and leggy, several inches over six feet tall, and he absolutely took her breath away. It must be true, she thought wildly, what everyone said about Americans and vitamin pills.

"The trunk's full, so I'm gonna have to throw your cases in the back seat with Skeet there."

"That's fine. Anywhere will do." As he walked toward her, she turned the full force of her smile on him. She couldn't help it; the response was automatic, programmed into her Serritella genes. Not appearing at her best before a man this spectacular, even if he was a backwoods bumpkin, suddenly seemed more painful than the blisters on her feet. At that moment she would have given anything she owned for half an hour in front of a mirror with the contents of her cosmetic case and the white linen Mary McFadden that was hanging in a Piccadilly resale shop right next to her periwinkle blue evening pajamas.

He stopped where he was and stared down at her.

For the first time since she'd left London, she felt as if she'd arrived in home territory. The expression on his face confirmed a fact she had discovered long ago—men were men the world over. She peered upward with innocent, radiant eyes. "Something the matter?"

"Do you always do that?"

"Do what?" The dimple in her cheek deepened.

"Proposition a man less than five minutes after you meet him."

"Proposition!" She couldn't believe she'd heard him correctly, and she exclaimed indignantly, "I was most certainly not propositioning you."

"Honey, if that smile wasn't a proposition, I don't know what one is." He picked up her cases and carried them to the other side of the car. "Normally I wouldn't mind, you understand, but it strikes me as just short of foolhardy to be hanging out your advertising when you're in the middle of nowhere with two strange men who might be pervert scum, for all you know."

"My *advertising!*" She stomped her foot on the road. "Put those suitcases down this minute! I wouldn't go anywhere with you if my life depended on it."

He glanced around at the scrub pine and the deserted road. "From the looks of things, it's getting mighty close."

She didn't know what to do. She needed help, yet his behavior was insufferable, and she hated the idea of demeaning herself by getting in the car. He took the choice away from her when he pulled open the back door and unceremoniously shoved the luggage at Skeet.

"Be careful with those," she cried, racing up to the car. "They're Louis Vuitton!"

"You picked a real live one this time, Dallie," Skeet muttered from the back.

"Don't I just know it," Dallie replied. He climbed behind the wheel, slammed the door, and then leaned out the window to look at her. "If you want to retain possession of your luggage, honey, you'd better get inside real quick, because in exactly ten seconds, I'm slipping the old Riviera into gear and me and Mr. Vee-tawn won't be anything to you but a distant memory."

She limped around the back of the car to the passenger door on the other side, tears struggling to reach the surface. She felt humiliated, frightened, and—worst of all—helpless. A hairpin slid down the back of her neck and fell into the dirt.

Unfortunately, her discomfiture was just beginning. Hoopskirts, she quickly discovered, had not been designed to fit into a modern automobile. Refusing to look at either of her rescuers to see how they were reacting to her difficulties, she finally eased onto the seat backside first and then gathered the unwieldy volume of material into her lap as best she could.

Dallie freed the gearshift from a spillover of crinolines. "You always dress for comfort like this?"

She glared at him, opening her mouth to deliver one of her

famous snappy rejoinders only to discover that nothing sprang to mind. They rode for some time in silence while she stared doggedly ahead, her eyes barely making it over the top of her mountain of skirts, the stays in the bodice digging into her waist. As grateful as she was to be off her feet, her position made the constriction of the corset even more unbearable. She tried to take a deep breath, but her breasts rose so alarmingly that she settled for shallow breaths instead. One sneeze, she realized, and she was a centerfold.

"I'm Dallas Beaudine," the man behind the wheel announced. "Folks call me Dallie. That's Skeet Cooper in the back."

"Francesca Day," she replied, permitting her voice to thaw ever so slightly. She had to remember that Americans were notoriously informal. What was considered boorish on the part of an Englishman was regarded as normal behavior in the States. Besides, she couldn't resist bringing this gorgeous country bumpkin at least partway to his knees. This was something she was good at, something that couldn't possibly go wrong on this day when everything else had fallen apart. "I'm grateful to you for rescuing me," she said, smiling at him over the top of her skirts. "I'm afraid I've had an absolutely beastly few days."

"You mind telling us about it?" Dallie inquired. "Skeet and I've been traveling a lot of miles lately, and we're getting tired of each other's conversation."

"Well, it's all quite ridiculous, really. Miranda Gwynwyck, this perfectly odious woman—the brewery family, you know—persuaded me to leave London and accept a part in a film being shot at the Wentworth plantation."

Skeet's head popped up just behind her left shoulder, and his eyes were alive with curiosity. "You a movie star?" he inquired. "There's something about you that's been lookin' familiar to me, but I can't quite place it."

"Not actually." She thought about mentioning Vivien Leigh to him and then decided not to bother.

"I got it!" Skeet exclaimed. "I knew I'd seen you before. Dallie, you'll never guess who this is."

Francesca looked back at him warily.

"This here's 'Bereft Francesca'!" Skeet declared with a hoot of laughter. "I knew I recognized her. You remember, Dallie. The one goin' out with all those movie stars."

"No kidding," Dallie said.

"How on earth—" Francesca began, but Skeet interrupted her.

"Say, I was real sorry to hear about your mama and that taxicab."

Francesca stared at him speechlessly.

"Skeet's a fan of the tabloids," Dallie explained. "I don't much like them myself, but they do make you think about the power of mass communications. When I was a kid, we used to have this old blue geography book, and the first chapter was called 'Our Shrinking World.' That just about says it, doesn't it? Did you have geography books like that in England?"

"I—I don't think so," she replied weakly. A moment of silence passed and she had the horrifying feeling that they might be waiting for her to supply the details of Chloe's death. Even the thought of sharing something so intimate with strangers appalled her, so she quickly returned to the subject at hand as if she'd never been interrupted. "I flew halfway across the world, spent an absolutely miserable night in the most horrible accommodations you could imagine, and was forced to wear this absolutely hideous dress. Then I discovered that the picture had been misrepresented to me."

"Porno flick?" Dallie inquired.

"Certainly not!" she exclaimed. Didn't these rural Americans take even the briefest moment to examine a thought before they passed it on to their mouths? "Actually, it was one of those horrid films about"—she felt ill even saying the word—"vampires."

"No kidding!" Skeet's admiration was evident. "Do you know Vincent Price?"

Francesca pressed her eyes closed for a moment and then reopened them. "I haven't had the pleasure."

Skeet tapped Dallie on the shoulder. "Remember old Vincent when he used to be on 'Hollywood Squares'?

Sometimes his wife was on with him. What's her name? She's one of those fancy English actresses, too. Maybe Francie knows her."

"Francesca," she snapped. "I detest being called anything else."

Skeet sank back into the seat and she realized she had offended him, but she didn't care. Her name was her name, and no one had the right to alter it, especially not today when her hold on the world seemed so precarious.

"So, what are your plans now?" Dallie asked.

"To return to London as soon as possible." She thought of Miranda Gwynwyck, of Nicky, of the impossibility of continuing as she was. "And then I'm getting married." Without realizing it, she had made her decision, made it because she could see no alternative. After what she had endured during the past twenty-four hours, being married to a wealthy brewer no longer seemed like such a terrible fate. But now that the words had been spoken, she felt depressed instead of relieved. Another hairpin fell out; this one tumbled down her front and stuck in a ruffle. She distracted herself from her glum thoughts by asking Skeet for her cosmetic case. He passed it forward without a word. She pushed it deep into the folds of her skirt and flipped open the lid.

"My God . . ." She almost wept when she saw her face. Her heavy eye makeup looked grotesque in natural light, she had eaten off her lipstick, her hair was falling every which way, and she was dirty! Never in all her twenty-one years had she primped in front of a man other than her hairdresser, but she had to get *herself* back, the person she recognized!

Grabbing a bottle of cleansing lotion, she set to work repairing the mess. As the heavy makeup came off, she felt a need to distance herself from the two men, to make them understand that she belonged to a different world. "Honestly, I look a fright. This entire trip has been an absolute nightmare." She pulled off her false eyelashes, moisturized her eyelids, and applied a light dusting of highlighter along with taupe shadow and a dab of mascara. "Normally I use this wonderful German mascara called Ecarte, but Cissy

Kavendish's maid—a really impossible woman from the West Indies—forgot to pack it, so I'm slumming with an English brand."

She knew she was talking too much, but she didn't seem to be able to stop herself. She swept a Kent brush over a cake of toffee blusher and shaded the area just beneath her cheekbones. "I'd give almost anything for a really good facial right now. There's this wonderful place in Mayfair that uses thermal heat and all sorts of other incredibly miraculous things they combine with massage. Lizzy Arden does the same thing." She quickly outlined her lips with a pencil, filled them in from a pot of rosy beige gloss, and checked the overall effect. Not terrific, but at least she almost looked like herself again.

The growing silence in the car was making her increasingly uneasy, so she kept talking to fill it. "It's always difficult when you're in New York trying to decide between Arden's and Janet Sartin. Naturally, I'm talking about Janet Sartin on Madison Avenue. I mean, one can go to her salon on Park, but it isn't quite the same, is it?"

Everything was quiet for a moment.

Finally, Skeet spoke. "Dallie?"

"Uh-huh?"

"Do you think she's done yet?"

Dallie pulled off his sunglasses and set them back on the dashboard. "I have a feeling she's just warming up."

She looked over at him, embarrassed by her own behavior and angry with his. Couldn't he see that she was having the most miserable day of her life, and try to make things a bit easier for her? She hated the fact that he didn't seem impressed by her, hated the fact that he wasn't trying to impress her himself. In some strange way that she couldn't quite define, his lack of interest seemed more disorienting than anything else that had happened to her.

She returned her attention to the mirror and began snatching the pins from her hair, silently admonishing herself to stop worrying about Dallas Beaudine's opinion. Any moment now they'd stumble on civilization. She'd call a taxi to take her to the airport in Gulfport and then book herself on the next flight to London. Suddenly she remembered her embarrassing financial problem and then, just as quickly, found the solution. She would simply call Nicholas and have him wire her the money for her air fare.

Her throat felt scratchy and dry, and she coughed. "Could you roll up the windows? This dust is dreadful. And I'd really like something to drink." She eyed a small Styrofoam cooler in the back. "I don't suppose there's an off chance that you might have a bottle of Perrier stashed away in there?"

A moment of pregnant silence filled the interior of the Riviera.

"Shoot, ma'am, we're fresh out," Dallie said finally. "I'm afraid old Skeet finished the last bottle right after we pulled that liquor store holdup over in Meridian."

Chapter
8

Dallie was the first to admit that he didn't always treat women well. Part of it was him, but part of it was them, too. He liked down-home women, good-time women, low-down women. He liked women he could drink with, women who could tell dirty jokes without lowering their voices, who'd boom out that old punch line right across the sweating beer pitchers, wadded-up cocktail napkins, and Waylon Jennings on the jukebox—never wasting a moment's thought on how some blue-haired club lady in the next town might be listening in. He liked women who didn't fuss around with tears and arguments because he was spending all his time hitting a couple hundred balls with his three-wood at the driving range instead of taking them to a restaurant that served snails. He liked women, in fact, who were pretty much like men. Except beautiful. Because, most of all, Dallie liked beautiful women. Not phony fashion-model beautiful, with all that makeup and those bony boys' bodies that gave him the creeps, but sexy beautiful. He liked breasts and hips, eyes that laughed and teeth that sparkled, lips that parted wide. He liked women he could love and leave. That's the way he was, and that's what made him pretty much turn mean on every woman he had ever cared about.

But Francesca Day was going to be the exception. She made him turn mean just by being there.

"Is that a filling station?" Skeet asked, sounding happy for the first time in miles.

Francesca peered ahead and breathed a silent prayer of thanksgiving as Dallie slowed the car. Not that she'd actually believed that story about the liquor store holdup, but she had to be careful. They pulled up in front of a ramshackle wooden building with flaking paint and a hand-lettered "Live Bate" sign leaning against a rusted pump. A cloud of dust drifted in through the car window as the tires crunched on the gravel. Francesca felt as if she'd been traveling for aeons; she was perishing of thirst, dying of starvation, and she had to use the lavatory.

"End of the line," Dallie said, turning off the ignition. "There'll be a phone inside. You can call one of your friends from there."

"Oh, I'm not going to call a friend," she replied, extracting a small calfskin handbag from her cosmetic case. "I'm calling a taxi to take me to the airport in Gulfport."

A loud groan emanated from the back. Dallie slumped down in his seat and tipped his hat forward over his eyes.

"Is something wrong?" she inquired.

"I don't even know where to start," Dallie muttered.

"Don't say a word," Skeet announced. "Just let her out, slip the Riviera into gear, and drive away. The guy pumping gas can handle it. I mean it, Dallie. Only a fool sets out to make a double bogey on purpose."

"What's wrong?" Francesca asked, beginning to feel alarmed.

Dallie tilted the brim of his cap back with his thumb. "For starters, Gulfport is about two hours behind you. We're in Louisiana now, halfway to New Orleans. If you wanted to go to Gulfport, why were you walking west instead of east?"

"How was I supposed to know I was walking west?" she replied indignantly.

Dallie slammed the heels of his hands against the steering wheel. "Because the goddamn sun was setting in front of your eyes, that's how!"

"Oh." She thought for a moment. There was no reason for her to panic; she would simply find another way. "Doesn't New Orleans have an airport? I can fly from there."

"How do you intend to *get* there? And if you mention a

taxi again, I swear to God I'll throw both pieces of that Louie Vee-tawn right over into the scrub pine! You're out in the middle of nowhere, lady, don't you understand that? There aren't any taxicabs out here! This is backwoods Louisiana, not Paris, France!"

She sat up more stiffly and bit down on the inside of her lip. "I see," she said slowly. "Well, perhaps I could pay you to take me the rest of the way." She glanced down at her handbag, worry furrowing her brow. How much cash did she have left? She'd better call Nicholas right away so he could have money waiting for her in New Orleans.

Skeet pushed open the door and stepped out. "I'm gonna get me a bottle of Dr Pepper while you sort this out, Dallie. But I'm tellin' you one thing—if she's still in this car when I get back, you can find somebody else to haul your Spauldings around on Monday morning." The door slammed shut.

"What an impossible man," Francesca said with a sniff. She looked sideways at Dallie. He wouldn't really leave her, would he, just because that horrid sidekick of his didn't like her? She turned to him, her tone placating. "Just let me make a telephone call. It won't take a minute."

She extricated herself from the car as gracefully as she could and, hoops swaying, walked inside the ramshackle building. Opening her handbag, she took out her wallet and quickly counted her money. It didn't take long. Something uncomfortable slithered along the base of her spine. She only had eighteen dollars left . . . eighteen dollars between herself and starvation.

The receiver was sticky with dirt, but she paid no attention as she snatched it from its cradle and dialed 0. When she was finally connected with an overseas operator, she gave Nicholas's number and reversed the charges. While she waited for the call to go through, she tried to distract herself from her growing uneasiness by watching Dallie get out of the car and wander over to the owner of the place, who was loading some old tires into the back of a dilapidated truck and regarding all of them with interest. What a waste, she thought, her eyes straying back to Dallie—putting a face like that on an ignorant hillbilly.

Nicholas's houseboy finally answered, but her hopes of

rescue were short-lived as he refused the call, announcing that his employer was out of town for several weeks. She stared at the receiver and then placed another call, this one to Cissy Kavendish. Cissy answered, but she was no more inclined to accept the call than Nicholas's houseboy. That awful bitch! Francesca fumed as the line went dead.

Beginning to feel genuinely frightened, she mentally ran through her list of acquaintances only to realize that she hadn't been on the best of terms with even her most loyal admirers in the last few months. The only other person who might lend her money was David Graves, who was away in Africa somewhere shooting a picture. Gritting her teeth, she placed a third collect call, this one to Miranda Gwynwyck. Somewhat to her surprise, the call was accepted.

"Francesca, how nice to hear from you, even though it's after midnight and I was sound asleep. How's your film career coming? Is Lloyd treating you well?"

Francesca could almost hear her purring, and she clenched the receiver more tightly. "Everything's super, Miranda; I can't thank you enough—but I seem to have a small emergency, and I need to get in touch with Nicky. Give me his number, will you?"

"Sorry, darling, but he's incommunicado at the moment with an old friend—a glorious blond mathematician who adores him."

"I don't believe you."

"Francesca, even Nicky has his limits, and I do believe you finally reached them. But give me your number and I'll have him return your call when he gets back in two weeks so he can tell you himself."

"Two weeks won't do! I have to talk to him now."

"Why?"

'That's private," she snapped.

"Sorry, I can't help."

"Don't do this, Miranda! I absolutely must—" The line went dead just as the owner of the service station walked in the door and flipped the dial on a greasy white plastic radio. The voice of Diana Ross suddenly filled Francesca's ears, asking her if she knew where she was going to. "Oh, God . . ." she murmured.

And then she looked up to see Dallie walking around the

front of the car toward the driver's side. "Wait!" She dropped the receiver and raced out the door, her heart banging against her ribs, terrified that he would drive off and leave her.

He stopped where he was and leaned back against the hood, crossing his arms over his chest. "Don't tell me," he said. "Nobody was home."

"Well, yes . . . no. You see, Nicky, my fiancé—"

"Never mind." He pulled off his cap by the brim and shoved his hand through his hair. "I'll drop you off at the airport. Only you have to promise that you won't *talk* on the way."

She bristled, but before she had time to reply, he jerked his thumb toward the passenger door. "Hop in. Skeet wanted to stretch his legs, so we'll pick him up down the road."

She had to use the toilet before she went anywhere, and she would die if she didn't change her clothes. "I need a few minutes," she said. "I'm sure you won't mind waiting." Since she wasn't sure of any such thing, she turned the full force of her charm on him—green cat's eyes, soft mouth, a small, helpless hand on his arm.

The hand was a mistake. He looked down at it as if she'd put a snake there. "I got to tell you, Francie—there's something about the way you go about doing things that pretty much rubs me the wrong way."

She snatched away her hand. "Don't call me that! My name is Francesca. And don't imagine I'm exactly enamored with you, either."

"I don't imagine you're exactly enamored with anybody except yourself." He pulled a piece of bubble gum from his shirt pocket. "And Mr. Vee-tawn, of course."

She gave him her most withering glare, went to the back door of the car, and pulled it open to extract her suitcase, because absolutely nothing—not abysmal poverty, Miranda's betrayal, or Dallie Beaudine's insolence—was going to make her stay in her torturous pink outfit a moment longer.

He slowly unwrapped his piece of bubble gum as he watched her struggling with the suitcase. "If you turn it on its side there, Francie, I think it'll be easier to get out."

She clamped her teeth together to keep from calling him every vile name in her vocabulary and jerked on the suitcase, putting a long scratch in the leather as it banged into the door handle. I'll kill him, she thought, dragging the suitcase toward a rusted blue and white rest room sign. I'll kill him and then I'll stomp on his corpse. Grasping a chipped white porcelain knob that hung loose from its plate, she pushed on the door, but it refused to budge. She tried two more times before it finally swung inward, squealing on its hinges. And then she gulped.

The room was terrible. Dirty water lay in the recesses of the broken floor tiles revealed by a dim bare light bulb hanging from the ceiling by a cord. The toilet was encrusted with filth, its lid had disappeared, and the seat was broken in half. As she stood looking at the noisome room, the tears that had been threatening all day finally broke loose. She was hungry and thirsty, she had to use the toilet, she didn't have any money, and she wanted to *go home*. Dropping the suitcase outside in the dirt, she sat down on it and began to cry. How could this be happening to her? She was one of the ten most beautiful women in Great Britain!

A pair of cowboy boots appeared in the dust at her side. She began crying harder, burying her face in her hands and releasing great gulping sobs that seemed to come all the way from her toes. The boots took a few steps to the side, then tapped impatiently in the dirt.

"This kickup gonna take much longer, Francie? I want to fetch Skeet before the 'gators get him."

"I went out with the Prince of Wales," she said with a sob, finally looking up at him. "He fell in love with me!"

"Uh-huh. Well, they say there's a lot of inbreeding—"

"I could have been *queen!*" The word was a wail as tears dripped off her cheeks and onto her breasts. "He adored me, everybody knew it. We went to balls and the opera—"

He squinted against the fading sun. "Do you think you could sorta skip through this part and get to the point?"

"I have to go to the *loo!*" she cried, pointing a shaky finger toward the rusty blue and white sign.

He left her side and then reappeared a moment later. "I see what you mean." Digging two rumpled tissues from his pocket, he let them flutter down into her lap. "I think you'll be safer out back behind the building."

She looked down at the tissues and then up at him and began sobbing again.

He took several chomps on his gum. "That domestic mascara of yours sure is falling down on the job."

Leaping up from the suitcase, tissues dropping to the ground, she shouted at him, "You think all this is amusing, don't you? You find it hysterically funny that I'm trapped in this awful dress and I can't go home and Nicky's gone off with some dreadful mathematician Miranda says is glorious—"

"Uh-huh." Her suitcase fell forward under the pressure of Dallie's boot toe. Before Francesca had a chance to protest, he had knelt down and flipped open the catches. "This is a god-awful mess," he said when he saw the chaos inside. "You got any jeans in here?"

"Under the Zandra Rhodes."

"What's a zanderoads? Never mind, I found the jeans. How about a T-shirt? You wear T-shirts, Francie?"

"There's a blouse," she sniffed. "Greige with cocoa trim—a Halston. And a Hermès belt with an art deco buckle. And my Bottega Veneta sandals."

He propped one arm across his knee and looked up at her. "You're startin' to push me again, aren't you, darlin'?"

Dashing away her tears with the back of her hand, she stared down at him, not having the faintest idea what he was talking about. He sighed and got back up. "Maybe you'd better find what you want yourself. I'll amble back to the car and wait for you. And try not to take too long. Old Skeet's already gonna be hotter than a Texas tamale."

As he turned to walk away, she sniffed and bit on her lip. "Mr. Beaudine?" He turned. She dug her fingernails into her palms. "Would it be possible—" Gracious, this was humiliating! "That is to say, perhaps you might— Actually, I seem to—" What was *wrong* with her? How had an ignorant hillbilly managed to intimidate her so badly that she couldn't seem to form the simplest sentence?

"Spit it out, honey. I got my heart set on findin' a cure for cancer before the decade's over, or at least having a cold

Lone Star and a chili dog by the time Landry's boys hit the Astroturf for the division championship."

"Stop it!" She stamped her foot in the dirt. "Just stop it! I don't have any idea what you're talking about, and even a blind idiot could see that I can't possibly get out of this dress by myself, and if you ask me, the person who talks too much around here is *you!*"

He grinned, and she suddenly forgot her misery under the force of that devastating smile, crinkling the corners of his mouth and eyes. His amusement seemed to come from a place deep inside, and as she watched him she had the absurd feeling that an entire world of funniness had somehow managed to pass her by. The idea made her feel more out of sorts than ever. "Hurry up, will you?" she snapped. "I can barely breathe."

"Turn around, Francie. Undressing women is one of my particular talents. Even better than my bunker shot."

"You're not undressing me," she sputtered, as she turned her back to him. "Don't make it sound so sordid."

His hands paused on the hooks at the back of her dress. "What exactly would you call it?"

"Performing a helpful function."

"Sort of like a maid?" The row of hooks began to ease open.

"Rather like that, yes." She had the uneasy feeling that she'd just taken another giant step in the wrong direction. She heard a short, vaguely malevolent chuckle that confirmed her fears.

"Something about you is sort of growin' on me, Francie. It's not often life gives you the opportunity to meet living history."

"Living history?"

"Sure. French Revolution, old Marie Antoinette. All that let-them-eat-cake stuff."

"What," she asked, as the last of the hooks fell open, "would someone like you know about Marie Antoinette?"

"Until a little over an hour ago," he replied, "not much."

They picked Skeet up about two miles down the road, and as Dallie had predicted, he wasn't happy. Francesca found herself banished to the back seat, where she sipped from a bottle of something called Yahoo chocolate soda, which she'd taken from the Styrofoam cooler without waiting for an invitation. She drank and brooded, remaining silent, as requested, all the way into New Orleans. She wondered what Dallie would say if he knew that she didn't have a plane ticket, but she refused even to consider telling him the truth. Picking at the corner of the Yahoo label with her thumbnail, she contemplated the fact that she didn't have a mother, money, a home, or a fiancé. All she had left was a small remnant of pride, and she desperately wanted the chance to wave it at least once before the day was over. For some reason, pride was becoming increasingly important to her when it came to Dallie Beaudine.

If only he weren't so impossibly gorgeous, and so obviously unimpressed with her. It was infuriating . . . and irresistible. She had never walked away from a challenge where a man was concerned, and it grated on her to be forced to walk away from this one. Common sense told her she had bigger problems to worry about, but something more visceral said that if she couldn't manage to attract the admiration of Dallie Beaudine she would have lost one more chunk of herself.

As she finished her chocolate soda, she figured out how to get the money she needed for her ticket home. Of course! The idea was so absurdly simple that she should have thought of it right away. She looked over at her suitcase and frowned at the scratch on the side. That suitcase had cost something like eighteen hundred pounds when she'd bought it less than a year before. Flipping open her cosmetic case, she riffled through the contents looking for a cake of eye shadow approximately the same butternut shade as the leather. When she found it, she unscrewed the lid and gently dabbed at the scratch. It was still faintly visible when she was done, but she felt satisfied that only a close inspection would reveal the flaw.

With that problem out of the way and the first airport sign in sight, she returned her thoughts to Dallie Beaudine, trying to understand his attitude toward her. The whole problem—the only reason everything was going so badly between them—was that she looked so awful. This had temporarily thrown him into the superior position. She let her eyelids drift shut and played out a fantasy in her mind in which she would appear before him well rested, hair freshly arranged in shining chestnut curls, makeup impeccable, clothes wonderful. She would have him on his knees in seconds.

The current argument, in what seemed to be an ongoing series between Dallie and that horrid companion of his, distracted her from her reverie.

"I don't see why you're so hell-bent on making Baton Rouge tonight," Skeet complained. "We've got all day tomorrow to get to Lake Charles in time for your round Monday morning. What difference does an extra hour make?"

"The difference is I don't want to spend any more time driving on Sunday than I have to."

"I'll drive. It's only an extra hour, and there's that real nice motel where we stayed last year. Don't you have a dog or something to check on there?"

"Since when did you give a damn about any of my dogs?"

"A cute little mutt with a black spot over one eye, wasn't it? Had some kind of a bad leg."

"That was in Vicksburg."

"You sure?"

"Of course I'm sure. Listen, Skeet, if you want to spend tonight in New Orleans so you can go over to the Blue Choctaw and see that red-haired waitress, why don't you just come out and say it instead of beating around the bush like this, going on about dogs and bad legs like some kind of goddamn hypocrite."

"I didn't say anything about a red-haired waitress or wanting to go to the Blue Choctaw."

"Yeah. Well, I'm not going with you. That place is an invitation to a fight, especially on Saturday night. The women all look like mud wrestlers and the men are worse. I damn near busted a rib the last time I went there, and I've had enough aggravation for one day."

"I told you to leave her with the guy at the filling station, but you wouldn't listen to me. You never listen to me. Just like last Thursday. I told you that shot from the rough was a hundred thirty-five yards; I'd paced it off, and I told you, but you ignored me and picked up that eight-iron just like I hadn't said a word."

"Just be quiet about it, will you? I told you right then I was wrong, and I told you the next day that I was wrong, and I been telling you twice a day ever since, so shut up!"

"That's a rookie's trick, Dallie, not trusting your caddy for the yardage. Sometimes I think you're deliberately trying to lose tournaments."

"Francie?" Dallie said over his shoulder. "You got any more of those fascinating stories about mascara you want to tell me right now?"

"Sorry," she said sweetly. "I'm all out. Besides, I'm not supposed to chat. Remember?"

"Too late anyway, I guess," Dallie sighed, pulling up to the airport's main terminal. With the ignition still running, he got out of the car and came around to open her door. "Well, Francie, I can't say it hasn't been interesting." After she stepped out, he reached into the back seat, removed her cases, and set them next to her on the sidewalk. "Good luck with your fiancé and the prince and all those other high rollers you run around with."

"Thank you," she said stiffly.

He took a couple of quick chews on his bubble gum and grinned. "Good luck with those vampires, too."

She met his amused gaze with icy dignity. "Good-bye, Mr. Beaudine."

"Good-bye, Miss Francie Pants."

He'd gotten the last word on her. She stood on the pavement in front of the terminal and faced the undeniable fact that the gorgeous hillbilly had scored the final point in a game she'd invented. An illiterate—probably illegitimate—backwoods bumpkin had outwitted, outtalked, and outscored the incomparable Francesca Serritella Day.

What was left of her spirit staged a full-scale rebellion, and she gazed up at him with eyes that spoke volumes in the history of banned literature. "It's too bad we didn't meet under different circumstances." Her pouty mouth curled into a wicked smile. "I'm absolutely certain we'd have tons in common."

And then she stood on tiptoe, curled into his chest, and lifted her arms until they encircled his neck, never for a moment letting her gaze drop from his. She tilted up her perfect face and offered up her soft mouth like a jeweled chalice. Gently drawing his head down with the palms of her hands, she placed her lips over his and then slowly parted them so that Dallie Beaudine could take a long, unforgettable drink.

He didn't even hesitate. He jumped right in just as if he'd been there before, bringing with him all the expertise he'd gained over the years to meet and mingle with all of hers. Their kiss was perfect—hot and sexy—two pros doing what they did best, a tingler right down to the toes. They were both too experienced to bump teeth or mash noses or do any of those other awkward things less practiced men and women are apt to do. The Mistress of Seduction had met the Master, and to Francesca the experience was as close to perfect as anything she'd ever felt, complete with goose bumps and a lovely weakness in her knees, a spectacularly perfect kiss made even more perfect by the knowledge that she didn't have to give a moment's thought to the awkward aftermath of having implicitly promised something she had no intention of delivering.

The pressure of the kiss eased, and she slid the tip of her tongue along his bottom lip. Then she slowly pulled away. "Good-bye, Dallie," she said softly, her cat's eyes slanting up at him with a mischievous glitter. "Look me up the next time you're in Cap Ferret."

Just before she turned away, she had the pleasure of seeing a slightly bemused expression take over his gorgeous face.

"I should be used to it by now," Skeet was saying as Dallie climbed back behind the wheel. "I should be used to it, but I'm not. They just fall all over you. Rich ones, poor ones, ugly ones, fancy ones. Don't make no difference. It's like they're all a bunch of homing pigeons circling in to roost. You got lipstick on you."

Dallie wiped the back of his hand over his mouth and then looked down at the pale smear. "Definitely imported," he muttered.

From just inside the door of the terminal, Francesca watched the Buick pull away and suppressed an absurd pang of regret. As soon as the car was out of sight, she picked up her cases and walked back outside until she came to a taxi stand with a single yellow cab. The driver got out and loaded her cases into the trunk while she settled in the back. As he got behind the wheel, he turned to her. "Where to, ma'am?"

"I know it's late," she said, "but do you think you could find a resale shop that's still open?"

"Resale shop?"

"Yes. Someplace that buys designer labels . . . and a really extraordinary suitcase."

Chapter
9

New Orleans—the city of "Stella, Stella, Stella for star," of lacy ironwork and Old Man River, Confederate jasmine and sweet olive, hot nights, hot jazz, hot women—lay at the bottom of the Mississippi like a tarnished piece of jewelry. In a city noted for its individuality, the Blue Choctaw managed to remain common. Gray and dingy, with a pair of neon beer signs that flickered painfully in a window dulled by exhaust fumes, the Blue Choctaw could have been located near the seediest part of any American city—near the docks, the mills, the river, skirting the ghetto. It bumped up to the bad side, the never-after-dark, littered sidewalks, broken street lamps, no-good-girls-allowed part of town.

The Blue Choctaw had a particular aversion to good girls. Even the women the men had left at home weren't all that good, and the men sure as hell didn't want to find better ones sitting on the red vinyl bar stools next to them. They wanted to find girls like Bonni and Cleo, semi-hookers who wore strong perfume and red lipstick, who talked tough and thought tough and helped a man forget that Jimmy Asshole Carter was sure enough going to get himself elected President and give all the good jobs to the niggers.

Bonni twirled the yellow plastic sword in her mai-tai and peered through the noisy crowd at her friend and rival Cleo Reznyak, who was shoving her tits up against Tony Grasso as he pushed a quarter in the jukebox and punched in C-24. There was a mean mood in the smoky air of the Blue Choctaw that night, meaner than usual, although Bonni didn't try to put her finger on its source. Maybe it was the sticky heat that wouldn't let go; maybe it was the fact that Bonni had turned thirty the week before and the last of her illusions had just about disappeared. She knew she wasn't smart, wasn't pretty enough to get by on her looks, and she didn't have the energy to improve herself. She was living in a broken-down trailer park, answering the telephone at Gloria's Hair Beautiful, and it wasn't going to get any better.

For a girl like Bonni, the Blue Choctaw represented a shot at the good times, a few laughs, the occasional big spender who would pick up the tab for her mai-tais, take her to bed, and leave a fifty-dollar bill on the dresser next morning. One of those big spenders was sitting at the other end of the bar . . . with his eye on Cleo.

She and Cleo had an agreement. They stood together against any newcomers who tried to sink their butts too comfortably onto the Blue Choctaw's bar stools, and they didn't poach on each other's territory. Still, the spender at the bar tempted Bonni. He had a big belly and arms strong enough to show that he held a steady job, maybe working on one of the offshore drilling rigs—a man out for a good time. Cleo had been getting more than her fair share of men lately, including Tony Grasso, and Bonni was tired of it.

"Hi," she said, wandering over and sliding up on the stool next to him. "You're new around here, aren't you?"

He looked her over, taking in her carefully arranged helmet of sprayed blond hair, her plum eye shadow, and deep, full breasts. As he nodded, Bonni could see him forgetting about Cleo.

"Been in Biloxi the last few years," he replied. "What're you drinking?"

She gave him a kittenish smile. "I'm partial to mai-tais." After he gestured toward the bartender for her drink, she crossed her legs. "My ex-husband spent some time in Biloxi. I don't suppose you ran into him? A cheap son of a bitch named Ryland."

He shook his head—didn't know anybody by that name —and moved his arm so that it brushed along the side of her tits. Bonni decided they were going to get along fine, and she turned her body just far enough so she didn't have to see the accusing expression in Cleo's eyes.

An hour later the two of them had it out in the little girls' room. Cleo bitched for a while, jerking a comb through her tough black hair and then tightening the posts on her best pair of fake ruby earrings. Bonni apologized and said she hadn't known Cleo was interested.

Cleo studied her suspiciously. "You know I'm getting tired of Tony. All he does is complain about his wife. Shit, I haven't had a good laugh out of him in weeks."

"The guy at the bar—his name's Pete—he's not much for laughs either," Bonnie admitted. She pulled a vial of Tabu from her purse and generously sprayed herself. "This place sure is going to hell."

Cleo fixed her mouth and then stepped back to scrutinize her work. "You said it there, honey."

"Maybe we should go up north. Up to Chicago or someplace."

"I been thinking about St. Louis. Someplace where the fucking men aren't all married."

It was a topic they'd discussed many times, and they continued to discuss it as they left the ladies' room, weighing the advantages of the oil boom in Houston, the climate in Los Angeles, the money in New York, and knowing all the time they'd never leave New Orleans.

The two women pushed through the group of men congregated near the bar, their eyes busy, no longer paying attention to each other even though they continued to talk. As they searched out their prey, Bonni began to realize something had changed. Everything seemed quieter, although the bar was still full, people were talking, and the jukebox blared out "Ruby." Then she noticed that a lot of heads were turning toward the doorway.

Pinching Cleo hard on the arm, she nodded her head. "Over there," she said.

Cleo looked in the direction Bonni had indicated and came to a sudden stop. "Kee-rist."

They hated her on sight. She was everything they weren't—a woman right off the fashion pages, beautiful as a New York model, even in a pair of jeans; expensive-looking, stylish, and snooty, with an expression on her face like she'd just smelled something bad, and they were it. She was the kind of woman who didn't belong anywhere near a place like the Blue Choctaw, a hostile invader who made them feel ugly, cheap, and worn out. And then they saw the two men they'd left not ten minutes earlier walking right toward her.

Bonni and Cleo looked at each other for a moment before they headed in the same direction, their eyes narrowed, their stomachs bitter with determination.

Francesca remained oblivious to their approach as she searched the hostile environment of the Blue Choctaw with an uneasy gaze, concentrating all her attention on trying to peer through the thick smoke and press of bodies to catch sight of Skeet Cooper. A tiny, apprehensive muscle quivered at her temple, and her palms were damp. Never had she felt so out of her element as she did in this seedy New Orleans bar.

The sound of raucous laughter and too-loud music attacked her ears. She felt hostile eyes inspecting her, and she gripped her small Vuitton cosmetic case more tightly, trying not to remember that it contained all she had left in the world. She tried to blot out the memory of the horrible places the taxi driver had taken her, each one more repulsive than the last, and none of them bearing the slightest resemblance to the resale shop in Piccadilly where the clerks wore gently used designer originals and served tea to their customers. She had thought it such a good idea to sell her clothes; she hadn't imagined she would end up in some dreadful pawnshop parting with her suitcase and the rest of her wardrobe for three hundred and fifty dollars just so she could pay her taxi fare and have enough money left to survive on for another few days until she got hold of Nicky. A Louis Vuitton suitcase full of designer originals let go for three hundred and fifty dollars! She couldn't spend two nights at a really good hotel for that amount.

"Hi, honey."

Francesca jumped as two disreputable-looking men came up to her, one with a stomach that strained the buttons of his plaid shirt, the other a greasy-looking character with enlarged pores.

"You look like you could use a drink," the heavy one said.

"Me and my new buddy Tony here'd be happy to buy you a couple of mai-tais."

"No, thank you," she replied, looking anxiously about for Skeet. Why wasn't he here? A needle-sharp shower of resentment pricked at her. Why hadn't Dallie given her the name of his motel instead of forcing her to stand in the doorway of this horrible place, the name of which she'd barely been able to dredge up after spending twenty minutes poring over a telephone book? The fact that she needed to find him had printed itself indelibly in her brain while she was making another series of fruitless calls to London trying to locate Nicky or David Graves or one of her other former companions, all of whom seemed to be out of town, recently married, or not taking her calls.

Two tough-faced women sidled up to the men in front of her, their hostility evident. The blonde leaned into the man with the stomach. "Hey, Pete. Let's dance."

Pete didn't take his eyes off Francesca. "Later, Bonni."

"I wanna dance now," Bonni insisted, her mouth hard.

Pete's gaze slithered over Francesca. "I said later. Dance with Tony."

"Tony's dancin' with me," the black-haired woman said, curling short purple fingernails over the other man's hairy arm. "Come on, baby."

"Go away, Cleo." Shaking off the purple fingernails, Tony pressed his hand on the wall just next to Francesca's head and leaned toward her. "You new in town? I don't remember seeing you around here before."

She shifted her weight, trying to catch sight of a red bandanna headband while she avoided the unpleasant smell of whiskey mixed with cheap after-shave.

The woman named Cleo sneered. "You don't think a snotty bitch like her's gonna give you the time of day, do you, Tony?"

"I thought I told you to get lost." He gave Francesca an oily smile. "Sure you wouldn't like a drink?"

"I'm not thirsty," Francesca said stiffly. "I'm waiting for someone."

"Looks like you got stood up," Bonni purred. "So why don't you get lost."

A blast of warm air from outside hit the damp back of her

blouse as the door opened, admitting three more rough-faced men, none of whom was Skeet. Francesca's uneasiness grew. She couldn't stand in the doorway all night, but she recoiled at the thought of going any farther inside. Why hadn't Dallie told her where he was lodging? She couldn't stay alone in New Orleans with only three hundred and fifty dollars between herself and starvation while she waited for Nicky to finish his fling. She had to find Dallie now, before he left! "Excuse me," she said abruptly, sliding between Tony and Pete.

She heard a short, unpleasant laugh from one of the women, and then a mutter from Tony. "It's your fault, Bonni," he complained. "You and Cleo scared her away just when—" The rest was mercifully lost as she slid through the crowd toward the back, looking for an inconspicuous table.

"Hey, honey—"

A quick glance over her shoulder told her that Pete was following her. She squeezed between two tables, felt someone's hand brush her bottom, and made a dash for the lavatory. Once inside, she sagged against the door, her cosmetic case clutched to her chest. Outside, she heard the sound of breaking glass and she jumped. What a hideous place! Her opinion of Skeet Cooper sank even lower. Suddenly she remembered Dallie's reference to a red-haired waitress. Although she hadn't spotted anyone who fit that description, she hadn't really been looking. Maybe the bartender could give her some information.

The door next to her opened abruptly, and the two tough-faced women came in. "Look what we got here, Bonni Lynn," the one named Cleo sneered.

"Well, if it ain't Miss Rich Bitch," Bonni replied. "What's the matter, honey? Did you get tired of working the hotel trade and decide to come down here to slum it?"

Francesca's jaw tightened. These awful women had pushed her far enough. Lifting her chin, she stared at Bonni's harsh plum eye shadow. "Have you been this rude from birth, or is it a more recent occurrence?"

Cleo laughed and turned to Bonni. "My, my. Didn't she just tell you off." She studied Francesca's cosmetic case. "What do you have in there that's so important?"

"None of your business."

"Got your jewels in there, honey?" Bonni suggested. "The sapphires and diamonds your boyfriends buy you? Tell me, how much do you charge to pull a trick?"

"A trick!" Francesca couldn't mistake her meaning and before she could stop herself, her hand shot out and slapped the woman across her pancaked cheek. "Don't you ever—"

She didn't get any further. With a howl of rage, Bonni curled her fingers into talons and whipped them through the air, ready to grab two handfuls of Francesca's hair. Francesca instinctively thrust her cosmetic case forward, using it to block the other woman's movement. The case caught Bonni at the waist, knocking the wind out of her and forcing her to teeter for a moment on her imitation alligator heels before she lost her balance. As she tumbled to the floor, Francesca felt a moment of primitive satisfaction that she'd finally been able to punish someone for all the dreadful things that had happened to her that day. The moment fled as she saw the look on Cleo's face, and realized that she had put herself in actual danger.

She rushed out the door, but Cleo caught her and grabbed her wrist before she reached the jukebox. "No, you don't, bitch," she snarled, pulling her back toward the lavatory.

"Help!" Francesca cried, as her entire life flashed before her. "Please, someone, help me!"

She heard an unpleasant masculine laugh, and as Cleo shoved her forward, she realized that no one was leaping to her defense. Those two awful women planned to physically assault her in the lavatory, and no one seemed to care! Panicked, she swung her cosmetic case, intent on pushing Cleo away, but hitting someone's tattoo instead. He yelled.

"Get that case away from her," Cleo demanded, her voice harsh with outrage. "She just slapped Bonni."

"Bonni had it coming," Pete called out over the final chorus of "Rhinestone Cowboy" and the comments of the interested onlookers. To Francesca's overwhelming relief, he started toward her, obviously intent on rescue. And then she realized the man with the tattooed arm had other ideas.

"Stay out of this!" the tattoo called over to Pete as he wrenched the case from her hands. "This is between the girls."

"No!" Francesca cried. "It's not between the girls. Actually, I don't even know this person, and I—"

She screamed as Cleo sank her hands into her hair and began twisting her head in the general direction of the lavatory. Her eyes began to tear and her neck snapped backward. This was barbaric! Awful! They would murder her!

In that instant, she felt several strands of her hair being pulled from her scalp. *Her beautiful chestnut hair!* Reason left her and blind fury took over. She went wild, releasing a screech as she swung out. Cleo grunted as Francesca's hand caught her in an abdomen that had lost its tone. The pressure on Francesca's scalp immediately eased, but she had only a moment to catch her breath before she saw Bonni coming toward her, ready to pick up where Cleo had left off. A table crashed to the floor nearby, glass shattering. She was dimly aware that the fight had spread, and that Pete had leaped to her rescue, wonderful Pete of the plaid shirt and beer belly, wonderful, marvelous, adorable Pete!

"You bitch!" Bonni cried, reaching out for anything she could grab, which happened to be the pearl buttons set into the cocoa trim on Francesca's greige Halston blouse. The front gave way; the shoulder seam split. Once again Francesca felt her hair being pulled, and once again she swung, locking her other hand around Bonni's head and grabbing some hair herself.

Suddenly it seemed as if the fight had surrounded her—chairs scraped over the floor, a bottle flew through the air, someone screamed. She felt one of the fingernails on her right hand tear. Ribbons of fabric hung from the front of her blouse, exposing her ecru lace bra, but she had no time to worry about modesty as Bonni's sharp rings scraped her neck. Francesca gritted her teeth against the pain and pulled harder. At the same time she had the sudden and horrifying realization that she—Francesca Serritella Day, darling of the international set, pet of the society columnists, almost Princess of Wales—was at the heart, the very center, the absolute core, of a barroom brawl.

Across the room, the door of the Blue Choctaw swung open and Skeet walked in, followed by Dallie Beaudine.

Dallie stood there for a moment, took in what was happening, saw the people involved, and shook his head with disgust. "Aw, hell." With a long, put-upon sigh, he began to shoulder his way through the crowd.

Never in her entire life had Francesca been so glad to see anyone, except at first she didn't realize it was him. When he touched her shoulder, she released Bonni, swung around, and hit him as hard as she could in the chest.

"Hey!" he yelled, rubbing the spot where she'd landed. "I'm on your side . . . I guess."

"Dallie!" She threw herself into his arms. "Oh, Dallie, Dallie, Dallie! My wonderful Dallie! I can't believe it's you!"

He pulled her off. "Easy, Francie, you're not out of here yet. Why the hell—"

He never finished. Someone who looked like an extra in an old Steve Reeves movie came at him with a right hook, and Francesca watched in horror as Dallie sprawled on the floor. Spotting her cosmetic case sitting in splendid isolation on the jukebox, she snatched it up and banged it into the side of the awful man's head. To her horror, the clasp gave way, and she watched helplessly as her wonderful blushers and shadows and creams and lotions flew about the room. A box of her specially blended translucent powder sent up a scented cloud that soon had everyone coughing and sliding and quickly put a damper on the fight.

Dallie staggered to his feet, threw a couple of punches of his own, and then grabbed her arm. "Come on. Let's get out of here before they decide to eat you for a bedtime snack."

"My makeup!" She scrambled toward a cake of frosted peach eye shadow, even though she knew it was a ridiculous thing to do with her blouse falling off, a bloody scratch on her neck, two fingernails broken, and her very life in danger. But recovering the eye shadow suddenly became more important to her than anything in the world, and she was willing to fight them all to get it back.

He whipped his arm around her waist and lifted her feet off the floor. "To hell with your makeup!"

"No! Put me down!" She had to have the eye shadow. Little by little, every single item she owned was being taken away from her, and if she let just one more thing disappear, one more possession slip out of her life, she might very well disappear herself, fading away like the Cheshire cat until nothing was left, not even her teeth.

"Come on, Francie!"

"No!" She fought Dallie as she'd fought the rest, flailing her legs in the air, kicking his calves, screaming out, "I want it! I have to have it."

"You're gonna get it, all right!"

"Please, Dallie," she begged. "Please!"

The magic word had never failed her before, and it didn't now. Muttering under his breath, he leaned forward with his arm still around her and snatched up the eye shadow. As he straightened, she grabbed it from him and then reached out, just managing to grasp the open lid of her cosmetic case before he pulled her away. By the time she had snapped the lid shut, she'd lost a bottle of almond-scented moisturizer and broken a third fingernail, but she had managed to avoid spilling out her calfskin handbag along with its three hundred and fifty dollars. And she had her precious frosted peach eye shadow.

Skeet propped the door open and Dallie carried her through. As he set her down on the pavement, she heard sirens. He immediately snatched her back up and dragged her toward the Riviera.

"Can't she even walk by herself?" Skeet asked, catching the keys that Dallie pitched to him.

"She likes to argue." Dallie glanced toward the flashing lights that weren't all that far away. "Commissioner Deane Beman and the PGA are only going to put up with so much from me this year, so let's get the hell out of here." Shoving her none too gently into the back seat, he jumped in after her and closed the door.

They rode in silence for several minutes. Her teeth began to chatter from the aftereffects of the fight, and her hands shook as she tried to pull the front of her blouse together and tuck some of the torn ends into her bra. It didn't take her long to realize the task was hopeless. A lump lodged in her throat. She hugged her arms over her chest and yearned for some expression of sympathy, some concern for her condition, a small sign that someone cared about her.

Dallie reached under the seat in front of him and pulled

out an unopened bottle of scotch. After breaking the seal with his thumbnail, he unscrewed the top, took a long swallow, and then looked thoughtful. Francesca prepared herself for the questions to come and made up her mind to answer each one with as much dignity as possible. She bit her bottom lip to keep it from trembling.

Dallie leaned toward Skeet. "I didn't see anything of that red-haired waitress. Did you get a chance to ask about her?"

"Yeah. The bartender said she went off to Bogalusa with some guy who works for the power company."

"Too bad."

Skeet glanced into the rearview mirror. "Seems the guy only had one arm."

"No kidding? Did the bartender tell you how a thing like that happened?"

"Industrial accident of some kind. A few years back the guy worked for a tool and die outfit up near Shreveport and got his arm caught in a press. Crushed that sucker flatter than a pancake."

"Guess it didn't make any difference to his love life with that waitress of yours." Dallie took another swallow. "Women are funny 'bout things like that. Take that lady we met last year in San Diego after the Andy Williams—"

"Stop it!" Francesca cried, unable to hold back her outcry. "Are you so callous that you don't have the simple decency to ask me if I'm all right? That was a barroom brawl back there! Don't you realize that I could have been killed?"

"Probably not," Dallie said. "Somebody most likely would've put a stop to it."

She drew back her hand and hit his arm as hard as she could.

"Ouch." He rubbed the spot she had struck.

"Did she just hit you?" Skeet inquired indignantly.

"Yeah."

"You gonna hit her back?"

"I'm thinking."

"I would if I was you."

"I know *you* would." He looked at her and his eyes darkened. "I would, too, if I thought she was going to be part of my life for any longer than about the next two and a half minutes."

She stared at him, wishing she could take back her impulsive blow, unable to believe what she'd just heard. "Exactly what are you saying?" she demanded.

Skeet sped through a yellow light. "How far is it to the airport from here?"

"Clear across town." Dallie leaned forward and clasped his hand over the back of the seat. "In case you weren't paying attention earlier, the motel's up another light and down a block."

Skeet stepped down on the accelerator and the Riviera shot forward, throwing Francesca back against the seat. She glared at Dallie, trying to shame him into apologizing so she could magnanimously forgive him. She waited the rest of the way to the motel.

They turned into the well-lit parking lot, and Skeet swung around to the side, stopping in front of a line of brightly painted metal doors stamped with black numbers. He shut off the ignition, and then he and Dallie climbed out. She watched incredulously as first one car door slammed and then the other.

"See you in the morning, Dallie."

"See you, Skeet."

She leaped out after them, her case clutched in her hand, trying unsuccessfully to hold her blouse closed. "Dallie!"

He pulled a room key from the pocket of his jeans and turned. Greige silk slithered through her fingers as she closed the car door. Couldn't he see how helpless she was? How much she needed him? "You have to help me," she said, staring at him with eyes so pitifully large they seemed to eat up her small face. "I put my life in jeopardy going to that bar just to find you."

He looked at her breasts and the ecru silk bra. Then he pulled his faded navy T-shirt over his head and tossed it to her. "Here's the shirt off my back, honey. Don't ask for anything more."

She watched incredulously as he walked into his motel room and shut the door—shut the door in her face! The panic that had been building inside her throughout the day burst free, flooding every part of her body. She had never experienced such fear, she had no way of coping with it, and so she converted it into something she understood—a burning flare of red-hot anger. No one treated her like this! No one! She'd make him deal with her! She'd make him pay!

She dashed to his door and banged her case against it, hitting it once, twice, wishing it were his horrid, ugly face. She kicked at it, cursed it, let her anger detonate, let it blaze bright and righteous in one never-to-be-forgotten display of the temper that had made her a legend.

The door swung open and he stood on the other side, his chest bare and his ugly face scowling at her. She'd show him a scowl! She'd show him that he'd never even imagined what a scowl looked like! "You bastard!" She shot past him and flung her case across the room, where it shattered the television screen in a satisfying explosion of glass. "You depraved, moronic bastard!" She kicked over a chair. "You callous son of a bitch!" She upended his suitcase.

And then she let herself go.

Screaming out insults and accusations, she tossed ashtrays and pillows, threw lamps, and pulled the drawers from the desk. Every slight she had suffered in the past twenty-four hours, every indignity, came to the surface—the pink dress, the Blue Choctaw, the peach eye shadow. . . . She punished Chloe for dying, Nicky for deserting her; she assaulted Lew Steiner, attacked Lloyd Byron, mutilated Miranda Gwynwyck, and most of all, she annihilated Dallie Beaudine. Dallie, the most beautiful man she had ever met, the only man who wasn't impressed by her, the only man who'd ever slammed a door in her face.

Dallie watched for a moment, his hands planted on his hips. A can of shaving cream flew past him and hit the mirror. "Unbelievable," he muttered. He stuck his head out the door. "Skeet! Come over here. You got to see this."

Skeet was already on his way. "What's going on? It sounds like—" He stopped dead in the open doorway, staring at the destruction taking place in front of him. "Why is she doin' that?"

"Damned if I know." Dallie ducked a flying copy of the Greater New Orleans telephone directory. "Damnedest thing I ever saw in my life."

"Maybe she thinks she's a rock star. Hey, Dallie! She's goin' for your three-wood!"

Dallie moved like the athlete he was, and in two long strides he had her.

Francesca felt herself being upended. For a moment her legs hung free, and then something hard jabbed into her stomach as she felt herself being tossed over his shoulder. "Put me down! Put me down, you bastard!"

"Not hardly. That's the best three-wood I ever owned."

They began to move. She screamed as he carried her outside, his shoulder pushing into her stomach, his arm clamped around the backs of her knees. She heard voices and she was dimly aware of doors opening and bathrobed bodies peering out.

"I never saw a woman so scared of a little old mouse in all my life," Dallie called out.

She banged her fists against his bare back. "I'll have you arrested!" she screamed. "I'll sue you! Bastard! I'll sue you for every penny—" He veered sharply to the right. She saw a wrought-iron fence, a gate, underwater lights—

"No!" She let out a bloodcurdling scream as he pitched her into the very deepest part of the motel swimming pool.

Chapter
10

Skeet walked up next to Dallie, and the two men stood on the edge of the pool watching her. Finally Skeet made an observation. "She's not coming up real fast."

Dallie tucked one thumb into the pocket of his jeans. "Doesn't look like she can swim. I should've figured."

Skeet turned to him. "Did you hear the peculiar way she says 'bastard'? Like 'bah-stud.' I can't say it the way she does. Real peculiar."

"Yeah. That fancy accent of hers sure does manage to screw up good American cusswords."

The splashing in the pool gradually began to slow down. "You gonna jump in and save her any time in the next century?" Skeet inquired.

"Suppose I'd better. Unless you'd consider doing it."

"Hell, no. I'm going to bed."

Skeet turned to walk out the gate, and Dallie sat down on the edge of a lounge chair to pull off his boots. He watched for a moment to see how much struggle she had left, and when he judged the time to be about right, he wandered over to the edge and dived in.

Francesca had just realized how much she didn't want to die. Despite the movie, her poverty, the loss of all her possessions, she was too young. Her whole life stretched before her. But as the awful weight of the water pressed

140

down on her, she understood that it was happening. Her lungs burned and her limbs no longer responded to any command. She was dying, and she hadn't even lived yet.

Suddenly something caught her around the chest and began dragging her upward, holding her close, not letting her go, pulling her to the surface, saving her! Her head burst through the water and her lungs grabbed the air. She sucked it in, coughing and choking, grabbing at the arms around her for fear they would let her go, sobbing and crying with the pure joy of still being alive.

Without quite being aware how it had happened, she found herself being pulled up on the deck, the last shreds of her greige silk blouse staying in the water. But even when she felt the solid concrete surface beneath her, she wouldn't let Dallie go.

When she could finally speak, her words came out in small choked gasps. "I'll never forgive you . . . I hate you. . . ." She clung to his body, painted herself on his bare chest, threw her arms around his shoulders, held him as tight as she had ever held anything in her life. "I hate you," she choked out. "Don't let me go."

"You really did get shook up there, didn't you, Francie?"

But she was beyond replying. All she could do was hold on for dear life. She held on to him as he carried her back into the motel room, held on to him while he talked to the motel manager who was waiting for them, held on as he pulled her case from the rubble, fumbled through it, and carried her to another room.

He leaned over to lay her on the bed. "You can sleep here for the—"

"No!" The now-familiar wave of panic returned.

He tried to pry her arms from his neck. "Aw, come on, Francie, it's almost two in the morning. I want to get at least a few hours' sleep before I have to wake up."

"No, Dallie!" She was crying now, gazing straight into those Newman-blue eyes and crying her heart out. "Don't leave me. I know you'll drive away if I let you go. I'll wake up tomorrow and you'll be gone and I won't know what to do."

"I won't drive away until I talk to you," he said finally, pulling her arms free.

"Promise?"

He pulled off the sodden Bottega Veneta sandals, which had miraculously stayed on her feet, and pitched them to the floor, along with the dry T-shirt he'd brought with him. "Yeah, I promise."

Even though he'd given his word, he sounded reluctant, and she made a small inarticulate sound of protest as he went out the door. Didn't she promise all sorts of things and then promptly forget about them? How did she know he wouldn't do the same? "Dallie?"

But he was gone.

Somewhere she found the energy to pull off her wet jeans and underwear, letting them fall in a heap beside the bed before she slid under the covers. She pushed her wet head into the pillow, closed her eyes, and in the instant before she fell asleep, wondered whether she might not have been better off if Dallie had left her on the bottom of the swimming pool.

Her sleep was deep and hard, but she still jolted awake barely four hours later when the first trickle of light seeped through the heavy draperies. Throwing off the covers, she jumped unsteadily from the bed and stumbled naked toward the window, every muscle in her body aching. Only after she'd pushed back the drapery and looked outside at the dreary, rain-soaked day did her stomach steady. The Riviera was still there.

Her heartbeat resumed its normal rhythm, and she slowly made her way toward the mirror, instinctively doing what she had done every morning of her life for as long as she could remember, greeting her reflection to assure herself that the world had not changed during the night, that it still orbited in a predestined pattern around the sun of her own beauty.

She let out a strangled cry of despair.

If she'd had more sleep, she might have handled the shock better, but as it was, she could barely comprehend what she saw. Her beautiful hair hung in tangled mats around her face, a long scratch marred the graceful curve of her neck, bruises had popped out on her flesh, and her bottom lip—her perfect bottom lip—was puffed up like a pastry shell.

Panic-stricken, she rushed to her case and inventoried her

remaining possessions: a travel-size bottle of René Garraud bath gel, toothpaste (no sign of a toothbrush), three lipsticks, her peach eye shadow, and the useless dispenser of birth control pills Cissy's maid had packed. Her handbag yielded up two shades of blusher, her lizard-skin wallet, and an atomizer of Femme. Those, along with the faded navy T-shirt Dallie had thrown at her the night before and the small pile of soggy clothes on the floor, were her possessions . . . all she had left in the world.

The enormity of her losses was too devastating to comprehend, so she rushed to the shower where she did as much as she could with a brown bottle of motel shampoo. She then used the few cosmetics she had left to try to reconstruct the person she'd been. After pulling on her uncomfortably soggy jeans and struggling into her wet sandals, she spritzed Femme under her arms and then slid on Dallie's T-shirt. She looked down at the word written in white on her left breast and wondered what an AGGIES was. Another mystery, another unknown to make her feel like an intruder in a strange land. Why had she never felt like this in New York? Without shutting her eyes, she could see herself rushing along Fifth Avenue, dining at La Caravelle, walking through the lobby of the Pierre, and the more she thought about the world she'd left behind, the more disconnected she felt from the world she'd entered. A knock sounded, and she quickly combed her hair with her fingers, not quite daring to risk another peek in the mirror.

Dallie stood leaning against the door frame wearing a sky blue windbreaker beaded with rainwater and bleached-out jeans that had a frayed hole at the side of one knee. His hair was damp and curled up at the ends. Dishwater blond, she thought disparagingly, not true blond. And he needed a really good cut. He also needed a new wardrobe. His shoulders pulled at the seams of his jacket; his jeans would have disgraced a Calcutta beggar.

It was no use. No matter how clearly she saw his flaws, no matter how much she needed to reduce him to the ordinary in her own eyes, he was still the most impossibly gorgeous man she had ever seen.

He leaned one hand against the door frame and looked down at her. "Francie, ever since last night, I've been trying to make it obvious to you in as many ways as I could that I don't want to hear your story, but since you're hell-bent on telling it and since I'm getting pretty close to desperate to get rid of you, let's do it right now." With that, he walked into her room, slumped down in a straight-backed chair, and put his boots up on the edge of the desk. "You owe me someplace in the neighborhood of two hundred bucks."

"Two hundred—"

"You pretty well trashed that room last night." He leaned back in the chair until only the rear legs were on the floor. "A television, two lamps, a few craters in the Sheetrock, a five-by-four picture window. The total came to five hundred sixty dollars, and that was only because I promised the manager I'd play eighteen holes with him the next time I come through. There only seemed to be a little over three hundred in your wallet—not enough to take care of all that."

"My wallet?" She tore at the latches of her case. "You got into my wallet! How could you do something like that? That's my property. You should never have—" By the time she'd pulled her wallet from her purse, the palms of her hands were as clammy as her jeans. She opened it and gazed inside. When she could finally speak, her voice was barely a whisper. "It's empty. You've taken all my money."

"Bills like that have to be settled real quick unless you want to catch the attention of the local *gendarmes.*"

She sagged down on the end of the bed, her sense of loss so overwhelming that her body seemed to have gone numb. She had hit bottom. Right at this moment. Right *now.* Everything was gone—cosmetics, clothes, the last of her money. She had nothing left. The disaster that had been picking up speed like a runaway train ever since Chloe's death had finally jumped the track.

Dallie tapped a motel pen on the top of the desk. "Francie, I couldn't help but notice that you didn't have any credit cards tucked away in that purse of yours . . . or any plane ticket either. Now, I want to hear you tell me real quick that you've got that ticket to London put away somewhere inside Mr. Vee-tawn, and that Mr. Vee-tawn is closed up in one of those twenty-five-cent lockers at the airport."

She hugged her chest and stared at the wall. "I don't know what to do," she choked out.

"You're a big girl, and you'd better come up with something real fast."

"I need help." She turned to him, pleading for understanding. "I can't handle this by myself."

The front legs of his chair banged to the floor. "Oh, no you don't! This is your problem, lady, and you're not going to push it off on me." His voice sounded hard and rough, not like the laughing Dallie who'd picked her up at the side of the road, or the knight in shining armor who'd saved her from certain death at the Blue Choctaw.

"If you didn't want to help me," she cried out, "you shouldn't have offered me that ride. You should have left me, like everyone else."

"Maybe you better start thinking about why everybody wants to get rid of you so bad."

"It's not my fault, don't you see? It's circumstances." She began to tell him all of it, beginning with Chloe's death, stumbling over her words in her haste to get them out before he walked away. She told him how she'd sold everything to pay for her ticket home only to realize that even if she did have a ticket, she couldn't possibly go back to London without money, without clothes, with the news of her humiliation in that terrible movie on everyone's lips so that they were all laughing at her. She realized right then that she had to stay where she was, where no one knew her, until Nicky got back from his sordid fling with the blond mathematician and she had a chance to talk to him over the telephone. That's why she'd set out to find Dallie at the Blue Choctaw. "Don't you see? I can't go back to London until I know Nicky will be right there at the airport waiting for me."

"I thought you told me he was your fiancé?"

"He is."

"Then why is he having a fling with a blond mathematician?"

"He's sulking."

"Jesus, Francie—"

She rushed over to kneel down beside his chair and looked up at him with her heart-stopping eyes. "It's not my fault, Dallie. Really. The last time I saw him, we had this awful quarrel just because I turned down his marriage proposal." A great stillness came over Dallie's face and she realized he had misinterpreted what she'd said. "No, it's not what you're thinking! He'll marry me! We've quarreled hundreds of times and he always proposes again. It's just a matter of getting hold of him on the telephone and telling him I forgive him."

Dallie shook his head. "Poor son of a bitch," he muttered.

She tried to glare at him, but her eyes were too teary, so she stood and turned her back, struggling for control. "What I need, Dallie, is some way to endure the next few weeks until I can talk to Nicky. I thought you could help me, but last night you wouldn't talk to me, and you made me so angry, and now you've taken my money." She spun on him, her voice catching on a sob. "Don't you see, Dallie? If you'd just been reasonable, none of this would have happened."

"I'll be goddamned." Dallie's boots hit the floor. "You're getting ready to blame all this on me, aren't you? Jesus, I hate people like you. No matter what happens, you manage to shift the blame to somebody else."

She jumped up. "I don't have to listen to this! All I wanted was some help."

"And a small bit of cash to go with it."

"I can return every penny in a few weeks."

"If Nicky takes you back." He stretched out his legs again, crossing them at the ankles. "Francie, you don't seem to realize that I'm a stranger with no obligation to you. I don't do all that good a job of taking care of myself, and I'm sure as hell not going to take you on, even for a few weeks. To tell you the truth, I don't even like you."

She looked at him, bewilderment imprinted on her face. "You don't like me?"

"I really don't, Francie." His burst of anger had faded, and he spoke calmly and with such obvious conviction that she knew he was telling the truth. "Look, honey, you're a real traffic stopper with that face of yours, and even though you're a little on the puny side, you kiss great. I can't deny that I had a few wayward thoughts about what the two of us might have been able to accomplish underneath the covers, and if you had a different personality I could even see myself losing my head over you for a few weeks. But the thing of it is, you don't have a different personality, and the way you are is pretty much a composite of all the bad qualities of every man and woman I ever met, with none of the good qualities thrown in to even things out."

She sank down on the end of the bed, hurt enveloping her. "I see," she said quietly.

He stood and pulled out his wallet. "I don't have a lot of ready cash right now. I'll cover the rest of the motel bill with plastic and leave fifty dollars to hold you for a few days. If you get around to paying me back, send me a check in care of General Delivery, Wynette, Texas. If you don't get around to it, I'll know things didn't work out between you and Nicky, and hope greener pastures turn up soon."

With that speech, he tossed the motel key on the desk and walked out the door.

She was finally alone. She stared down at a dark stain that looked like an outline of Capri on the motel carpet. Now. *Now* she'd hit bottom.

Skeet leaned out the passenger window as Dallie approached the Riviera. "You want me to drive?" he asked. "You can crawl in the back and try for a few hours' sleep."

Dallie opened the driver's door. "You drive too damned slow, and I don't feel like sleeping."

"Suit yourself." Skeet settled in and handed Dallie a Styrofoam coffee cup with the lid still snapped on. Then he gave him a slip of pink paper. "The cashier's phone number."

Dallie crumpled the paper and pushed it into the ashtray, where it joined two others. He pulled on his cap. "You ever heard of *Pygmalion,* Skeet?"

"Is he the guy who played right tackle for Wynette High?"

Dallie used his front teeth to pull the lid off his coffee cup while he turned the key in the ignition. "No, that was Pygella, Jimmy Pygella. He moved to Corpus Christi a few years back and opened up a Midas muffler shop. *Pygmalion*'s this play by George Bernard Shaw about a Cockney flower girl who gets made over into a real lady." He flipped on the windshield wipers.

"Don't sound too interesting, Dallie. The play I liked was

that *Oh! Calcutta!* we saw in St. Louis. Now that was real good."

"I know you liked that play, Skeet. I liked it, too, but you see it's not generally regarded as a great piece of literature. It doesn't have a lot to say about the human condition, if you follow me. *Pygmalion,* on the other hand, says that people can change . . . that they can get better with a little direction." He threw the car into reverse and backed out of the parking place. "It also says that the person directing that change doesn't get anything for his trouble but a load of grief."

Francesca, her eyes wide and stricken, stood in the open door of the motel room clutching her case to her chest like a teddy bear and watched the Riviera pull out of the parking place. Dallie was really going to do it. He was going to drive away and leave her all by herself, even though he'd admitted he'd thought about going to bed with her. Until now, that had always been enough to hold any man to her side, but suddenly it wasn't. How could that be? What was happening to her world? Bewilderment underscored her fear. She felt like a child who'd learned her colors wrong and just found out that red was really yellow, blue was really green—only now that she knew what was wrong, she couldn't imagine what to do about it.

The Riviera swung around to the exit, waited for a break in the traffic, and then began to move out onto the wet road. The tips of her fingers had gone numb, and her legs felt weak, as if all the muscles had lost their strength. Drizzle dampened her T-shirt, a lock of hair fell forward over her cheek. "Dallie!" She started to run as fast as she could.

"The thing of it is," Dallie said, looking up into his rearview mirror, "she doesn't think about anybody but herself."

"Most self-centered woman I ever encountered in my life," Skeet agreed.

"And she doesn't know how to do a damn thing except maybe put on makeup."

"She sure as hell can't swim."

"She doesn't have even one lick of common sense."

"Not a lick."

Dallie uttered a particularly offensive oath and slammed on the brakes.

Francesca reached the car, gasping for breath in small sobs. "Don't! Don't leave me alone!"

The strength of Dallie's anger took her by surprise. He vaulted out of the door, tore the case from her hands, and then backed her up against the side of the car so that the door handle jabbed into her hip.

"Now you listen to me, and you listen good!" he shouted. "I'm taking you under duress, and you stop that goddamn sniveling right now!"

She sobbed, blinking against the drizzle. "But I'm—"

"I said to *stop* it! I don't want to do this—I got a real bad feeling about it—so from this minute on, you'd better do exactly what I say. *Everything* I say. You don't ask me any questions; you don't make any comments. And if you give me one minute of that fancy horseshit of yours, you'll be out on your skinny ass."

"All *right,"* she cried, her pride hanging in tatters, her voice strangling on her humiliation. "All right!"

He looked at her with a contempt he made no effort to disguise, then jerked open the back door. She turned to scramble inside, but just as she bent forward, he drew back his hand and cracked her hard across her bottom. "There's more where that came from," he said, "and my hand's just itching for the next shot."

Every mile of the ride to Lake Charles felt like a hundred. She turned her face to the window and tried to pretend she was invisible, but when occupants of other cars looked idly over at her as the Riviera sped past, she couldn't suppress the illogical feeling that they knew what had happened, that they could actually see how she had been reduced to begging for help, see that she had been struck for the first time in her life. *I won't think about it,* she told herself as they sped past flooded rice fields and swampland covered with slimy green algae. *I'll think about it tomorrow, next week, any time but now when I might start crying again and he might stop the car and set me out on the highway.* But she couldn't help thinking about it, and she bit a raw place on the inside of her already battered bottom lip to keep from making the smallest sound.

She saw a sign that said Lake Charles, and then they crossed a great curved bridge. In the front seat, Skeet and Dallie talked on and off, neither of them paying any attention to her.

"The motel's right up there," Skeet finally remarked to Dallie. "Remember when Holly Grace showed up here last year with that Chevy dealer from Tulsa?"

Dallie grunted something Francesca didn't quite catch as he pulled into the parking lot, which didn't look all that different from the one they'd left less than four hours earlier, and swung around toward the office. Francesca's stomach growled, and she realized she hadn't had anything to eat since the evening before when she'd grabbed a hamburger after pawning her suitcase. Nothing to eat . . . and no money to buy anything with. And then she wondered who Holly Grace might be, but she was too demoralized to feel more than a passing curiosity.

"Francie, I'd already pushed my credit card limit pretty close to the edge before I met you, and that little romp of yours just about finished the job. You're going to have to share a room with Skeet."

"No!"

"No!"

Dallie sighed and flicked off the ignition. "All right, Skeet. You and I'll share a room until we get rid of Francie."

"Not hardly." Skeet threw open the door of the Riviera. "I haven't shared a room with you since you turned pro, and I'm not gonna start now. You stay up half the night and then make enough noise in the morning to wake the dead." He climbed out of the car and headed toward the office, calling back over his shoulder, "Since you're the one who's so all-fired anxious to bring Miss Fran-chess-ka along, you can damn well sleep with her yourself."

Dallie swore the entire time he was unloading his suitcase and carrying it inside. Francesca sat on the edge of one of the room's two double beds, her back straight, her feet side by side, knees pressed together, like a little girl on her best behavior at a grown-up party. From the next room she heard the sound of a television announcer reporting on an anti-nuclear group protesting at a missile site; then someone flipped the channel to a ball game and "The Star-Spangled Banner" rang out. Bitterness welled up inside her as the music brought back the memory of the round button she had spotted on the taxi driver's shirt: AMERICA, LAND OF OPPORTUNITY. What kind of opportunity? The opportunity to pay for food and shelter with her body in some sordid motel room? Nothing came entirely free, did it? And her body was all she had left. By coming into this room with Dallie, hadn't she implicitly promised to give him something in return?

"Will you stop looking like that!" Dallie threw his suitcase on the bed. "Believe me, Miss Fancy Pants, I don't have any designs on your body. You stay on your side of the room, as far out of my sight as possible, and we'll do just fine. But first I want my fifty bucks back."

She had to salvage some morsel of her self-respect when she handed him back his money, so she tossed her head, flicking her hair back over her shoulders as if she hadn't a care in the world. "I gather you're some sort of golfer," she remarked offhandedly, trying to show him that his surliness didn't affect her. "Would that be a vocation or an avocation?"

"More like an addiction, I guess." He grabbed a pair of slacks from his suitcase and then reached for the zipper on his jeans.

She spun around, quickly turning her back to him. "I—I think I'll stretch my legs a bit, take a turn around the parking lot."

"You do that."

She circled the parking lot twice, reading bumper stickers, studying newspaper headlines through the glass doors of the dispensers, gazing sightlessly at the front-page photograph of a curly-haired man screaming at someone. Dallie didn't seem to expect her to go to bed with him. What a relief that was. She stared at the neon vacancy sign, and the longer she stared, the more she wondered why he didn't desire her. What was wrong? The question nagged like an itch. She might have lost her clothes, her money, all of her possessions, but she still had her beauty, didn't she? She still had her allure. Or had she somehow lost that, too, right along with her luggage and her makeup?

Ridiculous. She was exhausted, that was all, and she couldn't think straight. As soon as Dallie left for the golf course, she would go to bed and sleep until she felt like herself again. A few remnant sparks of optimism flickered inside her. She was merely tired. A decent night's sleep and everything would be fine.

Chapter
11

Naomi Jaffe Tanaka slammed the palm of her hand down on the heavy glass top of her desk. "No!" she exclaimed into the telephone, her intense brown eyes snapping with displeasure. "She isn't even close to what we have in mind for the Sassy Girl. If you can't do better than her, I'll find a model agency that can."

The voice on the other end of the line grew sarcastic. "Do you want some phone numbers, Naomi? I'm sure the people at Wilhelmina will do a wonderful job for you."

The people at Wilhelmina refused to send Naomi anyone else, but she had no intention of sharing that particular piece of news with the woman on the phone. She pushed blunt, impatient fingers through her dark hair, which had been cut as short and sleek as a boy's by a famous New York hairdresser intent on redefining the word "chic." "Just keep looking." She shoved the most recent issue of *Advertising Age* away from the edge of her desk. "And next time try to find someone with some personality in her face."

As she put down the receiver, fire sirens screamed up Third Avenue, eight floors below her corner office at Blakemore, Stern, and Rodenbaugh, but Naomi paid no attention. She had lived with the noises of New York City all her life and hadn't consciously heard a siren since last winter when the two gay members of the New York City

Ballet who lived in the apartment above her had lit their fondue pot too near a pair of Scalamandré chintz curtains. Naomi's husband at the time, a brilliant Japanese biochemist named Tony Tanaka, had illogically blamed her for the incident and refused to talk to her for the rest of the weekend. She divorced him soon after—not just because of his reaction to the fire, but because living with a man who wouldn't share even the most elementary of his feelings had grown too painful for a wealthy Jewish girl from the Upper East Side of Manhattan, who in the never-to-be-forgotten spring of 1968 had helped take over the dean's office at Columbia and hold it for the People.

Naomi tugged on the black and silver caviar beads she was wearing with a gray flannel suit and silk blouse, clothes she would have scorned in those fiery, close-fisted days of Huey and Rennie and Abbie when her passions had focused on anarchy instead of market share. For the last few weeks, as the news reports about her brother Gerry's latest antinuclear escapade had surfaced, stray memories of that time kept flickering into her mind like old photographs, and she found herself experiencing a vague nostalgia for the girl she had been, the little sister who had tried so hard to earn her big brother's respect that she had endured sit-ins, love-ins, lie-ins, and one thirty-day jail sentence.

While her twenty-four-year-old big brother had been shouting revolution from the steps of Berkeley's Sproal Hall, Naomi had begun her freshman year at Columbia three thousand miles away. She had been her parents' pride and joy—pretty, popular, a good student—their consolation prize for having produced "the other one," the son whose antics had disgraced them and whose name was never to be mentioned. At first Naomi had buried herself in her studies, staying far away from Columbia's radical students. But then Gerry had arrived on campus and he had hypnotized her, right along with the rest of the student body.

She had always adored her brother, but never more so than on that winter day when she had watched him standing like a young blue-jeaned warrior at the top of the library steps trying to change the world with his impassioned tongue. She had studied those strong Semitic features surrounded by a great halo of curly black hair and couldn't believe the two of them had come from the same womb. Gerry had full lips and a bold nose unredeemed by the plastic surgeon who had reshaped hers. Everything about him was larger than life, while she felt merely ordinary. Lifting his strong arms over his head, he had pumped his fists in the air and tossed his head back, his teeth flashing like white stars against his olive skin. She had never seen anything more wondrous in her life than her big brother exhorting the masses to rebellion that day at Columbia.

Before the year was over, she had become part of Columbia's militant student group, an act that had finally won her brother's approval but had resulted in a painful estrangement from her parents. Disillusionment had settled in slowly over the next few years as she fell victim to the Movement's rampant male chauvinism, its disorganization, and its paranoia. By her junior year she had severed her contacts with its leaders, and Gerry had never forgiven her. They had seen each other only once in the past two years, and they had argued the entire time. Now she spent her days praying he wouldn't do something so irredeemably awful that everyone at the agency would find out he was her brother. Somehow she couldn't imagine a firm as conservative as BS&R appointing the sister of a nationally renowned radical as its first female vice-president.

She pulled her thoughts away from her past life and looked down at her present one—the layout spread on her desktop. As always, she felt the rush of satisfaction that told her she had done a good job. Her experienced eye approved the Sassy bottle design, a frosted glass teardrop topped by a wave-shaped navy blue stopper. The perfume flagon would be elegantly packaged in a shiny navy box imprinted with the hot pink letters of the slogan she had created—"SASSY! For Free Spirits Only." The exclamation point after the product name had been her idea, and one that particularly pleased her. Still, despite the success of both the packaging and the slogan, the spirit of the campaign was missing because Naomi hadn't been able to perform one simple task: she hadn't been able to find the Sassy Girl.

Her intercom buzzed, and her secretary reminded her that she had a meeting with Harry R. Rodenbaugh, senior vice-president and board member of BS&R. Mr.

Rodenbaugh had specifically requested that she bring along the new Sassy layout. Naomi groaned to herself. As one of BS&R's two creative directors, she'd been handling perfume and cosmetic accounts for years, and she'd never had so much trouble. Why did the Sassy account have to be the account that Harry Rodenbaugh had made his pet project? Harry, who desperately wanted one last Clio to his credit before he retired, insisted on a fresh face to represent the new product, a model who was spectacular but not recognizable to fashion magazine readers.

"I want personality, Naomi, not just another cookie cutter model's face," he had told her when he called her on his Persian carpet the week before. "I want a long-stemmed American Beauty rose with a few thorns on her. This campaign is all about the free-spirited American woman, and if you can't deliver anything closer to target than these overused children's faces you've been shoving under my nose for the past three weeks, then I don't see how you could possibly handle a position as a BS&R vice-president."

The sly old bastard.

Naomi gathered up her papers the same way she did everything, with quick, concentrated movements. Tomorrow she would start contacting all the theatrical agencies and look for an actress instead of a model. Better male chauvinists than Harry R. Rodenbaugh had tried to keep her down, and not one of them had succeeded.

As Naomi passed her secretary's desk, she stopped to pick up an Express Mail package that had just arrived, and in the process knocked a magazine onto the floor. "I'll get it," her secretary said, as she reached down.

But Naomi had already picked it up, her critical eye caught by the series of candid photographs on the page that had fallen open. She felt a prickle go up the back of her neck—an instinctive reaction that told her more clearly than any focus group when she was onto something big. Her Sassy Girl! Profile, full-face, three-quarters—each photograph was better than the last. On the floor of her secretary's office, she had found her American Beauty rose.

And then she scanned the caption. The girl wasn't a professional model, but that wasn't necessarily a bad thing.

She flipped to the front cover and frowned. "This magazine's six months old."

"I was cleaning out my bottom drawer, and—"

"Never mind." She turned back to the photographs and tapped the page with her index finger. "Make some phone calls while I'm in my meeting and see if you can locate her. Don't make any contact; just find out where she is."

But when Naomi returned from her meeting with Harry Rodenbaugh it was only to discover that her secretary hadn't been able to come up with anything. "She seems to have dropped out of sight, Mrs. Tanaka. No one knows where she is."

"We'll find her," Naomi said. The wheels in her mind were already clicking away as she mentally shuffled through her list of contacts. She glanced down at her Rolex oyster watch and calculated time differentials. Then she snatched up the magazine and headed into her office. As she dialed her telephone, she looked down at the series of pictures. "I'm going to find you," she said to the beautiful woman looking up from the pages. "I'm going to find you, and when I'm done, your life will never be the same."

The walleyed cat followed Francesca back to the motel. It had dull gray fur with bald patches around its bony shoulders from some long-ago fight. Its face had been squashed to the side, and one eye was misshapen, the iris rolled back into the cat's head so that only the milky white showed. To add to his unsavory appearance, he had lost the tip of one ear. She wished the animal had chosen someone else to follow along the highway, and she quickened her steps as she turned into the parking lot. The cat's unrelenting ugliness disturbed her. She had this illogical feeling that she didn't want to be around anything so ugly, that some of that ugliness might rub off on her, that people are judged by the company they keep.

"Go away!" she commanded.

The animal gave her a faintly malevolent look, but didn't alter its path. She sighed. With the way her luck had gone lately, what did she expect?

She had slept through her first afternoon and night in

Lake Charles, only dimly aware of Dallie coming into the room and making a racket, then making another racket when he left the next morning. By the time she had come fully awake, he'd been gone for several hours. Nearly faint with hunger, she had rushed through her bath, afterward making free use of Dallie's toiletries. Then she had picked up the five dollars he had left her for food and, staring down at the bill, made one of the most difficult decisions of her life.

In her hand she now carried a small paper sack containing two pairs of cheap nylon underpants, a tube of inexpensive mascara, the smallest bottle of nail polish remover she could find, and a package of emery boards. With the few cents that remained, she had purchased the only food she could afford, a Milky Way candy bar. Thick and heavy, she could feel its satisfying weight at the bottom of the paper sack. She had wanted real food—capon, wild rice, a mound of salad with blue cheese dressing, a wedge of truffle cake—but she had needed underpants, mascara, salvation for her disgraceful fingernails. As she had walked the mile back along the highway, she thought of all the money she had thrown away over the years. Hundred-dollar shoes, thousand-dollar gowns, money flying from her hands like cards from a magician's fingertips. For the price of a simple silk scarf, she could have eaten like a queen.

Since Francesca didn't have the price of a scarf, she had decided to make the most of her culinary moment, humble though it might be. A shady tree grew beside the motel, complete with a rusted lawn chair. She was going to sit in the chair, enjoy the warmth of the afternoon, and consume the chocolate bar morsel by morsel, savoring each bite to make it last. But first she had to get rid of the cat.

"Shoo!" she hissed, stomping her foot on the asphalt. The cat tilted its lopsided head at her and stood its ground. "Go away, you bloody beast, and find someone else to bother." When the animal wouldn't move, she expelled her breath in disgust and stomped toward the lawn chair. The cat followed. She ignored it, refusing to let this ugly animal ruin her pleasure in the first food she'd eaten since Saturday evening.

Kicking off her sandals as she sat down, she cooled the

bottoms of her feet in the grass while she dug into the bag for her candy bar. It felt as precious as a bar of gold bullion in her hand. Carefully unwrapping it, she dampened her finger to pick up a few errant chocolate slivers that fell out of the wrapper onto her jeans. Ambrosia . . . She slid the corner of the bar into her mouth, sank her teeth through the chocolate shell and into the nougat, and bit through. As she chewed, she knew she had never tasted anything so wonderful in her life. She had to force herself to take another slow bite instead of stuffing it all into her mouth.

The cat emitted a deep, gravelly sound, which Francesca guessed was some perverted form of a meow.

She glared at it, standing near the tree trunk watching her with its one good eye. "Forget it, beast. I need this more than you do." She took another bite. "I'm not an animal person, so you don't have to stare at me like that. I've no affection for anything that has paws and doesn't know how to flush."

The animal didn't move. She noticed its protruding ribs, the dullness of its fur. Was it her imagination or did she sense a certain sad resignation in that ugly, walleyed face? She took another small bite. The chocolate no longer tasted nearly as good. If only she didn't know how terrible hunger pangs felt.

"Dammit to bloody hell!" She jerked a chunk off the end of the bar, broke it into small pieces, and laid them on top of the wrapper. As she placed it all on the ground, she glared at the animal. "I hope you're satisfied, you miserable cat."

The cat walked over to the chair, bent his battered head to the chocolate, and consumed every morsel as if he were doing her a favor.

Dallie got back from the course after seven that evening. By that time she had repaired her fingernails, counted the cinder blocks on the walls of the room, and read Genesis. When he came through the door, she was so desperate for human company that she jumped up from her chair, only restraining herself at the last moment from running over to him.

"There's the ugliest cat I've ever seen in my life out there," he said, throwing his keys down on the dresser.

"Damn, I hate cats. Only animal in the world that I can't stand is a cat." Since at that particular moment, Francesca wasn't too fond of the species herself, she didn't offer any argument. "Here," he said, tossing a sack at her. "I brought you some dinner."

She let out a small cry as she grabbed the sack and tore it open. "A hamburger! Oh, God . . . chips, lovely chips! I adore you." She pulled out the french fries and immediately shoved two into her mouth.

"Jeez, Francie, you don't have to act as if you're starving to death. I left you money for lunch."

He pulled a change of clothes from his suitcase and disappeared into the bathroom for a shower. By the time he returned in his customary uniform of jeans and T-shirt, she had appeased her hunger but not her desire for company. However, she saw with alarm that he was getting ready to go out again.

"Are you leaving already?"

He sat down on the end of the bed and pulled on his boots. "Skeet and me have an appointment with a man named Pearl."

"At this time of night?"

He chuckled. "Mr. Pearl keeps real flexible hours."

She had the feeling that she had missed something, but she couldn't imagine what. Pushing aside the food rubble, she jumped to her feet. "Could I go with you, Dallie? I can sit in the car while you have your appointment."

"I don't think so, Francie. This kind of meeting can sometimes go on till the wee hours."

"I don't mind. Really I don't." She hated herself for pressing on, but she didn't think she could stand being shut up in the room much longer without anyone to talk to.

"Sorry, Fancy Pants." He shoved his wallet into his back pocket.

"Don't call me that! I hate it!" He lifted one eyebrow in her direction, and she quickly changed the subject. "Tell me about the golf tournament. How did you do?"

"Today was just a practice round. The Pro-Am's on Wednesday, but the actual tournament doesn't get going until Thursday. Did you make any progress getting hold of Nicky?"

She shook her head, not anxious to pursue that particular topic. "How much could you earn if you win this tournament?"

He picked up his cap and set it on his head, where the American flag over the bill stared back at her. "Only about ten thousand. This isn't much of a tournament, but the club pro's a friend of mine, so I play every year."

An amount she would have considered paltry a year before suddenly seemed like a fortune. "But that's wonderful. Ten thousand dollars! You simply have to win, Dallie."

He looked at her with a curiously blank face. "Why's that?"

"Why, so you can have the money, of course."

He shrugged. "As long as the Riviera's running smooth, I don't care too much about money, Francie."

"That's ridiculous. Everybody cares about money."

"I don't." He went out the door and then almost immediately reappeared. "Why's there a hamburger wrapper out here, Francie? You haven't been feeding that ugly cat, have you?"

"Don't be ridiculous. I detest cats."

"Now, that's the first sensible thing you've said since I met you." He gave her a small, approving nod and shut the door. She kicked the desk chair with the toe of her sandal and once again began counting the cinder blocks.

"Pearl is a *beer!*" she screamed five nights later when Dallie returned near dusk from playing in the semifinal round of the tournament. She waved the shiny magazine advertisement in his face. "All these nights when you've left me alone in this godforsaken room with nothing but television to keep me company, you've been out drinking beer in some sleazy bar."

Skeet set Dallie's clubs in the corner. "You've got to get up pretty early in the morning to put one over on Miss Fran-chess-ka. You shouldn't have left your old magazines lying around, Dallie."

Dallie shrugged and rubbed a sore muscle in his left arm. "Who figured she could read?"

Skeet chuckled and left the room. A stab of hurt shot through her at Dallie's comment. Uncomfortable memories of some of the unkind remarks she'd made returned to nag at her, remarks that had seemed clever at the time, but now seemed merely cruel. "You think I'm awfully funny, don't you?" she said quietly. "You enjoy telling jokes I don't understand and making references that go right past me. You don't even have the courtesy to mock me behind my back; you make fun of me right to my face."

Dallie unbuttoned his shirt. "Jeez, Francie, don't make such a big deal out of it."

She slumped down on the edge of the bed. He hadn't looked at her—not once since he'd walked into the room had he looked at her, not even when he was talking to her. She'd become invisible to him—sexless and invisible. Her fears that he would expect her to sleep with him in return for sharing the room now seemed ridiculous. He wasn't attracted to her at all. He didn't even like her. As he stripped off his shirt, she stared at his chest, lightly covered with hair and well muscled. The cloud of depression that had been following her for days settled lower.

He pulled off his shirt and tossed it on the bed. "Listen, Francie, you wouldn't like the kind of place Skeet and I patronize. There aren't any tablecloths, and all the food is deep-fried."

She thought of the Blue Choctaw and knew he was probably right. Then she looked toward the lighted television screen where something called "I Dream of Jeannie" was coming on for the second time that day. "I don't care, Dallie. I love fried food, and tablecloths are passé anyway. Just last year Mother gave a party for Nureyev and she used placemats."

"I'll bet they didn't have a map of Louisiana printed on them."

"I don't think Porthault does maps."

He sighed and scratched his chest. Why wouldn't he *look* at her? She stood. "That was a joke, Dallie. I can make jokes, too."

"No offense, Francie, but your jokes aren't too funny."

"They are to me. They are to my friends."

"Yeah? Well, that's another thing. We have different taste in friends, and I know you wouldn't like my drinking buddies. A few of them are golfers, some of them are locals, most of them say things like 'I seen' a lot. They're not your kind of people."

"To be totally honest," she said, glancing toward the television screen, "anyone who doesn't sleep in a bottle is my kind of person."

Dallie smiled at that and disappeared into the bathroom to take his shower. Ten minutes later, the door flew open and he exploded into the bedroom with a towel knotted around his hips and his face red beneath his tan. "Why is my toothbrush wet?" he roared, shaking the offending object in her face.

Her wish had come true. He was looking at her now, staring right through her—and she didn't like it one bit. She took a step back and tucked her bottom lip between her teeth in an expression she hoped looked charmingly guilty. "I'm afraid I had to borrow it."

"Borrow it! That's the most disgusting thing I've ever heard."

"Yes, well you see I seemed to have lost mine, and I—"

"Borrow it!" She backed farther away as she saw that he was building up steam. "We're not talking about a cup of sugar here, sister! We're talking about a frigging toothbrush, the most personal possession a person can own!"

"I've been sanitizing it," she explained.

"You've *been* sanitizing it," he repeated ominously. "'Been' implies that this wasn't a one-shot occurrence. 'Been' implies that we have a whole history of extended use."

"Not *extended,* actually. I mean, we've only known each other a few days."

He threw the toothbrush at her, hitting her in the arm. "Take it! Take the fucking thing! I've ignored the fact that you've gotten into my clothes, that you've screwed up my razor, that you haven't put the cap back on my deodorant! I've ignored the mess you make around this place, but I goddamn well am not going to ignore this."

She realized then that he was truly angry with her, and that, unwittingly, she had stepped over some invisible line. For a reason she couldn't comprehend, this business about the toothbrush was important enough that he'd decided to make an issue of it. She felt a wave of undiluted panic sweep through her. She had pushed him too far, and he was going to kick her out. In the next few seconds, he would lift his hand, point his finger toward that door, and tell her to get out of his life forever and ever.

She hurried across the room. "Dallie, I'm sorry. Really I am." He gave her a stony glare. She lifted her hands and pressed them lightly to his chest, her fingers splayed, the short, unpolished nails slightly yellowed from years of being hidden by carmine varnish. Tilting her head up, she gazed directly into his eyes. "Don't be angry with me." She shifted her weight closer so that her legs were pressing against his, and then she tucked her head into his chest and rested her cheek against his bare skin. No man could resist her. Not really. Not when she put her mind to it. She just hadn't put her mind to it, that was all. Hadn't Chloe raised her from birth to enchant men?

"What are you doing?" he asked.

She didn't reply; she just leaned against him, soft and compliant as a sleepy kitten. He smelled clean, like soap, and she inhaled the scent. He wasn't going to kick her out. She wouldn't let him. If he kicked her out, she wouldn't have anything or anyone left. She would vanish. Right now Dallie Beaudine was all she had left in the world, and she would do anything to keep him. Her hands crept up over his chest. She stood on tiptoe and circled his neck with her arms, then slid her lips along the line of his jaw and pressed her breasts into his chest. She could feel him growing hard beneath the towel, and she felt a renewed sense of her own power.

"Exactly what do you have in mind with all this?" he asked quietly. "A little tag team wrestling under the sheets?"

"It's inevitable, isn't it?" She forced herself to sound offhand. "Not that you haven't been a perfect gentleman about it, but we *are* sharing the same room."

"I've got to tell you, Francie, that I don't think it's a good idea."

"Why not?" She let her eyelashes perform as best they could wearing only dime-store mascara, and moved her hips closer to his body, the perfect coquette, a woman created only for the pleasure of men.

"It's pretty obvious, isn't it?" His hand slid up to encircle her waist and his fingers gently kneaded her skin. "We don't like each other. Do you want to have sex with a man who doesn't like you, Francie? Who won't respect you in the morning? Because that's the way it's going to end up if you keep on moving against me like that."

"I don't believe you anymore." Her old confidence returned in a pleasant rush. "I think you like me more than you want to admit. I think that's why you've been doing such a good job of avoiding me this past week, why you won't look at me."

"This doesn't have anything to do with liking," Dallie said, his other hand caressing her hip, his voice growing low and husky. "It has to do with physical proximity."

His head dipped, and she could feel him getting ready to kiss her. She slipped out of his arms and smiled seductively. "Just give me a few minutes." Stepping away from him, she headed toward the bathroom.

As soon as she was inside, she leaned back against the door and took a deep, shaky breath, trying to suppress her nervousness at what she was committing herself to do. This was it. This was her chance to cement Dallie to her, to make certain he didn't kick her out, to be sure he kept feeding her and taking care of her. But it was more than that. Having Dallie make love to her would let her feel like herself again, even if she was no longer quite sure who that was.

She wished she had one of her Natori nightgowns with her. And champagne, and a beautiful bedroom with a balcony that looked out over the sea. She caught sight of herself in the mirror and moved closer. She looked terrible. Her hair was too wild, her face too pale. She needed clothes, she needed makeup. Dabbing toothpaste on her finger, she swished it inside her mouth to freshen her breath. How could she let Dallie see her in those dreadful dime-store underpants? With trembling fingers, she tugged at the fastening of her jeans and stripped them down over her legs. She let out a soft moan as she saw the red marks on her skin near her navel where the waistband had pinched her too tightly. She didn't want Dallie to see her with creases. Rubbing at the marks with her fingers, she tried to make them go away, but that only made her skin redder. She would turn out the lights, she decided.

Quickly, she peeled off her T-shirt and bra and wrapped

herself in a towel. Her breath came quick and fast. As she pulled off her cheap nylon underpants, she saw a small patch of downy hair near her bikini line that she'd missed when she'd shaved her legs. Propping her leg up on the toilet seat, she slid the blade of Dallie's razor over the offensive spot. There, that was better. She tried to think what else she could do to improve herself. She repaired her lipstick and then blotted it with a square of toilet paper so it wouldn't smear when they kissed. She bolstered her confidence by reminding herself what a superb kisser she was.

Something inside her deflated like an old balloon, leaving her feeling limp and shapeless. What if he didn't like her? What if she wasn't any good, just like she hadn't been any good with Evan Varian or the sculptor in Marrakech? What if— Her green eyes looked back at her from the mirror as a dreadful thought occurred to her. What if she smelled bad? She grabbed her atomizer of Femme from the back of the toilet, opened her legs, and spritzed.

"Just what in the goddamn hell do you think you're doing?"

Spinning around, she saw Dallie standing inside the door, one hand on his towel-covered hip. How long had he been standing there? What had he seen? She straightened guiltily. "Nothing. I—I'm not doing anything."

He looked at the bottle of Femme hanging like a weight in her hand. "Isn't there anything about you that's real?"

"I—I don't know what you mean."

He took a step farther into the bathroom. "Are you test-marketing new uses for perfume, Francie? Is that what you're doing?" Resting the palm of one hand against the wall, he leaned toward it. "You got your designer blue jeans, your designer shoes, your designer luggage. Now Miss Fancy Pants has got her some designer pussy."

"Dallie!"

"You're the ultimate consumer, honey—the advertising man's dream. Are you going to put little gold designer initials on it?"

"That's not funny." She slammed the bottle down on the back of the toilet and clutched the towel tightly in her hand. Her skin felt hot with embarrassment.

He shook his head with a world-weariness that she found

insulting. "Come on, Francie, get your clothes on. I said I wouldn't do it, but I can't help myself. I'm taking you with me tonight."

"What accounts for this magnanimous change of heart?" she snapped.

He turned and walked out into the bedroom, so that his words drifted back over his shoulder. "The truth of it is, darlin', I'm afraid if I don't let you see a slice of the real world pretty soon, you're going to do yourself some actual harm."

Chapter
12

The Cajun Bar and Grill was a decided improvement over the Blue Choctaw, although it still wasn't the sort of place Francesca would have chosen as the site for a coming-out ball. Located about ten miles south of Lake Charles, it rested beside a two-lane highway in the middle of nowhere. It had a screen door that banged every time someone came through and a squeaky paddle-wheel fan with one bent blade. Behind the table where they were sitting, an iridescent blue swordfish had been nailed to the wall along with an assortment of calendars and an advertisement for Evangeline Maid bread. The placemats were exactly as Dallie had described them, although he had neglected to mention the scalloped edges and the legend printed in red beneath the map of Louisiana: "God's Country."

A pretty brown-eyed waitress in jeans and a tank top came to the table. She inspected Francesca with a combination of curiosity and ill-concealed envy, then turned to Dallie. "Hey, Dallie. I hear you're only one stroke off the lead. Congratulations."

"Thanks, honey. The course has been real good to me this week."

"Where's Skeet?" she asked.

Francesca gazed innocently at the chrome and glass sugar dispenser in the middle of the table.

"Something wasn't sitting right in his stomach, so he decided to stay back at the motel." Dallie gave Francesca a stony look and then asked her if she wanted something to eat.

A litany of wonderful foods flicked through her head—lobster consommé, duckling paté with pistachios, glazed oysters—but she was a lot smarter than she had been five days before. "What do you recommend?" she asked him.

"The chili dog's good, but the crawfish are better."

What in God's name were crawfish? "Crawfish would be fine," she told him, praying they wouldn't be deep-fried. "And could you recommend something green to go along with it? I'm beginning to worry about scurvy."

"Do you like key lime pie?"

She looked at him. "That's a joke, isn't it?"

He grinned at her and then turned to the waitress. "Get Francie here a big salad, will you, Mary Ann, and a side dish of beefsteak tomatoes all sliced up. I'll have the pan-fried catfish myself and some of those dill pickles like I had yesterday."

As soon as the waitress had moved away, two well-groomed men in slacks and polo shirts came over to the table from the bar. It was quickly evident from their conversation that they were touring golf pros playing in the tournament with Dallie and that they had come over to meet Francesca. They positioned themselves on either side of her and before long were giving her lavish compliments and teaching her how to extract the sweet meat from the boiled crawfish that soon arrived on a heavy white platter. She laughed at all their stories, flattered them outrageously, and, in general, had them both eating out of her hand before either had finished his first beer. She felt wonderful.

Dallie, in the meantime, was occupied with a couple of female fans at the next table, both of whom said they worked as secretaries at one of Lake Charles's petrochemical plants. Francesca watched surreptitiously as he talked to them, his chair tilted back on two legs, navy blue cap tipped back on his blond head, beer bottle propped on his chest, and that lazy grin spreading over his face when one of them told him an off-color joke. Before long, they had launched into a series of nauseating double entendres about his "putter."

Even though she and Dallie were involved in separate conversations, Francesca began to have the feeling that there was some connection between them, that he was as conscious of her as she was of him. Or maybe it was just wishful thinking. Her encounter with him at the motel had left her shaken. When she curled into his arms, she had sent them flying across some invisible barrier, and now it was too late to turn back, even if she was absolutely certain she wanted to.

Three brawny rice farmers whom Dallie introduced as Louis, Pat, and Stoney pulled up their chairs to join them. Stoney couldn't tear himself away from Francesca and kept refilling her glass from a bottle of bad Chablis that one of the golfers had bought her. She flirted with him shamelessly, gazing into his eyes with an intensity that had brought far more sophisticated men to their knees. He shifted in his chair, tugging unconsciously at the collar of his plaid cotton shirt while he tried to act as if beautiful women flirted with him every day.

Eventually the individual pockets of conversation disappeared and the members of the group joined together and began telling funny stories. Francesca laughed at all their anecdotes and drank another glass of Chablis. A warm haze induced by alcohol and a general sense of well-being enveloped her. She felt as if the golfers, the petrochemical secretaries, and the rice farmers were the best friends she had ever had. The men's admiration warmed her, the women's envy renewed her sagging self-confidence, and Dallie's presence at her side energized her. He made them laugh with a story about an unexpected encounter he'd had with an alligator on a Florida golf course, and she suddenly wanted to give something back to all of them, some small part of herself.

"*I* have an animal story," she said, beaming at her new friends. They all looked at her expectantly.

"Oh, boy," Dallie murmured at her side.

She paid no attention. She folded one arm on the edge of the table and gave them her dazzling wait-until-you-hear-this smile. "A friend of my mother's opened this lovely new lodge near Nairobi," she began. When she saw a vague blankness on several faces, she amended, "Nairobi . . . in Kenya. Africa. A group of us flew down to spend a week or so there. It was a super place. A lovely long veranda looked out on this beautiful swimming pool, and they served the best rum punches you can imagine." She sketched out a pool and a platter of rum punches with a graceful gesture of her hand.

"The second day there, some of us piled into one of the Land-Rovers with our cameras and drove outside the city to take photographs. We'd been gone for about an hour when the driver rounded a bend—not going all that fast, actually —and this ridiculous *warthog* leaped out in front of us." She paused for effect. "Well, there was this awful thump as the Land-Rover hit the poor creature and it *dropped* to the road. We all jumped out, of course, and one of the men, a really *odious* French cellist named Raoul"—she rolled her eyes so they would all understand exactly the sort of person Raoul had been—"brought his camera with him and took a photograph of that poor, ugly warthog lying in the road. Then, I don't know what made her do it, but my mother said to Raoul, 'Wouldn't it be funny if we took a picture of the warthog wearing your Gucci jacket!' " Francesca laughed at the memory. "Naturally, everyone thought this was amusing, and since there was no blood on the warthog to ruin the jacket, Raoul agreed. Anyway, he and two of the other men put the jacket on the animal. It was dreadfully insensitive, of course, but everyone laughed at the sight of this poor dead warthog in this marvelous jacket."

She grew vaguely aware that the area around them had fallen completely silent and that the slight blankness in the expressions of the people around the table hadn't altered. Their lack of response made her more determined to force them to love her story, to love her. Her voice grew more animated, her hands more descriptive. "So there we were, standing on the road looking down at this poor creature. Except—" She paused for a moment, caught her bottom lip between her teeth to build the suspense, and then went on, "Just as Raoul lifted his camera to take the picture, the warthog *leaped* to his feet, *shook* himself, and *ran off* into the trees." She laughed triumphantly at the punch line, tilted her head to the side, and waited for them to join her.

They smiled politely.

Her own laughter faded as she realized they had missed the point. "Don't you see?" she exclaimed with a touch of desperation. "Somewhere in Kenya today there's this poor warthog running around a game preserve, and he's wearing *Gucci!*"

Dallie's voice finally floated above the dead silence that had irreparably fallen. "Yep, that sure is some story, Francie. What do you say you and me dance?" Before she could protest, he'd grabbed her none too gently by the arm and pulled her toward a small square of linoleum in front of the jukebox. As he began to move to the music, he said softly, "A general rule of living life with real people, Francie, is not to end any sentences with the word 'Gucci.' "

Her chest seemed to fill up with a terrible heaviness. She had wanted to make them like her, and she'd only made a fool of herself. She had told a story that they hadn't found funny, a story that she suddenly saw through their eyes and realized she should never have told in the first place.

Her composure had been held together by only the lightest thread and now it broke. "Excuse me," she said, her voice sounding thick even to her own ears. Before Dallie could try to stop her, she pushed her way through the maze of tables and out the screen door. The fresh air invaded her nostrils, its moist nighttime scent mingling with the smell of diesel fuel, creosote, and fried food from the kitchen at the back. She stumbled, still light-headed from the wine, and steadied herself by leaning against the side of a pickup truck with mud-encrusted tires and a gun rack on the back. The sounds of "Behind Closed Doors" drifted out from the jukebox.

What was happening to her? She remembered how hard Nicky had laughed when she'd told him the warthog story, how Cissy Kavendish had wiped the tears from her eyes with Nigel MacAllister's handkerchief. A wave of homesickness swept over her. She'd attempted to get through to Nicky again today on the telephone, but no one had answered, not even the houseboy. She tried to imagine Nicky sitting in the Cajun Bar and Grill, and failed miserably. Then she tried to imagine herself sitting at the foot of the Hepplewhite table in Nicky's dining room wearing the Gwynwyck family emeralds, and succeeded admirably. But when she imagined the other end of the table—the place where Nicky should have been sitting—she saw Dallie Beaudine instead. Dallie, with his faded blue jeans, too-tight T-shirts, and movie star face, lording it over Nicky Gwynwyck's eighteenth-century dinner table.

The screen door banged, and Dallie came out. He walked to her side and held out her purse. "Hey, Francie," he said quietly.

"Hey, Dallie." She took the purse and looked up at the night sky spangled with floating stars.

"You did real fine in there."

She gave a soft, bitter laugh.

He inserted a toothpick in the corner of his mouth. "No, I mean it. Once you realized you'd made a jackass of yourself, you behaved with a little dignity for a change. No scenes on the dance floor, just a quiet exit. Everybody was real impressed. They want you to come back in."

She deliberately mocked him. "Not hardly."

He chuckled just as the screen door banged and two men appeared. "Hey, Dallie," they called out.

"Hey, K.C., Charlie."

The men climbed into a battered Jeep Cherokee and Dallie turned back to her. "I think, Francie, that I don't not like you as much as I used to. I mean, you're still pretty much a pain in the ass most of the time and not, strictly speaking, my kind of woman, but you do have your moments. You really went after that warthog story in there. I liked the way you gave it everything you had, even after it was pretty obvious that you were digging a real deep grave for yourself."

A clatter of dishes sounded from inside as the jukebox launched into the final chorus of "Behind Closed Doors." She dug the heel of her sandal into the hard-packed gravel. "I want to go home," she said abruptly. "I despise it here. I want to go back to England where I understand things. I want my clothes and my house and my Aston Martin. I want to have money again and friends who like me." She wanted her mother, too, but she didn't say that.

"Feeling real sorry for yourself, aren't you?"

"Wouldn't you if you were in my position?"

"Hard to say. I guess I can't imagine being real happy living that kind of sybaritic life."

She didn't precisely know what "sybaritic" meant, but she got the general idea, and it irritated her that someone whose spoken grammar could most charitably be described as substandard was using a word she didn't entirely understand.

He propped his elbow on the side of the pickup. "Tell me something, Francie. Do you have anything remotely resembling a life plan stored away in that head of yours?"

"I intend to marry Nicky, of course. I've already told you that." Why did the prospect depress her so?

He pulled out the toothpick and tossed it away. "Aw, come off it, Francie. You don't any more want to marry Nicky than you want to get your hair mussed up."

She rounded on him. "I don't have much choice in the matter, do I, since I don't have two shillings left to rub together! I have to marry him." She saw him opening his mouth, getting ready to spew out another one of his odious lower-class platitudes, and she cut him off. "Don't say it, Dallie! Some people were brought into this world to earn money and others were meant to spend it, and I'm one of the latter. To be brutally honest, I wouldn't have the slightest idea how to support myself. You've already heard what happened when I tried acting, and I'm too short to make any money at fashion modeling. If it comes down to a choice between working in a factory and marrying Nicky Gwynwyck, you can bloody well be certain which one I'm going to choose."

He thought about that for a moment and then said, "If I can make two or three birdies in the final round tomorrow, it looks like I'll pick up a little spare change. You want me to buy you that plane ticket home?"

She looked at him standing so close to her, arms crossed over his chest, only that fabulous mouth visible beneath the shadowing bill of his cap. "You'd do that for me?"

"I told you, Francie. As long as I can buy gas and pick up the bar tab, money doesn't mean anything to me. I don't even like money. To tell you the truth, even though I consider myself a true American patriot, I'm pretty much a Marxist."

She laughed at that, a reaction which told her more clearly than anything that she'd been spending too much time in his company. "I'm grateful for the offer, Dallie, but as much as I'd love to take you up on it, I need to stay around a bit longer. I can't go back to London like this. You don't know my friends. They'd dine out for weeks on the story of my transformation into a pauper."

He leaned back against the truck. "Nice batch of friends you've got there, Francie."

She felt as if he'd rapped his knuckles on a hollowness inside her, a hollowness she had never permitted herself to dwell on. "Go back inside," she said. "I'm going to stay out here for a while."

"I don't think so." He turned his body toward her, so that his T-shirt brushed against her arm. A yellow bug light by the screen door cast a slanted ochre shadow across his face, subtly changing his features, making him look older but no less splendid. "I think you and I have something more interesting to do tonight, don't we?"

His words produced an uncomfortable fluttering in the pit of her stomach, but being coy was as much a part of her as the Serritella cheekbones. Even though one part of her wanted to run back to hide in the Cajun Bar and Grill rest room, she gave him her most innocently inquisitive smile. "Oh? What's that?"

"A little tag team wrestling maybe?" His mouth curled in a slow, sexy smile. "Why don't you just climb into the front seat of the Riviera so we can be on our way."

She didn't want to climb into the front seat of the Riviera. Or maybe she did. Dallie stirred unfamiliar feelings in her body, feelings she would have been all too happy to act upon if only she were one of those women who was really *good* at sex, one of those women who didn't mind all the mess and the thought of having someone else's perspiration drip on her body. Still, even if she wanted to, she could hardly back out now without looking a total fool. As she walked over to the car and opened the door, she tried to convince herself that, since *she* didn't perspire, a man as gorgeous as Dallie just might not either.

She watched as he walked around the front of the Riviera, whistling tunelessly and digging the keys out of his back pocket. He seemed in no particular hurry. There wasn't any macho swagger to his stride, none of the cock-of-the-walk strut she'd noticed in the sculptor in Marrakech before he'd taken her to bed. Dallie acted casual, ordinary, as if going to bed with her were an everyday occurrence, as if it didn't matter all that much to him, as if he'd been there a thousand times before and she was just one more female body.

He got into the Riviera, turned on the ignition, and began fiddling with the radio dial. "Do you like country music, Francie, or is easy listening more your speed? Damn. I forgot to give Stoney that pass for tomorrow like I promised him." He opened the door. "I'll be back in a minute."

She watched him walk across the parking lot and noticed that he still wasn't moving with any urgency. The screen door opened and the golfers came out. He stopped and talked to them, sticking a thumb in the rear pocket of his jeans and propping his boot up on the concrete step. One of the golfers drew an imaginary arc through the air, and then a second one right below it. Dallie shook his head, pantomimed a golf swing, and then drew two imaginary arcs of his own.

She slumped dejectedly down in the seat. Dallie Beaudine certainly didn't look like a man swept away by unbridled passion.

When he finally got back to the Riviera, she was so rattled she couldn't even look at him. Were the women in his life so gorgeous that she was merely one of the crowd? A bath would fix everything, she told herself as he started the car. She would run the water as hot as she could stand it so that the bathroom would fill with steam and the humidity would make her hair form those soft little tendrils around her face. She would put on a touch of lipstick and some blusher, spray the sheets with perfume, and cover one of the lamps with a towel so the light would fall softly, and—

"Something wrong, Francie?"

"What makes you ask?" she replied stiffly.

"You've pretty much laminated yourself to that door handle over there."

"I like it here."

He fiddled with the radio dial. "Suit yourself. So what's it going to be? Country or easy listening?"

"Neither. I like rock." She had a sudden inspiration, and she immediately acted upon it. "I've loved rock for as long as I can remember. The Rolling Stones are my very favorite group. Most people don't know it, but Mick wrote three songs for me after we spent some time together in Rome."

Dallie didn't look particularly impressed, so she decided to embellish. After all, it wasn't too much of a lie, since Mick Jagger certainly knew her well enough to say hello. She lowered her voice into a breathless, confiding whisper. "We stayed in this wonderful apartment that overlooked the Villa Borghese. Everything was absolutely super. We had complete privacy, so we could even make love outside on the terrace. It didn't last, of course. He has this terrible ego— not to mention Bianca—and I met the prince." She paused. "No, that's not right. I met Ryan O'Neal, and *then* I met the prince."

Dallie looked over at her, gave his head a slow shake as if he were clearing water from his ears, and then returned his attention to the road. "You like making love outside, do you, Francie?"

"Of course, don't most women?" Actually, she couldn't imagine anything worse.

They drove for several miles in silence. Suddenly he swung the wheel to the right and turned off the highway onto a narrow dirt road that headed directly into a stand of bald cypresses hung with beards of Spanish moss. "What are you doing? Where are you going!" she exclaimed. "Turn the car around this minute! I want to go back to the motel."

"I think you might like this spot, being such a sexual adventuress and all." He pulled in among the cypresses and turned off the ignition. Strange insect sounds drifted through the open window on his side.

"That looks like a swamp out there," she cried desperately.

He peered through the windshield. "I believe you're right. We'd better not get too far from the car; most 'gators seem to feed at night." He pulled off his cap, set it on the dashboard, and turned to her. He waited expectantly.

She pushed herself a little more closely against the door handle.

"Do you want to go first, or do you want me to?" he finally asked.

She kept her reply cautious. "Go first doing what?"

"Warming up. You know—foreplay. Since you've had all those big-time lovers, you've got me a little intimidated here. Maybe you'd better set the pace."

"Let's—let's forget this. I—I think maybe I made a mistake. Let's go back to the motel."

"Not a good idea, Francie. Once you make that crossover into the Promised Land, you can't really turn back without making things awkward."

"Oh, I don't think so. I don't think it'll be awkward at all. It wasn't actually the Promised Land, just a small flirtation. I mean, it certainly won't be awkward for me, and I'm positive it won't be awkward for—"

"Yes, it will. It'll be so awkward I probably won't even be able to play half-decent golf tomorrow. I'm a professional athlete, Francie. Professional athletes have fine-tuned bodies, like well-oiled engines. One little speck of awkwardness'll throw everything off stride. Like dirt. You could cost me a good five strokes tomorrow, darlin'."

His accent had gotten unbelievably thick, and she suddenly realized she was being conned. "Damn it, Dallie! Don't do this to me. I'm nervous enough as it is without your making fun of me."

He laughed, put his arm around her shoulder, and pulled her close in a friendly sort of hug. "Why don't you just say you're nervous instead of going through all that fancy stuff of yours? You make everything so hard on yourself."

It felt nice being in his arms, but she couldn't quite forgive him for teasing. "That's easy for you to say. You're obviously comfortable in every conceivable sort of bed, but I'm not." She took a breath and spit out exactly what was on her mind. "Actually . . . I don't even like sex." There. She'd said it. Now he could really laugh at her.

"Now, why's that? Something that feels as good as sex and doesn't cost any money should be right up your alley."

"I'm just not an athletic person."

"Uh-huh. Well, that explains it, all right."

She couldn't entirely forget the swamp. "Could we go back to the motel, Dallie?"

"I don't think so, Francie. You'll be closing yourself up in the bathroom and worrying about your makeup and reaching for that perfume bottle of yours." He lifted the hair on the side of her neck and, leaning over, nuzzled his lips against her skin. "You ever necked in the back seat of a car before?"

She closed her eyes against the delicious sensation he was arousing. "Does one of the royal family's limousines count?"

He caught her earlobe gently between his teeth. "Not unless the windows fogged up."

She wasn't sure who moved first, but somehow Dallie's mouth was on hers. His hands moved up along the back of her neck and plowed through her hair from beneath, spreading it out over his bare forearms. He imprisoned her head in the palms of his hands and tilted it farther back so that her mouth opened involuntarily. She waited for the invasion of his tongue, but it didn't come. Instead, he played with her bottom lip. Her own hands crept around his ribs to his back and unconsciously slipped beneath his T-shirt so she could feel his strong bare skin. Their mouths played together and Francesca lost all desire to try to maintain the upper hand. Before long, she found herself receiving his tongue with pleasure—his beautiful tongue, his beautiful mouth, his beautiful taut skin beneath her hands. She devoted herself to the kiss, concentrating only on the feelings he was arousing without giving a thought to what would happen next. His mouth slid away from hers and traveled to her neck. She giggled softly.

"Do you have something you want to share with the rest of the class," he murmured into her skin, "or is this a private joke?"

"No, I'm just having fun." She smiled as he kissed her neck and tugged on the rosette of material at her waist securing the long tail of the T-shirt. "What's an Aggies?" she asked.

"An Aggie? Somebody like me who went to college at Texas A&M is an Aggie."

She pulled back abruptly, her amazement etching itself in the perfect arch of her eyebrows. "You went to a university? I don't believe it!"

He looked at her with a mildly aggravated expression. "I've got a bachelor of arts degree in English literature. Do you want to see my diploma or can we get back to work here?"

"English literature?" She burst out in laughter. "Oh, Dallie, that's incredible! You barely speak the language."

He was clearly offended. "Well, now, that's real nice. That's a real nice thing to say to somebody."

Still laughing, she tossed herself into his arms, moving so suddenly that she knocked him off balance and bumped him back into the steering wheel. Then she said the most astonishing thing.

"I could eat you up, Dallie Beaudine."

It was his turn to laugh, but he didn't get very far with it because her mouth was all over his. She forgot about being scared and about not being any good at sex as she lifted herself to her knees and leaned on him.

"I'm running out of maneuvering room here, honey," he finally said against her mouth. Pulling away, he opened the door of the Riviera and got out. Then he extended his hand for her.

She let him help her out, but instead of opening the back door so they could resettle in roomier quarters, he pinned her hips with his thighs against the side of the Riviera and drew her into another kiss. The dome light left on by the open door produced a dim area of illumination around the car that made the darkness beyond seem even more impenetrable. The vague image of her open-toed sandals and alligators lurking beneath a car flickered through her mind. Without losing one moment of the kiss, she draped her arms over his shoulders and pulled herself up so that one of her legs was wrapped tightly around the back of one of his and her other foot was planted firmly on top of his cowboy boot.

"I *do* like the way you kiss," he murmured. His left hand slid up along her bare spine and unfastened her bra while his right reached between their bodies to tug at the snap on her jeans.

She could feel herself getting nervous again, and it didn't have anything to do with alligators. "Let's go buy some champagne, Dallie. I—I think some champagne will help me relax."

"I'll relax you." He pulled the snap open and began working on the zipper.

"Dallie!" she exclaimed. "We're outside."

"Uh-huh. Just you, me, and the swamp." The zipper gave.

"I—I don't think I'm ready for this." Reaching under her loose T-shirt, he cupped her breast in his hand and let his lips trail over her cheek to her mouth. Panic began beating inside her. He rubbed her nipple with his thumb and she moaned softly. She wanted him to think she was wonderful—a spectacular lover—and how could she do that in the middle of a swamp? "I—I need champagne. And soft lights. I need sheets, Dallie."

He withdrew his hand from her breast and settled it gently around the side of her neck. Gazing down into her eyes, he said, "No, you don't, honey. You don't need anything but yourself. You've got to start understanding that, Francie. You've got to start relying on yourself instead of all these props you think you need to set up around you."

"I-I'm afraid." She tried to make her words sound defiant, but didn't quite succeed. Unwrapping herself from his legs and stepping down off his cowboy boot, she confessed everything. "It might seem silly to you, but Evan Varian said I was frigid, and there was this Swedish sculptor in Marrakech—"

"You want to hold on to that part of the story for a while?"

She felt some of her fight coming back, and she glared at him. "You brought me here on purpose, didn't you? You brought me here because you knew I'd hate it." She took several steps back and pointed a shaky finger toward the Riviera. "I'm not the sort of woman you make love to in the back seat of a car."

"Who said anything about a back seat?"

She stared at him for a moment and then exclaimed, "Oh, no! I'm not lying down on that creature-infested ground. I mean it, Dallie."

"I don't much like the ground myself."

"Then how? Where?"

"Come on, Francie. Stop plotting and planning and trying to make sure you always have your best side turned to the camera. Let's just kiss a little bit so things can take their natural course."

"I want to know *where*, Dallie."

"I know you do, honey, but I'm not going to tell you because you'll start worrying about whether it's color-coordinated or not. For once in your life, take a chance at doing something where you may not come out looking your best."

She felt as if he had held a mirror up in front of her—not a very large mirror and one with clouded glass, but a mirror nonetheless. Was she as vain as Dallie seemed to believe? As calculating? She didn't want to think so, and yet . . . She stuck out her chin and began defiantly peeling down her jeans. "All right, we'll do it your way. But just don't expect anything spectacular from me." The slim denim pantlegs caught on her sandals. She bent over to struggle with them, but the heels stuck in the folds. She gave the jeans another tug and tightened the snare. "Is this turning you on, Dallie?" she fumed. "Do you like watching me? Are you getting excited? Dammit! Dammit to bloody hell!"

He started to move toward her, but she looked up at him through the veil of her hair and bared her teeth. "Don't you dare touch me. I mean it. I'll do it myself."

"We're not getting off to a real promising start here, Francie."

"You go to hell!" Jeans hobbling her ankles, she hopped the three steps back to the car, sat down hard on the front seat, and finally extricated herself from the pants. Then she stood up in T-shirt, underpants, and sandals. "There! And I'm not taking another thing off until I feel like it."

"Sounds fair to me." He opened his arms to her. "You want to cuddle up here for a minute and catch your breath."

She did. She really did. "I suppose."

She curled into his chest. He held her for a moment, and then he tilted back her head and began kissing her again. She'd sunk so low in her own estimation that she didn't even try to impress him; she just let him do the work. After a while, she realized that it felt nice. His tongue touched hers and his splayed hand pressed against the bare skin of her back. She lifted her arms and wrapped them around his neck. He reached under her shirt again and his thumbs began to toy with the sides of her breasts and then slid over onto the nipples. It felt so good—shivery and warm at the same time. Had the sculptor played with her breasts? He must have, but she didn't remember. And then Dallie pushed her T-shirt above her breasts and began teasing her with his mouth—his beautiful, wonderful mouth. She sighed as he sucked gently on one nipple and then the other. Somewhat to her surprise, she realized her own hands were once again beneath his shirt, kneading his bare chest. He picked her up in his arms, walked forward with her curled into his chest, and then laid her down.

Over the trunk of his Riviera.

"Absolutely not!" she exclaimed.

"Give it a chance," he replied.

She opened her mouth to tell him that nothing in the world would convince her to be mauled while she was stretched out on the trunk of a car, but he seemed to take her open mouth as some sort of invitation. Before she could frame her words he started kissing her again. Without quite knowing how it happened, she heard herself moan as his kisses grew deeper, hotter. She arched her neck to him, opened her mouth, thrust her tongue, and forgot about her demeaning position. He reached down and encircled her ankle with his fingers, then pulled her leg up. "Right here," he crooned softly. "Put your foot right up here next to the license plate, honey."

She did just as he asked.

"Move your hips forward a little bit. That's good." His voice sounded thick, not as calm as usual, and his breathing was faster than normal as he rearranged her. She pulled at his T-shirt, wanting to feel his bare skin against her breasts.

He peeled it over his head and then began tugging at her underpants.

"Dallie . . ."

"It's all right, darlin'. It's all right." Her underpants disappeared and her bottom settled on cold metal dusted with road grit. "Francie, that package of birth control pills I spotted in your case wasn't just there for decoration, now, was it?"

She shook her head, unwilling to break the mood by offering any lengthy explanations. When her periods had unaccountably stopped a few months ago, her physician had told her to quit taking her birth control pills until they resumed. He had assured her that she couldn't get pregnant until then, and at the moment that was all that mattered.

Dallie's hand closed over the inside of one of her thighs. He moved it slightly away from the other and began stroking her skin lightly, each time coming closer to the one part of her that she didn't find all that beautiful, the one part of her that she would just as soon have kept hidden away, except that it felt so warm and quivery and strange. "What if somebody comes?" she cried as he brushed against her.

"I'm hoping somebody will," he replied huskily. And then he stopped brushing, stopped teasing, and touched her . . . really touched her. Inside.

"Dallie . . ." Her voice was half moan, half cry.

"Feel good?" he muttered, his fingers sliding gently in and out.

"Yes. Yes."

While he played with her, she closed her eyes against the slice of Louisiana moon above her head so that nothing would distract her from the wonderful feelings that were rushing through her body. She turned her cheek and didn't even feel the dirt from the trunk rub against her skin. His hands grew less patient. They spread her legs farther apart and pulled her hips closer to the edge. Her feet were balanced precariously on the bumper, separated by a Texas license plate and some dusty chrome. He fumbled with the front of his jeans and she heard the zipper give. He lifted her hips.

When she felt him push inside her, she gave a small gasp. He bent over her, his feet still on the ground, but drew back slightly. "Am I hurting you?"

"Oh, no. It—it feels so good."

"It's supposed to, honey."

She wanted him to believe she was a wonderful lover—to do everything right—but the whole world seemed to be sliding away from her, making everything dizzy, wavery, and mushy with warmth. How could she concentrate when he was touching her that way, moving like that? She suddenly wanted to feel more of him. Lifting her foot from the bumper, she wrapped one knee around his hips, the other around his leg, pushing against him until she had absorbed as much of him as she could.

"Easy, honey," he said. "Take your time." He began moving inside her slowly, kissing her, and making her feel as good as she'd ever felt in her life. "You with me, darlin'?" he murmured softly in her ear, the sound slightly hoarse.

"Oh, yes . . . yes. Dallie . . . my wonderful Dallie . . . my lovely Dallie . . ." A cacophony of sound seemed to explode in her head as she came and came and came.

He heaved hard, and something halfway between a moan and groan escaped him. The sound gave her a feeling of power, touched fire to her excitement, and she came again. He quivered over her for a wonderfully interminable length of time and then grew heavy.

She turned her cheek so that it pressed against his hair, felt him dear and beautiful and real against her, inside her. She noticed that their skin was stuck together and that his back felt moist beneath her hands. She felt a small drop of perspiration fall from him onto her bare arm and realized she didn't care. Was this what it meant to be in love? she wondered dreamily. Her eyelids drifted open. She was in love. Of course. Why hadn't she realized it long before this? That was what was wrong with her. That was why she'd been feeling so unhappy. She was in love.

"Francie?" he murmured.

"Yes?"

"You all right?"

"Oh, yes."

He eased himself up on one arm and smiled down at her. "Then how 'bout we head for the motel and try it again on top of those sheets you were so set on?"

On the drive back, she sat in the middle of the front seat and leaned her cheek against his shoulder while she chewed a piece of Double Bubble and daydreamed about their future.

Chapter
13

Naomi Jaffe Tanaka let herself into her apartment, a Mark Cross briefcase in one hand and a bag from Zabar's perched on her opposite hip. Inside the bag was a container of golden figs, a sweet Gorgonzola, and a crusty loaf of French bread, all she needed for a perfect working night dinner. She set down her briefcase and placed the sack on the black granite counter in her kitchen, leaning it against the wall, which had been painted with a hard burgundy enamel. The apartment was expensive and stylish, exactly the sort of place where the vice-president of a major advertising agency should live.

Naomi frowned as she pulled out the Gorgonzola and set it on a pink glazed porcelain plate. Only one small stumbling block lay between her and the vice-presidency she craved—finding the Sassy Girl. Just that morning, Harry Rodenbaugh had sent her a stinging memo threatening to turn the account over to one of the agency's "more aggressive men" if she couldn't produce her Sassy Girl in the next few weeks.

She kicked off her gray suede pumps and nudged them out of the way with a stockinged toe while she removed the rest of her purchases from the sack. How could it be so difficult to find one person? Over the past few days, she and her secretary had made dozens of phone calls, but not one of them had run the girl to ground. She was out there, Naomi knew, but where? She rubbed her temples, but the pressure did nothing to relieve the headache that had been plaguing her all day.

After depositing the figs in the refrigerator, she picked up her pumps and headed wearily out of the kitchen. She would take a shower, put on her oldest bathrobe, and pour herself a glass of wine before she started on the work she'd brought home. With one hand, she began unfastening the pearl buttons at the front of her dress, while with the elbow of her other arm, she flicked on the living room light switch.

"What's doin', sis?"

Naomi shrieked and spun toward her brother's voice, her heart jumping in her chest. "My God!"

Gerry Jaffe lounged on the couch, his shabby jeans and faded blue work shirt out of place against the silky rose upholstery. He still wore his black hair in an Afro. He had a small scar on his left cheekbone and tired brackets around those full lips that had once driven all of her female friends wild with lust. His nose was the same—as big and bold as an eagle's. And his eyes were deep black nuggets that still burned with the fire of the zealot.

"How did you get in here?" she demanded, her heart pounding. She felt both angry and vulnerable. The last thing she needed in her life right now was another problem, and Gerry's reappearance could only mean trouble. She also hated the feeling of inadequacy she always experienced when Gerry was around—a little sister who once again didn't measure up to her brother's standards.

"No kiss for your big brother?"

"I don't want you here."

She received a brief impression of an enormous weariness hanging over him, but it vanished almost immediately. Gerry had always been a good actor. "Why didn't you call first?" she snapped. And then she remembered that Gerry had been photographed by the newspapers a few weeks before outside the naval base in Bangor, Maine, leading a demonstration against stationing the Trident nuclear submarine there. "You've been arrested again, haven't you?" she accused him.

"Hey, what's another arrest in the Land of the Free, the

Home of the Brave?" Uncoiling himself from the sofa, he held out his arms to her and gave her his most charming Pied Piper grin. "Come on, sweetie. How 'bout a little kiss?"

He looked so much like the big brother who used to buy her candy bars when she had asthma attacks that she nearly smiled. But her temporary softening was a mistake. With a monstrous growl, he vaulted over her glass and marble coffee table and came for her.

"Gerry!" She backed away from him, but he kept coming. Baring his teeth, he turned his hands into claws and came lurching toward her in his best Frankensteinian manner. "The Four-Eyed Fang-Toothed Phantom walks again," he growled.

"I said stop it!" Her voice rose in pitch until it was shrill. She couldn't deal with the Fang-Toothed Phantom now—not with the Sassy Girl and the vice-presidency and her headache all plaguing her. Despite the passing years, her brother never changed. He was the same old Gerry—larger than life, just as outrageous as ever. But she wasn't nearly as charmed.

He lurched toward her, his face comically distorted, eyes rolling, playing the game he'd teased her with for as long as she could remember. "The Fang-Toothed Phantom lives off the flesh of young virgins." He leered.

"Gerry!"

"Succulent young virgins!"

"Stop it!"

"Juicy young virgins!"

Despite her irritation, she giggled. "Gerry, don't!" She backed away toward the hallway, not taking her eyes off him as he advanced inexorably toward her. With an inhuman shriek he made his lunge. She screamed as he caught her up into his arms and began spinning her in a circle. Ma! she wanted to shout. Ma, Gerry's teasing me! In a sudden rush of nostalgia, she wanted to call out for protection to the woman who now turned her face away whenever her older child's name was mentioned.

Gerry sank his teeth into her shoulder and bit her just hard enough so that she would squeal again, but not hard enough to hurt her. Then he stiffened. "What's this?" he cried in outrage. "This is awful stuff. This isn't a virgin's flesh." He took her over to the sofa and dumped her unceremoniously. "Shit. Now I'm going to have to settle for pizza."

She loved him and she hated him, and she wanted to hug him so much that she jumped up off the sofa and gave him a sucker punch right in the arm.

"Ow! Hey, nonviolence, sis."

"Nonviolence, my ass! What the hell is wrong with you, barging in here like this? You're so damned irresponsible. When are you going to grow up?"

He didn't say anything; he just stood there looking at her. The fragile good humor between them faded. His Rasputin eyes took in her expensive dress and the stylish pumps that had fallen to the floor. Pulling out a cigarette, he lit it, still watching her. He had always had the ability to make her feel inadequate, personally responsible for the sins of the world, but she refused to squirm at the disapproval that gradually came over his expression as he surveyed the material artifacts of her world. "I mean it, Gerry," she went on. "I want you out of here."

"The old man must finally be proud of you," he said tonelessly. "His little Naomi has turned into a fine capitalist pig, just like all the rest."

"Don't start on me."

"You never told me how he reacted when you married that Jap." He gave a bark of cynical laughter. "Only my sister Naomi could marry a Jap named Tony. God, what a country."

"Tony's mother is American. And he's one of the leading biochemists in the country. His work has been published in every important—" She broke off, realizing she was defending a man she no longer even liked. This was exactly the sort of thing Gerry did to her.

Slowly she turned back to face him, taking some time to study his expression more closely. The weariness she thought she had glimpsed earlier seemed once again to have settled over him, and she had to remind herself it was merely another act. "You're in trouble again, aren't you?"

Gerry shrugged.

He really did look tired, she thought, and she was still her mother's daughter. "Come on out to the kitchen. Let me get you something to eat." Even with Cossacks trying to break down the door of the cottage, the women in her family would make everyone sit down to a five-course dinner.

While Gerry smoked, she fixed him a roast beef sandwich, adding an extra slice of Swiss cheese, just the way he liked it, and putting out a dish of the figs she had bought for herself. She set the food in front of him and then poured herself a glass of wine, watching surreptitiously as he ate. She could tell he was hungry, just as she could tell that he didn't want her to see exactly how hungry, and she wondered how long it had been since he'd eaten a decent meal. Women used to stand in line for the honor of feeding Gerry Jaffe. She imagined they still did, since her brother continued to have more than his fair share of sex appeal. It used to enrage her to see how casually he treated the women who fell in love with him.

She made him another sandwich, which he demolished as efficiently as he'd eaten the first one. Settling down on the stool next to him, she felt an illogical stab of pride. Her brother had been the best of them all, with Abbie Hoffman's sense of the comic, Tom Hayden's discipline, and Stokely Carmichael's fiery tongue. But now Gerry was a dinosaur, a sixties radical transplanted into the Age of Me First. He attacked nuclear missile silos with a ball-peen hammer and shouted power to the people whose hearing had been blocked by the headsets of their Sony Walkmans.

"How much do you pay for this place?" Gerry asked as he crumpled his napkin and got up to walk over to the refrigerator.

"None of your business." She absolutely refused to listen to his lecture on the number of starving children she could feed on her monthly rent.

He pulled out a carton of milk and took a glass from the cupboard. "How's Ma?" His question was casual, but she wasn't fooled.

"She's having a little trouble with arthritis, but other than that, she's okay." Gerry rinsed out the glass and set it in the top rack of her dishwasher. He had always been neater than she was. "Dad's good, too," she said, suddenly unable to tolerate the idea of making him ask. "You know he retired last summer."

"Yeah, I know. Do they ever ask about . . ."

Naomi couldn't help herself. She got up from the stool and walked over to rest her cheek against her brother's arm. "I know they think about you, Ger," she said softly. "It's just—it's been hard on them."

"You'd think they'd be proud," he said bitterly.

"Their friends talk," she replied, knowing how lame the excuse was.

He gave her a brief, awkward hug and then quickly moved away, going back into the living room. She found him standing next to the window, pushing the draperies back with one hand and lighting a cigarette with the other.

"Tell me why you're here, Gerry. What do you want?"

For a moment he stared out over the Manhattan skyline. Then he stuck his cigarette into the corner of his mouth, pressed the palms of his hands together in an attitude of prayer, and sketched a small bow before her. "Just a little sanctuary, sis. Just a little sanctuary."

Dallie won the Lake Charles tournament.

"Of course you won the damned thing," Skeet grumbled as the three of them walked into the motel room on Sunday night with a silver urn-shaped trophy and a check for ten thousand dollars. "The tournament doesn't amount to a hill of beans, so you naturally have to play some of the best damned golf you've played in two months. Why can't you do this kind of thing at Firestone or anyplace they got a TV camera pointed at you, do you mind telling me that?"

Francesca kicked off her sandals and sagged down onto the end of the bed. Even her bones were tired. She had walked all eighteen holes of the golf course so she could cheer Dallie on as well as discourage any petrochemical secretaries who might be following him too closely. Everything was going to change for Dallie now that she loved him, she had decided. He would start playing for her, just as he'd played today, winning tournaments, making all sorts of money to support them. They'd been lovers for less than a day, so she knew the idea of Dallie supporting her on a permanent basis was premature, but she couldn't help thinking about it.

Dallie began pulling the tail of his golf shirt out of his light gray slacks. "I'm tired, Skeet, and my wrist hurts. Do you mind if we save this for later?"

"That's what you always say. But there isn't any saving it till later 'cause you won't ever talk about it. You go on——"

"Stop it!" Francesca jumped up from the bed and rounded on Skeet. "You leave him alone, do you hear? Can't you see how tired he is? You act as if he lost the bloody tournament today instead of winning it. He was magnificent."

"Magnificent my sweet aunt," Skeet drawled. "That boy didn't play with three-quarters of what he's got, and he knows it better than anybody. How about you take care of your makeup, Miss Fran-chess-ka, and you let me take care of Dallie?" He stalked to the door and slammed it as he went out.

Francesca confronted Dallie. "Why don't you fire him? He's impossible, Dallie. He makes everything so difficult for you."

He sighed and stripped his shirt over his head. "Leave it alone, Francie."

"That man is your employee, and yet he acts as though you're working for him. You need to put a stop to it." She watched as he walked over to the brown paper sack he'd brought back to the room with him and pulled out a six-pack of beer. He drank too much, she realized, even though he never seemed to show any signs of it. She had also seen him take a few pills that she doubted were vitamins. As soon as the time was right, she would persuade him to stop both practices.

He peeled a can from its plastic ring and popped the top. "Trying to come between Skeet and me isn't a good idea, Francie."

"I'm not trying to come between you. I just want to make things easier for you."

"Yeah? Well, forget it." He drained his beer and stood up. "I'm going to take a shower."

She didn't want him to be angry with her, so she curved

her mouth into an irresistibly sexy smile. "Need any help with those hard-to-reach places?"

"I'm tired," he said irritably. "Just leave me alone." He walked into the bathroom and shut the door, but not before he'd seen the hurt in her eyes.

Stripping off his clothes, he turned the shower on full blast. The water sluiced over his sore shoulder. Closing his eyes, he ducked under the shower head, thinking about that lovesick look he'd spotted on her face. He should have figured she would start imagining she was in love with him. Everything was packaging to her. She was exactly the sort of woman who couldn't see any further than his pretty face. Dammit, he should have left things like they were between them, but they'd been sleeping in the same room for nearly a week and her accessibility had been driving him crazy. How much could he expect from himself? Besides, something about her had gotten to him last night when she'd told that stupid warthog story.

Even so, he should have kept his jeans zipped. Now she was going to cling to him like a string of bad luck, expecting hearts and flowers and all that other horseshit, none of which he had the slightest intention of giving to her. There was no way, not when he had Wynette looming up in front of him and Halloween beating at his door, and not when he could think of a dozen women he liked a whole lot better. Still—although he had no intention of telling her about it—she was one of the best-looking women he'd ever met. Even though he realized it was a mistake, he suspected he would be back in bed with her before too much more time had passed.

You're a real bastard, aren't you, Beaudine?

The Bear loomed up from the back recesses of Dallie's brain with a corona of Jesus-light shining around his head. The goddamn Bear.

You're a loser, chum, the Bear whispered in that flat midwestern drawl of his. *A two-bit loser. Your father knew it and I know it. And Halloween's coming up, just in case you forgot. . . .*

Dallie hit the cold water faucet with his fist and drowned out the rest.

But things with Francesca didn't get any easier, and the next day their relationship wasn't improved when, just the other side of the Louisiana-Texas border, Dallie began complaining about hearing a strange noise coming from the car.

"What do you think that is?" he asked Skeet. "I had the engine tuned not three weeks ago. Besides, it seems to be coming from the back. Do you hear that?"

Skeet was engrossed in an article about Ann-Margret in the newest issue of *People* and he shook his head.

"Maybe it's the exhaust." Dallie looked over his shoulder at Francesca. "Do you hear anything back there, Francie? Funny grating kind of noise?"

"I don't hear a thing," Francesca replied quickly.

Just then a loud rasp filled the interior of the Riviera. Skeet's head shot up. "What's that?"

Dallie swore. "I know that sound. Dammit, Francie. You've got that ugly walleyed cat back there with you, don't you?"

"Now, Dallie, don't get upset," she pleaded. "I didn't mean to bring him along. He just followed me into the car and I couldn't get him out."

"Of course he followed you!" Dallie yelled into the rearview mirror. "You've been feeding him, haven't you? Even though I told you not to, you've been feeding that damned walleyed cat."

She tried to make him understand. "It's just— He's got such bony ribs and it's hard for me to eat when I know he's hungry."

Skeet chuckled from the passenger seat and Dallie rounded on him. "What do you think is so goddamn funny, you mind telling me that?"

"Not a thing," Skeet replied, grinning. "Not a thing."

Dallie pulled off onto the shoulder of the interstate and threw open his door. He twisted to the right and leaned over the back of the seat to see the cat huddled on the floor next to the Styrofoam cooler. "Get him out of here right now, Francie."

"He'll get hit by a car," she protested, not entirely certain why this cat, who hadn't given her even the smallest sign of affection, had earned her protection. "We can't let him out on the highway. He'll be killed."

"The world'll be a better place," Dallie retorted. She glared at him. He leaned over the seat and made a swipe at the cat. The animal arched his back, hissed, and sank his teeth into Francesca's ankle.

She let out a yelp of pain and screeched at Dallie. "Now see what you've done!" Pulling her foot into her lap, she inspected her injured ankle and then shrieked down at the cat, "You bloody ingrate! I hope he throws you in front of a bloody Greyhound bus."

Dallie's scowl changed to a grin. After a moment's thought, he shut the door of the Riviera and glanced over at Skeet. "I guess maybe we should let Francie keep her cat after all. It'd be a shame to break up a matched set."

For people who liked small towns, Wynette, Texas, was a good place to live. San Antonio, with its big-city lights, lay only a little more than two hours southeast, as long as the person behind the wheel didn't pay too much attention to the chicken-shit double-nickel speed limit the bureaucrats in Washington had pushed down the throats of the citizens of Texas. The streets of Wynette were shaded with sumac trees, and the park had a marble fountain with four drinking spouts. The people were sturdy. They were ranchers and farmers, about as honest as Texans got, and they made sure the town council was controlled by enough conservative Democrats and Baptists to keep away most of the ethnics looking for government handouts. All in all, once people settled in Wynette, they tended to stay.

Before Miss Sybil Chandler had taken it in hand, the house on Cherry Street had been just another Victorian nightmare. Over the course of her first year there, she had painted the dull gray gingerbread trim Easter egg shades of pink and lavender and hung ferns across the front porch in plant hangers she had macraméd herself. Still not satisfied, she had pursed her thin schoolteacher's lips and stenciled a chain of leaping jackrabbits in palest tangerine around the front window frames. When she was finished, she had signed her work in small neat letters next to the mail slot in the door. This effect had pleased her so much she had added a condensed *curriculum vitae* in the door panel beneath the mail slot:

> The Work of Miss Sybil Chandler
> Retired High School Teacher
> Chairperson, Friends of Wynette Public Library
> Passionate Lover of W. B. Yeats,
> E. Hemingway, and Others
> Rebel

And then, thinking it all sounded rather too much like an epitaph, she had covered what she'd written with another jackrabbit and contented herself with only the first line.

Still, that last word she'd painted on the door had lingered in her mind, and even now it filled her with pleasure. *"Rebel,"* from the Latin *rebellis.* What a lovely sound it had and how wonderful if such a word actually were to be inscribed on her tombstone. Just her name, the dates of her birth and her demise (the latter far into the future, she hoped), and that one word, "Rebel."

As she thought of the great literary rebels of the past, she knew it was hardly likely such an awe-inspiring word would ever be applied to her. After all, she had begun her rebellion only twelve years before, when, at the age of fifty-four, she'd quit the teaching job she'd held for thirty-two years in a prestigious Boston girls' school, packed her possessions, and moved to Texas. How her friends had clucked and tutted, believing she'd lost her senses, not to mention a sizable portion of her pension. But Miss Sybil hadn't listened to any of them, since she had been quite simply dying from the stifling predictability of her life.

On the airplane from Boston to San Antonio, she'd changed her clothes in the rest room, stripping the severe wool suit from her thin, juiceless body and shaking out the neat knot that confined her salt-and-pepper hair. Re-outfitted in her first pair of blue jeans and a paisley dashiki, she had returned to her seat and spent the rest of the flight admiring her calf-high red leather boots and reading Betty Friedan.

Miss Sybil had chosen Wynette by closing her eyes and stabbing at a map of Texas with her index finger. The school board had hired her sight unseen from her résumé, over-joyed that so highly acclaimed a teacher wanted a position in their small high school. Still, when she'd shown up for her initial appointment dressed in a floral-print muumuu, three-inch-long silver earrings, and her red leather boots, the superintendent had considered firing her just as quickly as he'd hired her. Instead, she eased his mind by spearing him with her small no-nonsense eyes and telling him she would not permit any slackers in her classroom. A week later she began teaching, and three weeks after that she lacerated the library board for having removed *The Catcher in the Rye* from their fiction collection.

J. D. Salinger reappeared on the library shelves, the senior English class raised their SAT verbal scores one hundred points over the previous year's class, and Miss Sybil Chandler lost her virginity to B. J. Randall, who owned the town's GE appliance store and thought she was the most wonderful woman in the world.

All went well for Miss Sybil until B.J. died and she was forced to retire from teaching at the age of sixty-five. She found herself wandering listlessly around her small apartment with too much time on her hands, too little money, and no one to care about. Late one night she wandered beyond the bounds of her small apartment into the center of town. That was where Dallie Beaudine had found her sitting on the curb at Main and Elwood in the middle of a thunderstorm clad only in her nightgown.

Now she glanced at the clock as she hung up the telephone from her weekly long-distance conversation with Holly Grace and then took a brass watering can into the living room of Dallie's Victorian Easter egg house to tend the plants. Only a few more hours and her boys would be home. Stepping over one of Dallie's two mongrel dogs, she set down her watering can and took her needlepoint to a sunny window seat where she allowed her mind to slip back through the years to the winter of 1965.

She had just finished quizzing her remedial sophomore English class on *Julius Caesar* when the door of the room opened and a lanky young man she had never seen before sauntered in. She immediately decided that he was much too handsome for his own good, with a swaggering walk and an insolent expression. He slapped a registration card down on her desk and, without waiting for an invitation, made his way to the back of the room and slouched down into an empty seat, letting his long legs sprawl out across the aisle. The boys regarded him cautiously; the girls giggled and craned their necks to get a better look. He grinned at several of them, openly assessing their breasts. Then he leaned back in his chair and went to sleep.

Miss Sybil bided her time until the bell rang and then called him to her desk. He stood before her, one thumb tucked in the front pocket of his jeans, his expression determinedly bored. She examined the card for his name, checked his age—nearly sixteen—and informed him of her classroom rules: "I do not tolerate tardiness, gum chewing, or slackers. You will write a short essay for me introducing yourself and have it on my desk tomorrow morning."

He studied her for a moment and then withdrew his thumb from the pocket of his jeans. "Go fuck yourself, lady."

This statement quite naturally caught her attention, but before she could respond, he had swaggered from the room. As she stared at the empty doorway, a great flood of excitement rose inside her. She had seen a blaze of intelligence shining in those sullen blue eyes. Astonishing! She immediately realized that more than insolence was eating away at this young man. He was another rebel, just like herself!

At precisely seven-thirty that evening, she rapped on the door of a run-down duplex and introduced herself to the man who had been listed on the registration card as the boy's guardian, a sinister-looking character who couldn't have been thirty himself. She explained her difficulty and the man shook his head dejectedly. "Dallie's starting to go bad," he told her. "The first few months we were together, he was all right, but the kid needs a house and a family. That's why I told him we were gonna settle here in Wynette for a while. I thought getting him into school regular might calm him down, but he got hisself suspended the first day for hitting the gym teacher."

Miss Sybil sniffed. "A most obnoxious man. Dallas made an excellent choice." She heard a soft shuffling noise behind her and hastily amended, "Not that I approve of violence, of course, although I should imagine it's sometimes quite satisfying." Then she turned and told the lanky, too-handsome boy slouched in the doorway that she had come to supervise his homework assignment.

"And what if I tell you I'm not doing it?" he sneered.

"I should imagine your guardian would object." She regarded Skeet. "Tell me, Mr. Cooper, what is your position regarding physical violence?"

"Don't bother me none," Skeet replied.

"Do you think you might be capable of physically restraining Dallas if he doesn't do as I ask?"

"Hard to say. I've got him on weight, but he's got me on height. And if he's hurt too much, he won't be able to hustle the boys at the country club this weekend. All in all, I'd say no."

She didn't give up hope. "All right, then, Dallas, I'm asking you to do your assignment voluntarily. For the sake of your immortal soul."

He shook his head and stuck a toothpick in his mouth.

She was quite disappointed, but she hid her feelings by rummaging in the tie-dyed tote bag she'd brought with her and pulling out a paperback book. "Very well, then. I observed your visual exchanges with the young ladies in the class today and came to the conclusion that anyone as obviously interested in sexual activity as you should read about it from one of the world's great writers. I'll expect an intelligent report from you in two days." With that, she thrust a copy of *Lady Chatterley's Lover* into his hand and left the house.

For nearly a month she relentlessly dogged the small apartment, thrusting banned books at her rebellious student and badgering Skeet to put tighter reins on the boy. "You don't understand," Skeet finally complained in frustration. "Regardless of the fact that no one wants him back, he's a runaway and I'm not even his legal guardian. I'm an ex-con he picked up in a gas station rest room, and he's been pretty much taking care of me, instead of the other way around."

"Nevertheless," she said, "you're an adult and he is still a minor."

Gradually Dallie's intelligence won out over his sullenness, although later he would insist she had just worn him down with all her dirty books. She talked him back into school, moved him into her college-bound class, and tutored him whenever he wasn't playing golf. Thanks to her efforts, he graduated with honors at age eighteen and was accepted at four different colleges.

After he left for Texas A&M, she missed him dreadfully, although he and Skeet continued to make Wynette their home base and he came to see her during vacations when he wasn't playing golf. Gradually, however, his responsibilities took him farther away for longer stretches of time. Once they didn't see each other for nearly a year. In her dazed state, she had barely recognized him the night he found her sitting in the thunderstorm on the curb at Main and Elwood wearing her nightgown.

Francesca had somehow imagined Dallie living in a modern apartment built next to a golf course instead of an old Victorian house with a central turret and pastel-painted gingerbread trim. She gazed at the windows of the house in disbelief as the Riviera turned the corner and slipped into a narrow gravel driveway. "Are those rabbits?"

"Two hundred fifty-six of them," Skeet said. "Fifty-seven if you count the one on the front door. Look, Dallie, that rainbow on the garage is new."

"She's going to break her fool neck one of these days climbing those ladders," Dallie grumbled. Then he turned to Francesca. "You mind your manners, now. I mean it, Francie. None of your fancy stuff."

He was talking to her as if she were a child instead of his lover, but before she could retaliate, the back door flew open and an incredible-looking old lady appeared. With her long gray ponytail flying behind her and a pair of reading glasses bobbing on the gold neck chain that hung over her daffodil yellow sweat suit, she rushed toward them, crying out, "Dallas! Oh, my, my! Skeet! My goodness!"

Dallie climbed out of the car and enveloped her small,

thin body in a bear hug. Then Skeet grabbed her away to the accompaniment of another chorus of my-my's.

Francesca emerged from the back seat and looked on curiously. Dallie had said his mother was dead, so who was this? A grandmother? As far as she knew, he had no relatives except the woman named Holly Grace. Was this Holly Grace? Somehow Francesca doubted it. She'd gotten the impression Holly Grace was Dallie's sister. Besides, she couldn't envision this eccentric-looking old lady showing up at a motel with a Chevy dealer from Tulsa. The cat slipped from the back seat, looked around disdainfully with his one good eye, and disappeared under the back steps.

"And who is this, Dallas?" the woman inquired, turning to Francesca. "Please introduce me to your friend."

"This is Francie . . . Francesca," Dallie amended. "Old F. Scott would have loved her, Miss Sybil, so if she gives you any trouble, let me know." Francesca darted him an angry glare, but he ignored her and continued his introduction. "Miss Sybil Chandler . . . Francesca Day."

Small brown eyes gazed at her, and Francesca suddenly felt as if her soul was being examined. "How do you do?" she replied, barely able to keep herself from squirming. "It's a pleasure to meet you."

Miss Sybil beamed at the sound of her accent, then extended her hand for a hearty shake. "Francesca, you're British! What a delightful surprise. Pay no attention to Dallas. He can charm the dead, of course, but he's a complete scoundrel. Do you read Fitzgerald?"

Francesca had seen the movie of *The Great Gatsby*, but she suspected that wouldn't count. "I'm afraid not," she said. "I don't read much."

Miss Sybil gave a disapproving cluck. "Well, we'll soon fix that, won't we? Bring the suitcases inside, boys. Dallas, are you chewing gum?"

"Yes, ma'am."

"Please remove it along with your hat before you come inside."

Francesca giggled as the old woman disappeared through the back door.

Dallie flicked his gum into a hydrangea bush. "Just you wait," he said to Francesca ominously.

Skeet chuckled. "Looks like ol' Francie's gonna take some of the heat off us for a change."

Dallie smiled back. "You can almost see Miss Sybil rubbing her hands together just waiting to get at her." He looked at Francesca. "Did you mean it when you said you haven't read Fitzgerald?"

Francesca was beginning to feel as if she'd confessed to a series of mass murders. "It's not a crime, Dallie."

"It is around here." He chuckled maliciously. "Boy, are you ever in for it."

The house on Cherry Street had high ceilings, heavy walnut moldings, and light-flooded rooms. The old wooden floors were scarred in places, a few cracks marred the plaster walls, and the interior decoration lacked even a modest sense of coordination, but the house still managed to project a haphazard charm. Striped wallpaper coexisted alongside floral, and the odd mix of furniture was enlivened by needlework pillows and afghans crocheted in multicolored yarns. Plants set in handmade ceramic pots filled dark corners, cross-stitch samplers decorated the walls, and golf trophies popped up everywhere—as doorstops, bookends, weighing down a stack of newspapers, or simply catching the light on a sunny windowsill.

Three days after her arrival in Wynette, Francesca slipped out of the bedroom Miss Sybil had assigned to her and crept across the hallway. Beneath a T-shirt of Dallie's that fell to the middle of her thighs, she wore a rather astonishing pair of silky black bikini underpants that had miraculously appeared in the small stack of clothing Miss Sybil had lent her to supplement her wardrobe. She had slipped into them half an hour earlier when she'd heard Dallie come up the stairs and go into his bedroom.

Since their arrival, she'd barely seen him. He left for the driving range early in the morning, from there went to the golf course and then God knew where, leaving her with no one but Miss Sybil for company. Francesca hadn't been in the house for a day before she'd found a copy of *Tender Is the Night* pressed into her hands along with a gentle admonition to refrain from pouting when things didn't go her way. Dallie's abandonment upset her. He acted as if nothing had happened between them, as if they hadn't spent a night making love. At first she had tried to ignore it, but now she had decided that she had to start fighting for what she wanted, and what she wanted was more lovemaking.

She tapped the tip of one unpainted fingernail softly on the door opposite her own, afraid Miss Sybil would awaken and hear her. She shuddered at the thought of what the disagreeable old woman would do if she knew Francesca had wandered across the hall to Dallie's bedroom for illicit sex. She would probably chase her from the house screaming "Harlot!" at the top of her lungs. When Francesca heard no response from the other side of the door, she tapped a bit harder.

Without warning, Dallie's voice boomed out from the other side, sounding like a cannon in the still of the night. "If that's you, Francie, come on in and stop making so damned much noise."

She darted inside the bedroom, hissing like a tire losing its air. "Shh! She'll hear you, Dallie. She'll know I'm in your room."

He stood fully dressed, hitting golf balls with his putter across the carpet toward an empty beer bottle. "Miss Sybil's eccentric," he said, eyeing the line of his putt, "but she's not even close to being a prude. I think she was disappointed when I told her we wouldn't be sharing a room."

Francesca had been disappointed, too, but she wasn't going to make an issue of it now, when her pride had already been stung. "I've barely seen you at all since we got here. I thought maybe you were still angry with me about Beast."

"Beast?"

"That bloody cat." A trace of annoyance crept into her voice. "He bit me again yesterday."

Dallie smiled, then sobered. "Actually, Francie, I thought it might be better if we kept our hands to ourselves for a while."

Something inside her gave a small lurch. "Why? What do you mean?"

The ball pinged against the glass as his putt found its mark. "I mean that I don't think you can handle a whole lot more trouble in your life right now, and you should know that I'm pretty much unreliable where women are concerned." He used the head of the putter to reach out for another ball and draw it close. "Not that I'm proud of it, you understand, but that's the way things are. So if you've got any ideas about rose-covered bungalows or His and Her bath towels, you might want to get rid of them."

Enough of the old proud Francesca still lingered that she managed to slip a condescending laugh past the lump in her throat. "Rose-covered bungalows? Really, Dallie, what on earth can you be thinking of? I'm going to marry Nicky, remember? This is my last fling before I'm permanently shackled." Except she wasn't going to marry Nicky. She'd placed another call last night, hoping that he would have returned by now and she could talk him into advancing her a small loan so she wouldn't be so dependent on Dallie for money. Her call woke the houseboy, who said Mr. Gwynwyck was away on his honeymoon. Francesca had stood with the receiver in her hand for some time before she'd hung up the phone.

Dallie looked up from the floor. "Are you telling me the truth? No His and Hers? No long-term plans?"

"Of course I'm telling the truth."

"Are you sure? There's something funny in your face when you look at me."

She tossed herself down into a chair and gazed around the room as if the caramel-colored walls and floor-to-ceiling bookcases were far more interesting than the man in front of her. "Fascination, darling," she said airily, draping a bare leg over the arm of the chair and arching her foot. "You are, after all, rather one of a kind."

"It's nothing more than fascination?"

"Gracious, Dallie. I don't mean to insult you, but I'm hardly the kind of woman who would fall in love with an impoverished Texas golf pro." Yes, I am, she admitted silently. I'm exactly that kind of woman.

"Now, you do have a point there. To tell you the truth, I can't imagine you falling in love with an impoverished anybody."

She decided the time had come to salvage another small remnant of her pride, so she stood and stretched, revealing the bottom edge of the black silk underpants. "Well, darling,

I think I'll leave, since you seem to have other things to occupy your time."

He looked at her for a minute as if he were making up his mind about something. Then he gestured toward the opposite side of the room with his putter. "Actually, I thought you might want to help me out here. Go on and stand over there, will you?"

"Why?"

"Just you never mind. I'm the man. You're the woman. You do what I say."

She made a face, then did as he asked, taking her time as she moved.

"Now slip off that T-shirt," he ordered.

"Dallie!"

"Come on, this is serious, and I don't have all night."

He didn't look at all serious, so she obediently pulled off the T-shirt, taking her time and feeling a warm rush through her body as she revealed herself to him.

He took in her bare breasts and the silky black bikini underpants. Then he gave an admiring whistle. "Now, that's nice, honey. That is *real* inspiring stuff. This is going to work out even better than I thought."

"What's going to work out?" she inquired warily.

"Something all us golf pros do for practice. You arrange yourself lying down in the position of my choice on the carpet right there. When you're ready, you slip off those panties, call out some specific part of your body, and I see how close I can get with my putt. It's the best exercise in the world for improving a golfer's concentration."

Francesca smiled and planted one hand on her bare hip. "And I can just imagine how much fun it is to fetch the balls when you're done."

"Damn, but you British women are smart."

"Too smart to let you get away with this."

"I was afraid you'd say that." He propped his putter up against a chair and began to walk toward her. "Guess we'll just have to find something else to occupy our time."

"Like what?"

He reached out and pulled her into his arms. "I don't know. But I'm thinking real hard."

Later, as she lay in his arms drowsy from lovemaking, she considered how strange it was that a woman who had turned down the Prince of Wales had fallen in love with Dallie Beaudine. She tilted her head so that her lips touched his bare chest and gave his skin a soft kiss. Just before she drifted off to sleep, she told herself that she would make him care for her. She would become exactly the woman he wanted her to be, and then he would love her as much as she loved him.

Sleep didn't come so easily to Dallie—either that night or for the next few weeks. He could feel Halloween beating down on him, and he lay awake trying to distract himself by playing a round of golf in his head or thinking about Francesca. For a woman who painted herself as one of the world's great sophisticates just because she'd run around Europe eating snails, Miss Fancy Pants would have learned a hell of a lot more, in his opinion, if she'd spent a few half-times on a stadium blanket under the bleachers at Wynette High.

She didn't seem to have logged enough hours between the bedposts to really relax with him, and he could see her worrying about whether she had her hands in the right place or whether she was moving in a way that would please him. It was hard for him to enjoy himself with all that single-minded dedication coming his way.

He knew she had half convinced herself she was in love with him, even though it wouldn't take her more than twenty-four hours back in London before she would have forgotten his name. Still, he had to admit that when he finally got her on that plane, part of him was actually going to miss her, despite the fact that she was a feisty little thing who wasn't giving up her stuck-up ways easy. She couldn't pass a mirror without spending a day and a half looking at herself, and she left a mess everywhere she went, as if she expected some servant to come along after her and clean up. Even so, he had to admit that she seemed to be making an effort. She ran errands into town for Miss Sybil and took care of that damned walleyed cat and tried to get along with Skeet by telling him stories about all the movie stars she'd met. She'd even started reading J. D. Salinger. More important, she finally seemed to be getting the idea that the world hadn't been created just for her benefit.

One thing he knew for sure. He would be sending old Nicky back a hell of a better woman than the one Nicky'd sent him.

Chapter
14

Naomi Jaffe Tanaka had to restrain herself from jumping up from her desk and dancing a jig as she set down her telephone. She'd found her! After an incredible amount of work, she'd finally found her Sassy Girl! Quickly she called in her secretary and dictated a list of instructions.

"Don't try to contact her; I want to approach her in person. Just double-check my information to make certain it's right."

Her secretary looked up from her steno pad. "You don't think she'll turn you down, do you?"

"I hardly think so. Not for the kind of money we're offering." But for all her confidence, Naomi was a natural worrier, and she knew she wouldn't relax until she had a signature on the dotted line of an ironclad contract. "I want to fly out as quickly as possible. Let me know as soon as the arrangements are set."

After her secretary left her office, Naomi hesitated for a moment and then dialed the number of her apartment. The phone rang again and again, but she refused to hang up. He was there; her luck wasn't good enough to make him magically disappear. She should never have agreed to let him stay in her apartment. If anyone at BS&R found out—"Answer, dammit."

The line clicked. "Saul's Whorehouse and Crematorium. Lionel speaking."

"Can't you just say hello like a normal person?" she snapped. Why was she putting herself through this? The police wanted Gerry for questioning, but he had received a tip that they planned to frame him on trumped-up charges of drug dealing, so he refused to go in to talk to them. Gerry didn't even smoke grass anymore, let alone deal in drugs, and she hadn't had the heart to turn him back out on the street. She also retained enough of her old distrust of the police to be unwilling to submit him to the unpredictability of the legal system.

"Talk to me nice or I'll hang up," he said.

"Terrific," she retorted. "If I get really nasty, does that mean you'll move out?"

"You got a letter from Save the Children thanking you for your contribution. Fifty lousy bucks."

"Dammit, you have no business reading my mail."

"Trying to buy your way into heaven, sis?"

Naomi refused to jump to his bait. There was a moment of silence, and then he made a grudging apology. "Sorry. I'm so bored I can't stand myself."

"Did you look over that information on law school I left out for you?" she asked casually.

"Aw, shit, don't start this again."

"Gerry . . ."

"I'm not selling out!"

"Just think about it, Gerry. Going to law school isn't selling out. You could do more good by working inside the system—"

"Knock it off, okay, Naomi? We've got a world out there that's ready to blow itself up. Adding another lawyer to the system isn't going to change a thing."

Despite his vehement protests, she sensed that the idea of going to law school wasn't as distasteful to him as he pretended. But she knew he needed time to think it over, so she didn't press him. "Look, Gerry, I have to go out of town for a few days. Do me a favor and try to be gone when I get back."

"Where are you going?"

She looked down at the memo pad on her desk and smiled

to herself. In twenty-four hours, the Sassy Girl would be signed, sealed, and delivered. "I'm going to a place called Wynette, Texas," she said.

Clad in jeans, sandals, and one of Miss Sybil's brightly colored cotton blouses, Francesca sat next to Dallie in a honky-tonk called the Roustabout. After nearly three weeks in Wynette, she had lost count of the number of evenings they had spent at the town's favorite night spot. Despite the raucous country band, the cloud of low-hanging smoke, and the tacky orange and black Halloween crepe paper hanging from the bar, she had discovered she actually liked the place.

Everyone in Wynette knew the town's most famous golfer, so the two of them always entered the honky-tonk to a chorus of "Hey, Dallie's" ringing out over the Naugahyde stools and the twang of the steel guitars. But tonight, for the first time, there had been a few "Hey, Francie's" thrown in, pleasing her inordinately.

One of the Roustabout's female patrons pushed her witch's mask to the top of her head and planted a boisterous kiss on Skeet's cheek. "Skeet, you old bear, I'm going to get you to the altar yet."

He chuckled. "You're too young for me, Eunice. I couldn't keep up with you."

"You said a mouthful there, honey." Eunice let out a shriek of laughter and then went off with a friend who was unwisely dressed in a harem costume that left her chubby midriff bare.

Francesca smiled. Although Dallie had been in a surly mood all evening, she was having fun. Most of the Roustabout's patrons were wearing their standard outfits of jeans and Stetsons, but a few wore Halloween costumes and all the bartenders had on glasses with rubber noses.

"Over here, Dallie!" one of the women called out. "We're going to bob for apples in a bucket of draft."

Dallie slammed the front legs of his chair down to the floor, grabbed Francesca's arm, and muttered, "Christ, that's all I need. Quit talking, dammit. I want to dance."

She hadn't been talking, but his expression was so grim that she didn't bother pointing that out. She just got up and followed him. As he dragged her across the floor toward the jukebox, she found herself remembering the first night he'd brought her to the Roustabout. Had it only been three weeks ago?

Her memories of the Blue Choctaw had still been fresh that night, and she was nervous. Dallie had dragged her onto the dance floor and, over her protests, insisted on teaching her the Texas two-step and the Cotton-Eyed Joe. After twenty minutes, her face had felt flushed and her skin had been damp. She had wanted nothing more than to escape to the rest room and repair the damage. "I've danced enough, Dallie," she had told him.

He had steered her toward the center of the wooden dance floor. "We're just warming up."

"I'm quite warm enough, thank you."

"Yeah? Well, I'm not."

The tempo of the music had picked up and Dallie's hold on her waist had tightened. She had begun to hear Chloe's voice taunting her over the country music, telling her that no one would love her if she didn't look beautiful, and she had felt the first flutters of uneasiness spread out inside her. "I don't want to dance anymore," she had insisted, trying to pull away.

"Well, that's just too bad, because I do." Dallie had snatched up his bottle of Pearl as they passed by their table. Without losing a beat, he had taken a drink, then pressed the bottle to her lips and tilted it up.

"I don't—" She had swallowed and choked as beer splashed into her mouth. He had raised the bottle to his own mouth again and emptied it. Sweaty tendrils had clung to her cheeks and beer had run down her chin. "I'm going to leave you," she had threatened, her voice rising. "I'm going to walk off this floor and out of your life forever if you don't let me go right now."

He had paid no attention. He had held on to her damp hands and pressed her body up against his.

"I want to sit down!" she had demanded.

"I don't really care what you want." He had moved his hands high up under her arms, right where the perspiration had soaked through her blouse.

"Please, Dallie," she had cried, mortified.

"Just shut your mouth and move your feet."

She had continued to plead with him, but he ignored her. Her lipstick had disappeared, her underarms had become a public disgrace, and she had felt absolutely certain that she was going to cry.

Just then, right in the middle of the dance floor, Dallie had stopped moving. He had looked down at her, dipped his head, and kissed her full on her beery mouth. "Damn, you're pretty," he had whispered.

She remembered those gentle words now as he pulled her none too gently through the orange and black paper streamers toward the jukebox. After three weeks of posturing, posing, and trying to work miracles with dime store cosmetics, she had only once wrung a compliment about her appearance out of him—and that had been when she looked terrible.

He bumped into two men on his way to the jukebox and didn't bother to apologize. What was the matter with him tonight? Francesca wondered. Why was he acting so surly? The band had taken a break, and he dug into the pocket of his jeans for a quarter. A chorus of groans rang out along with a few catcalls.

"Don't let him do it, Francie," Curtis Molloy called out.

She tossed him a mischievous smile over her shoulder. "Sorry, luv, but he's bigger than I am. Besides, he gets dreadfully ornery if I argue with him." The combination of her British accent with their lingo made them laugh, as she'd known it would.

Dallie punched the same two buttons he'd been punching all night whenever the band stopped playing, then set his bottle of beer on top of the jukebox. "I haven't heard Curtis blabber so much in years," he told Francesca. "You really got him going. Even the women are starting to like you." His words sounded more grudging than pleased.

She ignored his bad mood as the rock tune began to play. "What about you?" she asked saucily. "Do you like me, too?"

He moved his athlete's body to the first chords of "Born to Run," dancing to Springsteen's music as gracefully as he did the Texas two-step. "Of course I like you," he scowled.

"I'm not so much of an alley cat that I'd still be sleeping with you if I didn't like you a whole lot better than I used to. Damn, I love this song."

She had hoped for a somewhat more romantic declaration, but with Dallie she'd learned to settle for what she could get. She also didn't share his enthusiasm for the song he kept playing on the jukebox. Although she couldn't understand all of the lyrics, she gathered that the part about tramps like us who were born to run might be what Dallie liked so much about the song. The sentiment didn't fit well with her own vision of domestic bliss, so she shut out the lyrics and concentrated on the music, matching her body movements to Dallie's as she was learning to do so well in their own deep night bedroom dance. He looked into her eyes and she looked into his, and the music swept up around them. She felt as if some kind of invisible lock had snapped them together, and then the mood was broken as her stomach gave one of its queer pitches.

She wasn't pregnant, she told herself. She couldn't be. Her doctor had told her very clearly that she couldn't get pregnant until she started having her menstrual periods again. But her recent nausea had worried her enough that the day before at the library she'd looked through a Planned Parenthood pamphlet on pregnancy when Miss Sybil wasn't watching. To her dismay, she had read the exact opposite and she found herself desperately counting back to that first night she and Dallie had made love. It had been almost a month ago exactly.

They danced again and then went back to their table, the palm of his hand cupped over the small of her back. She enjoyed his touch, the sensation of a woman being protected by the man who cared about her. Maybe it wouldn't be so bad if she actually was pregnant, she thought as she sat down at the table. Dallie wasn't the kind of man who would slip her a few hundred dollars and drive her to the local abortionist. Not that she had any desire to have a baby, but she was beginning to learn that everything had a price. Maybe pregnancy would make him commit himself to her, and once he made that commitment everything would be wonderful. She would encourage him to stop drinking so much and apply himself more. He would begin to win tournaments and make enough money so they could buy a house in a city somewhere. It wouldn't be the sort of fashionable international life she'd envisioned for herself, but she didn't need all that running about anymore, and she knew she would be happy as long as Dallie loved her. They would travel together, and he would take care of her, and everything would be perfect.

But the picture wouldn't quite crystallize in her mind, so she took a sip from her bottle of Lone Star.

A woman's voice with a drawl as lazy as a Texas Indian summer penetrated her thoughts. "Hey, Dallie," the voice said softly, "make any birdies for me?"

Francesca sensed the change in him, an alertness that hadn't been there a moment before, and she lifted her head.

Standing next to their table and gazing down at him with mischievous blue eyes stood the most beautiful woman Francesca had ever seen. Dallie jumped up with a soft exclamation and enveloped her in his arms. Francesca had the sensation of time frozen in place as the two dazzling blond creatures pressed their heads together, beautiful American thoroughbreds in home-grown denim and worn cowboy boots, superhumans who suddenly made her feel incredibly small and ordinary. The woman wore a Stetson pushed back on a cloud of blond hair that fell in sexy disarray to her shoulders, and she'd left three buttons on her plaid shirt unfastened to reveal more than a little of the impressive swell of her breasts. A wide leather belt encircled her small waist, and tight jeans fit her hips so closely they made a V at her crotch before clinging in a smooth line down a nearly endless expanse of long, trim leg.

The woman looked into Dallie's eyes and said something so quietly only Francesca overheard. "You didn't think I'd leave you alone for Halloween, did you, baby?" she whispered.

The fear that had seemed like a cold fist clutching Francesca's heart abruptly eased as she realized how much alike they looked. Of course . . . she shouldn't have been so startled. Of course they looked alike. This woman could only be Dallie's sister, the elusive Holly Grace.

A moment later, he confirmed her identity. Releasing the tall blond goddess, he turned to Francesca. "Holly Grace, this is Francesca Day. Francie, I'd like you to meet Holly Grace Beaudine."

"How do you do?" Francesca extended her hand and smiled warmly. "I would have recognized you as Dallie's sister anywhere; you two look so much alike."

Holly Grace pulled the brim of the Stetson forward a bit on her head and studied Francesca with clear blue eyes. "Sorry to disappoint you, honey, but I'm not Dallie's sister."

Francesca regarded her quizzically.

"I'm Dallie's wife."

Chapter
15

Francesca heard Dallie call out her name. She began to move faster, her eyes nearly blinded with tears. The soles of her sandals slipped on the gravel as she ran through the parking lot toward the highway. But her short legs were no match for his long ones, and he caught up with her before she could reach the road.

"You mind telling me what's going on here?" he shouted, catching her shoulder and spinning her around. "Why'd you run out, cussing at me like that and embarrassing yourself in front of all those people who were starting to think you were a real human being?"

He was yelling at her as if she were the one at fault, as if she were the liar, the deceiver, the treacherous snake who'd turned love into betrayal. She drew back her arm and slapped his face as hard as she could.

He slapped her back.

Although he was mad enough to hit her, he wasn't mad enough to hurt her, so he struck her with only a small portion of his strength. Still, she was so small that she lost her balance and bumped into the side of a car. She grabbed the sideview mirror with one hand and pressed the other to her cheek.

"Jesus, Francie, I hardly touched you." He rushed over and reached out for her arm.

"You bastard!" She spun on him and slapped him again, this time catching him on the jaw.

He grabbed both of her arms and shook her. "You settle down now, do you hear me? You settle down before you get hurt."

She kicked him hard in the shin, and the leather of his oldest pair of cowboy boots didn't protect him from the sharp edge of her sandal. "Goddammit!" he yelped.

She drew back her foot to kick him again. He thrust out his uninjured leg and tripped her with it, sending her down into the gravel.

"Bloody bastard!" she screamed, tears and dirt mingling on her cheeks. "Bloody, wife-cheating bastard! You'll pay for this!" Ignoring the stinging in the heels of her hands and the dirty scratches on her arms, she began to push herself back up to go after him again. She didn't care if he hurt her, if he killed her. She hoped he would. She wanted him to kill her. She was going to die anyway from the horrible pain spreading inside her like a deadly poison. If he killed her, at least the pain would be over quickly.

"Stop it, Francie," he yelled, as she staggered to her feet. "Don't come any closer or you'll really get hurt."

"You bloody bastard," she sobbed, wiping her nose on her wrist. "You bloody *married* bastard! I'm going to make you pay!" Then she went after him again—a pampered little British house cat charging a full-grown, free-roaming all-American mountain lion.

Holly Grace stood in the middle of the crowd that had gathered outside the front door of the Roustabout to watch. "I can't believe Dallie didn't tell her about me," she said to Skeet. "It doesn't usually take him more than thirty seconds to work my existence into any conversation he has with a woman he's attracted to."

"Don't be ridiculous," Skeet growled. "She knew about you. We talked about you in front of her a hundred times—that's what's making him so mad. Everybody in the world knows the two of you've been married since you was teenagers. This is just one more example of what a fool that woman is." Worry etched a frown between his shaggy eyebrows as Francesca landed another blow. "I know he's trying to hold her off without hurtin' her too much, but if one of those kicks lands too close to his danger zone, she's gonna find herself in a hospital bed and he's gonna end up in jail for assault and battery. See what I told you about her, Holly Grace? I never knew a woman as much trouble as that one."

Holly Grace took a swig from Dallie's bottle of Pearl, which she'd picked up off the table, then remarked to Skeet, "If word of this little altercation makes its way to Mr. Deane Beman, Dallie's gonna get his ass kicked right off the pro tour. The public doesn't much like football players beating up women, let alone golfers."

Holly Grace watched as the floodlights caught the sheen of tears on Francesca's cheeks. Despite Dallie's determination to hold that little girl off, she kept going right back after him. It occurred to Holly Grace that there might be more to Miss Fancy Pants than what Skeet had told her on the telephone. Still, the woman couldn't have much sense. Only a fool would go after Dallas Beaudine without holding a loaded gun in one hand and a blacksnake whip in the other. She winced as one of Francesca's kicks managed to catch him behind the knee. He quickly retaliated and then managed to immobilize her partially by pinioning both her elbows behind her back and clamping her to his chest.

Holly Grace spoke quietly to Skeet. "She's getting ready to kick him again. We'd better step in before this goes any further." She handed off her beer bottle to the man standing next to her. "You take her, Skeet. I'll handle Dallie."

Skeet didn't argue about the distribution of duties. Although he didn't relish the idea of trying to calm down Miss Fran-chess-ka, he knew Holly Grace was the only person with half a shot at handling Dallie when he really kicked up. They quickly crossed the parking lot, and when they reached the struggling pair, Skeet said, "Give her to me, Dallie."

Francesca let out a strangled sob of pain. Her face was pressed against Dallie's T-shirt. Her arms, twisted behind her back, felt as if they were ready to pop from their sockets. He hadn't killed her. Despite the pain, he hadn't killed her after all. "Leave me alone!" she screamed into Dallie's chest. No one suspected she was screaming at Skeet.

Dallie didn't move. He gave Skeet a frozen stare over the

top of Francesca's head. "Mind your own goddamn business."

Holly Grace stepped forward. "Come on, baby," she said lightly. "I got about a thousand things I've been saving up to tell you." She began stroking Dallie's arm in the easy, proprietary manner of a woman who knows she has the right to touch a particular man in any way she wants. "I saw you on television at the Kaiser. Your long irons were looking real good for a change. If you ever learn how to putt, you might even be able to play half-decent golf someday."

Gradually, Dallie's grip on Francesca eased, and Skeet cautiously reached out to draw her away. But at the instant Skeet touched her, Francesca sank her teeth into the hard flesh of Dallie's chest, clamping down on his pectoral muscle.

Dallie yelled just long enough for Skeet to whip Francesca into his own arms.

"Crazy bitch!" Dallie shouted, drawing back his arm and taking a lunge toward her. Holly Grace jumped in front of him, using her own body as a shield, because she couldn't stand the thought of Dallie getting kicked off the tour. He stopped, put a hand on her shoulder, and rubbed his chest with a knotted fist. A vein throbbed in his temple. "Get her out of my sight! I mean it, Skeet! Buy her a plane ticket home, and don't you ever let me see her again!"

Just before Skeet dragged her away, Francesca heard the echo of Dallie's voice coming from behind her, much softer now, and gentler. "I'm sorry," he said.

Sorry . . . The word was repeated in her head like a bitter refrain. Only those two small words of apology for destroying what was left of her life. And then she heard the rest of what he was saying.

"I'm sorry, Holly Grace."

Francesca let Skeet put her into the front seat of his Ford and sat without moving as he turned out onto the highway.

They drove in silence for several minutes before he finally said, "Look, Francie, I'm gonna pull into the gas station down the road and call one of my friends who works over at the county clerk's office to see if she'll put you up for the night. She's a real nice lady. Tomorrow morning I'll come on over with your things and take you to the airport in San Antonio. You'll be back in London before you know it."

She made no response and he looked over at her uneasily. For the first time since he'd met her, he felt sorry for her. She was a pretty little thing when she wasn't talking, and he could see that she was hurt real bad. "Listen, Francie, there wasn't any reason for you to get so riled up about Holly Grace. Dallie and Holly Grace are just one of those facts of life, like beer and football. But they stopped making judgments about each other's bedroom lives a long time ago, and if you hadn't gotten Dallie so mad with all that carrying on, he probably would have kept you around a while longer."

Francesca winced. Dallie would have kept her around—like one of his mongrel dogs. She swallowed tears and bile as she thought how much she had shamed herself.

Skeet stepped down harder on the accelerator, and a few minutes later they pulled into the gas station. "You just sit here and I'll be right back."

Francesca waited until Skeet had gone inside before she slipped from the car and began to run. She ran down the highway, dodging the headlights of the cars, running through the night as if she could run away from herself. A cramp in her side finally made her slow her pace, but she still didn't stop.

She wandered for hours through the deserted streets of Wynette, not seeing where she was going, not caring. As she walked past vacant stores and night-quiet homes, she felt as if the last part of her old self had died . . . the best part, the eternal light of her own optimism. No matter how bleak things had been since Chloe's death, she had always felt her difficulties were only temporary. Now she finally understood they weren't temporary at all.

Her sandal slipped in the dirty orange pulp of a jack-o'-lantern that had been smashed on the street, and she fell, bruising her hip on the pavement. She lay there for a moment, her leg twisted awkwardly beneath her, pumpkin ooze mixing with the dried blood from the scratches on her forearm. She wasn't the kind of woman men abandoned—she was the one who did the abandoning. Fresh tears began to fall. What had she done to deserve this? Was she so terrible? Had she hurt people so badly that this was to be her punishment? A dog barked in the distance, and far down the street an upstairs light flicked on in a bathroom window.

She couldn't think what to do, so she lay in the dirt and the pumpkin pulp and cried. All her dreams, all her plans, everything . . . gone. Dallie didn't love her. He wasn't going to marry her. They weren't going to live together happily ever after forever and ever.

She didn't remember making the decision to start walking again, but after a while she realized her feet were moving and she was heading down a new street. And then in the darkness she stumbled over the curb and looked up to see that she was standing in front of Dallie's Easter egg house.

Holly Grace pulled the Riviera into the driveway and shut off the ignition. It was nearly three in the morning. Dallie was slumped down in the passenger seat, but although his eyes were closed, she didn't think he was asleep. She got out of the car and walked around to the passenger door. Half afraid he would slump out onto the ground, she braced the door with her hip as she pulled it slowly open. He didn't move.

"Come on, baby," she said, reaching down and tugging on his arm. "Let's get you tucked in."

Dallie muttered something indecipherable and let one leg slide to the ground.

"That's right," she encouraged him. "Come on, now."

He stood and draped his arm around her shoulders as he'd done so many times before. Part of Holly Grace wanted to pull away and hope that he would fold up on the ground like an old accordion, but the other part of her wouldn't let him go for anything in the world—not a shot at being southwestern regional sales manager, not a chance to replace her Firebird with a Porsche, not even a bedroom encounter with all four of the Statler Brothers at the same time—because Dallie Beaudine was the person she almost loved best of anybody in the world. Almost, but not quite, since the person she'd learned to love best was herself. Dallie had taught her that a long time ago. Dallie had taught her a lot of good lessons he'd never been able to learn himself.

He suddenly pulled away from her and began walking around the side of the house toward the front. His steps were slightly unsteady, but considering how much he'd had to drink, he was doing pretty well. Holly Grace watched him for a moment. Six years had passed, but he still wouldn't let Danny go.

She rounded the front of the house in time to see him slump down on the top porch step. "You go on to your mama's now," he said quietly.

"I'm staying, Dallie." She climbed the steps, then pulled off her hat and tossed it over onto the porch swing.

"Go on, now. I'll come over and see you tomorrow."

He was speaking more distinctly than he usually did, a sure indication of just how drunk he really was. She sat down next to him and gazed out into the darkness, deciding to force the issue. "You know what I was thinkin' about today?" she asked. "I was thinkin' about how you used to walk around with Danny up on your shoulders, and he'd hold on to your hair and squeal. And every once in a while, his diaper'd leak so that when you put him down you'd have a wet spot on the back of your shirt. I used to think that was so funny—my pretty-boy husband goin' around with baby pee on the back of his T-shirt." Dallie didn't respond. She waited a moment and then tried again. "Remember that awful fight we had when you took him to the barbershop and got all his baby curls cut off? I threw your Western Civ book at you, and we made love on the kitchen floor . . . only neither of us had swept it in a week and all Danny's Cheerio rejects got ground into my back, not to mention a few other places."

He spread his legs and put his elbows on his knees, bending his head. She touched his arm, her voice soft. "Think about the good times, Dallie. It's been six years. You got to let go of the bad and think about the good."

"We were crummy parents, Holly Grace."

She tightened her grip on his arm. "No, we weren't. We loved Danny. There's never been a little boy who was loved as much as he was. Remember how we used to tuck him in bed with us at night, even though everybody said he'd grow up queer?"

Dallie lifted his head and his voice was bitter. "What I

remember is how we'd go out at night and leave him alone with all those twelve-year-old baby-sitters. Or drag him along when we couldn't find anybody to stay with him—prop that little plastic seat of his up in the corner of some booth in a bar and feed him potato chips, or put Seven-Up in his bottle if he started to cry. Christ . . ."

Holly Grace shrugged and let go of his arm. "We weren't even nineteen when Danny was born. Not much more than kids ourselves. We did the best we knew how."

"Yeah? Well, it wasn't fucking good enough!"

She ignored his outburst. She had done a better job of coming to terms with Danny's death than Dallie had, although she still had to look away when she caught a glimpse of a mother picking up a little towheaded boy. Halloween was the hardest for Dallie because that was the day Danny had died, but Danny's birthday was hardest for her. She gazed at the dark, leafy shapes of the pecan trees and remembered how it had been that day.

Although it had been exam week at A&M and Dallie had a paper to write, he was out hustling some cotton farmers on the golf course so they could buy a crib. When her water had broken, she had been afraid to go to the hospital by herself so she'd driven to the course in an old Ford Fairlane she'd borrowed from the engineering student who lived next door to them. Although she had folded a bath towel to sit on, she'd still soaked through onto the seat.

The greenskeeper had gone after Dallie and returned with him in less than ten minutes. When Dallie had seen her leaning against the side of the Fairlane, wet patches staining her old denim jumper, he had vaulted out of the electric cart and run over to her. "Shoot, Holly Grace," he'd said, "I just drove the green on number eight—landed not three inches from the cup. Couldn't you have waited a while longer?" Then he'd laughed and picked her up, wet jumper and all, and held her against his chest until a contraction made her cry out.

Thinking about it now, she felt a lump growing in her throat. "Danny was such a beautiful baby," she whispered to Dallie. "Remember how scared we were when we brought him home from the hospital?"

His reply was low and tight. "People need a license to keep a dog, but they let you take a baby out of a hospital without asking a single question."

She jumped up from the step. "Dammit, Dallie! I want to *mourn* our baby boy. I want to *mourn* him with you tonight, not listen to you turn everything bitter."

He slumped forward for a moment, his head dropping. "You shouldn't have come. You know how I get this time of year."

She let the palm of her hand come to rest on the top of his head like a baptism. "Let Danny go this year."

"Could you let him go if you were the one who'd killed him?"

"I knew about the cistern cover, too."

"And you told me to fix it." He stood up slowly, wandering over to the porch railing. "You told me twice that the hinge was broken and that the neighborhood boys kept pulling it off so they could throw stones down inside. You weren't the one who stayed home with Danny that afternoon. You weren't the one who was supposed to be watching him."

"Dallie, you were studying. It's not like you were passed out drunk on the floor when he slipped outside."

She shut her eyes. She didn't want to think about this part—about her little two-year-old baby boy toddling across the yard to that cistern, looking down into it with his boundless curiosity. Losing his balance. Falling forward. She didn't want to imagine that little body struggling for life in that dank water, crying out. What had her baby thought about at the end, when all he could see was a circle of light far above him? Had he thought about her, his mother, who wasn't there to pull him safely into her arms, or had he thought about his daddy, who kissed him and roughhoused with him and held him so tight that he would squeal? What had he thought about at that last moment when his small lungs had filled with water?

Blinking against the sting of tears, she went over to Dallie and circled his waist from behind. Then she rested her forehead against the back of his shoulder. "God gives us life as a gift," she said. "We don't have any right to add our own conditions."

He began to shudder, and she held on to him as best she could.

Francesca watched them from the darkness beneath the pecan tree that stood next to the porch. The night was quiet, and she had heard every word. She felt sick . . . even worse than when she'd run from the Roustabout. Her own pain now seemed frivolous compared to theirs. She hadn't known Dallie at all. She had never seen anything more than the laughing, wisecracking Texan who refused to take life seriously. He'd hidden a wife from her . . . the death of his son. As she looked at the two grief-stricken figures standing on the porch, the intimacy between them seemed as solid as the old house itself—an intimacy brought about by living together, by sharing happiness and tragedy. She realized then that she and Dallie had shared nothing except their bodies, and that love had depths to it she hadn't even imagined.

Francesca watched as Dallie and Holly Grace disappeared into the house. For a fraction of a moment, the very best part of her hoped they would find some comfort with each other.

Naomi had never been to Texas before, and if she had anything to say about the matter, she would never come here again. As a pickup truck sped past her in the right lane going at least eighty, she decided that some people were not meant to venture beyond predictable city traffic jams and the comforting scent of exhaust being belched out by crawling yellow cabs. She was a city girl; the open road made her nervous. Or maybe it wasn't the highway at all. Maybe it was Gerry huddled next to her in the passenger seat of her rental Cadillac, scowling through the windshield like an ill-tempered toddler.

When she had returned to her apartment the night before to pack a suitcase, Gerry had announced that he was going to Texas with her. "I've got to get out of this place before I go crazy," he had exclaimed, thrusting one hand through his hair. "I'm going to Mexico for a while—live underground. I'll fly to Texas with you tonight—the cops at the airport won't be looking for a couple traveling together—and then I'll make arrangements to cross the border. I've got some friends in Del Rio. They'll help me. It'll be good in Mexico. We'll get our movement reorganized."

She had told him he couldn't go with her, but he refused to listen. Since she couldn't physically restrain him, she had found herself boarding the Delta flight to San Antonio with Gerry at her side, holding her arm.

She stretched in the driver's seat, inadvertently pressing down on the gas pedal so that the car accelerated slightly. Next to her, Gerry plunged his hands deep into the pockets of a pair of gray flannel slacks he'd procured from somewhere. The outfit was supposed to make him look like a respectable businessman but fell somewhat short of the mark since he had refused to cut his hair. "Relax," she said. "Nobody's paid any attention to you since we got here."

"The cops'll never let me get away this easy," he said, glancing nervously over his shoulder for the hundredth time since they had pulled out of the hotel garage in San Antonio. "They're playing with me. They'll let me get so close to the Mexican border that I can smell it, and then they'll close in on me. Frigging pigs."

The sixties paranoia. She'd almost forgotten about it. When Gerry had learned about the FBI wiretaps, he'd believed that every shadow hid a cop, that every new recruit was an informer, that the mighty J. Edgar Hoover himself was personally searching for evidence of subversive activity in the Kotex the women in the anti-war movement tossed into the garbage. Although at the time there had been reason for caution, in the end the fear had been more exhausting than the reality. "Are you sure the police even care?" Naomi said. "Nobody looked at you twice when you got on the plane."

He glared at her and she knew that she had insulted him by belittling his importance as a fugitive—Macho Gerry, the John Wayne of the radicals. "If I'd been by myself," he said, "they'd have noticed fast enough."

Naomi wondered. For all Gerry's insistence that the police were out to get him, they certainly didn't seem to be looking very hard. It made her feel strangely sad. She remembered the days when the police had cared a great deal about the activities of her brother.

The Cadillac topped a grade, and she saw a sign announcing the city limits of Wynette. A spurt of excitement went through her. After all this time, she would finally see her Sassy Girl. She hoped she hadn't made a mistake by not calling ahead, but she felt instinctively that this first connection needed to be made in person. Besides, photographs sometimes lied. She had to see this girl face to face.

Gerry looked at the digital clock on the dashboard. "It's not even nine o'clock yet. She's probably still in bed. I don't see why we had to leave so early."

She didn't bother answering. Nothing ever had any importance to Gerry except his own mission to save the world single-handedly. She pulled into a service station and asked for directions. Gerry hunched down in the seat, hiding himself behind an open road map in case the pimply-faced kid standing by the gas pumps was really a crack government agent out to catch Public Enemy Number One.

As she pulled the car back out onto the street, she said, "Gerry, you're thirty-two years old. Aren't you getting tired of living like this?"

"I'm not going to sell out, Naomi."

"If you ask me, running off to Mexico comes closer to selling out than staying around and trying to work inside the system."

"Just shut up about it, will you?"

Was it only her imagination or did Gerry sound less sure of himself? "You'd be a wonderful lawyer," she pressed on. "Courageous and incorruptible. Like a medieval knight fighting for justice."

"I'll think about it, okay?" he snapped. "I'll think about it after I get to Mexico. Remember that you promised to get me over closer to Del Rio before nightfall."

"God, Gerry, can't you think about anything but yourself?"

He looked at her with disgust. "The world's getting ready to blow itself up, and all you care about is selling perfume."

She refused to get into another shouting match with him,

and they rode in silence the rest of the way to the house. As Naomi pulled up in the Cadillac, Gerry glanced nervously over his shoulder toward the street. When he saw nothing suspicious, he relaxed enough to lean forward and study the house. "Hey, I like this place." He gestured toward the painted jackrabbits. "It gives out great vibes."

Naomi gathered up her purse and briefcase. Just as she was getting ready to open the car door, Gerry caught her arm. "This is important to you, isn't it, sis?"

"I know you don't understand, Gerry, but I love what I do."

He nodded slowly and then smiled at her. "Good luck, kid."

The sound of a car door slamming woke Francesca. At first she couldn't think where she was, and then she realized that—like an animal going into a cave to die alone—she had crawled into the back seat of the Riviera and fallen asleep. Memories of the night before washed over her, bringing a fresh wave of pain. She straightened and moaned softly as the muscles in various parts of her body protested her change in position. The cat, who was curled up on the floor beneath her, lifted his misshapen head and meowed.

Then she saw the Cadillac.

She caught her breath. For as long as she could remember, big, expensive cars had always brought wonderful things into her life—expensive men, fashionable places, glittering parties. An illogical surge of hope swept through her. Maybe one of her friends had tracked her down and come to take her back to her old life. She brushed her hair from her face with a dirty, shaking hand, let herself out of the car, and walked cautiously around to the front of the house. She couldn't face Dallie this morning, and she especially couldn't face Holly Grace. As she crept up the front steps, she told herself not to get her hopes up, that the car might have brought a magazine writer to interview Dallie, or even an insurance salesman—but every muscle in her body felt tense with expectation. She heard an unfamiliar woman's voice through the open door and stepped to one side so she could listen unobserved.

". . . have been looking everywhere for her," the woman was saying. "I was finally able to track her down through inquiries about Mr. Beaudine."

"Imagine going to all that trouble just for a magazine advertisement," Miss Sybil replied.

"Oh, no," the woman's voice protested. "This is much more important. Blakemore, Stern, and Rodenbaugh is one of the most important advertising agencies in Manhattan. We're planning a major campaign to launch a new perfume, and we need an extraordinarily beautiful woman as our Sassy Girl. She'll be on television, billboards. She'll make public appearances all over the country. We plan to make her one of the most familiar faces in America. Everyone will know about the Sassy Girl."

Francesca felt as if she had just been given back her life. The Sassy Girl! They were looking for her! A surge of joy pulsed through her veins like adrenaline as she absorbed the astonishing realization that she would now be able to walk away from Dallie with her head held high. This fairy godmother from Manhattan was about to give her back her self-respect.

"But I'm afraid I don't have any idea where she is," Miss Sybil said. "I'm sorry to have to disappoint you after you've driven so far, but if you'll give me your business card, I'll pass it on to Dallas. He'll see that she gets it."

"No!" Francesca grabbed the screen door handle and pulled it open, illogically afraid the woman would vanish before she could get to her. As she rushed inside, she saw a thin, dark-haired woman in a navy business suit standing next to Miss Sybil. "No!" Francesca exclaimed. "I'm here! I'm right—"

"What's going on?" a throaty voice drawled. "Hey, how ya doin', Miss Sybil? I didn't get a chance to say hi last night. You got any coffee made?"

Francesca froze in the doorway as Holly Grace Beaudine came down the stairs, long bare legs stretching out from beneath one of Dallie's pale blue dress shirts. She yawned, and Francesca's altruistic feelings toward her from the night before vanished. Even bare of makeup and with sleep-tousled hair, she looked extraordinary.

Francesca cleared her throat and stepped into the living room, making everyone aware of her presence.

The woman in the gray suit audibly gasped. "My God! Those photographs didn't do you justice." She walked forward, smiling broadly. "Let me be the first to offer my congratulations to our beautiful new Sassy Girl."

And then she held out her hand to Holly Grace Beaudine.

Chapter
16

Francesca might have been invisible for all the attention anyone paid her. She stood numbly just inside the doorway while the woman from Manhattan clucked over Holly Grace, talking about exclusive contracts and time schedules and a series of photographs that had been taken of her when she appeared at a charity benefit in Los Angeles as the date of a famous football player.

"But I sell sporting goods," Holly Grace exclaimed at one point. "At least I did until I got involved in a small labor dispute a few weeks back and staged an unofficial walkout. You don't seem to realize that I'm not a model."

"You will be when I've finished with you," the woman insisted. "Just promise me you won't disappear again without leaving a phone number. From now on, always let your agent know where you are."

"I don't have an agent."

"I'll fix that, too."

There would be no fairy godmother for her, Francesca realized. No one to take care of her. No magical modeling contracts appearing at the last moment to save her. She caught sight of her reflection in a mirror Miss Sybil had framed with seashells. Her hair was wild, her face scraped and bruised. She looked down and saw the dirt and dried blood streaking her arms. How had she ever thought she could get through life on the strength of her beauty alone? Compared to Holly Grace and Dallie, she was second rate. Chloe had been wrong. Looking pretty wasn't enough—there was always someone prettier.

Turning away, she let herself silently out the door.

Nearly an hour passed before Naomi Tanaka left and Holly Grace went into Dallie's bedroom. There had been some confusion over Naomi's rental car, which seemed to have disappeared while Naomi was inside the house, and Miss Sybil had ended up driving her to Wynette's only hotel. Naomi had promised to give Holly Grace until the next day to look over the contract and consult her lawyer. Not that there was any doubt in Holly Grace's mind about signing. The amount of money they were offering her was staggering—a hundred thousand dollars for doing nothing more than wiggling around in front of a camera and shaking hands at department-store perfume counters. She remembered her days in Bryan, Texas, living with Dallie in student housing and trying to scratch together enough money to pay for groceries.

Still dressed in Dallie's blue shirt and holding a coffee mug in each hand, she closed the door to his bedroom with her hip. The bed looked like a war zone, with all the covers pulled out from the bottom and tangled around his hips. Even asleep, Dallie couldn't seem to find any peace. She set his coffee mug down on the nightstand and then took a sip from her own.

The Sassy Girl. It sounded just right to her. Even the timing was right. She was tired of battling the good ol' boys at SEI, tired of having to work twice as hard as everyone else to go the same distance. She was ready for a fresh start in her life, a chance to make big money. Long ago she had decided that when opportunity knocked on her door, she would be standing right there to answer it.

Taking her coffee over to the old armchair, she sat down and crossed her foot over her bare knee. Her thin gold ankle bracelet caught the sunlight, sending an ambulating serpentine reflection onto the ceiling above her head. Glittering images flashed in her mind—designer clothes, fur coats, famous New York restaurants. After all her work, all these years of butting her head against stone walls, the chance of a lifetime had finally dropped right in her lap.

Cuddling the warm mug in her hand, she looked over at Dallie. People who knew about their separate lives and separate home addresses always asked why they hadn't gotten divorced. They couldn't understand that Holly Grace and Dallie still liked being married to each other. They were family.

Her gaze traveled down along the hard curve of his calf, the sight of which had once produced so many stirrings of lust inside her. When had they last made love? She couldn't remember. All she knew was that the minute she and Dallie climbed into bed together, all their old troubles came back to haunt them. Holly Grace was once again a helpless young girl in need of protection, and Dallie was a teenage husband trying desperately to support a family while failure hung over him like a dark cloud. Now that they'd begun to make it a practice to stay out of each other's beds, they'd discovered the relief of letting go of those old parts of themselves. Lovers were a dime a dozen, they had finally decided, but best friends were hard to find.

Dallie moaned and turned over onto his stomach. She left him alone for a few more minutes while he pushed his face into the pillows and stretched out his legs. Finally, she got up and walked over to sit on the edge of the bed. Putting down her own mug, she picked up his. "I brought you some coffee. Drink this down and I guarantee you'll feel almost like a human being by the time next week rolls around."

He eased himself into the pillows wedged up against the headboard and, with his eyes still half closed, held out his hand. She gave him the mug and then pushed back a rumpled thatch of blond hair that had fallen over his forehead. Even with messy hair and stubble on his chin, he managed to look gorgeous. His morning appearance used to aggravate her when they first got married. She would wake up looking like the wrath of God, and he would look like a movie star. He always told her she looked her prettiest in the morning, but she never believed him. Dallie wasn't objective where she was concerned. He thought she was the most beautiful woman in the world, no matter how bad she looked.

"Have you seen Francie this morning?" he muttered.

"I saw her for about three seconds in the living room a little bit ago, and then she ran away. Dallie, I don't mean to criticize your taste in women, but she seems flighty to me." Holly Grace leaned back into the pillows and pulled up her knees, chuckling at the memory of the scene in the Roustabout parking lot. "She really did go after you last night, didn't she? I've got to give her credit for that. The only other woman I know who could go one on one with you like that is me."

He turned his head and glared at her. "Yeah? Well, that's not all the two of you have in common. You both talk too damn much in the morning."

Holly Grace ignored his bad temper. Dallie was always grouchy when he woke up, but she liked to talk in the morning. Sometimes she could pry interesting tidbits out of him if she kept at him before he was fully conscious. "I have to tell you that I think she's the most interesting stray you've picked up in a long time—almost better than that midget clown who used to travel with the rodeo. Skeet told me how she trashed your motel room in New Orleans. I sure wish I'd seen that." She propped her elbow up on the pillow next to his head and tucked her foot up beneath her hip. "Just out of curiosity, why didn't you tell her about me?"

He stared at her for a moment over the top of his mug and then pulled it away from his mouth without sipping. "Don't be ridiculous. She knew about you. I talked about you in front of her all the time."

"That's what Skeet said, but I'm wondering whether in any of those conversations you happened to use the exact word 'wife'?"

"Of course I did. Or Skeet did." He shoved his fingers through his hair. "I don't know . . . somebody did. Maybe Miss Sybil."

"Sorry, baby, but it looked to me like she was hearing the bad news for the very first time."

He impatiently set his mug down. "Hell, what's the difference? Francie's too much in love with herself to care about anybody else. She's past history as far as I'm concerned."

Holly Grace wasn't surprised. The fight in the parking lot

the night before had looked just about as final as a parting could be . . . unless the two fighters loved each other to the point of desperation, the way she and Dallie used to.

He abruptly shoved back the covers and got out of bed wearing nothing more than his white cotton briefs. She let herself enjoy the sight of those tight muscles rippling across his shoulders and the strength in the backs of his thighs. She wondered what man had first come up with the notion that women didn't enjoy looking at men's bodies. Probably some egghead Ph.D. with four chins and a potbelly.

Dallie turned and caught her studying him. He scowled, even though she knew he probably enjoyed it. "I've got to locate Skeet and make sure he gave her money for a plane ticket home. If she roams around by herself for too long, she's bound to get into more trouble than she can handle."

Holly Grace looked at him more closely, and an unaccustomed pang of jealousy hit her. It had been a long time since she'd minded Dallie having other women, especially since she collected more than her fair share of good-looking men. But she didn't like the idea of having him care too much about any woman who didn't meet with her approval, which showed exactly what kind of narrow-minded Christian she was. "You really liked her, didn't you?"

"She was all right," he replied noncommittally.

Holly Grace wanted to know more, like how good Miss Fancy Pants could really be in bed after Dallie had already had the best. But she knew that he would call her a hypocrite, so she set aside her curiosity for the moment. Besides, now that he was finally awake, she could tell him her really important news. Moving to a cross-legged position in the middle of the bed, she filled him in on her morning.

He reacted just about the way she had expected he would. She told him he could go straight to hell.

He said he was glad about the job, but her *attitude* bothered him.

"My *attitude* is my own damn business," she retorted.

"One of these days you're going to learn that happiness isn't wrapped up in a dollar bill, Holly Grace. There's more involved than that."

"Since when did you get to be such an expert on happiness? It should be pretty much apparent to anyone who isn't half brain-dead that rich is better than poor and that just because you intend to be a failure all your life doesn't mean I'm going to be one, too."

They kept on hurting each other like that for a while, then they spent a few minutes stomping around the bedroom without talking. Dallie made a phone call to Skeet; Holly Grace went into the bathroom and got dressed. In the old days they would have broken their stony silence with angry lovemaking, trying unsuccessfully to use their bodies to solve all the problems that their minds couldn't handle. But now they didn't touch each other, and gradually their anger ran out of steam. Finally, they went downstairs together and shared the rest of Miss Sybil's coffee.

The man behind the wheel of the Cadillac frightened Francesca, although he was handsome in a scary sort of way. He had curly black hair, a compact body, and dark, angry eyes, which kept darting nervously toward the rearview mirror. She had an uncomfortable feeling that she'd seen that face someplace before, but she couldn't remember where. Why hadn't she stopped to think more clearly when he'd offered her a ride instead of just jumping into the Cadillac? Like a fool, she had barely looked at him; she'd just climbed in. When she had asked him what he'd been doing in front of Dallie's house, he had said he was a chauffeur and that his passenger didn't need him any longer.

She tried to shift her feet out from under the cat, but he planted his weight more firmly across them and she gave up. The man looked over at her through a cloud of cigarette smoke and then glanced again into the rearview mirror. His nervousness bothered her. He was acting like some sort of fugitive. She shivered. Maybe he wasn't really a chauffeur. Maybe this was a stolen car. If only she'd let Skeet drive her to the airport in San Antonio this wouldn't have happened. Once again she'd made the wrong choice. Dallie had been right every one of the dozen times he'd told her she didn't have any common sense.

Dallie . . . She bit her lip and pulled her cosmetic case closer to her hip. While she had sat numbly in the kitchen, Miss Sybil had gone upstairs and gotten her things together for her. Then Miss Sybil had handed her an envelope containing enough money to buy an airplane ticket to London, along with a little extra to tide her over. Francesca had stared down at the envelope, knowing that she couldn't take it, not now that she had begun to think about things like pride and self-respect. If she took the envelope she would be nothing more than a whore being paid off for services rendered. If she didn't take it . . .

She had taken the envelope and felt as if something bright and innocent had died forever inside her. She couldn't meet Miss Sybil's eyes as she slipped the money inside her case. The lock clicked and her stomach rebelled. Dear God, what if she really was pregnant? Only by swallowing hard could she prevent herself from losing the slice of toast Miss Sybil had forced her to eat. The elderly woman's voice had been kinder than usual as she said that Skeet would drive her to the airport.

Francesca had shaken her head and announced in her haughtiest voice that she had already made plans. Then, before she could further humiliate herself by clinging to Miss Sybil's thin chest and begging her to tell her what to do, she had grabbed her case and run out the door.

The Cadillac hit a rut, jolting her to one side, and she realized that they had left the highway. She stared out at the rutted, unpaved road that lay like a dusty ribbon across the flat, bleak landscape. They had left the hill country behind some time before. Shouldn't they be close to San Antonio by now? The knot in her stomach twisted tighter. The Cadillac bounced again, and the cat shifted its weight on her feet and looked up at her with a baleful glare, as if she were personally responsible for the bumpy ride. After several more miles had slipped by, she said, "Are you certain this is right? This road doesn't look very well traveled."

The man lit a fresh cigarette from the butt of his old one, then snatched up the map that lay on the seat between them.

Francesca was wiser now than she had been a month before, and she studied the shadows thrown by a few scraggly mesquite. "West!" she exclaimed after a few moments. "We're going west. This isn't the way to San Antonio."

"It's a shortcut," he said, tossing down the map.

She felt as if her throat were closing up. Rape . . . murder . . . an escaped convict and a mutilated female body left at the side of the road. She couldn't take any more. She was heartsick and exhausted, and she had no resources left to deal with another catastrophe. She fruitlessly searched the flat horizon for the sight of another car. All she could see was the tiny skeletal finger of a radio antenna standing miles in the distance. "I want you to let me out," she said, trying to keep her tone normal, as if being murdered on a deserted road by a crazed fugitive were the furthest thing from her mind.

"I can't do that," he said. And then he looked over at her, his eyes hard black marbles. "Just stay with me till we get closer to the Mexican border, and then I'll let you go."

Dread coiled like a snake in the pit of her stomach.

He took a deep drag on the cigarette. "Look, I'm not going to hurt you, so you don't have to get nervous. I'm a completely nonviolent person. I just need to get to the border, and I want two people in the car instead of one. There was a woman with me earlier, but while I was waiting for her, this cop car turned onto the street. And then I saw you walking down the sidewalk with that suitcase in your hand. . . ."

If he had meant to reassure her with his explanation, it didn't work. She realized that he truly was a fugitive, just as she'd feared. She tried to suppress the hysteria creeping through her, but she couldn't control it. As he slowed the car for another rut, she grabbed for the door handle.

"Hey!" He hit the brake and caught her by the arm. The car skidded to a full stop. "Don't do that. I'm not going to hurt you."

She tried to twist away from him, but his fingers bit into her arm. She screamed. The cat jumped up from the floor, landing with its rump on her leg and its front paws on the seat. "Let me out!" she screeched.

He held her fast, talking with the cigarette clamped in his mouth. "Hey, it's okay. I just need to get nearer the border before—"

To her, his eyes looked dark and menacing. "No!" she shrieked. "I want out!" Her fingers had turned clumsy with fear, and the door handle refused to give. She pushed harder, trying to throw the force of her body against it. The cat, disturbed by all the activity, arched his back and spat, then sank his front claws into the man's thigh.

The man gave a yelp of pain and pushed at the animal. The cat yeowed and sank his claws deeper.

"Leave him alone," Francesca shouted, turning her attention from the door to the assault on her cat. She slapped at the man's arm while the cat maintained its bloody grip on his leg, hissing and spitting all the time.

"Get him off me!" the man yelled. He threw up his elbow to defend himself and accidentally knocked the cigarette out of his mouth. Before he could catch it, the cigarette wedged itself inside the open collar of his shirt. He swatted at it with his hand, yelling again as the burning tip began to sear his skin.

His elbow hit the horn.

Francesca pounded on his chest.

The cat began to climb his arm.

"Get out of here!" he screamed.

She grabbed for the door handle. This time it gave, and as it swung open, she vaulted out, the cat springing after her.

"You're crazy, you know that, lady!" the man screamed, yanking the cigarette from his shirt with one hand and rubbing at his leg with the other.

She spotted her case, abandoned on the seat, and raced forward with her arm extended to claim it. He saw what she was doing and immediately slid across the seat to pull the door shut before she could reach it.

"Give me my case," she yelled.

"Get it yourself!" He flipped her his middle finger, threw the car into gear, and hit the accelerator. The tires spun, spitting out a great cloud of dust that immediately engulfed her.

"My case!" she yelled as he peeled away. *"I need my case!"* She began running after the Cadillac, choking in the dust and calling out. She ran until the car had faded to a small dot on the horizon. Then she collapsed to her knees in the middle of the road.

Her heart was pumping like a piston in her chest. She caught her breath and laughed, a wild, broken sound that was barely human. Now she'd done it. Now she'd really done it. And this time there was no good-looking blond savior to come to her rescue. A deep-throated rasp sounded next to her. She was alone except for a walleyed cat.

She started to shake and crossed her arms over her chest as if she could hold herself together. The cat wandered off to the side of the road and began picking its way delicately through the brush. A jackrabbit darted out from a clump of dried grass. She felt as if chunks of her body were flying away into the hot, cloudless sky—pieces of her arms and legs, her hair, her face. . . . Since she had come to this country, she had lost everything. Everything she owned. Everything she was. She had lost it all, and now she had lost herself. . . .

Twisted verses from the Bible invaded her brain, verses half learned from long-forgotten nannies, something about Saul on the road to Damascus, struck down into the dirt, blinded and then reborn. At that moment Francesca wanted to be reborn. She felt the dirt beneath her hands and wanted a miracle that would make her new again, a miracle of biblical proportions . . . a divine voice calling down to her with a message. She waited, and she, who never thought to pray, began to pray. "Please, God . . . make a miracle for me. Please, God . . . send me a voice. Send me a messenger. . . ."

Her prayer was fierce and strong, her faith—the faith of despair—immediate and boundless. God would answer her. God must answer her. She waited for her messenger to appear in white robes with a seraphic voice to point out the path to a new life. "I've learned my lesson, God. Really I have. I'll never be spoiled and selfish again." She waited, eyes squeezed shut, tears making paths in the dust on her cheeks. She waited for the messenger to appear, and an image began to form in her mind, vague at first and then growing more solid. She strained to look into the dimmest corners of her consciousness, strained to peer at her messenger. She strained and saw . . .

Scarlett O'Hara.

She saw Scarlett lying in the dirt, silhouetted against a Technicolor hillside. Scarlett crying out, "As God is my witness, I'll never go hungry again."

Francesca choked on her tears and a hysterical bubble of laughter rose from her chest. She fell back onto her heels and slowly let the laughter consume her. How typical, she thought. And how appropriate. Other people prayed and got thunderbolts and angels. She got Scarlett O'Hara.

She stood up and started to walk, not knowing where she was going, just moving. The dust drifted like powder over her sandals and settled between her toes. She felt something in her back pocket and, reaching in to investigate, pulled out a quarter. She gazed down at the coin in her hand. Alone in a foreign country, homeless, possibly pregnant—mustn't forget *that* calamity waiting to happen—she stood in the middle of a Texas road with only the clothes on her back, twenty-five cents in her hand, and a vision of Scarlett O'Hara in her head.

A strange euphoria began to consume her—an audaciousness, a sense of limitless possibilities. This was America, land of opportunity. She was tired of herself, tired of what she had become, ready to begin anew. And in all the history of civilization, had anyone ever been given such an opportunity for a fresh start as she faced at this precise moment?

Black Jack's daughter looked down at the money in her hand, tested its weight for a moment, and considered her future. If this was to be a fresh start, she wouldn't carry any baggage from the past. Without giving herself a chance to reconsider, she drew back her arm and flung the quarter away.

The country was so vast, the sky so tall, that she couldn't even hear it land.

Chapter
17

Holly Grace sat on the green wooden bench at the driving range and watched Dallie hitting practice balls with his two-iron. It was his fourth basket of balls, and he was still slicing all his shots to the right—not a nice power fade but an ugly slice. Skeet was slouched down at the other end of the bench, his old Stetson pulled down over his eyes so he wouldn't have to watch.

"What's wrong with him?" Holly Grace asked, pushing her sunglasses up on top of her head. "I've seen him play with a hangover lots of times, but not like this. He's not even trying to correct himself; he's just hitting the same shot over and over."

"You're the one who can read his mind," Skeet grunted. "You tell me."

"Hey, Dallie," Holly Grace called out, "those are about the worst two-iron shots in the entire history of golf. Why don't you forget about that little British girl and concentrate on earning yourself a living?"

Dallie teed up another ball with the head of his iron. "How 'bout you just mind your own business?"

She stood and tucked the back of her white cotton camisole into the waistband of her jeans before she wandered over to him. The pink ribbon threaded through the lacy border of the camisole turned up in the breeze and nestled into the hollow between her breasts. As she passed the end tee, a man practicing his drives got caught up in his backswing and completely missed the ball. She gave him a sassy smile and told him he'd do lots better if he kept his head down.

Dallie stood in the early afternoon sunshine, his hair golden in the light. She squinted at him. "Those cotton farmers up in Dallas are gonna take you to the cleaner's this weekend, baby. I'm giving Skeet a brand-new fifty-dollar bill and telling him to bet it all against you."

Dallie leaned over and picked up the beer bottle sitting in the center of a pile of balls. "What I really love about you, Holly Grace, is the way you always cheer me on."

She stepped into his arms and gave him a friendly hug, enjoying his particular male smell, a combination of sweaty golf shirt and the damp, leathery scent of warm club grips. "I call 'em like I see 'em, baby, and right now you're just short of terrible." She stepped away and looked straight into his eyes. "You're worried about her, aren't you?"

Dallie gazed out at the 250-yard sign and then back at Holly Grace. "I feel responsible for her; I can't help it. Skeet shouldn't have let her get away like that. He knows how she is. She lets herself get tangled up in vampire movies, she fights in bars, sells her clothes to loan sharks. Christ, she took me on in the parking lot last night, didn't she?"

Holly Grace studied the thin white leather straps criss-crossing the toes of her sandals and then looked at him thoughtfully. "One of these days, we've got to get ourselves a divorce."

"I don't see why. You're not planning on getting married again, are you?"

"Of course not. It's just—maybe it's not good for either one of us, going on like this, using our marriage to keep us out of any other emotional involvements."

He regarded her suspiciously. "Have you been reading *Cosmo* again?"

"That does it!" Slamming her sunglasses down over her eyes, she stomped over to the bench and grabbed her purse. "There's no talking to you. You are so narrow-minded."

"I'll pick you up at your mama's at six," Dallie called after her as she headed toward the parking lot. "You can take me out for barbecue."

As Holly Grace's Firebird pulled out of the parking lot, Dallie handed Skeet his two-iron. "Let's go on over to the course and play a few holes. And if I even look like I'm thinking about using that club, you just take out a gun and shoot me."

But even without his two-iron, Dallie played poorly. He knew what the problem was, and it didn't have anything to do with his backswing or his follow-through. He had too many women on his mind, was what it was. He felt bad about Francie. Try as he might, he couldn't actually remember having told her he was married. Still, that wasn't any excuse for the way she'd carried on the night before in the parking lot, acting as if they'd already taken a blood test and made a down payment on a wedding ring. Dammit, he'd told her he wouldn't get serious. What was wrong with women that you could tell them straight to their faces that you would never marry them, and they'd nod just as sweet as pie and say they understood what you were saying and that they felt exactly the same way, but all the time they were picking out china patterns in their heads? It was one of the reasons he didn't want to get a divorce. That and the fact that he and Holly Grace were family.

After two double bogeys in a row, Dallie called it quits for the day. He got rid of Skeet and then wandered around the course for a while, poking at the underbrush with an eight-iron and shagging lost balls just like he'd done when he was a kid. As he pulled a brand-new Top-Flite out from under some leaves, he realized it must be nearly six, and he still had to shower and change before he picked up Holly Grace. He'd be late, and she'd be mad. He'd been late so many times Holly Grace had finally given up fighting with him about it. Six years ago he'd been late. They were supposed to be at the funeral home at ten o'clock to pick out a toddler-size coffin, but he hadn't shown up until noon.

He blinked hard. Sometimes the pain still cut through him as sharp and swift as a brand-new knife. Sometimes his mind would play tricks on him and he would see Danny's

245

face as clearly as his own. And then he would see Holly Grace's mouth twist into a horrible grimace as he told her that her baby was dead, that he'd let their sweet little blond-haired baby boy die.

He drew back his arm and took a vicious slice at a clump of weeds with his eight-iron. He wouldn't think about Danny. He would think about Holly Grace instead. He would think about that long-ago autumn when they were both seventeen, the autumn they'd first set each other on fire. . . .

"Here she comes! Holy shit, Dallie, will you look at those tits!" Hank Simborski fell back against the brick wall out behind the metal shop where Wynette High's troublemakers gathered each day at lunchtime to smoke. Hank grabbed his chest and punched Ritchie Reilly with his elbow. "I'm dying, Lord! I'm dyin'! Just give me one squeeze on those tits so I can go a happy man!"

Dallie lit his second Marlboro from the butt of the first and looked through the smoke at Holly Grace Cohagan walking toward them with her nose stuck up in the air and her chemistry book clutched against her cheap cotton blouse. Her hair was pulled back from her face with a wide yellow headband. She wore a navy blue skirt and white diamond-patterned tights like the ones he'd seen stretched over a set of plastic legs in the window at Woolworth's. He didn't like Holly Grace Cohagan, even though she was the best-looking senior girl at Wynette High. She acted superior to the rest of the world, which made him laugh because everybody knew she and her mama lived off the charity of her uncle Billy T Denton, pharmacist at Purity Drugs. Dallie and Holly Grace were the only really dirt-poor kids in senior college prep, but she acted like she fit in with the others, while he hung out with guys like Hank Simborski and Ritchie Reilly so everybody knew he didn't give a damn.

Ritchie stepped away from the wall and moved forward to catch her attention, puffing up his chest to compensate for the fact that she stood a head taller than he did. "Hey, Holly Grace, want a cigarette?"

Hank sauntered forward, too, trying to look cool but not quite making it because his face had started to turn red. "Have one of mine," he offered, pulling out a pack of Winstons. Dallie watched Hank lean forward on the balls of his feet, trying to give himself another inch of height, which still wasn't enough to draw even with an Amazon like Holly Grace Cohagan.

She looked at both of them like they were piles of dog shit and began to sweep by. Her attitude pissed Dallie off. Just because Ritchie and Hank got into a little trouble now and then and weren't in college prep didn't mean she had to treat them like maggots or something, especially since she was wearing dime-store tights and a ratty old navy skirt he'd seen her wear a couple hundred times before. With the Marlboro dangling from the corner of his mouth, Dallie swaggered forward, shoulders hunched into the collar of his denim jacket, eyes squinted against the smoke, a mean, tough look on his face. Even without the two-inch heels on his scuffed cowboy boots, he was the one boy in the senior class tall enough to make Holly Grace Cohagan look up.

He stepped directly into her path and curled his top lip in a trace of a sneer so she'd know exactly what kind of bad-ass she was dealing with. "My buddies offered you a smoke," he said, real soft and low.

She curled her lip right back at him. "I turned them down."

He squinted a little more against the smoke and looked even meaner. It was about time she remembered that she was back behind the school with a real man, and that none of those squeaky-clean college-prep boys who were always drooling over her were around to come to her rescue. "I didn't hear you say 'no, thank you,'" he drawled.

She stuck up her chin and looked him straight in the eye. "I heard you're queer, Dallie. Is that true? Somebody said you're so pretty they're going to nominate you for home-coming queen."

Hank and Ritchie snickered. Neither of them had the nerve to tease Dallie about his looks since he'd beaten them up when they first tried it, but that didn't mean they couldn't enjoy watching someone else go after him. Dallie clenched his teeth. He hated his face, and he'd done his best to ruin it with a sullen expression. So far, only Miss Sybil Chandler had seen through him. He intended to keep it that way.

"You shouldn't listen to gossip," he sneered. "I know I didn't listen when I heard that you'd been putting out for every rich boy in the senior class." It was a lie. Part of Holly Grace's appeal lay in the fact that nobody had managed to get any further with her than a few incomplete gropes and some tongue-kissing.

Her knuckles gradually turned white as she clutched her chemistry book, but other than that she didn't betray a flicker of emotion at what he'd said. "Too bad you won't ever be one of them," she jeered.

Her attitude infuriated him. She made him feel small and unimportant, less than a man. No woman would have ever talked like that to his old man, Jaycee Beaudine, and no woman was going to talk like that to him. He moved his body closer so he could hover over her and she would feel the threat of six feet of solid male steel getting ready to run her down. She took a quick step to one side, but he was too fast. Pitching his cigarette down on the blacktop, he side-stepped with her and then moved closer, so that she either had to retreat or bump against him. Gradually, he backed her up against the brick wall.

Behind him, Hank and Ritchie made smacking noises with their mouths and let out catcalls, but Dallie didn't pay any attention. Holly Grace still held up her chemistry book gripped in her hands so that instead of feeling her breasts against his chest, he felt only the hard corners of the book and the contours of her knuckles. He braced his hands against the wall on either side of her head and leaned into her, pinning her hips to the wall with his own and trying not to pay any attention to the sweet scent of her long blond hair, which reminded him of flowers and fresh spring air. "You wouldn't know what to do with a real man," he sneered, moving his hips against her. "And you're too busy wrestling the pants off those rich boys to find out."

He waited for her to back down, to lower those clear blue eyes and look upset so he could let her go.

"You're a pig!" she spat out, glaring at him defiantly.

"And you're too ignorant to know how pitiful you really are."

Ritchie and Hank began to hoot. Dallie wanted to punch them . . . punch her. . . . He would make her deal with him! "Is that so?" he scoffed. Abruptly, he slid his hand down along her side to the hem of her navy skirt, keeping her body pinned against the wall so she couldn't get away. She blinked. Her eyelids opened and closed once, twice. She didn't say anything, didn't struggle. He pushed his hand up beneath her dress and touched her leg through the diamond-patterned white tights, not letting himself think about how much he'd been wanting to touch her legs, how much time he'd spent dreaming about those legs.

She set her jaw and gritted her teeth and didn't say a word. She was as tough as nails, ready to take on any man who looked at her. Dallie thought he could probably take her right then, right against the wall. She wasn't even fighting him. She probably wanted it. That's what Jaycee had told him—that women liked a man who took what he wanted. Skeet said it wasn't true, that women wanted a man who respected them, but maybe Skeet was just too soft.

Holly Grace glared at him, and something pounded hard in his chest. He curled his hand closer to the inside of her thigh. She didn't move. Her face was a picture of defiance. Everything about her told him how tough she was—her eyes, the flare of her nostrils, the set of her jaw. Everything except the small, helpless quiver that had begun to destroy the corner of her mouth.

He backed away abruptly, stuffing his hands into the pockets of his jeans and hunching his shoulders. Ritchie and Hank snickered. Too late, he realized that he should have moved more slowly. Now it looked as if she'd gotten the best of him, as if he'd been the one to retreat. She glared at him like he was a bug she'd just squashed under her foot, and then she walked away.

Hank and Ritchie started to tease him, so he began to brag about how she was practically begging for it and how lucky she would be if he ever decided to give it to her. But all the time he was talking, his stomach kept twisting on him as if he'd eaten something bad, and he couldn't forget that helpless quiver spoiling the corner of her soft pink mouth.

That evening he found himself hanging around in the alley behind Purity Drugs where she worked for her uncle after school. He leaned his shoulders against the wall of the store and dug the heel of his boot into the dirt and thought about how he should be meeting Skeet at the driving range right now and practicing shots with his three-wood. Except right now he didn't care about his three-wood. He didn't care about golf or hustling the boys at the country club or anything but trying to redeem himself in the eyes of Holly Grace Cohagan.

A ventilation grid was set into the outside wall of the store a few feet above his head. Occasionally he heard a sound coming from the storeroom on the other side—a box being dropped, Billy T calling out an order, the distant ringing of the telephone. Gradually the sounds had died down as closing time approached, until now he could hear Holly Grace's voice so clearly he knew she must be standing right beneath the grid.

"You go on, Billy T. I'll lock up."

"I'm in no hurry, honey bun."

In his imagination, Dallie could see Billy T with his white pharmacist's coat and his florid face looking down his big putty nose at the high school boys when they came in to buy rubbers. Billy T would pull a pack of Trojans off the shelf behind him, lay them on the counter, and then, like a cat playing with a mouse, cover them with his hand and say, "If you buy those, I'll tell your mama." Billy T had tried that crap with Dallie the first time he'd ever come into the store. Dallie had looked him straight in the eye and said he was buying them so he could fuck his mama. That had shut up old Billy T.

Holly Grace's voice drifted out of the vent. "I'm going home, then, Billy T. I have a lot of studying to do for tomorrow." Her voice sounded strange, tight and overly polite.

"Not yet, honey," her uncle answered, his voice as slick as oil. "You've been slipping out on me early all week. The front's all locked up. You come on over here, now."

"No, Billy T, I don't—" She stopped speaking abruptly, as if something had settled over her mouth. Dallie straightened against the wall, his heart pounding in his chest. He heard the unmistakable sound of a moan and he squeezed his eyes shut. Christ . . . that's why she was holding out on all the senior boys. She was giving it to her uncle. Her own uncle.

A white-hot rage settled over him. Without any idea what he planned to do once he was inside, he flung himself at the back door and swung it open. Empty cartons and packages of paper towels and toilet paper lined the walls of the back hallway. He blinked his eyes, adjusting them to the dim light. The storage room was on his left, the door partly ajar, and he could hear Billy T's voice. "You're so pretty, Holly Grace. Yes . . . Oh, yes . . ."

Dallie's hands curled into fists at his sides. He walked toward the doorway and looked inside. He felt sick.

Holly Grace was sprawled on an old ripped couch, her white Woolworth's tights down around her ankles, one of Billy T's hands pushed up under her skirt. Billy T knelt by the couch, huffing and puffing like a steam engine while he tried to pull her tights the rest of the way off and feel her up at the same time. His back was to the doorway so he couldn't see Dallie watching them. Holly Grace lay with her head turned toward the door, eyes squeezed shut, just like she didn't want to lose a minute of what old Billy T was doing to her.

Dallie couldn't make himself look away and as he watched, the last of any romantic notions he might have had about her died away. Billy T got her tights off and started fumbling with the buttons on her blouse. He finally jerked it open and pushed up her bra. Dallie saw the flash of one of Holly Grace's breasts. The shape was distorted from the pressure of the bra band, but he could still see that it was round and full, just like he'd imagined, with a dusky nipple all puckered tight.

"Oh, Holly Grace," Billy T moaned, still kneeling on the floor in front of her. He pushed her skirt up to her waist and fumbled with the front of his trousers. "Tell me how much you want it. Tell me how good I am."

Dallie thought he was going to be sick, but he couldn't move. He couldn't turn away from the sight of those long graceful legs sprawled so awkwardly on the couch. "Tell me," Billy T was saying. "Tell me how much you need it, honey bun."

Holly Grace didn't open her eyes, didn't say a word. She just turned her face into the old plaid pillow on the couch. Dallie felt a prickle travel along his spine, a creeping of gooseflesh, as if somebody had just walked over his grave.

"Tell me!" Billy T said, louder this time. And then, abruptly, he drew back his fist and hit her in the stomach.

She gave a strangled, horrible cry and her body convulsed. Dallie felt as if Jaycee's fist had just landed in his own stomach, and a bomb went off in his head. He sprang forward, every nerve in his body ready to explode. Billy T heard a sound and turned, but before he could move, Dallie had shoved him to the concrete floor. Billy T looked up at him, his fat face puckered with disbelief like some comic book villain. Dallie drew back his foot and kicked him hard in the stomach.

"You p-punk," Billy T gasped, clutching his stomach and trying to get out the words at the same time. "Sh-shit-eating punk—"

"No!" Holly Grace screamed, as Dallie started after him again. She jumped up from the couch and raced to Dallie, grabbing his arm as he stood there. "No, don't do this!" Her face contorted with fear as she tried to pull him toward the door. "You don't understand," she cried. "You're only making it worse!"

Dallie spoke to her real quietly. "You pick up your clothes and go on out into the hall now, Holly Grace. Me and Billy T are going to have ourselves a little talk."

"No . . . please—"

"Go on, now."

She didn't move. Even though Dallie couldn't think of anything he wanted to do more than gaze at her beautiful, stricken face, he made himself look at Billy T instead. Although Billy T outweighed him by a hundred pounds, the pharmacist was all fat and Dallie didn't think he would have much trouble beating him into a bloody pulp.

Billy T seemed to know it, too, because his little pig eyes were distorted with fear as he fumbled with the zipper on his pants and tried to struggle to his feet. "You get him out of here, Holly Grace," he panted. "Get him out of here, or I'll make you pay for this."

Holly Grace gripped Dallie's arm, pulling so hard toward the door that he had trouble keeping his balance. "Go away, Dallie," she pleaded, her voice coming out in frightened gasps. "Please . . . please go away. . . ."

She was barefoot, her blouse unbuttoned. As he extricated himself from her grasp, he saw a yellow bruise on the inner curve of her breast, and his mouth went dry with the old fear of childhood. He reached out and pushed the blouse away from her breast, breathing a soft curse as he saw the network of bruises that marred her skin, some of them old and faded, others fresh. Her eyes were wide and tortured, begging him not to say anything. But as he gazed into them, the supplication disappeared and was replaced by defiance. She yanked the front of her dress closed and glared at him as if he'd just peeked into her diary.

Dallie's voice wasn't more than a whisper. "Did he do that to you?"

Her nostrils flared. "I fell." She licked her lips and some of her defiance faded as her eyes nervously darted toward her uncle. "It's—it's all right, Dallie. Me and Billy T . . . It—it's all right."

Suddenly her face seemed to crumple and he could feel the weight of her misery as if it were his own. He took a step away from her toward Billy T, who had risen to his feet, although he was still bent slightly forward, holding his pig stomach. "What did you say you'd do to her if she told?" Dallie asked. "How'd you threaten her?"

"None of your goddamn business," Billy T sneered, trying to edge sideways to the door.

Dallie blocked the path. "What'd he say he'd do to you, Holly Grace?"

"Nothing." Her voice sounded dead and flat. "He didn't say anything."

"You whisper one word about this and I'll call the sheriff on you," Billy T screeched at Dallie. "I'll say you broke into my store. Everybody in this town knows you're a punk, and it'll be your word against mine."

"Is that so?" Without warning, Dallie picked up a carton marked FRAGILE and threw it with all his strength against the wall behind Billy T's head. The sound of breaking glass reverberated in the storeroom. Holly Grace sucked in her breath and Billy T began to curse.

"What did he say he'd do to you, Holly Grace?" Dallie asked again.

"I—I don't know. Nothing."

He slammed another carton into the wall. Billy T let out a scream of fury, but he was too cowardly to take on Dallie's young strength. "You stop that!" he shrieked. "You stop that right now!" Sweat had broken out all over his face, and his voice had grown high-pitched with impotent rage. "Stop that, you hear me!"

Dallie wanted to sink his fists into that soft fat, to punch Billy T until there was nothing left, but something inside him held back. Something inside him knew that the best way to help Holly Grace was to break the conspiracy of silence Billy T used to hold her prisoner.

He picked up another carton and balanced it lightly in his hands. "I've got the rest of the night, Billy T, and you've got a whole store out there for me to wreck." He threw the carton against the wall. It split open and a dozen bottles shattered, filling the air with the pungent smell of rubbing alcohol.

Holly Grace had been strung tight for too long, and she broke first. "Stop, Dallie! No more! I'll tell you, but then you've got to promise to go away. Promise me!"

"I promise," he lied.

"It's—it's my mama." The expression on her face begged him for understanding. "He's going to send my mama away if I say anything! He'll do it, too. You don't know him."

Dallie had seen Winona Cohagan in town a few times, and she had reminded him of Blanche DuBois, a character in one of the plays Miss Chandler had given him to read over the summer. Vague and pretty in a faded way, Winona fluttered when she talked, dropped packages, forgot people's names, and in general acted like an incompetent fool. He knew she was the sister of Billy T's invalid wife, and he had heard she took care of Mrs. Denton while Billy T was working.

Holly Grace went on, letting loose a flood of words. Like water from a dam that had finally broken, she could no longer hold back. "Billy T says Mama's not right in the head, but that's a lie. She's just a little flighty. But he says if I don't do what he wants, he'll send her away, put her in a state mental hospital. Once people get in those places, they don't ever leave. Don't you see? I can't let him do that to my mama. She needs me."

Dallie hated seeing that helpless look in her eyes, and he slammed another carton into the wall because he was only seventeen himself and he wasn't exactly sure how to make that look go away. But he found that the destruction didn't help, so he yelled at her. "Don't you ever be such a fool again, you hear me, Holly Grace? He's not going to send your mama away. He's not going to do a goddamn thing, because if he does, I'm going to kill him with my bare hands."

She stopped looking so much like a whipped puppy, but he could see that Billy T had bullied her for too long and that she still didn't believe him. He made his way through the rubble and grabbed the shoulders of Billy T's white pharmacist's jacket. Billy T whimpered and threw up his hands to protect his head. Dallie shook him. "You aren't ever going to touch her again, are you, Billy T?"

"No!" he blubbered. "No, I won't touch her! Let me go. Make him let me go, Holly Grace!"

"You know if you ever touch her again, I'll come and get you, don't you?"

"Yes . . . I—"

"You know I'll kill you if you ever touch her again."

"I know! Please—"

Dallie did what he'd been wanting to do since he'd first looked into the storage room. He drew back his fist and slammed it into Billy T's fat pig face. Then he hit him half a dozen more times until he saw enough blood to make himself feel better. He stopped before Billy T passed out, and got real close to his face. "You go ahead and call the police on me, Billy T. You go ahead and have me arrested, because while I'm sitting in that jail cell over at the sheriff's office, I'm going to be telling everybody I know about the dirty little games you've been playing in here. I'm going to tell every cop I see, every do-good lawyer. I'm going to tell the people who sweep out my cell and the juvenile officer who investigates my case. It won't take long for the word to spread. People'll pretend not to believe it, but they'll be thinking about it every time they look at you and wondering if it's true."

Billy T didn't say anything. He just lay there whimpering and trying to hold his bleeding face together in the palms of his pudgy hands.

"Come on, Holly Grace. You and me have somebody we got to talk to." Dallie scooped up her shoes and her tights and, taking her gently by the arm, led her from the storage room.

If he had expected gratitude from her, she quickly let him know exactly how wrong he was. When she heard what he intended to do, she started to yell at him. "You promised, you liar! You promised you wouldn't tell anybody!"

He didn't say anything, didn't try to explain, because he could see the fear in her eyes and he figured if he were in her place, he'd be scared, too.

Winona Cohagan twisted her hands in the ruffle of her frilly pink apron as she sat in the living room of Billy T's house listening to Dallie talk. Holly Grace stood by the stairs, her mouth white and pinched as if she wanted to die of shame. For the first time Dallie realized that she hadn't cried once. From the moment he had burst into the storage room, she had remained dry-eyed and stricken.

Winona didn't spend any time cross-examining either of them, so Dallie got the idea that someplace deep in her heart she might have suspected Billy T was a pervert. But the quiet misery in her eyes told him that she had no idea her daughter had been his victim. He also saw right away that Winona loved Holly Grace and that she wasn't going to let anyone hurt her daughter, no matter what it might cost her. When he finally walked toward the front door to leave the house, he figured Winona, for all her flightiness, would do what was right.

Holly Grace didn't look at him as he left, and she didn't say thank you.

For the next few days she was absent from school. He, Skeet, and Miss Sybil paid an after-hours visit to Purity Drugs. They let Miss Sybil do most of the talking, and by the time she was done, Billy T had gotten the idea that he couldn't stay in Wynette any longer.

When Holly Grace finally came back to school, she stared right through Dallie as if he didn't exist. He didn't want her to know how much he was hurt by her stuck-up attitude, so he flirted with her best friend and made sure there were good-looking girls around him whenever he thought he might run into her. It didn't work as well as he'd hoped, because every time he ran into her, she had a rich college-prep boy at her side. Still, sometimes he thought he caught a flicker of something sad and old in her eyes, so he finally swallowed his pride and went up to her and asked her if she wanted to go to the homecoming dance with him. He asked her like he didn't much care whether she went with him or not, like he was doing her a big fat favor by even thinking about taking her. He wanted to make sure that when she turned him down, she would understand he didn't really give a damn and that he'd only asked her because he didn't have anything better to do.

She said she'd go.

Chapter
18

Holly Grace looked up at the anniversary clock on the mantel and swore under her breath. Dallie was late as usual. He knew she was leaving for New York City in two days and that they wouldn't see each other for a while. Couldn't he be on time just once? She wondered if he had set out after that British girl. It would be just like him to go off without saying a word.

She had dressed for the evening in a silky peach-colored turtleneck, which she'd tucked into a pair of brand-new stretch jeans. The jeans had tight cigarette legs whose length she had accented with a pair of three-inch heels. She never wore jewelry because putting earrings and necklaces near her great mane of blond hair was, she felt, a clear case of gilding the lily.

"Holly Grace, honey," Winona remarked from her armchair on the other side of the living room. "Have you seen my crossword puzzle book? I had it right here, and now I can't seem to find it."

Holly Grace retrieved the book from beneath the evening newspaper and sat down on the arm of her mother's chair to offer her advice on twenty-three across. Not that her mother needed advice, any more than she had really lost her crossword puzzle book, but Holly Grace didn't begrudge her the attention she wanted. As they worked on the puzzle together, she put her arm around Winona's shoulders and leaned down to rest her cheek on top of her mother's faded blond curls, taking in the faint scent of Breck shampoo and Aqua Net hair spray. In the kitchen, Ed Graylock, Winona's husband of three years, was puttering with a broken toaster and singing "You Are So Beautiful" along with the radio. His voice kept fading out on the high notes, but he came on strong as soon as Joe Cocker slid back into his range. Holly Grace felt her heart swell with love for these two—big Ed Graylock, who had finally given Winona the happiness she deserved, and her pretty, flighty mother.

The anniversary clock chimed seven. Giving in to the vague nostalgia that had been plaguing her all day, Holly Grace stood up and gave Winona's cheek a peck. "If Dallie ever gets here, tell him I'll be at the high school. And don't wait up for me; I'll probably be late." She grabbed her purse and headed for the front door, calling out to Ed that she would invite Dallie for breakfast in the morning.

The high school was locked up for the night, but she banged on the door by the metal shop until the custodian let her in. Her heels clicked on the concrete ramp that led into the back hallway, and as the old smells assaulted her, her footsteps seemed to be tapping out the rhythm of "R-E-S-P-E-C-T" with the Queen of Soul wailing right in her ear. She started to hum the song softly under her breath, but before she knew it she was humming "Walk Away Renée" instead and she'd rounded the corner to the gym, and then the Young Rascals were singing "Good Lovin'" and it was homecoming 1966 all over again. . . .

Holly Grace had barely said more than three words to Dallie Beaudine since he'd picked her up for the football game in a burgundy 1964 Cadillac El Dorado that she knew for certain didn't belong to him. It had deep velour seats, automatic windows and an AM/FM stereo radio blaring out, "Good love. . . ." She wanted to ask him where he got the car, but she refused to be the one to talk first.

Leaning back into the velour seat, she crossed her legs and tried to look like she rode in El Dorados all the time, like maybe the El Dorado had been invented just for her to ride in. But it was hard to pretend something like that when she was so nervous and when her stomach was growling because all she'd had to eat for dinner was half a can of Campbell's chicken noodle soup. Not that she minded. Winona couldn't really cook anything more complicated on the illegal hot plate they kept in the small back room they'd rented from Agnes Clayton the day they'd left Billy T's house.

On the horizon in front of them, the night sky glowed with a patch of light. Wynette was proud of being the only high school in the county with a lighted stadium. Everybody from the surrounding towns drove over to see Wynette play on Friday nights after their own high school game had ended. Since tonight was homecoming and the Wynette Broncos were playing last year's regional champions, the crowd was even bigger than normal. Dallie parked the El Dorado on the street several blocks away from the stadium.

He didn't say anything as they walked along the sidewalk, but when they reached the high school, he slipped his hand into the pocket of a navy blazer that looked brand new and pulled out a pack of Marlboros. "Want a cigarette?"

"I don't smoke." Her voice came out tight with disapproval, like Miss Chandler's when she talked about double negatives. She wished she could speak the words all over again, say something like, "Sure, Dallie, I'd love a smoke. Why don't you light one up for me?"

Holly Grace spotted some of her friends as they headed into the parking lot and nodded at one of the boys she'd turned down for a date that evening. She noticed that the other girls wore new wool skirts or A-line dresses bought just for the occasion, along with low square-heeled pumps that had wide grosgrain bows stretched across the toes. Holly Grace had on the black corduroy skirt that she'd worn to school once a week since her junior year and a plaid cotton blouse. She also noticed that all the other boys held hands with their dates, but Dallie had shoved his hands in the pockets of his slacks. Not for long, she thought bitterly. Before the evening was through, those hands would be all over her.

They joined the crowd moving across the parking lot toward the stadium. Why had she said she would go out with him? Why had she said yes when she knew what he wanted from her—a boy with Dallie Beaudine's reputation, who'd seen what he'd seen.

They drew up next to the table where the Pep Club was selling big yellow mums with little gold footballs dangling from the maroon and white ribbons. Dallie turned to her and asked grudgingly, "You want a flower?"

"No, thank you." Her voice echoed back at her, distant and haughty.

He stopped walking so suddenly the boy behind him bumped into his back. "Don't you think I can afford it?" he sneered at her under his breath. "Don't you think I've got enough money to buy you a goddamn three-dollar flower?" He pulled out an old brown wallet curled in the shape of his hip and slapped a five-dollar bill down on the table. "I'll take one of those," he said to Mrs. Good, the Pep Club adviser. "Keep the change." He shoved the mum at Holly Grace. Two yellow petals drifted down onto the cuff of her blouse.

Something snapped inside her. She thrust the flower back at him and returned his attack in an angry whisper. "Why don't you pin it on! That's why you bought it, isn't it? So you can grab a feel right now instead of having to wait till the dance!"

She stopped, horrified by her outburst, and dug the fingernails of her free hand into her palm. She found herself silently praying that he would understand how she felt and give her one of those melty looks she'd seen him give other girls, that he would say he was sorry and that sex wasn't what he'd asked her out for. That he would say he liked her as much as she liked him and that he didn't blame her for what he'd seen Billy T doing.

"I don't have to take this crap from you!" He knocked the flower out of her hand, turned his back on the stadium, and strode angrily away from her toward the street.

She looked down at the flower lying in the gravel, ribbons trailing in the dust. As she knelt to pick it up, Joanie Bradlow swept past her in a butterscotch jumper and dark brown Capezio flats. Joanie had practically thrown herself at Dallie the whole first month of school. Holly Grace had heard her giggling about him in the rest room: "I know he runs around with the wrong crowd, but, ohgod, he's so gorgeous. I dropped my pencil in Spanish and he picked it up and I thought, ohgod, I'm going to die!"

Misery formed a hard, tight lump inside her as she stood alone, the bedraggled mum clasped in her hand, while the crowd jostled past her toward the stadium. Some of her classmates called out a greeting and she gave them a bright smile and a cheery wave of her hand, as if her date had just left her for a minute to go to the rest room and she was waiting for him to come back any second now. Her old corduroy skirt hung like a lead curtain from her hips, and even knowing that she was the prettiest girl in the senior class didn't make her feel any better. What good was it to be pretty when you didn't have nice clothes and everybody in town knew that your mama had sat on a wooden bench most of yesterday afternoon at the county welfare office?

She knew she couldn't keep standing there with that stupid smile on her face, but she couldn't go into the bleachers, either, not by herself on homecoming night. And she couldn't start walking back to Agnes Clayton's boardinghouse until everybody was seated. While no one was looking, she slipped around the side of the building and then dashed inside through the door by the metal shop.

The gym was deserted. A caged ceiling light cast striped shadows through the canopy of maroon and white crepe paper streamers that hung limply from the girders, waiting for the dance to begin. Holly Grace stepped inside. Despite the decorations, the smell was the same as always—decades of gym classes and basketball games, reams of absence excuses and late passes, dust, old sneakers. She loved gym class. She was one of the best girl athletes in the school, the first to be chosen for a team. She loved gym. Everybody dressed the same.

A belligerent voice startled her. "You want me to take you home, is that what you want?"

She spun around to see Dallie standing just inside the gym doors leaning against the center post. His long arms were hanging stiffly at his side and he had a scowl on his face. She noticed that his slacks were too short and that she could see an inch or so of dark socks. The ill-fitting slacks made her feel a little better.

"Do you want to?" she asked.

He shifted his weight. "Do you want me to?"

"I don't know. Maybe. I guess."

"If you want me to take you home, just say so."

She gazed down at her hands where the dirty white ribbon on the mum was woven through her fingers. "Why did you ask me to go out with you?"

He didn't say anything, so she lifted her head and looked over at him. He shrugged.

"Yeah, okay," she replied briskly. "You can take me home."

"Why'd you say you'd go out with me?"

She shrugged.

He looked down at the toes of his loafers. After a moment's pause, he spoke so quietly she could barely hear him. "I'm sorry about the other day."

"What do you mean?"

"With Hank and Ritchie."

"Oh."

"I know it's not true about you and all those other guys."

"No, it's not."

"I know that. You made me mad."

A little flicker of hope flared inside her. "It's okay."

"It's not. I shouldn't have said what I did. I shouldn't have touched your leg like that. It was just that you made me mad."

"I didn't mean to—make you mad. You can be sort of scary."

His head shot up and for the first time all evening, he looked pleased. "I can?"

She couldn't help smiling. "You don't have to act so proud of yourself. You're not that scary."

He smiled, too, and it made his face so beautiful her mouth went dry.

They looked at each other like that for a while, and then she remembered about Billy T and what Dallie had seen and what he must expect of her. Her brief happiness faded. She walked over to the first row of bleachers and sat down. "I know what you think, but it's not true. I—I couldn't help what Billy T was doing to me."

He looked at her as if she'd grown horns. "I know that.

Did you think I really thought you liked what he was doing?"

Her words came out in a rush. "But you made it seem like it was so *easy* to get him to stop. You say a few words to Mama and it's all over. But it wasn't easy for me. I was afraid. He kept hurting me, and I was afraid he'd hurt Mama like that before he sent her away. He said nobody'd believe me if I told, that Mama would hate me."

Dallie walked over and sat down next to her. She could see where the leather was scuffed on the toes of his loafers and he'd tried to polish over the marks. She wondered if he hated being poor as much as she did, if poverty gave him the same sense of helplessness.

Dallie cleared his throat. "Why'd you say that about me pinning the flower on you? About grabbing a feel? Do you think that's the way I am because of how I was talking the other day in front of Hank and Ritchie?"

"Not exactly."

"Then why?"

"I figured maybe—that after what you saw with Billy T, maybe you'd expect me to . . . you know, to maybe—have sex with you tonight."

Dallie's head shot up and he looked indignant. "Then why'd you say you'd go out with me? If you thought that was all I wanted from you, why the hell did you say you'd go out with me?"

"I guess because someplace inside me, I hoped I was wrong."

He stood up and glared at her. "Yeah? Well, you sure were wrong. You sure as hell were wrong! I don't know what's wrong with you. You're the prettiest girl at Wynette High. And you're smart. Don't you know I've liked you since the first day in English class?"

"How was I supposed to know that when you scowled every time you looked at me?"

He couldn't quite meet her eyes. "You just should have known, that's all."

They didn't say anything more. They left the building and walked back across the parking lot to the stadium. A big cheer went up from the bleachers and the loudspeaker announced, "First down. Wynette."

Dallie took her hand and tucked it, along with his own, into the pocket of his navy blazer.

"Are you mad at me for being late?"

Holly Grace spun around toward the door of the gym. For a fraction of a moment she felt disoriented as she gazed at the twenty-seven-year-old Dallie leaning against the center post, looking bigger and more solid, so much more handsome than the sullen seventeen-year-old kid she'd fallen in love with. She recovered quickly.

"Of course I'm mad. As a matter of fact, I just told Bobby Fritchie I'd go out with him tonight for surf and turf instead of waiting around for you." She pulled her purse off her shoulder and let it dangle from her fingers. "Did you find out anything about that little British girl?"

"Nobody's seen her. I don't think she's still in Wynette. Miss Sybil gave her the money I left, so she should be on her way back to London by now."

Holly Grace could see he was still worried. "I think you care more about her than you're letting on. Although to tell you the truth—other than the fact that she's knockout gorgeous—I don't see exactly why."

"She's different, is all. I'll tell you one thing. I never in all my life got involved with a woman so different from me. Opposites may attract in the beginning, but they don't stick together too well."

She looked at him, a brief sadness in her eyes. "Sometimes people who are the same don't do too good a job of it, either."

He walked over to her, moving in that slow, sexy way that used to melt her bones. He pulled her into his arms to dance, humming "You've Lost That Lovin' Feelin'" into her ear. Even with improvised music, their bodies moved together perfectly, as if they'd been dancing with each other for a million years. "Damn, you're tall when you wear those shoes," he complained.

"Kinda makes you nervous, doesn't it? Having to look at me straight on."

"If Bobby walks in here and sees you wearing those high heels on his new basketball floor, you're on your own."

"It's still hard for me to think of Bobby Fritchie as

Wynette's basketball coach. I remember hanging around the office door while the two of you served morning detention."

"You're a liar, Holly Grace Beaudine. I never served a morning detention in my life. I used to take swats instead."

"You did, too, and you know it. Miss Sybil raised so much hell every time any of the teachers gave you swats that they got tired of tangling with her."

"You remember it your way, and I'll remember it mine." Dallie rested his cheek against hers. "Seeing you here reminds me of that homecoming dance. I don't think I ever sweat so much in my life. All the time we were dancing, I kept having to put more space between us because of the effect you were having on me. All I could think about was getting you alone in that El Dorado I'd borrowed, except I knew that even after I had you alone, I couldn't touch you because of the way we'd talked. Most miserable night I ever spent in my life."

"As I remember, your miserable nights didn't last too long. I must have been the easiest girl in the county. Damn, I got so I couldn't think about anything except having sex with you. I needed to wash the feel of Billy T off me so bad I was willing to go to hell for it. . . ."

Holly Grace lay back on the narrow bed in Dallie's shabby room, her eyes pressed shut as he pushed his finger up inside her. He groaned and rubbed himself against her thigh. The denim of his jeans felt rough against the bare skin of her leg. Her panties lay on the linoleum floor next to the bed along with her shoes, but other than that she was still more or less dressed—white blouse unbuttoned to the waist, bra unfastened and pushed to the side, wool skirt modestly covering Dallie's hand while it explored between her legs.

"Please . . ." she whispered. She arched against his palm. His breathing sounded heavy and strangled in her ear, his hips moved rhythmically against her thigh. She didn't think she could stand it any longer. Over the past two months, their petting sessions had grown heavier and heavier until they could think of nothing else. But still they held back— Holly Grace because she didn't want him to think she was fast, Dallie because he didn't want her to think he was like Billy T.

Suddenly she crumpled her hand into a fist and hit him behind the shoulder. He jerked away, his lips wet and swollen from kissing her, his chin red. "Why'd you do that?"

"Because I can't stand this anymore!" she exclaimed. "I want to do it! I know it's wrong. I know I shouldn't let you, but I just can't stand it anymore. I feel like I'm on fire." She tried to make him understand. "All those months, Billy T made me do it. All those months he hurt me. Don't I have the right, just once, to choose for myself?"

Dallie looked at her for a long time to make sure she was serious. "I don't want you to think— I love you, Holly Grace. I love you more than I ever loved anybody in my entire life. I'll still love you even if you say no."

Sitting up, she pulled off her blouse and slipped her bra straps down over her shoulders. "I'm tired of saying no."

Even though they had touched each other everywhere, they'd made it a rule to keep most of their clothes on, so it was the first time he'd seen her bare from the waist up. He looked at her with awe and then reached out and stroked a gentle finger down over her breast. "You're so beautiful, baby," he said, his voice choked.

A surge of wonder shot through her at the emotion in his expression and she found that she wanted to give everything she had to this boy who treated her with so much tenderness. She leaned forward, thrust her thumbs into the tops of her knee socks, and stripped them off. Then she unfastened the waistband of her skirt, lifting up her hips to slip it down. He pulled off his T-shirt and his jeans, then slid down his briefs. She drank in the beauty of his thin young body as he lay down beside her and tenderly wound his fingers through her hair. She lifted her head off the crumpled pillow to kiss him and slid her tongue into his mouth. He groaned and accepted it. Their kisses grew deeper until they were moaning and sucking on each other's lips and tongues, their long legs twisting together, their blond hair dampened with sweat.

"I don't want you to get pregnant," he whispered into her mouth. "I'll just—I'll just put it in a little bit."

But of course he didn't, and it was the best thing she'd ever felt. She uttered a low moan deep in her throat as she came, and he quickly followed, shuddering in her arms as if he'd been shot through with a bullet. The whole thing was over in less than a minute.

By graduation day they were using rubbers, but by that time, she was already pregnant and he refused to help her find the money for an abortion. "Abortion is wrong when two people love each other," he shouted, pointing his finger at her. And then his voice had softened. "I know we planned to wait until I graduated from A&M, but we'll get married now. Except for Skeet, you're the only good thing that's ever happened to me in my life."

"I can't have a baby now," she cried. "I'm seventeen! I'm going to San Antonio to get a job. I want to make something of myself. Having a baby now will ruin my whole life."

"How can you say that? Don't you love me, Holly Grace?"

"Of course I do. But loving's not always enough."

As she saw the agony in his eyes, that familiar helpless feeling closed around her. It stayed with her right through the wedding in Pastor Leary's study.

Dallie quit humming in the middle of the chorus to "Good Vibrations" and came to a stop on the free-throw line. "Did you really tell Bobby Fritchie you'd go out with him tonight?"

Holly Grace had been performing an intricate harmony, and she continued singing for a few measures without him. "Not exactly. But I thought about it. I get so aggravated when you're late."

Dallie let her go and gave her a long look. "If you really want a divorce, you know I'll go along with it."

"I know." She walked over to the bleachers and sat down, stretching out her legs in front of her and putting a small scratch in Coach Fritchie's new varnish with the heel of her shoe. "Since I don't have any plans to get married again, I'm happy with things just like they are."

Dallie smiled and walked forward along the center court line to sit on the bleachers beside her. "I hope New York City works out for you, baby. I really do. You know I want to see you happy about more than I want anything in the world."

"I know you do. Same goes for me."

She began to talk about Winona and Ed, about Miss Sybil and the other things they usually discussed whenever they were together in Wynette. He only listened with half his mind. The other half was remembering two teenagers with troubled pasts, a baby, and no money. Now he realized that they hadn't had a chance, but they had loved each other, and they had put up a good fight. . . .

Skeet took a construction job in Austin to help out as much as he could, but it wasn't union work so it didn't pay too well. Dallie worked for a roofer when he wasn't in class or trying to pick up some extra cash on the golf course. They had to send Winona money, and there was never enough.

Dallie had lived with poverty for so long it didn't bother him too much, but it was different for Holly Grace. She got this helpless, panicked look in her eyes that sank right into his veins and froze his blood. It made him feel that he was failing her, and he started arguments—bitter fights where he accused her of not doing her share. He said she didn't keep the house clean enough, or he told her she was too lazy to cook him a good meal. She countered by accusing him of not providing for his family, insisting that he should quit playing golf and study engineering instead.

"I don't want to be an engineer," he retorted during an especially fierce argument. Banging one of his books down on the scratched surface of the kitchen table, he added, "I want to study literature, and I want to play golf!"

She threw the dish towel at him. "If you want to play golf so bad, why are you wasting money studying literature?"

He threw the towel right back. "Nobody in my family ever graduated from college! I'm going to be the first." Danny started to cry at the angry sound of his father's voice. Dallie picked him up, buried his face in the baby's blond curls, and refused to look at Holly Grace. How could he explain that he had something to prove when even he didn't know what it was?

As similar as they were in so many ways, they wanted different things from life. Their fights began to escalate until they attacked each other's most vulnerable spots, and then they felt sick inside because of the way they hurt each other. Skeet said they fought because they were both so young that they were pretty much raising each other right along with Danny. It was true.

"I wish you'd stop walking around with that surly look on your face all the time," Holly Grace said one day as she dabbed Clearasil on one of the pimples that still occasionally popped out on Dallie's chin. "Don't you understand that the first step toward being a man is to stop pretending to be one."

"What do you know about being a man?" he replied, grabbing her around the waist and pulling her down on his lap. They made love, but a few hours later he was scolding her for not standing up straight.

"You walk around with your shoulders hunched over just because you think your breasts are too big."

"I do not," Holly Grace retorted hotly.

"Yes, you do and you know it." He tilted up her chin so she was looking him straight in the eye. "Baby, when are you going to stop blaming yourself for what ol' Billy T did to you?"

Eventually, Dallie's words took hold and Holly Grace let go of the past.

Unfortunately, all of their confrontations didn't end as well. "You've got an attitude problem," Dallie accused her at the end of several days of arguing about money. "Nothing is ever good enough for you."

"I want to be somebody!" she countered. "I'm the one stuck here with a baby while you go to college."

"As soon as I'm done, you can go. We've talked about it a hundred times."

"It'll be too late by then," she said. "My life will be half over."

Their marriage was already rocky, and then Danny died. Dallie's guilt after Danny's death was like a fast-growing cancer. Right away they moved from the house where it happened, but night after night he dreamed about the cistern cover. In his dreams he saw the broken hinge and he turned away toward the old wooden garage to get his tools so he could fix it. But he never made it to the garage. Instead, he found himself back in Wynette or standing next to the trailer outside Houston where he had lived while he was growing up. He knew he had to get back to that cistern cover, had to get it fixed, but something kept stopping him.

He would wake up covered with sweat, the sheets tangled around him. Sometimes Holly Grace was already awake, her shoulders shaking, her face turned into the pillow to muffle the sound of her crying. In all the time he'd known her nothing had ever made her cry. Not when Billy T hit her in the stomach with his fist; not when she was scared because they were just kids and they didn't have any money; not even at Danny's funeral where she had sat as if she was carved out of stone while he cried like a baby. But now that she was crying, he knew it was the worst sound he had ever heard.

His guilt was a disease, eating away at him. Every time he shut his eyes, he saw Danny running toward him on chubby legs, one strap of his denim coveralls falling down off his shoulder, bright blond curls alight in the sun. He saw those blue eyes wide with wonder and the long lashes that curled on his cheeks when he slept. He heard Danny's squeal of laughter, remembered the way he had sucked his fingers when he got tired. He saw Danny in his mind, and then he heard Holly Grace crying, and as her shoulders quaked helplessly, his guilt intensified until he thought he might die right along with Danny.

Eventually, she said she was going to leave him, that she still loved him but she'd gotten a job on the sales staff of a sports equipment company and she was leaving for Fort Worth in the morning. That night, the sound of her muffled crying awakened him again. He lay there for a while with his eyes open, and then he jerked her up out of the pillow and hit her across the face. He slapped her once, and then he slapped her again. After that, he pulled on his pants and ran right out of the house so that in years to come, Holly Grace Beaudine would remember she had a son of a bitch husband who hit her, not some stupid kid who had made her cry because he'd killed her baby.

After she left, he spent several months so drunk that he couldn't play golf, even though he was supposed to be getting ready for qualifying school for the pro tour. Skeet eventually called Holly Grace, and she came to see Dallie.

"I'm happy for the first time in a long time," she told him. "Why can't you be happy, too?"

It had taken years for them to learn to love each other in a new way. At first they had tumbled back into bed together, only to find themselves caught up in old arguments. Occasionally they had tried to live with each other for a few months, but they wanted different things from life and it never worked out. The first time he saw her with another man, Dallie wanted to kill him. But a cute little secretary had caught his eye, so he kept his fists to himself.

Over the years they talked about divorce, but neither of them did anything about it. Skeet meant everything in the world to Dallie. Holly Grace loved Winona with all her heart. But the two of them together—Dallie and Holly Grace—they were each other's real family, and people with childhoods as troubled as theirs didn't give up family easily.

Tempest-Tossed

Chapter
19

The building was a squat white rectangle of concrete with four dusty cars parked at the side next to a trash dumpster. A padlocked shack stood behind the dumpster, and fifty yards beyond that was the thin metal finger of the radio antenna that Francesca had been walking toward for nearly two hours. As Beast went off to explore, Francesca wearily climbed the two steps to the front door. Its glass surface was nearly opaque with dust and the smear of countless finger-prints. Decals advertising the Sulphur City Chamber of Commerce, the United Way, and various broadcasting associations covered much of the left side of the door, while the center held the gold call letters KDSC. The bottom half of the *C* was missing, so it might have been a *G*, but Francesca knew it wasn't because she had seen the *C* on the mailbox at the end of the lane when she turned in.

Although she could have positioned herself in front of the door to study her reflection, she didn't bother. Instead, she rubbed the back of her hand over her forehead, pushing aside the damp strands of hair that had stuck there, and brushed off her jeans as best she could. She couldn't do anything about the bloody scrapes on her arms, so she ignored them. Her earlier euphoria had faded, leaving exhaustion and a terrible apprehension.

Pushing open the front door, she found herself in a reception area overstuffed with six cluttered desks, nearly as many clocks, an assortment of bulletin boards, calendars, posters, and cartoons fixed to the walls with curling yellowed tape. A brown and gold striped Danish modern couch sat to her left, the center cushion concave from too much use. The room contained only one window, a large one that looked into a studio where an announcer wearing a headset sat in front of a microphone. His voice was piped into the office through a wall speaker and the volume was turned low.

A chubby red-haired chipmunk of a woman looked up at Francesca from the room's only occupied desk. "Can I help you?"

Francesca cleared her throat, her gaze traveling from the swaying gold crosses hanging from the woman's ears down over her polyester blouse, and then on to the black telephone sitting by her wrist. One call to Wynette and her immediate problems would be over. She would have food, a change of clothes, and a roof over her head. But the idea of running to Dallie for help had lost its old appeal. Despite her exhaustion and fear, something inside her had been unalterably changed back on that deserted dirt road. She was sick of being a pretty ornament getting blown away by every ill wind that swept in her direction. For better or for worse, she was going to take control of her own life.

"I wonder if I might speak with the person in charge," she said to the chipmunk. Francesca spoke carefully, trying her best to sound competent and professional, instead of like someone with a dirty face and dusty, sandaled feet who didn't have a dime in her pocket.

The combination of Francesca's bedraggled appearance and her upper-class British accent obviously interested the woman. "I'm Katie Cathcart, the office manager. Could you tell me what this is about?"

Could an office manager help her? Francesca had no idea, but decided she would be better off with the man at the top. She kept her tone friendly, but firm. "It's rather personal."

The woman hesitated, then got up and went into the office behind her. She reappeared a moment later. "As long as you

276

don't take too long, Miss Padgett'll see you. She's our station manager."

Francesca's nervousness took a quantum leap. Why did the station manager have to be a woman? At least with a man, she would have stood half a chance. And then she reminded herself that this was an opportunity for a fresh beginning—a new Francesca, one who wasn't going to try to slide through life using the tired old tricks of her former self. Straightening her shoulders, she walked into the station manager's office.

A gold metal nameplate on the desk announced the presence of CLARE PADGETT, an elegant name for an inelegant woman. In her early forties, she had a masculine, square-jawed face, softened only by the remains of a dab of red lipstick. Her graying brown hair was medium-length and blunt-cut. It looked as though it received nothing more than shampooing by way of attention. She held a cigarette like a man, pushed into the crook between the index and middle finger of her right hand, and when she lifted the cigarette to her mouth she didn't so much inhale the smoke as swallow it.

"What is it?" Clare asked abruptly. She spoke in a professional broadcaster's voice, rich and resonant, but without the slightest trace of friendliness. From the wall speaker behind the desk came the faint sound of the announcer reading a local news report.

Even though she hadn't been offered it, Francesca took the room's single straight-backed chair, deciding in an instant that Clare Padgett didn't look like the sort of person who would respect anyone she could step all over. As she gave her name, she positioned herself on the edge of the seat. "I'm sorry to appear without an appointment, but I wanted to inquire about a possible job." Her voice sounded tentative instead of assertive. What had happened to all that arrogance she used to carry around with her like a cloud of perfume?

After a brief inspection of Francesca's appearance, Clare Padgett returned her attention to her paperwork. "I don't have any jobs."

It was nothing more than Francesca had expected, but she

still felt as if she'd had the wind knocked out of her. She thought of that dusty ribbon of road stretching to the rim of the Texas horizon. Her tongue felt dry and swollen in her mouth. "Are you absolutely certain you don't have something? I'm willing to do anything."

Padgett sucked in more smoke and tapped at the top sheet of paper with her pencil. "What kind of experience do you have?"

Francesca thought quickly. "I've done some acting. And I have lots of experience with—uh—fashion." She crossed her ankles and tried to tuck the toes of her scuffed Bottega Veneta sandals behind the leg of the chair.

"That doesn't exactly qualify you for a job at a radio station, now, does it? Not even a rat-shit operation like this." She tapped her pencil a little harder.

Francesca took a deep breath and prepared to jump into water much too deep for a nonswimmer. "Actually, Miss Padgett, I don't have any radio experience. But I'm a hard worker, and I'm willing to learn." Hard worker? She'd never worked hard in her life.

In any case, Clare was unimpressed. She lifted her eyes and regarded Francesca with open hostility. "I was kicked off the air at a television station in Chicago because of someone like you—a cute little cheerleader who didn't know the difference between hard news and her panty size." She leaned back in her chair, her eyes narrow with disenchantment. "We call women like you Twinkies—little fluff balls who don't know the first thing about broadcasting, but think it would be oh-so-exciting to have a career in radio."

Six months before, Francesca would have swept from the room in a huff, but now she clamped her hands together in her lap and lifted her chin a shade higher. "I'm willing to do anything, Miss Padgett—answer the telephones, run errands . . ." She couldn't explain to this woman that it wasn't a career in broadcasting that attracted her. If this building had held a fertilizer factory, she would still have wanted a job.

"The only work I have is for someone to do the cleaning and odd jobs."

"I'll take it!" *Dear God, cleaning.*

"I don't think you're right for it."

Francesca ignored the sarcasm in her voice. "Oh, but I am. I'm a wonderful cleaner."

She had Clare Padgett's attention again, and the woman seemed amused. "Actually, I'd wanted someone Mexican. Are you a citizen?" Francesca shook her head. "Do you have a green card?"

Again she shook her head. She had only the vaguest idea what a green card was, but she was absolutely certain she didn't have one and she refused to start her new life with a lie. Maybe frankness would impress this woman. "I don't even have a passport. It was stolen from me a few hours ago on the road."

"How unfortunate." Clare Padgett was no longer making the smallest effort to hide how much she was enjoying the situation. She reminded Francesca of a cat with a helpless bird clasped in its mouth. Obviously Francesca, despite her bedraggled state, was going to have to pay for all the slights the station manager had suffered over the years at the hands of beautiful women. "In that case, I'll put you on the payroll at sixty-five dollars a week. You'll have every other Saturday off. The rest of the time you'll be here from sunup to sundown, the same hours we're on the air. And you'll be paid in cash. We've got truckloads of Mexicans coming in every day, so the first time you screw up, you're out."

The woman was paying slave wages. This was the sort of job illegal aliens took because they didn't have a choice. "All right," Francesca said, because she didn't have a choice.

Clare Padgett smiled grimly and led Francesca out to the office manager. "Fresh meat, Katie. Give her a mop and show her the bathroom."

Clare disappeared and Katie looked at Francesca with pity. "We haven't had anyone clean for a few weeks. It's pretty bad."

Francesca swallowed hard. "That's all right."

It wasn't all right, of course. She stood in front of a pantry in the station's tiny kitchenette, looking over a shelf full of cleaning products, none of which she had the slightest idea how to use. She knew how to play baccarat, and she could name the maître d's of the world's most famous restaurants, but she hadn't the faintest idea how to clean a bathroom. She read the labels as quickly as she could, and half an hour later Clare Padgett discovered her on her knees in front of a gruesomely stained toilet, pouring blue powdered cleanser on the seat.

"When you scrub the floor, make certain you get into the corners, Francesca. I hate sloppy work."

Francesca gritted her teeth and nodded. Her stomach did a small flip-flop as she prepared to attack the mess on the underside of the seat. Unbidden, she thought of Hedda, her old housekeeper. Hedda, with her rolled stockings and bad back, who'd spent her life on her knees cleaning up after Chloe and Francesca.

Clare sucked on her cigarette and then deliberately tossed it down next to Francesca's foot. "You'd better hustle, chicky. We're getting ready to close down for the day." Francesca heard a malevolent chuckle as the woman moved away.

A little later, the announcer who'd been on the air when Francesca arrived stuck his head in the bathroom and told her he had to lock up. Her heart lurched. She had no place to go, no bed to sleep in. "Has everybody left?"

He nodded and ran his eyes over her, obviously liking what he saw. "You need a lift into town?"

She stood and wiped her hair out of her eyes with her forearm, trying to seem casual. "No. Somebody's picking me up." She inclined her head toward the mess, her resolution not to begin her new life with lies already abandoned. "Miss Padgett told me I had to finish this tonight before I left. She said I could lock up." Did she sound too offhand? Not offhand enough? What would she do if he refused?

"Suit yourself." He gave her an appreciative smile. A few minutes later she let out a slow, relieved breath as she heard the front door close.

Francesca spent the night on the black and gold office sofa with Beast curled against her stomach, both of them poorly fed on sandwiches she had made from stale bread and a jar of peanut butter she found in the kitchenette. Exhaustion had seeped into the very marrow of her bones, but still she couldn't fall asleep. Instead, she lay with her eyes open, Beast's fur pushed into the V's between her fingers, thinking about how many more obstacles lay in her way.

The next morning she awakened before five and promptly threw up into the toilet she had so painstakingly cleaned the night before. For the rest of the day, she tried to tell herself it was only a reaction to the peanut butter.

"Francesca! Dammit, where is she?" Clare stormed from her office as Francesca flew out of the newsroom where she'd just finished delivering a batch of afternoon papers to the news director.

"I'm here, Clare," she said wearily. "What's the problem?"

It had been six weeks since she'd started work at KDSC, and her relationship with the station manager hadn't improved. According to the gossip she'd picked up from members of the small KDSC staff, Clare's radio career had been launched at a time when few women could get jobs in broadcasting. Station managers hired her because she was intelligent and aggressive, and then fired her for the same reason. She finally made it to television, where she fought bitter battles for the right to report hard news instead of the softer stories considered appropriate for women reporters.

Ironically, she was defeated by Equal Opportunity. In the early seventies when employers were forced to hire women, they bypassed battle-scarred veterans like Clare, with their sharp tongues and cynical outlooks, for newer, fresher faces straight off college campuses—pretty, malleable sorority girls with degrees in communication arts. Women like Clare had to take what was left—jobs for which they were overqualified, like running backwater radio stations. As a result, they smoked too much, grew increasingly bitter, and made life miserable for any females they suspected of trying to get by on nothing more than a pretty face.

"I just got a call from that fool at the Sulphur City bank," Clare snapped at Francesca. "He wants the Christmas promotions today instead of tomorrow." She pointed toward a box of bell-shaped tree ornaments printed with the name of the radio station on one side and the name of the bank on the other. "Get over there right away with them, and don't take all day like you did last time."

Francesca refrained from pointing out that she wouldn't have taken so long last time if four staff members hadn't dumped additional errands on her—everything from delivering overdue bills for air time to having a new water pump put in the station's battered Dodge Dart. She pulled on the red and black plaid car coat she'd bought at a Goodwill store for five dollars and then grabbed the key to the Dart from a cup hook next to the studio window. Inside, Tony March, the afternoon deejay, was cuing up a record. Although he hadn't been with KDSC very long, everyone knew he would be quitting soon. He had a good voice and a distinct personality. For announcers like Tony, KDSC, with its unimpressive 500-watt signal, was merely a stepping stone to better things. Francesca had already discovered that the only people who stayed at KDSC for very long were people like her who didn't have any other choice.

The car started after only three attempts, which was nearly a record. She backed around and headed out of the parking lot. A glance at the rearview mirror showed pale skin, dull hair snared at the back of her neck with a rubber band, and a red-rimmed nose from the latest in a series of head colds. Her car coat was too big for her, and she had neither the money nor the energy to improve her appearance. At least she didn't have to fend off many advances from the male staff members.

There had been few successes for her these past six weeks, but many disasters. One of the worst had occurred the day before Thanksgiving when Clare had discovered she was sleeping on the station couch and screamed at her in front of everyone until Francesca's cheeks burned with humiliation. Now she and Beast lived in a bedroom-kitchen combination over a garage in Sulphur City. It was drafty and badly furnished with discarded furniture and a lumpy twin bed, but the rent was cheap and she could pay it by the week, so she tried to feel grateful for every ugly inch of it. She had also gained the use of the station's Dodge Dart, although Clare made her pay for gas even when someone else took the car. It was an exhausting, hand-to-mouth existence, with no room for financial emergencies, no room for personal emergencies, and no—absolutely *no*—room for an unwanted pregnancy.

Her fists tightened on the steering wheel. By doing without almost everything, she had managed to save the one hundred and fifty dollars the San Antonio abortion clinic would charge her to get rid of Dallie Beaudine's baby. She refused to let herself think of the ramifications of her decision; she was simply too poor and too desperate to consider the morality of the act. After her appointment on Saturday, she would have averted one more disaster. That was all the introspection she allowed herself.

She finished running her errands in little more than an hour and returned to the station, only to have Clare yell at her for having gone off without washing her office windows first.

The following Saturday she got up at dawn and made the two-hour drive to San Antonio. The waiting room of the abortion clinic was sparsely furnished but clean. She sat down on a molded plastic chair, her hands clutching her black canvas shoulder bag, her legs pressed tightly together as if they were unconsciously trying to protect the small piece of protoplasm that would soon be taken from her body. The room held three other women. Two were Mexican and one was a worn-out blonde with an acned face and hopeless eyes. All of them were poor.

A middle-aged, Spanish-looking woman in a neat white blouse and dark skirt appeared at the door and called her name. "Francesca, I'm Mrs. Garcia," she said in lightly accented English. "Would you come with me, please?"

Francesca numbly followed her into a small office paneled in fake mahogany. Mrs. Garcia took a seat behind her desk and invited Francesca to sit in another molded plastic chair, differing only in color from the one in the waiting room.

The woman was friendly and efficient as she went over the forms for Francesca to sign. Then she explained the procedure that would take place in one of the surgical rooms down the hall. Francesca bit down on the inside of her lip and tried not to listen too closely. Mrs. Garcia spoke slowly and calmly, always using the word "tissue," never "fetus." Francesca felt a detached sense of gratitude. Ever since she had realized she was pregnant, she had refused to personify the unwelcome visitor lodged in her womb. She refused to connect it in her mind to that night in a Louisiana swamp. Her life had been pared down to the bone—to the marrow —and there was no room for sentiment, no room to build falsely romantic pictures of chubby pink cheeks and soft curly hair, no need *ever* to use the word "baby," not even in her thoughts. Mrs. Garcia began to speak of "vacuum aspiration," and Francesca thought of the old Hoover she pushed around the radio station carpet every evening.

"Do you have any questions?"

She shook her head. The faces of the three sad women in the waiting room seemed implanted in her mind—women with no future, no hope. Mrs. Garcia slid a booklet across the metal desktop. "This pamphlet contains information on birth control that you should read before you have intercourse again."

Again? The memory of Dallie's deep, hot kisses rushed back to her, but the intimate caresses that had once set her senses aflame now seemed to have happened to someone else. She couldn't imagine ever feeling that good again.

"I can't have this—this *tissue,"* Francesca said abruptly, interrupting the woman in midsentence as she showed her a diagram of the female reproductive organs.

Mrs. Garcia stopped what she was saying and inclined her head to listen, obviously accustomed to hearing the most private revelations pass across her desk.

Francesca knew she had no need to justify her actions, but she couldn't seem to stop the flow of words. "Don't you see that it's impossible?" Her fists clenched into knots in her lap. "I'm not a horrible person. I'm not unfeeling. But I can barely take care of myself and a walleyed cat."

The woman gazed at her sympathetically. "Of course you're not unfeeling, Francesca. It's your body, and only you can decide what's best."

"I've made up my mind," she replied, her tone as angry as if the woman had argued with her. "I don't have a husband or money. I'm barely hanging on to a job working for a boss who hates me. I don't even have any way to pay my medical bills."

"I understand. It's difficult—"

"You *don't* understand!" Francesca leaned forward, her eyes dry and furious, each word coming out like a hard, crisp pellet. "All my life I've lived off other people, but I'm not going to do that anymore. I'm going to make something of myself!"

"I think your ambition is admirable. You're obviously a competent young—"

Again Francesca pushed aside her sympathy, trying to explain to Mrs. Garcia—trying to explain to herself—what had brought her to this red brick abortion clinic in the poorest part of San Antonio. The room was warm, but she hugged herself as if she felt a chill. "Have you ever seen those pictures people put together on black velvet with little nails and different colored strings—pictures of bridges and butterflies, things like that?" Mrs. Garcia nodded. Francesca gazed at the fake mahogany paneling without seeing it. "I have one of those awful pictures fastened to the wall, right above my bed, this terrible pink and orange string picture of a guitar."

"I don't quite see—"

"How can someone bring a baby into the world when she lives in a place with a string picture of a guitar on the wall? What kind of mother would deliberately expose a helpless little baby to something so ugly?" *Baby.* She'd said the word. Twice she'd said it. A painful press of tears pricked at the backs of her eyelids but she refused to shed them. In the past year, she'd cried enough spoiled, self-indulgent tears to last a lifetime, and she wasn't going to cry any more.

"You know, Francesca, an abortion doesn't have to be the end of the world. In the future, the circumstances may be different for you . . . the time more convenient."

Her final word seemed to hang in the air. Francesca slumped back in the chair, all the anger drained out of her. Was that what a human life came down to, she wondered, a matter of convenience? It was inconvenient for her to have a baby right now, so she would simply do away with it? She looked up at Mrs. Garcia. "My friends in London used to schedule their abortions so they wouldn't miss any balls or parties."

For the first time Mrs. Garcia visibly bristled. "The women who come here aren't worried about missing a party, Francesca. They're fifteen-year-olds with their whole lives in front of them, or married women who already have too many children and absent husbands. They're women without jobs and without any hope of getting work."

But she wasn't like them, Francesca told herself. She wasn't helpless and broken anymore. These past few months she had proven that. She'd scrubbed toilets, endured abuse, fed and sheltered herself on next to nothing. Most people would have crumbled, but she hadn't. She had survived.

It was a new, tantalizing view of herself. She sat straighter in the chair, her fists gradually easing open in her lap. Mrs. Garcia spoke hesitantly. "Your life seems rather precarious at the moment."

Francesca thought of Clare, of the ugly rooms above the garage, of the string guitar, of her inability to call Dallie for help, even when she desperately needed it. "It *is* precarious," she agreed. Leaning over, she picked up her canvas shoulder bag. Then she rose from her chair. The impulsive, optimistic part of her that she thought had died months before seemed to have taken over her feet, seemed to be forcing her to do something that could only lead to disaster, something illogical, foolish. . . .

Something wonderful.

"May I have my money back, please, Mrs. Garcia? Take out whatever you need to cover your time today."

Mrs. Garcia looked worried. "Are you sure about your decision, Francesca? You're already ten weeks pregnant. You don't have much more time to undergo a safe abortion. Are you absolutely sure?"

Francesca had never been less sure of anything in her life, but she nodded.

She broke into a little run as she left the abortion clinic, and then a skip to cover the last few feet to the Dart. Her mouth curved in a smile. Of all the stupid things she had ever done in her life, this was the stupidest. Her smile grew wider. Dallie had been absolutely right about her—she didn't have a single ounce of common sense. She was poorer than a church mouse, badly educated, and living every minute on the cutting edge of disaster. But right now, at this very moment, none of that mattered, because some things in life were more important than common sense.

Francesca Serritella Day had lost most of her dignity and all of her pride. She wasn't going to lose her baby.

Chapter
20

Francesca discovered something rather wonderful about herself in the next few months. With her back pressed to the wall, a gun pointed to her forehead, a time bomb ticking in her womb, she learned that she was quite intelligent. She grasped new ideas easily, retained what she learned, and having had so few academic prejudices imposed upon her by teachers, never let preconceived notions limit her thinking. With her first months of pregnancy behind her, she also discovered a seemingly endless capacity for hard work, which she began taking advantage of by laboring far into the night, reading newspapers and broadcasting magazines, listening to tapes, and getting ready to take a small step up in the world.

"Do you have a minute, Clare?" she asked, sticking her head into the record library, a small tape cassette pressed into the damp palm of her hand. Clare was leafing through one of the *Billboard* reference books and didn't bother to look up.

The record library was actually nothing more than a large closet with albums lining the shelves, strips of colored tape affixed to their spines to indicate whether they fell into the category of male vocalists, female vocalists, or groups. Francesca had intentionally chosen the location because it was neutral territory, and she didn't want to give Clare the added advantage of being able to sit like God behind her desk while she decided the fate of the supplicant in the budget seat opposite her.

"I have all day," Clare replied sarcastically, as she continued to flip through the book. "As a matter of fact, I've been sitting in here for hours just twiddling my thumbs and waiting for someone to interrupt me."

It wasn't the most auspicious beginning, but Francesca ignored Clare's sarcasm and positioned herself in the center of the doorway. She was wearing the newest item in her wardrobe: a man's gray sweat shirt that hung in baggy folds past her hips. Out of sight beneath it, her jeans were unfastened and unzipped, held together with a piece of cord crudely sewn across the placket. Francesca looked Clare squarely in the eyes. "I'd like a shot at Tony's announcing job when he leaves."

Clare's eyebrows rose halfway up her forehead. "You *are* kidding."

"Actually, I'm not." Francesca lifted her chin and went on as if she had all the confidence in the world. "I've spent a lot of time practicing, and Jerry helped me make an audition tape." She held out the cartridge. "I think I can do the job."

A cruel, amused smile curled at the corners of Clare's mouth. "An interesting ambition, considering the fact that you have a noticeable British accent and you've never been in front of a microphone in your life. Of course, the little cheerleader who replaced me in Chicago hadn't ever been on the air either, and she sounded like Betty Boop, so maybe I should watch out."

Francesca kept a tight rein on her temper. "I'd like a chance anyway. My British accent will give me a different sound from everyone else."

"You clean toilets," Clare scoffed, lighting a cigarette. "That's the job you were hired for."

Francesca refused to flinch. "And I've been good at it, haven't I? Cleaning toilets and doing every other bloody job you've thrown at me. Now give me a shot at this one."

"Forget it."

Francesca couldn't play it safe any longer. She had her baby to think about, her future. "You know, I'm actually starting to sympathize with you, Clare."

"What do you mean by that?"

"You've heard the old proverb about not understanding another person until you've walked a mile in his shoes. I understand you, Clare. I know exactly what it's like to be discriminated against because of who you are, no matter how hard you work. I know what it's like to be denied a shot at a job—not from a lack of ability, but because of the personal prejudice of your employer."

"Prejudice!" A cloud of smoke emerged like dragon fire from Clare's mouth. "I've never been prejudiced in my life. I've been a *victim* of prejudice."

This was no time for retreat, and Francesca pressed harder. "You won't even take fifteen minutes to listen to an audition tape. I'd call that prejudice, wouldn't you?"

Clare's jaw snapped into a rigid line. "All right, Francesca, I'll give you your fifteen minutes." She snatched the cassette from her hand. "But don't hold your breath."

For the rest of the day, Francesca's insides felt like a quivering mass of aspic. She had to get this job. Not only did she desperately need the money but she absolutely had to succeed at something. Radio was a medium that functioned without pictures, a medium in which sage green eyes and a perfect profile held no significance. Radio was her testing ground, her chance to prove to herself that she would never again have to depend on her looks to get by.

At one-thirty, Clare stuck her head through the door of her office and beckoned to Francesca, who set down the fliers she'd been stacking in a carton and tried to walk into the office confidently. She couldn't quite pull it off.

"The tape isn't terrible," Clare said, settling into her chair, "but it's not much good either." She pushed the cartridge across the desktop.

Francesca stared down at it, trying to hide the crushing disappointment she felt.

"Your voice is too breathy," Clare went on, her tone brisk and impersonal. "You talk much too fast and you emphasize the strangest words. Your British accent is the only thing you have going for you. Otherwise, you sound like a bad imitation of every mediocre male disc jockey we've had at this station."

Francesca strained to hear some trace of personal animosity in her voice, some sense that Clare was being vindictive. But all she heard was the dispassionate assessment of a seasoned professional. "Let me do another tape," she pleaded. "Let me try again."

The chair squeaked as Clare leaned back. "I don't want to hear another tape; it won't be any different. AM radio is about people. If listeners want music, they tune into an FM station. AM radio has to be personality radio, even at a rat-shit station like this. If you want to make it in AM, you have to remember you're talking to *people,* not to a microphone. Otherwise you're just another Twinkie."

Francesca snatched up the tape and turned toward the door, the threads of her self-control nearly unraveling. How had she ever imagined she could break into radio without any training? One more delusion. One more sand castle she had built too near the water's edge.

"The best I can do is use you as a relief announcer on weekends if somebody can't make it."

Francesca spun around. "A relief announcer! You'll use me as a relief announcer?"

"Christ, Francesca. Don't act like I'm doing you any big favor. All it means is you'll end up working an afternoon shift on Easter Sunday when nobody's listening."

But Francesca refused to let Clare's testiness deflate her, and she let out a whoop of happiness.

That night she pulled a can of cat food from her only kitchen cupboard and began her nightly conversation with Beast.

"I'm going to make something of myself," she told him. "I don't care how hard I have to work or what I have to do. I'm going to be the best announcer KDSC has ever had." Beast lifted his hind leg and began grooming himself. Francesca glowered at him. "That is absolutely the most disgusting habit you have, and if you think you're going to do that around my daughter, you can think again."

Beast ignored her. She reached for a rusty can opener and fastened it over the rim of the can, but she didn't begin turning it at once. Instead, she stared dreamily ahead. She knew intuitively that she was going to have a daughter—a little star-spangled American baby girl who would be taught from the very beginning to rely on something more than the physical beauty she was predestined to inherit from her parents. Her daughter would be the fourth generation of Serritella females—and the best. Francesca vowed to teach her child all the things she had been forced to learn on her own, all the things a little girl needed to know so that she would never end up lying in the middle of a dirt road and wondering how she'd gotten there.

Beast disturbed her daydreams by batting her sneaker with his paw, reminding her of his dinner. She resumed opening the can. "I've absolutely made up my mind to call her Natalie. It's such a pretty name—feminine but strong. What do you think?"

Beast stared at the bowl of food that was being lowered toward him much too slowly, all his attention focused on his dinner. A small lump formed in Francesca's throat as she set it on the floor. Women shouldn't have babies when they had only a cat with whom to share their daydreams about the future. And then she shook off her self-pity. Nobody had forced her to have this baby. She had made the decision herself, and she wasn't going to start whining about it now. Lowering herself to the old linoleum floor, she sat cross-legged by the cat's bowl and reached out to stroke him.

"Guess what happened today, Beast? It was the most wonderful thing." Her fingers slipped through the animal's soft fur. "I felt my baby move. . . ."

Within three weeks of her interview with Clare, a flu epidemic hit three of the KDSC announcers and Clare was forced to let Francesca take over a Wednesday morning shift. "Try to remember you're talking to *people*," she barked as Francesca headed for the studio with her heart beating so rapidly she felt as if the blades of a helicopter were chopping away at her chest.

The studio was small and overheated. A control board lined the wall perpendicular to the studio window, while the opposite side housed cubbyholes filled with the records that were to be played that week. The room also contained a spinning wooden rack for tape cartridges, a large gray file box for live commercial copy, and, taped to every flat surface, an assortment of announcements and warnings. Francesca seated herself before the control board and clumsily settled the headset over her ears. Her hands wouldn't stop shaking. At small stations like KDSC, there were no engineers to operate the control board; announcers had to do it for themselves. Francesca had spent hours learning how to cue records, operate microphone switches, set voice levels, and use the three tape cartridge—or cart—decks, only two of which she was tall enough to reach from the stool in front of the mike.

As the AP news came to an end, she looked at the row of dials on her control board. In her nervousness, they seemed to be changing shape in front of her, melting like Dali watches until she couldn't remember what any of them were for. She forced herself to concentrate. Her hand flicked to the AP selector switch. She pushed the lever that opened her microphone and potted up the sound on the dial beneath. A trickle of perspiration slid between her breasts. She had to do well. If she messed up today, Clare would never give her a second chance.

As she opened her mouth to speak, her tongue seemed to stick to the roof of her mouth. "Hello," she croaked. "This is Francesca Day coming to you on KDSC with music for a Wednesday morning."

She was talking too fast, running all her words together, and she couldn't think of another thing to say even though she had rehearsed this moment in her mind a hundred times. In a panic, she released the record she was holding on the first turntable and potted up the sound, but she had cued it too close to the beginning of the song and it wowed as she let it go. She moaned audibly, and then realized she hadn't turned off her mike switch so that the moan had carried out over the air. She fumbled with the lever.

In the reception area, Clare watched her through the studio window and shook her head in disgust. Francesca imagined she could hear the word "Twinkie" coming through the soundproof walls.

Her nerves eventually steadied and she did better, but she had listened to enough tapes of good announcers over the past few months to know just how mediocre she was. Her back began to ache from the tension. When her stretch was finally up and she emerged from the studio limp with exhaustion, Katie gave her a sympathetic smile and muttered something about first-time jitters. Clare slammed out of her office and announced that the flu epidemic had spread to Paul Maynard, and she would have to put Francesca on the air again the following afternoon. She spoke so scathingly that Francesca wasn't left with any doubt about how she felt concerning the situation.

That night, as she used one of her four bent kitchen forks to push a clump of overcooked scrambled eggs around her plate, she tried for the thousandth time to figure out what she was doing wrong. Why couldn't she talk into a microphone the way she talked to people?

People. She set down her fork as she was struck by a sudden thought. Clare kept talking about people, but where were they? Impulsively, she jumped up from the table and began leafing through the magazines she had lifted from the station. Eventually, she cut out four photographs of people who looked like the sort who might listen to her show the next day—a young mother, a white-haired old lady, a beautician, and an overweight truck driver like the ones who traveled across the county on the state highway and picked up the KDSC signal for about forty miles. She stared at them for the rest of the evening, making up imaginary life histories and personal foibles. They would be her audience for tomorrow's show. Only these four.

The next afternoon she taped the pictures to the edge of the control board, dropping the old lady twice because her fingers were so clumsy. The morning disc jockey flicked on the AP news, and she sat down to adjust the headset. No more imitation deejay. She was going to do this her own way. She looked at the photographs in front of her—the young mother, the old woman, the beautician, and the truck driver. *Talk to them, dammit. Be yourself, and forget about everything else.*

The AP news ended. She stared into the friendly brown eyes of the young mother, flicked the switch on her microphone, and took a deep breath.

"Hello, everyone, it's Francesca here with music and chit-chat for a Thursday afternoon. Are you having an absolutely wonderful day? I hope so. If not, maybe we can do something about it." *God, she sounded like Mary Poppins.* "I'll be with you all afternoon, for better or for worse, depending on whether or not I can find the right microphone switch." That was better. She could feel herself relaxing a bit. "Let's begin our afternoon together with music." She looked over at her truck driver. He seemed like the sort of man Dallie would like, a beer drinker who enjoyed football and dirty jokes. She gave him a private smile. "Here's an absolutely dreary song I'm going to play for you from Debby Boone. I promise the tunes will get better as we go on."

She potted up the first turntable, turned down her mike, and as Debby Boone's sweet voice came over the monitor, glanced toward the studio window. Three startled faces had popped up like jack-in-the-boxes—Katie's, Clare's, and the news director's. Francesca bit her lip, got her first taped commercial ready, and began to count. She hadn't reached ten before Clare slammed through the studio door.

"Are you out of your mind? What do you mean, a *dreary* song?"

"Personality radio," Francesca said, giving Clare an innocent look and a carefree wave of her hand, as if the whole thing were nothing more than a lark.

Katie stuck her head in the door. "The phone lines are starting to light up, Clare. What do you want me to do?"

Clare thought for a moment and then rounded on Francesca. "All right, *Miss Personality.* Take the calls on the air. And keep your finger on the two-second delay switch, because listeners don't always watch their language."

"On the air? You can't be serious!"

"You're the one who decided to get cute. Don't sleep with sailors if you're afraid of a little VD." Clare stalked out of the studio and took a post by the window where she smoked and listened.

Debby Boone sang the final notes of "You Light Up My Life," and Francesca played a thirty-second commercial for a local lumberyard. When it was done, she hit the mike switch. *People,* she told herself. *You're talking to people.*

"The phone lines are open. Francesca, here. What's on your mind?"

"I think you're a devil worshiper," a crotchety woman's voice said from the other end. "Don't you know that Debby Boone wrote that song about the Lord?"

Francesca stared at the picture of the white-haired lady taped to the control board. How could that sweet old lady have turned on her like this? She bristled. "Did Debby tell you that personally?"

"Don't you sass me," the voice retorted. "We have to listen to all these songs about sex, sex, sex, and then something nice comes along and you make fun of it. Anybody who doesn't like that song doesn't love the Lord."

Francesca glared at her old lady. "That's an awfully narrow-minded attitude, don't you think?"

The woman hung up on her, the slam of the receiver sounding like a bullet passing through her headset. Belatedly, Francesca remembered that these were her listeners and she was supposed to be nice to them. She grimaced at the photograph of her young mother. "I'm sorry. Maybe I shouldn't have said that, but she sounded like a perfectly dreadful person, didn't she?"

Out of the corner of her eye, she could see Clare drop her head and clasp her forehead in the palm of her hand. She made a hasty amendment. "Of course, I've been awfully narrow-minded myself in the past, so I probably shouldn't cast stones." She hit the phone switch. "Francesca, here. What's on your mind?"

"Yeah . . . uh. This is Sam. I'm calling from the Diamond Truck Stop out on U.S. ninety? Listen . . . uh . . . I'm glad you said that about that song."

"You don't like it either, Sam?"

"Naw. As far as I'm concerned, that's about the biggest piece of faggot horseshit music—"

Francesca hit the two-second delay switch just in time. She spoke breathlessly, "You've got a rude mouth, Sam, and I'm cutting you off."

The incident unnerved her, and she knocked her carefully arranged pile of public service announcements to the floor just as the next caller identified herself as Sylvia. "If you think 'Light Up My Life' is so bad, why do you play it?" Sylvia asked.

Francesca decided that the only way she could be a success at this was to be herself—for better or for worse. She looked at her beautician. "Actually, Sylvia, I liked the song at first, but I've gotten tired of it because we play it so many times every day. It's part of our programming policy. If I don't play it once during my show, I could lose my job, and to be perfectly honest with you, my boss doesn't like me all that much anyway."

Clare's mouth opened in a silent scream from the other side of the window.

"I know exactly what you mean," her caller replied. And then to Francesca's surprise, Sylvia confessed that her last boss had made life miserable for her, too. Francesca asked a few sympathetic questions, and Sylvia, who was obviously the chatty sort, replied candidly. An idea began to form. Francesca realized that she had unwittingly hit a common nerve, and she quickly asked other listeners to phone in to talk about their experiences with their employers.

The lines remained lit for a good portion of the next two hours.

When her stretch was up, Francesca emerged from the studio with her sweat shirt sticking to her body and adrenaline still pumping through her veins. Katie, her expression slightly bemused, tilted her head toward the station manager's office.

Francesca resolutely squared her shoulders and walked in to find Clare talking on the telephone. "Of course, I understand your position. Absolutely. And thank you for calling. . . . Oh, yes, I certainly will talk to her." She put the receiver back in the cradle and glared at Francesca, whose feeling of elation had begun to dissolve. "That was the last gentleman you put on the air," Clare said. "The one you told your listeners sounded like 'the sort of baseborn chap who beats his wife and then sends her out to buy beer.'" Clare leaned back in her chair, crossing her arms over her flat bosom. "That 'baseborn chap' happens to be one of our biggest sponsors. At least he *used* to be one of our biggest sponsors."

Francesca felt sick. She'd gone too far. She'd gotten so carried away being herself and talking to her photographs that she'd forgotten to watch her tongue. Hadn't she learned anything these past few months? Was she predestined to go on like this forever, reckless and irresponsible, charging forward without ever once considering the consequences? She thought of the small piece of life nestled inside her. One of her hands instinctively closed over her waist. "I'm sorry, Clare. I didn't mean to let you down. I'm afraid I got carried away." She turned to the door, trying to get away so she could lick her wounds, but she didn't move quickly enough.

"Just where do you think you're going?"

"To the—the bathroom."

"Gawd. The Twinkie is melting at the first sign of trouble."

Francesca spun around. "Dammit, Clare!"

"Dammit, yourself! I told you after I listened to your audition tape that you were talking too fast. Now, I goddamn well want you to slow down before tomorrow."

"Talking too fast?" Francesca couldn't believe it. She had just lost KDSC a sponsor and Clare was yelling at her for talking too fast? And then the rest of what Clare had said registered. "Tomorrow?"

"You bet your sweet ass."

Francesca stared at her. "But what about the sponsor, the man who just called you?"

"Screw him. Sit down, chicky. We're going to make ourselves a radio show."

Within two months, Francesca's ninety-minute talk and interview program had been firmly established as the closest thing KDSC had ever had to a hit, and Clare's hostility toward Francesca had gradually settled into the same casual cynicism she adopted with the rest of the announcers. She continued to berate Francesca for practically everything—talking too fast, mispronouncing words, playing two public service spots back to back—but no matter how outrageous Francesca's comments were on the air, Clare never once censured her. Even though Francesca's spontaneity sometimes got them into trouble, Clare knew good radio when she heard it. She had no intention of killing the goose that was so unexpectedly laying a small golden egg for her backwater radio station. Sponsors began demanding air time on her show, and Francesca's salary quickly rose to one hundred thirty-five dollars a week.

For the first time in her life, Francesca discovered the satisfaction that came from doing a good job, and she received enormous pleasure from the realization that the other staff members genuinely liked her. The Girl Scouts asked her to speak at their annual mother-daughter banquet, and she talked about the importance of hard work. She adopted another stray cat and spent most of one weekend writing a series of public service announcements for the Sulphur City Animal Shelter. The more she opened up her life to other people, the better she felt about herself.

The only cloud on her horizon centered on her worry that Dallie might hear her radio show while he was traveling on U.S. 90 and decide to track her down. Just thinking about what an idiot she'd made of herself with him made her skin crawl. He had laughed at her, patronized her, treated her like a mildly retarded adult, and she had responded by jumping into bed with him and telling herself she was in love. What a spineless little fool she'd been! But she told herself she wasn't spineless any longer, and if Dallie Beaudine had the nerve to stick his nose back into her business, he would regret it. This was her life, her baby, and anybody who got in her way was in for a fight.

Acting on a hunch, Clare began to set up remote broadcasts for Francesca's show from such diverse locales as the local hardware store and the police station. At the hardware store, Francesca learned the correct use of a power drill. At the police station, she endured a mock jailing. Both broadcasts were runaway successes, primarily because Francesca made no secret of how much she hated each experience. She was terrified that the power drill would slip and bite through her hand. And the jail cell where they'd set up the remote was filled with the most hideous bugs she had ever seen.

"Oh, God, that one has pincers!" she moaned to her listeners as she raised her feet off the cracked linoleum floor. "I hate this place—I really do. It's no wonder criminals act so barbaric."

The local sheriff, who was sitting on the other side of the microphone gazing at her like a lovesick calf, squashed the offender with his boot. "Shoot, Miss Francesca, bugs like that don't hardly count. It's centipedes you got to watch out for."

The KDSC listeners heard something that sounded like a cross between a groan and a squeal, and they chuckled to themselves. Francesca had a funny way of reflecting their own human weaknesses. She said what was on her mind and, with surprising frequency, what was on theirs, too, although most of them didn't have the nerve to come out and acknowledge their shortcomings in public the way she did. You had to admire someone like that.

The ratings continued to rise, and Clare Padgett mentally rubbed her hands together with glee.

Using a part of the increase in her salary, Francesca bought an electric fan to try to dispel the stifling afternoon heat in her garage apartment, purchased a Cézanne museum poster to replace the string guitar, and made a down payment on a six-year-old Ford Falcon with body rust. The rest she tucked away in her very first savings account.

Although she knew her looks had improved now that she was eating better and worrying less, she paid little attention to the fact that a healthy glow had returned to her skin and a sheen to her hair. She had neither the time nor the interest to linger in front of a mirror, a pastime that had proved so completely useless to her survival.

The Sulphur City airport advertised a skydiving club, and Clare's normally testy temper took a turn for the worse. She knew a good programming idea when she saw one, but even she couldn't order a woman who was eight months pregnant to jump out of an airplane. Francesca's pregnancy greatly inconvenienced Clare, and as a result she made only the smallest concessions to it.

"We'll schedule the jump two months after your kid is born. That'll give you plenty of time to recover. We'll use a wireless mike so the listeners can hear you scream all the way down."

"I'm not jumping from an airplane!" Francesca exclaimed.

Clare fingered the pile of forms on her desk, part of her attempt to straighten out Francesca's affairs with the U.S. Bureau of Naturalization and Immigration. "If you want these forms filled out, you will."

"That's blackmail."

Clare shrugged. "I'm a realist. You probably won't be around for long, chicky, but while you are, I'm going to suck out every last drop of your blood."

This wasn't the first time Clare had alluded to her future,

and each time she did, Francesca felt a surge of anticipation pass through her. She knew the rule as well as anyone: people who were good didn't stay at KDSC for very long; they moved on to bigger markets.

She waddled out of Clare's office that day feeling pleased with herself. Her show had gone well, she had almost five hundred dollars tucked away in the bank, and a bright future seemed to be waiting for her on the not-so-distant horizon. She smiled to herself. All it took to succeed in life was a small bit of talent and a lot of hard work. And then she saw a familiar figure walking toward her from the front door, and the light went out of her day.

"Aw, hell," Holly Grace Beaudine drawled as she came to a stop in the center of the reception area. "That stupid son of a bitch knocked you up."

Chapter
21

The bubble of Francesca's self-satisfaction abruptly popped. Holly Grace planted five frosty mauve fingernails on the hip of a pair of elegantly tailored white summer trousers and shook her head in disgust. "That man doesn't have any more sense now than he did the day I married him."

Francesca winced as every head in the office turned her way. She felt her cheeks fill with color, and she had a wild urge to cross her hands over her bulging abdomen.

"Do you girls want to use my office to chat?" Clare stood just inside her doorway, obviously enjoying the mini-drama that had sprung up before her.

Holly Grace quickly sized up Clare as the person in authority and announced, "Us *girls* are gonna go someplace and have ourselves a stiff drink. That is, if you don't mind."

"Be my guest." Clare swept her hand toward the door. "I do hope you'll be ready to share some of this excitement with your listeners tomorrow, Francesca. I'm sure they'll be fascinated."

Francesca stayed several steps behind Holly Grace as they crossed the parking lot toward a sleek silver Mercedes. She had no desire to go anywhere with Holly Grace, but she could hardly play out this particular scene in front of her rabidly curious co-workers. The muscles in her shoulders had tightened into knots and she tried to relax them. If she let Holly Grace intimidate her so quickly, she would never recover.

The Mercedes had a pearl gray leather interior that smelled like new money. As Holly Grace got in, she gave the steering wheel a light pat and then pulled a pair of sunglasses from a purse that Francesca instantly recognized as Hermès. Francesca drank in every detail of Holly Grace's wardrobe, from the marvelous turquoise silk halter top that criss-crossed in the back before disappearing into the belted waistband of her beautifully cut trousers to the stunning Peretti chrome cuff bracelet and luscious silver kid Ferragamo sandals. The Sassy ads were everywhere, and so Francesca wasn't surprised to see how well Holly Grace was doing for herself. As casually as possible, Francesca draped her arm over the coffee stain that marred the front of her shapeless yellow cotton maternity dress.

As they rode silently toward Sulphur City, the pit of her stomach filled with dread. Now that she knew about Francesca's baby, Holly Grace would surely go to Dallie. What if he tried to make some claim on her baby? What was she going to do? She stared straight ahead and forced herself to think.

On the outskirts of Sulphur City, Holly Grace slowed down at two separate roadhouses, inspected them, and then drove on. Only when she reached the third and most disreputable-looking did she seem satisfied. "This place looks like it serves good Tex-Mex. I count six pickups and three Harleys. What do you say?"

Even the idea of food made Francesca feel nauseated; she just wanted to get their encounter over with. "Any place is fine with me. I'm not very hungry."

Holly Grace tapped her fingernails on the steering wheel. "The pickups are a real good sign, but you can't always tell with the Harleys. Some of those bikers keep themselves so stoned they wouldn't know the difference between good Tex-Mex and shoe leather." Another pickup pulled into the lot in front of them, and Holly Grace made up her mind. She nosed into a parking place and shut off the engine.

A few minutes later, the two women slid into a booth at the back of the restaurant—Francesca clumsily bumping her stomach against the edge of the table, Holly Grace settling in with a model's elegance. Above them, a set of steer horns and a rattlesnake skin had been nailed to the wall along with several old Texas license plates. Holly Grace pushed her sunglasses on top of her head and nodded toward the Tabasco bottle in the center of the table. "This place is gonna be real good."

A waitress appeared. Holly Grace ordered a tamale-enchilada-taco combination and Francesca ordered iced tea. Holly Grace made no comment about her lack of appetite. She leaned back in the booth, ran her fingers through her hair, and hummed along with the jukebox. Francesca had a vague sense of familiarity, as if she and Holly Grace had done this before. There was something about the tilt of her head, the lazy drape of her arm over the seat back, and the play of light on her hair. Then Francesca realized that Holly Grace reminded her of Dallie.

The silence between them lengthened until Francesca couldn't stand it any longer. A strong offense, she decided, was her only defense. "This isn't Dallie's baby."

Holly Grace regarded her skeptically. "I'm real good at counting."

"It isn't." She stared coldly across the table. "Don't try to make trouble for me. My life is none of your business."

Holly Grace toyed with her Peretti cuff bracelet. "I picked up your radio show when I was driving along Ninety on my way over to Hondo to see an old boyfriend, and I was so surprised to hear you that I almost ran off the road. You do a real good show." She looked up from the bracelet with clear blue eyes. "Dallie was pretty upset when you disappeared like that. Even though I can't blame you for being mad when you found out about me, you really shouldn't have left without talking to him first. He's sensitive."

Francesca thought of any number of responses to that and discarded them all. The baby kicked her hard beneath her ribs.

"You know, Francie, Dallie and I had a little baby boy once, but he died." No emotion was visible in Holly Grace's face. She was merely stating a fact.

"I know. I'm sorry." The words sounded stiff and inadequate.

"If you're having Dallie's baby and you don't let him know, you'd be pretty much of a low-life in my opinion."

"I'm not having his baby," Francesca said. "I had an affair in England, right before I came over. It's his baby, but he married a female mathematician before he knew I was pregnant." It was the story she'd invented in the car, the best she could come up with on short notice, and the only one Dallie might accept when word of this got back to him. She managed to give Holly Grace one of her old haughty looks. "Good gracious, you don't think I would have Dallie's baby without demanding some sort of financial support from him, do you? I'm not stupid."

She saw that she had struck a responsive chord and that Holly Grace was no longer so certain of herself. Francesca's iced tea arrived and she took a sip, then stirred it with her straw, trying to buy time. Should she give more details about Nicky to support her lie or should she keep quiet? Somehow she had to make her story stick.

"Dallie's funny about babies," Holly Grace said. "He doesn't believe in abortion, no matter what the circumstances, which is exactly the sort of hypocrisy I hate in a man. Still, if he knew you were having his baby, he'd probably get a divorce and marry you."

Francesca felt a stir of anger. "I'm not a charity case. I don't *need* to have Dallie marry me." She forced herself to speak more calmly. "Besides, whatever you may think of me, I'm not the kind of woman who'd make one man responsible for another's child."

Holly Grace played with the straw wrapper abandoned on the table. "Why didn't you get an abortion? I would have if I were you."

Francesca was surprised at how easily she could slip back behind her rich-girl facade. She gave a bored shrug. "Who remembers to look at a calendar from one month to the next? By the time I realized what had happened, it was too late."

They didn't say much else until Holly Grace's meal arrived on a platter the size of west Texas. "Are you sure you wouldn't like some of this? I'm supposed to lose four pounds before I go back to New York."

If Francesca hadn't been so much on edge, she would have

laughed as she watched food ooze over the sides of the plate and puddle onto the table. She tried to shift the course of the discussion by asking Holly Grace about her career.

Holly Grace dug into the exact center of her first enchilada. "Have you ever heard any of those talk shows where they interview famous models and all of them say that the job's glamorous, but it's a lot of hard work, too? As far as I can tell, every one of them is lying through her teeth, because I never made so much easy money in my life. In September, I'm even auditioning for a TV show." She set down her fork so she could heap green chili salsa over everything except her Ferragamo sandals. Shrugging her hair away from her face, she picked up her taco, but she didn't lift it to her mouth. Instead, she studied Francesca. "It's too bad you're so short. I know about a dozen photographers who'd think they'd died and gone to homo heaven if you were six inches taller . . . and not pregnant, of course."

Francesca didn't say anything, and Holly Grace fell silent, too. She set down her taco untasted and pierced the center of a mound of refried beans with her fork, twisting it back and forth until she'd made an indentation that looked like an angel's wing. "Dallie and I pretty much stay out of each other's love lives, but it doesn't seem to me I can do that in this case. I'm not absolutely sure you're telling the truth, but I can't exactly come up with a good reason why you'd lie."

Francesca felt a surge of hope, but she kept her expression carefully blank. "I don't really care whether you believe me or not."

Holly Grace continued to twist her fork back and forth in the beans, turning the angel's wing into a full circle. "He's sensitive on the subject of kids. If you're lying to me . . ."

Her stomach in a knot, Francesca took a calculated risk. "I suppose I'd be better off if I told you this *was* his baby. I could certainly use some cash."

Holly Grace bristled like a lioness springing to the defense of her cub. "Don't get any ideas about trying to put the screws to him, because I swear to God I'll testify in court to everything you've told me today. Don't think for one minute that I'll sit on the sidelines and watch Dallie pass out dollar bills to help you raise another man's kid. Got it?"

Francesca hid her relief behind an aristocratic arch of her

eyebrows and a bored sigh, as if this were all just too, too tedious for words. "God, you Americans are so full of melodrama."

Holly Grace's eyes turned as hard as sapphires. "Don't try to screw him over on this, Francie. Dallie and I may have an unorthodox marriage, but that doesn't mean we wouldn't take a bullet for each other."

Francesca pulled a six-shooter of her own from its holster and sighted down the barrel. "You're the one who forced this confrontation, Holly Grace. You can do whatever you want." I take care of myself, she thought fiercely. And I take care of what's mine.

Holly Grace didn't exactly look at her with new respect, but she didn't say anything, either. When their meal was finally over, Francesca grabbed the check, even though she couldn't afford to. For the next few days, she anxiously watched the front door of the station, but when Dallie failed to show up, she concluded that Holly Grace had kept her mouth shut.

Sulphur City was a small, graceless town whose only claim to fame lay in its Fourth of July celebration, which was considered the best in the county, mainly because the Chamber of Commerce rented a tilt-a-whirl every year from Big Dan's Traveling Wild West Show and set it up in the middle of the rodeo arena. In addition to the tilt-a-whirl, tents and awnings encircled the perimeter of the arena and spilled out into the gravel parking lot beyond. Beneath a green and white striped awning, Tupperware ladies showed off pastel lettuce crispers, while in the next tent the County Lung Association exhibited laminated photographs of diseased organs. The pecan growers badgered the Pentecostals, who were handing out tracts with pictures of monkeys on the covers, and children dashed in and out of the tents, snatching up buttons and balloons only to abandon them next to the animal pens, where they set off firecrackers and bottle rockets.

Francesca moved awkwardly through the crowd toward the KDSC remote tent, her toes pointed slightly outward, her hand pressed to the small of her back, which had been aching since yesterday afternoon. Although it was barely ten o'clock in the morning, the mercury had already reached ninety-four and perspiration had formed between her breasts. She gazed longingly toward the Kiwanis Sno-Cone machine, but she had to be on the air in ten minutes to interview the winner of the Miss Sulphur City contest and she didn't have time to stop. A middle-aged rancher with grizzled cheeks and a fat nose slowed his steps and gave her a long, appreciative look. She ignored him. With a full-term pregnancy sticking out in front of her like the *Hindenburg*, she could hardly be anybody's idea of a sex object. The man was obviously some sort of loony who was turned on by pregnant women.

She had almost reached the KDSC tent when the sound of a single trumpet came toward her from the area near the calf pens where the members of the high school band were warming up. She turned her head to see a tall young boy with a hank of light brown hair falling over his eyes and a trumpet pressed to his mouth. As the boy played the notes of "Yankee Doodle Dandy," he turned his head so that the bell of the instrument caught the sun. Francesca's eyes began to tear from the glare, but she couldn't bring herself to look away.

The moment hung suspended in time as the Texas sun burned above her, white and merciless. The smell of hot popcorn and dust mingled with the scent of manure and Belgian waffles. Two Mexican women, chattering in Spanish, passed by with children draped from their plump bodies like ruffled shawls. The tilt-a-whirl clattered along its noisy track, and the Mexican women laughed, and a string of firecrackers went off next to her as Francesca realized that she belonged to it all.

She remained perfectly still while the smells and the sights absorbed her. Somehow, without knowing it, she had become part of this vast, vulgar melting pot of a country—this place of rejects and discards. The hot breeze caught her hair and tossed it about her head so that it waved like a chestnut flag. At that moment, she felt more at home, more complete, more alive, than she ever had felt in England. Without quite knowing how it had happened, she had been absorbed by this hodgepodge of a country, transformed by it, until—

somehow—she, too, had become another feisty, single-minded, ragtag American.

"You better get out of this sun, Francie, before you suffer heat stroke."

Francesca whirled around to see Holly Grace ambling up next to her wearing designer jeans and eating a grape Popsicle. Her heart took a giant leap in the direction of her throat. She had not seen Holly Grace since their lunch together two weeks earlier, but she'd thought about her almost incessantly. "I assumed you'd be back in New York by now," she said warily.

"As a matter of fact, I'm on my way, but I decided to stop by here for a few hours to see how you're doing."

"Is Dallie with you?" She surreptitiously scanned the crowd behind Holly Grace.

To Francesca's relief, Holly Grace shook her head. "I decided not to say anything to him. He's playing in a tournament next week, and he doesn't need any distractions. You look like you're about ready to pop."

"I feel like it, too." Once again she tried to rub the ache from her back, and then, because Holly Grace looked sympathetic and she was feeling very much alone, she added, "The doctor thinks it'll be another week."

"Are you scared?"

She pressed her hand against her side where a small foot was pushing up. "I've been through so much this past year, I can't imagine that giving birth could be any worse." Glancing toward the KDSC tent, she saw Clare waving wildly toward her, and added wryly, "Besides, I'm looking forward to lying down for a few hours."

Holly Grace chuckled and fell in step next to her. "Don't you think it's about time you stopped working and took it easy?"

"I'd like to, but my boss won't give me any more than a month off with pay, and I don't want to start the clock running until the baby's born."

"That woman looks like she eats hardware for breakfast."

"Only the screws."

Holly Grace laughed, and Francesca felt a surprising sense of camaraderie with her. They walked toward the tent together, chatting awkwardly about the weather. A gust of hot air plastered her loose cotton dress to the mound of her stomach. A fire siren went off, and the baby gave her three hard kicks.

Suddenly a wave of pain ripped across her back, the sensation so fierce that her knees began to buckle. She instinctively reached out for Holly Grace. "Oh, dear—"

Holly Grace dropped her Popsicle and grabbed her waist. "Hang on."

Francesca moaned and leaned forward trying to catch her breath. A trickle of amniotic fluid began leaking along the insides of her legs. She leaned into Holly Grace and took a half-step, the sudden wetness squishing into her sandals. Clutching her abdomen, she gasped, "Oh, Natalie . . . you're not acting . . . much like a . . . lady."

Over by the calf pens, cymbals clashed and the boy with the trumpet once again turned the bell of his instrument into the blazing Texas sun and played for all he was worth:

I'm a Yankee Doodle Dandy,
Yankee Doodle do or die,
A real live nephew of my Uncle Sam,
Born on the Fourth of July. . . .

Lighting the Lamp

Chapter
22

He pressed himself flat against the wall, the switchblade clenched in his fist, his thumb next to the button. He didn't want to kill. He found no pleasure in drawing human blood, especially female blood, but the time always came when such a thing was necessary. Tilting his head to the side, he heard the sound he'd been waiting for, the soft ding of the elevator doors opening. Once the woman stepped out, her footsteps would be absorbed by the thick melon-colored carpet that covered the hallway in the expensive Manhattan co-op building, so he began to count softly to himself, every muscle in his body tense, ready to spring into action.

He brushed the pad of his thumb over the button of his switchblade, not hard enough to trigger it, but merely to reassure himself. The city was a jungle to him, and he was a jungle cat—a strong, silent predator who did what he had to.

No one remembered the name he had been born with—time and brutality had erased it. Now the world knew him only as Lasher.

Lasher the Great.

He kept counting, having already calculated the time it would take her to reach the turn in the hallway where he had flattened himself against the subdued paisley wallpaper. And then he caught the faint scent of her perfume. He poised himself to spring. She was beautiful, famous . . . and soon she would be dead!

He sprang forward with a mighty roar as the call for blood raged in his head.

She screamed and stumbled backwards, dropping her purse. He flicked the button on his switchblade with one hand and, looking up at her, pushed his glasses back up on the bridge of his nose with the other. "You're dead meat, China Colt!" Lasher the Great sneered.

"And you're dead *ass,* Theodore Day!" Holly Grace Beaudine leaned over to swat the seat of his camouflage pants with the palm of her hand, then clutched her chest through her down jacket. "Honest to God, Teddy, the next time you do that to me I'm going to take a switch to you."

Teddy, whose I.Q. had been measured in the vicinity of one hundred and seventy by the child study team at his former school in a fashionable suburb of Los Angeles, didn't believe her for a minute. But just to be on the safe side, he gave her a hug, not actually something he minded, since he loved Holly Grace almost as much as he loved his mother.

"Your show was great last night, Holly Grace. I loved the way you used those numbchucks. Will you teach me?" Every Tuesday night he was allowed to stay up and watch "China Colt," even though his mother thought it was too violent for an impressionable nine-year-old kid like himself. "Look at my new switchblade, Holly Grace. Mom bought it for me in Chinatown last week."

Holly Grace took it from his hand, inspected it, and then ran the end through the auburn hair that hung straight and fine over his pale forehead. "Looks more like a switch*comb* to me, buddy boy."

Teddy gave her a disgusted look and reclaimed his weapon. He pushed the black plastic frames of his glasses back up on his nose and messed up the bangs she had just straightened. "Come see my room. My new spaceship wallpaper is up." Without looking back, he took off down the hallway, sneakers flying, canteen banging against his side, Rambo T-shirt tucked into his camouflage pants, which were tightly belted high above his waist, just the way he liked them.

Holly Grace looked after him and smiled. God, she loved that little boy. He had helped fill that awful Danny-ache she

314

had thought she would never lose. But now as she watched him disappear, another ache nagged at her. It was December of 1986. Two months before, she had turned thirty-eight. How had she ever let herself get to be thirty-eight without having another child?

As she bent to pick up the purse she'd dropped, she found herself remembering the hellish Fourth of July when Teddy had been born. The air conditioning hadn't been working at the county hospital and the labor room where they put Francesca already contained five screaming, sweating women. Francesca lay on the narrow bed, her face as pale as death, her skin damp with sweat, and silently endured the contractions that racked her small body. It was her silent suffering that eventually got to Holly Grace—the quiet dignity of her endurance. Right then Holly Grace made up her mind to stand by Francesca. No woman should have a baby by herself, especially one who was so determined not to ask for help.

For the rest of the afternoon and into the evening, Holly Grace wiped Francesca's skin with damp, cool cloths. She held her hand and refused to leave her when they wheeled her into the delivery room. Finally, on that endless Fourth of July just before midnight, Theodore Day was born. The two women had gazed at his small, wrinkled form and then smiled at each other. At that moment, a bond of love and friendship had been formed that had lasted for nearly ten years.

Holly Grace's respect for Francesca had slowly grown over those years until she couldn't think of a person she admired more. For a woman who had started life with more than her fair share of character defects, Francesca had accomplished everything she'd set out to do. She had worked her way from AM radio to local television, gradually moving from smaller markets into bigger ones until she made it to Los Angeles, where her morning television program had eventually caught the attention of the network. Now she was the star of the New York–based "Francesca Today," a Wednesday night talk and interview show that had been chomping up the Nielsens for the past two years.

It hadn't taken viewers long to fall in love with Francesca's offbeat interviewing style, which, as far as Holly

Grace could figure out, was based almost entirely on her complete lack of interest in anything resembling journalistic detachment. Despite her startling beauty and the remnants of her British accent, she somehow managed to remind viewers of themselves. The others—Barbara Walters, Phil Donahue, even Oprah Winfrey—were always in control. Francesca, like millions of her fellow Americans, hardly ever was. She just leaped into the fray and tried her best to hang on, resulting in the most spontaneous television interview show Americans had seen in years.

Teddy's voice rang out from the apartment. "Hurry, Holly Grace!"

"I'm coming, I'm coming." As Holly Grace began walking toward Francesca's co-op apartment, her thoughts drifted back through the years to Teddy's six-month birthday, when she had flown to Dallas where Francesca had just taken a job at one of the city's radio stations. Although they had talked on the phone, it was the first time the two women had seen each other since Teddy's birth. Francesca greeted Holly Grace at her new apartment with a squeal of welcome accompanied by a loud smacking kiss on the cheek. Then she had proudly placed a wiggling bundle in Holly Grace's arms. When Holly Grace had looked down at the baby's solemn little face, any doubts that might have been lurking in her subconscious about Teddy's parentage evaporated. Not even in her wildest imagination could she believe her gorgeous husband had anything to do with the child in her arms. Teddy was adorable, and Holly Grace had instantly loved him with all her heart, but he was just about the ugliest baby she'd ever seen. He was certainly nothing at all like Danny. Whoever had fathered this homely little critter, it couldn't have been Dallie Beaudine.

As the years passed, age had improved Teddy's looks somewhat. His head was well shaped, but a fraction too large for his body. He had auburn hair, wispy-fine and straight as a board, eyebrows and eyelashes so pale they were almost invisible, and cheekbones that he couldn't seem to grow into. Sometimes when he turned his head a certain way, Holly Grace thought she caught a glimpse of how his face would look as a man—strong, distinctive, not unattractive. But until he grew into that face, not even his own mother ever made the mistake of bragging about Teddy's good looks.

"Come on, Holly Grace!" Teddy's head popped back out the paneled white doorway. "Get the lead out!"

"I'll get *your* lead out," she growled, but she walked the rest of the way more quickly. As she entered the foyer, she shrugged out of her down jacket and adjusted the sleeves of a snowy white sweat suit, the legs of which were stuffed into a pair of Italian boots hand tooled with bronze leather flowers. Her trademark blond hair fell well past her shoulders, its color now highlighted with pale silvery streaks. She was wearing a trace of sable brown mascara and a dab of blusher, but little other makeup. She regarded the fine lines that had begun to form at the corners of her eyes as character-building. Besides, it was her day off and she didn't have the patience.

The living room of Francesca's apartment had pale yellow walls, peach moldings, and an exquisite Heriz rug accented in navy. With its English country garden touches of cotton chintz and silk damask, the room was exactly the kind of tastefully elegant and outrageously expensive showplace *House and Garden* loved to feature on its glossy pages, except that Francesca refused to raise a child in a showcase and had, quite casually, sabotaged some of her decorator's best work. The Hubert Robert landscape over the Italian marble fireplace had given way to an elaborately framed crayon rendering of a bright red dinosaur (Theodore Day, circa 1981). A seventeenth-century Italian chest had been moved several feet off center to make room for Teddy's favorite orange vinyl beanbag chair, while the chest itself bore the Mickey Mouse telephone Teddy and Holly Grace had bought as a present for Francesca on her thirty-first birthday.

Holly Grace stepped inside, dropped her purse on a copy of *The New York Times,* and waved to Consuelo, the Spanish woman who took wonderful care of Teddy but left all the dishes for Francesca to wash up when she came home. As she turned away from Consuelo, Holly Grace noticed a girl curled up on the sofa engrossed in a magazine. The girl was sixteen or seventeen with badly bleached hair and a faded bruise on her cheek. Holly Grace stopped in her tracks and then rounded on Teddy with a vehement whisper, "Your mother did it again, didn't she?"

"Mom said to tell you not to scare her."

"This is what I get for going to California for three weeks." Holly Grace grabbed Teddy by the arm and pulled him back to his bedroom out of earshot. As soon as she had shut the door, she exclaimed in frustration, "Dammit, I thought you were going to talk to her? I can't believe she did this again."

Teddy walked over to the shoe box that held his stamp collection and fiddled with the lid. "Her name's Debbie, and she's pretty nice. But the welfare department finally found a foster home for her, so she's leaving in a few days."

"Teddy, that girl's a hooker. She probably has needle tracks in her arm." He began puffing his cheeks in and out, a habit he had when he didn't want to talk about something. Holly Grace groaned in frustration. "Look, honey, why didn't you call me in L.A. right away? I know you're only nine years old, but that genius I.Q. of yours has some responsibilities attached to it, and one of them is to try to keep your mother at least partially in touch with the world of reality. You know she doesn't have an ounce of common sense where this sort of thing is concerned—bedding down runaways, tangling with pimps. She leads with her heart instead of her head."

"I like Debbie," Teddy said stubbornly.

"You liked that Jennifer character, too, and she stole fifty bucks from your Pinocchio bank before she split."

"She left me a note telling me she'd pay it back, and she was the only one who ever took anything."

Holly Grace saw that she was fighting a losing battle. "You should at least have called me."

Teddy picked up the lid of his stamp collection box and put it over his head, decisively ending the conversation. Holly Grace sighed. Sometimes Teddy was sensible, and sometimes he acted just like Francesca.

Half an hour later, she and Teddy were inching their way through the traffic-snarled streets toward Greenwich Village. As Holly Grace stopped for a light, she thought about the beefy forward on the New York Rangers she was meeting for dinner that night. She was certain he would be terrific in bed, but the fact that she couldn't take advantage of it depressed her. AIDS really pissed her off. Just when women had finally gotten themselves as sexually liberated as men, this awful disease had to come along and stop all the fun. She used to enjoy her one-night stands. She would put her lover through all his best tricks and then kick him out before he had a chance to expect her to make breakfast for him. Whoever said sex with a stranger was demeaning had to be somebody who liked to cook breakfast. Resolutely, she pushed aside the stubborn image of a dark-haired man whose breakfast she had very much liked cooking. That affair had been temporary insanity on her part—a disastrous case of rampaging hormones blinding her judgment.

Holly Grace leaned on the horn as the light changed and a moron in a Dodge Daytona cut in front of her, barely missing the fender of her newest Mercedes. It seemed to her that AIDS had affected everybody with any sense. Even her ex-husband had been sexually monogamous for the past year. She frowned, still upset with him. She certainly didn't have anything against monogamy these days, but unfortunately Dallie was practicing it with someone named Bambi.

"Holly Grace?" Teddy said, looking over at her from the soft depths of the passenger seat. "Do you think it's right for a teacher to flunk a kid just because maybe that kid doesn't do a dumb science project for his gifted class like he's supposed to?"

"This doesn't exactly sound like a theoretical question," Holly Grace replied dryly.

"What's that mean?"

"It means you should have done your science project."

"This one was dumb." Teddy scowled. "Why would anybody want to go around killing a bunch of bugs and sticking them to a board with pins? Don't you think that's dumb?"

Holly Grace was beginning to get the drift. Despite Teddy's penchant for war games and filling every sheet of drawing paper he put his hands on with pictures of guns and knives, most of them dripping blood, the child was a pacifist at heart. She had once seen him carry a spider down seventeen floors in the elevator so he could release it on the street. "Did you talk to your mother about this?"

"Yeah. She called my gifted teacher to ask if I could draw the bugs instead of killing them, but when Miss Pearson said no, they ended up getting in an argument and Miss Pearson hung up. Mom doesn't like Miss Pearson. She thinks she puts too much pressure on us kids. Finally Mom said she'd kill the bugs for me."

Holly Grace rolled her eyes at the idea of Francesca killing anything. If any bugs had to be killed, she had a pretty strong notion who would end up doing the job. "That seems to solve your problem, then, doesn't it?"

Teddy looked over at her, a picture of offended dignity. "What kind of jerk do you think I am? What difference would it make to the bugs whether I killed them or she did? They'd still be dead because of me."

Holly Grace looked over at him and smiled. She loved this kid—she really did.

Naomi Jaffe Tanaka Perlman's quaint little mews house was set on a small cobbled Greenwich Village street that held one of New York's few surviving bishop's-crook lampposts. A tangle of winter-bare wisteria vines clung to the green shutters and white-painted brick of the house, which Naomi had purchased with some of the profits from the ad agency she'd started four years ago. She lived there with her second husband, Benjamin R. Perlman, a professor of political science at Columbia. As far as Holly Grace could see, the two of them had a marital match made in left-wing heaven. They gave money to every goosey cause that came their way, held cocktail parties for people who wanted to bust up the CIA, and worked in a soup kitchen once a week for relaxation. Still, Holly Grace had to admit that Naomi had never seemed more content. Naomi had told her that, for the first time in her life, she felt as if all the parts of herself had come together.

Naomi led them into her cozy living room, waddling more than Holly Grace thought necessary, since she was only five months pregnant. Holly Grace hated the gnawing envy that ate away at her every time she looked at Naomi's waddle, but she couldn't seem to help it, even though Naomi had been her good friend ever since their Sassy days. But every time she looked at Naomi, she couldn't help thinking that if she didn't have a baby soon, she would lose her chance forever.

". . . so she's going to fail me in science," Teddy concluded from the kitchen, where he and Naomi had gone for refreshments.

"But that's barbaric," Naomi replied. The blender whirred for a few moments and then shut off. ". . . think you should petition. This has to be a violation of your civil rights. I'm going to talk to Ben."

"That's all right," Teddy said. "I think Mom got me into enough trouble with my teacher as it is."

Moments later, they emerged from the kitchen, Teddy with a bottle of natural fruit soda in his hand and Naomi holding out a strawberry daiquiri to Holly Grace. "Did you hear about that bizarre insect assassination project at Teddy's school?" she asked. "If I were Francesca, I'd sue. I really would."

Holly Grace took a sip of her daiquiri. "I think Francesca might have a few more important things on her mind right now."

Naomi smiled, then glanced toward Teddy, who was disappearing into the bedroom to get Ben's chess set. "Do you think she'll do it?" she whispered.

"It's hard to say. When you see Francesca rolling around the floor in her jeans and giggling with Teddy like a fool, it seems pretty impossible. But when somebody upsets her, and she gets that snooty look on her face, you just know a few of her ancestors had to have had blue blood, and then you've got to think that it's a real possibility."

Naomi eased down in front of the coffee table, folding her legs so she looked like a pregnant Buddha. "I'm opposed to monarchy on principle, but I have to admit that Princess Francesca Serritella Day Brancuzi has a terrific ring."

Teddy returned with the chess set and began setting it up on the coffee table. "Concentrate this time, Naomi. You're almost as easy to beat as Mom."

Suddenly they all jumped as three sharp bangs sounded at the front door. "Oh, dear," Naomi said, glancing apprehensively toward Holly Grace. "I only know one person who knocks like that."

"Don't you dare let him in while I'm here!" Holly Grace jerked forward, splashing strawberry daiquiri down the front of her white sweat suit.

"Gerry!" Teddy shrieked, racing for the door.

"Don't open it," Holly Grace called out, jumping up. "No, Teddy!"

But it was too late. Not enough men passed through Teddy Day's life for him to give up a chance to be with any one of them. Before Holly Grace could stop him, he had flung open the door.

"Hey, Teddy!" Gerry Jaffe called out, offering the palms of his hands. "What's happenin', my man?"

Teddy slapped him ten. "Hey, Gerry! I haven't seen you in a couple of weeks. Where have you been?"

"In court, kiddo, defending some people who did a little damage to the Shoreham nuclear power plant."

"Did you win?"

"You might say that it was a draw."

Gerry never regretted the decision he'd reached in Mexico ten years before to come back to the United States, face the New York City cops and their trumped-up drug charge, and then, after his name was cleared, go on to law school. One by one, he had watched the leaders of the Movement change direction—Eldridge Cleaver's soul no longer on ice but dedicated to Jesus, Jerry Rubin sucking up to capitalism, Bobby Seale peddling barbecue sauce. Abbie Hoffman was still around, but he was caught up in environmental causes, which left it up to Gerry Jaffe, the last of the sixties radicals, to draw the attention of the world away from stainless-steel pasta machines and designer pizzas and back to the possibility of nuclear winter. With all his heart, Gerry believed that the future rested on his shoulders, and the heavier the weight of responsibility, the more he played the clown.

After giving Naomi a smack on the lips, he leaned down to speak directly to her belly. "Listen up, kid, this is Uncle Gerry talking. The world sucks. Stay in there as long as you can."

Teddy thought this was hysterically funny and began to roll on the floor, shrieking with laughter. This action brought him the attention of all the adults, so he laughed louder, until he ceased being cute and became merely annoying. Naomi believed in letting children express themselves, so she didn't reprimand him, and Holly Grace, who didn't believe any such thing, was too distracted by the sight of Gerry's impressive shoulders straining the seams of his worn leather bomber jacket to call Teddy to task.

In 1980, not long after Gerry had passed the New York Bar exam, he had given up his Afro, but he still wore his hair long in the back so that the dark curls, now lightly threaded with gray, fell over his collar. Beneath his leather jacket, he was wearing his normal work attire—baggy khaki trousers and a cotton fatigue sweater. A No Nukes button graced the jacket collar. His mouth was as full and sensuous as ever, his nose as bold, and his zealot's eyes still black and burning. That exact pair of eyes had done in Holly Grace Beaudine a year ago when she and Gerry had found themselves shoved into a corner together at one of Naomi's parties.

Holly Grace still had a hard time explaining to herself what it was about Gerry Jaffe that had made her fall in love with him. It certainly hadn't been his politics. She honestly believed in the importance of a strong military defense for the United States, a position that drove him wild. They had raging political arguments, which generally ended in some of the most incredible lovemaking she had experienced in years. Gerry, who had few inhibitions in public, had even fewer in the bedroom.

But her attraction to him was more than sexual. For one thing, he was as physically active as she. During the three months of their affair they had taken skydiving lessons together, gone mountain climbing, and even tried hang gliding. Being with him was like living in a never-ending adventure. She loved the excitement he engendered around him. She loved his passion and his zeal, the zest with which he ate his food, his uninhibited laughter, his unabashed sentimentality. She had once walked into the room and found him crying at a Kodak television commercial, and when she had teased him about it, he hadn't made a single excuse. She had even grown to love his male chauvinism. Unlike Dallie who, despite his good ol' boy demeanor, had always been the most liberated man she'd ever known, Gerry clung to ideas about male-female relationships that were firmly entrenched in the fifties. And Gerry always looked so befuddled when she confronted him with it, so crestfallen that he—the darling of the radicals—couldn't seem to comprehend one of the most basic principles of an entire social revolution.

"Hello, Holly Grace," he said, walking toward her.

She leaned over to put her sticky strawberry daiquiri on the coffee table and tried to look at him as if she couldn't quite remember his name. "Oh, hi, Gerry."

Her ploy didn't work. He came closer, his compact body advancing with a determination that sent a shiver of apprehension through her. "Don't you dare touch me, you commie terrorist," she warned, thrusting out her hand as if it held a crucifix that could ward him off.

He stepped past the coffee table.

"I mean it, Gerry."

"What are you afraid of, babe?"

"Afraid!" she scoffed, taking three steps back. "Me? Afraid of you? In your dreams, you left-wing pinko."

"God, Holly Grace, you've got a mouth on you." He stopped in front of her and without turning addressed his sister. "Naomi, could you and Teddy find something to do in the kitchen for a few minutes?"

"Don't even think about leaving, Naomi," Holly Grace ordered.

"Sorry, Holly Grace, but tension isn't good for a pregnant woman. Come on, Teddy. Let's go make some popcorn."

Holly Grace took a deep breath. This time she wouldn't allow Gerry to get the best of her, no matter what he did. Their affair had lasted for three months, and he'd taken advantage of her the entire time. While she had been falling in love, he had been merely using her celebrity as a way of getting his name in the newspapers so he could publicize his anti-nuclear activities. Holly Grace couldn't believe what a sucker she'd been. Old radicals never changed. They just got law degrees and updated their bag of tricks.

Gerry reached out to touch her, but physical contact with him tended to cloud her thinking, so she jerked her arm away before he could make contact. "Keep your hands to yourself, buster." She had survived these last few months without him very nicely, and she wasn't going to have a relapse now. She was too old to die twice in one year from a broken heart.

"Don't you think this separation has gone on long enough?" he said. "I miss you."

She gave him her coolest stare. "What's wrong? Can't you get your face on television, now that we're not an item anymore?" She used to love the way those dark curls brushed along the back of his neck. She remembered the texture of those curls—soft and silky. She would wrap them around her finger, touch them with her lips.

"Don't start on this, Holly Grace."

"Won't anybody let you make speeches on the nightly news, now that we've broken up?" she said nastily. "You really played our affair for all it was worth, didn't you? While I was mooning over you like a stupid fool, you were sending out press releases."

"You're really starting to piss me off. I love you, Holly Grace. I love you more than I've ever loved anyone in my life. We had something good going."

He was doing it. He was breaking her heart again. "The only good thing we had going was sex," she said fiercely.

"We had a hell of a lot more than sex!"

"Such as what? I don't like your friends, and I sure as hell don't like your politics. Besides, you know I hate Jews."

Gerry groaned and slumped down on the couch. "Oh, God, here we go again."

"I'm a dedicated anti-Semite. I really am, Gerry. I'm from Texas. I hate Jews, I hate blacks, and I think all gay men should be put in prison. Now what kind of future would I have with a left-wing pinko like you?"

"You don't hate Jews," Gerry said reasonably, as if he were speaking to a child. "And three years ago you signed a gay rights petition that was published in every newspaper in New York, and the year after that you had a highly publicized affair with a certain wide receiver for the Pittsburgh Steelers."

"He was very light-skinned," Holly Grace countered. "And he always voted Republican."

Slowly he got up from the couch, his expression both

troubled and tender. "Look, babe, I can't give up my politics, not even for you. I know you don't approve of our approach—"

"All of you people are so goddamn sanctimonious," she hissed. "You treat anyone who doesn't agree with your methods like a warmonger. Well, I've got news for you, buddy boy. No sane person likes living with nuclear weapons, but not everybody thinks it's a terrific idea for us to throw all our missiles away while the Soviets are still sitting on top of a whole toy box full of their own."

"Don't you think the Soviets—"

"I'm not listening to you." She grabbed her purse and called out for Teddy. Dallie had been right every one of those times he'd told her money couldn't buy happiness. She was thirty-seven years old and she wanted to nest. She wanted a baby while she could still have one, and she wanted a husband who loved her for herself, not just for the publicity she brought him.

"Holly Grace, please—"

"You go fuck yourself."

"Goddammit!" He grabbed her then, pulled her into his arms, and pressed his mouth to hers in a gesture that wasn't so much a kiss as a way of distracting himself from his desire to shake her until her teeth rattled. They were the same height, and Holly Grace worked out with weights, so Gerry had to use considerable strength to pin her arms to her sides. She finally stopped struggling so that he could work her over with his mouth the way he wanted to—the way she liked. Finally her lips parted enough so that he could slip his tongue inside.

"Come on, babe," he whispered. "Love me back."

She did, just for a moment, until she realized what she was doing. When Gerry felt her stiffen, he immediately slid his mouth to her neck where he took a long, sucking bite.

"You did it to me again," she yelped, squirming away from him and clasping her neck.

He had put his mark on her deliberately and he didn't apologize. "Every time you look at that mark, I want you to remember that you're throwing away the best thing that's ever happened to either one of us."

Holly Grace gave him a furious glare and then spun

around toward Teddy, who had just come into the room with Naomi. "Get your coat and tell Naomi good-bye."

"But Holly Grace—" Teddy protested.

"Now!" She bundled Teddy into his coat, grabbed her own, and propelled the two of them out the door without looking back.

As they disappeared, Gerry avoided the displeasure in his sister's eyes by pretending to study a metal sculpture on the mantel. Even though he was forty-two, he wasn't used to being the mature one in a relationship. He was used to women who mothered him, who agreed with his opinions, who cleaned his apartment. He wasn't used to a prickly Texas beauty who could outdrink him any day of the week and who would laugh in his face if he asked her to run a small load of wash. He loved her so much he felt as if a part of him had walked out of the house with her. What was he going to do? He couldn't deny that he'd taken advantage of the publicity from their affair. It was instinctive—the way he did things. For the past few years, the media had ignored his best efforts to draw attention to the cause, and it wasn't in his nature to turn his back on free publicity. Why couldn't she understand that it didn't have a damned thing to do with loving her—he was just seizing his opportunities as he'd always done.

His sister walked past him, and he once again leaned over to address her stomach. "This is Uncle Gerry speaking. If you're a male child in there, guard your balls because there are about a million women out here waiting to cut them off."

"Don't joke about it, Gerry," Naomi said, dropping down into one of the armchairs.

His mouth twisted. "Why not? You've got to admit this whole thing with Holly Grace is pretty goddamn funny."

"You're really screwing up," she said.

"It's impossible to argue with someone who doesn't make sense," he retorted belligerently. "She knows I love her, and she goddamn well knows it's not just for her famous name."

"She wants a baby, Gerry," Naomi said quietly.

He stiffened. "She just thinks she wants a baby."

"You're such a jerk. Every time the two of you get together, both of you go on and on about your political differences and who's using who. Just once, I'd like to hear one of you admit that most of the reason the two of you can't get it together is because she desperately wants to have a baby and you still haven't grown up enough to be a father."

He turned on his sister. "It doesn't have anything to do with not being grown up. I refuse to bring a kid into a world that has a mushroom cloud hanging over it."

She regarded him sadly, one hand clasped over her rounded stomach. "Who do you think you're kidding, Gerry? You're afraid to be a father. You're afraid you'll screw up as badly with your own kid as Dad did with you—God rest his soul."

Gerry didn't say anything, and he damn well wasn't going to let Naomi see him with tears in his eyes, so he just turned his back on her and stalked right out the door.

Chapter
23

Francesca smiled directly into the camera as the "Francesca Today" theme music faded and the show began. "Hello, everybody. I hope all of you have your television snacks nearby and that you've finished any urgent bathroom business, because I absolutely guarantee that you're not going to want to move from your seats once you meet our four young guests this evening."

She tilted her head toward the red light that had come on next to camera two. "Tonight we're broadcasting the last show in our series on the British nobility. As you know, we've had our high points and our low points since we've come to Great Britain—even I won't try to pretend that our last program was anything short of a giant bore—but we're back on track tonight."

Out of the corner of her eye, she saw that her producer, Nathan Hurd, had planted his hands on his hips, a sure sign that he was displeased. He hated it when she admitted on the air that one of their shows wasn't wonderful, but her famous royal guest on the last program had been incredibly long-winded and even her most impertinent questions hadn't livened him up. Unfortunately, that program, unlike the one they were now taping, had been broadcast live, so they hadn't been able to redo it.

"With me this evening are four attractive young people,

all of them children of famous peers of the British realm. Have you ever wondered what it would be like to grow up knowing that your life has already been mapped out for you? Do young royals ever feel like rebelling? Let's ask."

Francesca introduced her four guests, who were comfortably seated in the attractive living room arrangement that approximated the New York studio set where "Francesca Today" was normally taped. Then she turned her attention to the only child of one of Great Britain's most renowned dukes. "Lady Jane, have you ever thought about chucking family tradition and running off with the chauffeur?"

Lady Jane laughed, then blushed, and Francesca knew she had the beginnings of an entertaining show.

Two hours later, with the taping finished and her young guests' responses lively enough to keep the ratings up, Francesca stepped out of her taxi and entered the Connaught. Most Americans regarded Claridge's as the ultimate London hotel, but as someone who didn't want to be away from home in the first place, Francesca felt that the better choice was the tiny Connaught, which had only ninety rooms, the best service in the world, and a minimal chance of running into a rock star in the corridor.

Her tiny frame was swathed from chin to midcalf in an elegant black Russian sable, which was set off by a pair of perfect pear-shaped four-carat diamond stud earrings that sparkled through the windblown chestnut of her hair. The lobby, with its Oriental rugs and dark-paneled walls, was warm and inviting after the damp December streets of Mayfair. A magnificent staircase covered by a brass-bordered carpet circled upward six stories, its mahogany banisters gleaming with polish. Although she was exhausted from a hectic week, she managed a smile for the hall porter. The head of every man in the lobby turned as she made her way to the small elevator located near the desk, but she didn't notice.

Beneath the elegance of the sable and the expensive dazzle of the pear-shaped studs, Francesca's clothing was frankly funky. She had changed from her more conservative on-camera outfit into the clothes she had worn to the studio that morning—cropped, tight-fitting black leather pants accompanied by an oversize raspberry sweater appliquéd with a taupe teddy bear. Matching raspberry socks, neatly folded over at the tops, set off a pair of Susan Bennis flats. It was an outfit that Teddy especially liked, since cuddly-looking bears and leather-clad motorcycle gangs were among his favorite things. She frequently wore it when they went out for the day, whether to raid F.A.O. Schwarz for a chemistry set, to visit the Temple of Dendur at the Metropolitan, or to pay a call on a slimy-looking pretzel vendor in Times Square whose wares, Teddy insisted, were the best in Manhattan.

Despite her exhaustion, the thought of Teddy made Francesca smile. She missed him so much. It was awful being separated from her child, so awful that she had been seriously thinking about cutting down on her work schedule when her contract came up for renewal in the spring. What good was it to have a child if she couldn't spend time with him? The veil of depression that had been hanging over her for months settled lower. She had been so short-tempered lately, a sure sign that she was working too hard. But she hated to slow down when everything was going so well.

Stepping out of the elevator, she glanced at her watch and made a quick calculation. Yesterday Holly Grace had taken Teddy to Naomi's house, and today they were supposed to go to the South Street Seaport Museum. Maybe she could catch him before he left. She frowned as she remembered that Holly Grace had told her Dallas Beaudine was coming to New York. After all these years, the idea of Teddy and Dallie in the same town still made her nervous. It wasn't that she feared recognition; God knew there wasn't anything about Teddy that would remind Dallie of himself. It was simply that she disliked the thought of Dallie having anything to do with her son.

She slipped her sable over a satin-covered hanger and hung it in the closet. Then she placed a call to New York. To her delight, Teddy answered the phone.

"Day residence. Theodore speaking."

Just the sound of his voice made Francesca's eyes mist. "Hello, baby."

"Mom! Guess what, Mom? I went to Naomi's yesterday and Gerry showed up, and him and Holly Grace had another fight. Today she's taking me to the South Street

Seaport, and then we're going to her apartment and order Chinese. And you know my friend Jason . . ."

Francesca smiled as she listened to Teddy rattle on. When he finally paused for breath, she said, "I miss you, honey. Remember, I'll be home in a few days, and then we'll have two whole weeks of vacation together in Mexico. We're going to have such a good time." It was to be her first real vacation since she had signed her contract with the network, and the two of them had been looking forward to it for months.

"Will you swim in the ocean this time?"

"I'll wade," she conceded.

He gave a scornful masculine snort. "At least go up to your waist."

"I'll compromise on my knees, but no farther."

"You're really a chicken, Mom," he said solemnly. "A lot more chicken than me."

"You're absolutely right about that."

"Are you studying for your citizenship exam?" he said. "The last time I asked you the test questions, you messed up the whole part about bills getting passed into law."

"I'll study on the plane," she promised. Applying for American citizenship was something she had postponed far too long. She had always been too busy, too tightly scheduled, until one day she realized that she had lived in the country for ten years and had never cast a ballot. She had been ashamed of herself and, with Teddy helping her, had begun the lengthy application process that same week.

"I love you big heaps, honey," she said.

"Me, too."

"And will you be especially nice to Holly Grace tonight? I don't expect you to understand, but it upsets her when she sees Gerry."

"I don't know why. Gerry's cool."

Francesca was too wise to try to explain the subtleties of male-female relationships to a nine-year-old boy, especially one who thought all girls were jerks. "Just be extra nice to her, sweetie," she said.

When she had finished her phone call, she undressed and began getting ready for her evening with Prince Stefan

Marko Brancuzi. Wrapping herself in a silk robe, she walked into the tiled bathroom where plump cakes of her favorite soap sat by the roomy tub, along with her customary brand of American shampoo. The Connaught made it their business to know their guests' grooming preferences, along with the papers they read, how they wanted their coffee in the morning, and, in Francesca's case, the fact that Teddy collected bottle caps. A supply of unusual European beer caps always awaited her in a neatly tied parcel when she checked out. She'd never quite had the heart to tell them that Teddy's idea of collecting bottle caps was based more on quantity than on quality, with Pepsi currently beating out Coke by 394.

She eased herself into the hot bathwater and when her skin had adjusted to the temperature, settled back and shut her eyes. God, she was tired. She needed a vacation so badly. A small voice nagged at her, asking how much longer she was going to go on like this—leaving her child to fly all over the world at the drop of a hat, attending endless production meetings, skimming stacks of books every night before she went to sleep? Lately Holly Grace and Naomi had been with Teddy more than she had.

Thoughts of Holly Grace pushed her mind in a slow circle back to Dallas Beaudine.

Her encounter with him had taken place so long ago that it no longer seemed anything more than an accident of biology that he'd fathered Teddy. He wasn't the one who had given birth, or gone without nylons in those early years to pay for corrective baby shoes, or lost sleep worrying about raising a child whose I.Q. was a good forty points higher than her own. Francesca, not Dallie Beaudine, was responsible for the person Teddy had become. No matter how hard Holly Grace pushed, Francesca refused to let him back into even the smallest corner of her life.

"Aw, come on, Francie, it's been ten years," Holly Grace had complained the last time they'd talked about it. They had been lunching at the newly opened Aurora on East Forty-ninth, sitting on a leather banquette off to one side of the granite horseshoe bar. "In a few weeks Dallie's going to be in the city talking to the network about doing color commentary for their golf tournaments this spring. How about you relax your rules for a change and let me take Teddy to meet him? Teddy's heard stories about Dallie for years, and Dallie's curious about Teddy after listening to me ramble on about him so much."

"Absolutely not!" Francesca speared a morsel of duck *confit* lightly coated in hazelnut oil from her salad and made the excuse she always made when the topic came up, the only one Holly Grace seemed to accept. "That time with Dallie was the most humiliating period of my entire life, and I refuse to bring back even the smallest memory of it. I won't have any contact with him ever again—and that means keeping Teddy away, too. You know how I feel about this, Holly Grace, and you promised you wouldn't push me again."

Holly Grace was clearly exasperated. "Francie, that boy is going to grow up queer if you don't let him associate with more members of the male sex."

"You're all the father a boy needs," Francesca replied dryly, feeling both exasperation and deep affection for the woman who had stood by her through so much.

Holly Grace chose to take Francesca's remark seriously. "I sure haven't been able to make a success of his athletic career." She stared glumly toward the frosted globes hanging over the bar. "Honest to God, Francie, he's got more left feet than you do."

Francesca knew she was too defensive about Teddy's lack of a father, but she couldn't help herself. "I tried, didn't I? You made me pitch balls to him when he was four years old."

"And wasn't that a great moment in baseball history," Holly Grace replied with withering sarcasm. "Helen Keller pitching and Little Stevie Wonder catching. The two of you are the most uncoordinated—"

"You didn't do any better with him. He fell off that awful horse when you took him riding, and he broke his finger the first time you threw a football at him."

"That's one of the reasons I want him to meet Dallie. Now that Teddy's getting a little older, Dallie might have some ideas about what to do with him." Holly Grace extracted a sprig of watercress from beneath a flaky piece of smoked sea bass and munched on it contemplatively. "I don't know—it must be all that foreign blood Teddy's got. Damn, if Dallie really had been his father, we wouldn't have this problem. Athletic coordination is programmed in all the Beaudine genes."

A lot you know, Francesca thought with a wry smile, as she lathered her arms and then moved the soapy loofah over her legs. Sometimes she found herself wondering what wonderful, wayward chromosome had produced her son. She knew that Holly Grace was disappointed that Teddy wasn't better looking, but Francesca had always regarded Teddy's sweet, homely face as a gift. It would never occur to Teddy to rely on good looks to get through life. He would use his brain, his courage, and his sweet, sentimental heart.

The water in the tub was growing tepid, and she realized she had barely twenty minutes before the driver arrived to take her to Stefan's yacht for dinner. Although she was tired, she was looking forward to spending the night with Stefan. After several months of long-distance phone calls with only a few rushed face-to-face meetings, she felt that the time had definitely come to deepen their relationship. Unfortunately, working fourteen-hour days since she had arrived in London hadn't left her with any spare time for sexual frolicking. But with the last show on tape, all she had left to do tomorrow was stand in front of various British monuments for some tourist shots they planned to use at the end of the broadcast. She had made up her mind that before she flew back to New York, she and Stefan were going to spend at least two nights together.

Despite the pressures of the clock, she picked up the soap and absentmindedly rubbed it over her breasts. They tingled, reminding her of how glad she would be to end her year of self-imposed celibacy. It wasn't that she'd planned to be celibate for so long, it was just that she seemed psychologically incapable of bed-hopping. Holly Grace might mourn the passing of the one-night stand, but regardless of how much Francesca's healthy body nagged at her, she found sex without emotional attachment an arid, awkward business.

Two years ago, she had nearly married a charismatic

young California congressman. He was handsome, successful, and wonderful in bed. But he nearly went crazy whenever she brought home one of her runaways and he hardly ever laughed at her jokes, so she had finally stopped seeing him. Prince Stefan Marko Brancuzi was the first man she'd met since then whom she cared enough about to sleep with.

They had met several months before when she'd interviewed him on her show. She had found Stefan both charming and intelligent, and he had soon proven himself to be a good friend. But was caring the same thing as loving, she wondered, or was she just trying to find a way out of the dissatisfaction she had been feeling with her life?

Shaking off her melancholy mood, she toweled herself dry and slipped on her robe. Knotting the sash, she moved to the mirror, where she applied her makeup efficiently, allowing no time for either scrutiny or admiration. She took care of herself because it was her business to look good, but when people raved about her sage green eyes, her delicate cheekbones and gleaming chestnut hair, Francesca found herself withdrawing from them. Painful experience had taught her that being born with a face like hers was more of a liability than an asset. Strength of character came from hard work, not smoky-thick eyelashes.

Clothes, however, were another matter.

Surveying the four evening outfits she had brought with her, she passed up a silver-studded Kamali and a yummy Donna Karan, deciding instead on a strapless black silk faille designed by Gianni Versace. The gown bared her shoulders, cinched her waist, and then fell in soft, uneven tiers to mid-calf. Dressing quickly, she gathered up her purse and reached for her sable. As her fingers brushed the soft fur collar, she hesitated, wishing Stefan hadn't given her the coat. But he'd been so upset when she'd tried to refuse it that she'd eventually given in. Still, she disliked the idea of all those furry little animals dying so she could be fashionably dressed. Also, the lavishness of the gift subtly offended her sense of self-reliance.

With a stubborn set to her jaw, she passed over the fur for a flaming fuchsia shawl. Then, for the first time that evening, she really looked at herself in the mirror. Versace gown, pear-shaped diamond studs, black stockings sprinkled with a mist of tiny jet beads, slim Italian heels—all luxuries she had bought for herself. A smile tugged at the corners of her mouth as she draped the fuchsia shawl around her bare shoulders and made her way to the elevator.

God bless America.

Chapter
24

You're sellin' out, is what it is," Skeet said to Dallie, who was scowling at the back of the cab driver's neck as the taxi crawled down Fifth Avenue. "You can try to paint a pretty face on it, talkin' 'bout *new opportunities* and *expanding horizons,* but what you're doin' is giving up."

"What I'm doing is being realistic," Dallie answered with some irritation. "If you weren't so goddamn ignorant, you'd see that this is just about the chance of a lifetime." Riding in a car with someone else driving always put Dallie in a bad mood, but when he was stuck in a Manhattan traffic jam and the man behind the wheel could only speak Farsi, Dallie passed the point of being fit for human company.

He and Skeet had spent the last two hours at the Tavern on the Green, being wined and dined by the network brass, who wanted Dallie to sign an exclusive five-year contract to do color commentary during their golf tournaments. He had done some announcing for them the year before while he was recovering from a fractured wrist, and the audience response had been so favorable that the network had immediately gone after him. Dallie had the same humorous, irreverent attitude on the air as Lee Trevino and Dave Marr, currently the most entertaining of the color commentators. But as one of the network vice-presidents had remarked to his third wife, Dallie was a hell of a lot prettier than either one.

Dallie had made a sartorial concession to the importance of the occasion by putting on a navy suit, along with a respectable maroon silk tie neatly knotted at the collar of his pale blue dress shirt. Skeet, however, had settled for a corduroy jacket from J. C. Penney's along with a string tie he'd won in the fall of 1973 pitching dimes into goldfish bowls.

"You're sellin' out your God-given talent," Skeet insisted stubbornly.

Dallie whipped around to glower at him. "You're a damn hypocrite, is what you are. For as long as I can remember, you've been pushing Hollywood talent agents down my throat and trying to get me to pose for pinup pictures wearing nothing but my jockstrap, but now that I have an offer with a little dignity attached to it, you're getting all indignant."

"Those other offers didn't interfere with your *golf*. Dammit, Dallie, you wouldn't have missed a single tournament if you'd done a guest shot on 'The Love Boat' during the off season, but we're talking about something entirely different here. We're talkin' about you sitting up in an announcer's booth making wise-ass remarks about Greg Norman's pink shirts while Norman's out there making golf history. We're talking about the end of your professional career! I didn't hear those network honchos say anything about you coming up into the announcers' booth only on the days you don't make the cut, the way Nicklaus does, and some of the other big boys. They're talkin' about having you there full-time. In the announcers' booth, Dallie—not out on the golf course."

It was one of the longest speeches Dallie had ever heard Skeet make, and the sheer volume of words held him momentarily in check. But then Skeet muttered something under his breath, aggravating Dallie almost past the point of endurance. He managed to keep a rein on his temper only because he knew that these past few golf seasons had just about broken Skeet Cooper's heart.

It had all started a few years back when he'd been driving

home from a Wichita Falls bar and had almost killed a teenage kid riding a ten-speed bike. He'd given up taking illegal pharmaceuticals in the late seventies, but he'd continued his friendship with the beer bottle right up until that night. The boy ended up with nothing more serious than a broken rib, and the cops had gone a lot easier on Dallie than he'd deserved, but he'd been so badly shaken that he'd given up booze right after. It hadn't been easy, which told him just how much he'd been kidding himself about his drinking. He might never survive the cut at the Masters or finish in the money at the U.S. Classic, but he would be damned if he'd kill a kid because he drank too goddamn much.

To his surprise, going on the wagon had immediately improved his game, and the next month he'd taken a third in the Bob Hope, right in front of the television cameras. Skeet was so happy he almost cried. That night Dallie had overheard him talking to Holly Grace on the telephone. "I knew he could do it," Skeet had crowed. "You just watch. This is it, Holly Grace. He's going to be one of the greats. It's all going to come together for our boy now."

But it hadn't, not quite. And that's what was pretty much breaking Skeet's heart. Once or twice each season Dallie took a second or third in one of the majors, but it had become pretty obvious to everyone that, at thirty-seven, his best years were just about gone and the big championships would never be his.

"You got the skill," Skeet said, staring out the murky window of the cab. "You got the skill and you got the talent, but something inside you is keeping you from being a real champion. I just wish I knew what it was."

Dallie knew, but he wasn't saying. "Now you listen to me, Skeet Cooper. Everybody understands that watching golf on television is about as interesting as watching somebody sleep. Those network honchos are getting ready to pay me some semi-spectacular money to liven up their broadcasts, and I don't see any need to throw their generosity back in their faces."

"Those network honchos wear fancy cologne," Skeet grumbled, as if that said it all. "And since when did you get so all-fired concerned about money?"

"Since I looked at the calendar and saw that I was

thirty-seven years old, that's when." Dallie leaned forward and abruptly rapped on the glass separating him from the driver. "Hey, you! Let me out at the next corner."

"Just where do you think you're going?"

"I'm going to see Holly Grace, that's where. And I'm going by myself."

"It won't do you any good. She'll just say the same thing I been sayin'."

Dallie pushed open the door anyway and jumped out in front of Cartier. The cab pulled away, and he stepped directly into a pile of dog shit. It served him right, he thought, for eating a lunch that cost more than the yearly budget of most Third World nations.

Oblivious to the attention he was attracting from several female passersby, he began scraping the sole of his shoe on the curb. It was then that the Bear came up behind him, right there in the middle of Midtown. *You'd better sign while they still want you*, the Bear said. *How much longer are you going to kid yourself?*

I'm not kidding myself! Dallie started back up Fifth Avenue, heading toward Holly Grace's apartment.

The Bear stayed right with him, shaking his big blond head in disgust. *You thought giving up booze was going to guarantee you'd make those eagle putts, didn't you, boy? You thought it was going to be that simple. Why don't you tell old Skeet what's really holding you back? Why don't you just come right out and tell him you don't have the guts to be a champion?*

Dallie quickened his pace, doing his best to lose the Bear in the crowd. But the Bear was tenacious. He'd stuck around for a long time, and he wasn't going anyplace now.

Holly Grace lived in the Museum Tower, the luxury condominiums built above the Museum of Modern Art, which made her fond of announcing that she slept on top of some of the greatest painters in the world. The doorman recognized Dallie and let him into Holly Grace's apartment to wait for her. Dallie hadn't seen Holly Grace for several months, but they talked on the telephone frequently and not much happened in either life that didn't get discussed between them.

The apartment wasn't Dallie's style at all—too much

white furniture, with free-form chairs that didn't fit his lanky body, and some abstract art that reminded him of pond scum. He shucked off his coat and tie, then stuck a tape of *Born in the U.S.A.* into a cassette player he found in a cabinet that looked as if it was designed to hold dental equipment. He fast-forwarded the tape to "Darlington County," which, in his opinion, was one of the ten greatest American songs ever written. While the Boss sang about his adventures with Wayne, Dallie wandered about the spacious living room, finally coming to a stop in front of Holly Grace's piano. Since he'd last been in the apartment, she'd added a group of photographs in silver frames to the collection of glass paperweights that had always occupied the top of the piano. He noted several pictures of Holly Grace and her mother, a couple of photos of himself, some snapshots of the two of them together, and a photograph of Danny they'd had taken at Sears in 1969.

Dallie's fingers tightened around the edge of the frame as he picked it up. Danny's round face looked back at him, wide-eyed and laughing, a tiny bubble of drool frozen forever on the inside of his bottom lip. If Danny had lived, he would have been eighteen years old now. Dallie couldn't imagine it. He couldn't picture Danny at eighteen, as tall as himself, blond and lithe, as good-looking as his mother. In his mind, Danny would always be a toddler running toward his twenty-year-old father with a loaded diaper sagging down around his knees and his chubby arms extended in perfect trust.

Dallie replaced the photograph and looked away. After all these years, the ache was still there—not as acute, maybe, but still there. He distracted himself by studying a photograph of Francesca wearing bright red shorts and laughing mischievously into the camera. She was perched on a big rock, pushing her hair away from her face with one hand and propping a chubby baby between her legs with the other. He smiled. She looked happy in the picture. That time with Francesca had been a good time in his life, sort of like living inside a private joke. Still, maybe the laugh was on him now.

Who would have ever thought Miss Fancy Pants would turn out to be such a success? She'd done it on her own, too—he knew that from Holly Grace. She'd raised a baby without anyone to help her and made a career for herself. Of course, there'd been something special about her even ten years before—a feistiness, a way she had of charging at life straight on and going after what she wanted without any thought of the consequences. For a fraction of a moment it flashed through his mind that Francesca had taken life on at a full run while he was still hanging out at the fringes.

The idea didn't please him, and he rewound the Springsteen tape to distract himself. He then went into the kitchen and opened the refrigerator, bypassing Holly Grace's Miller Lite for a Dr Pepper. He'd always appreciated the fact that Francesca had been honest with Holly Grace about that baby of hers. It had been natural for him to wonder if the baby might not be his, and Francesca could certainly have pinned old Nicky's kid on him without too much trouble. But she hadn't done it, and he admired her for it.

Popping the lid on the Dr Pepper, he walked back to the piano and looked around for another picture of Francesca's son, but found only the one. He got a kick out of the fact that whenever the child was mentioned in an article about Francesca, he was always identified as the product of an unhappy early marriage—so unhappy that Francesca had refused to give the child his father's last name. As far as Dallie knew, he, Holly Grace, and Skeet were the only people who knew the marriage had never existed, but all of them had enough respect for what Francesca had done with herself to keep their mouths shut.

The unexpected friendship that had developed between Holly Grace and Francesca seemed to Dallie one of life's more interesting relationships, and he'd mentioned to Holly Grace more than once that he would like to drop in some time when the two of them were together to see how they got along. "I just can't picture it," he'd once said. "All I can see is you going on and on about the last Cowboys game while Francie talks about her Gucci shoes and admires herself in the mirror."

"She's not like that, Dallie," Holly Grace replied. "I mean, she *does* talk about her shoes, but that's not all."

"It just seems ironic," he answered, "that somebody like her should be raising a male child. I'll bet you anything he grows up strange."

Holly Grace hadn't liked that remark, so he'd stopped teasing her, but he could tell she was worried about the same thing. That's how he knew the kid was pretty much a sissy.

Dallie had rewound *Born in the U.S.A.* for the third time when he heard a key turn in the front door. Holly Grace called out, "Hey, Dallie. The doorman said he let you in. You weren't supposed to show up until tomorrow."

"I had a change of plans. Damn, Holly Grace, this place reminds me of a doctor's office."

Holly Grace had a peculiar look on her face as she walked in from the foyer, her blond hair sweeping over the collar of her coat. "That's exactly what Francesca always says. Honestly, Dallie, it's the spookiest thing. Sometimes the two of you give me the willies."

"Now, why's that?"

She tossed her purse down on a white leather couch. "You're not going to believe this, but you have these strange similarities. I mean, you and me, we're like two peas in a pod, right? We look alike, we talk alike. We have just about all the same interests—sports, sex, cars."

"Is there a point in here somewhere, because I'm starting to get hungry."

"Of course there's a point. You and Francesca don't like any of the same things. She loves clothes, cities, fancy people. Her stomach gets queasy if she sees somebody sweat, and her politics are definitely getting more liberal all the time—I guess maybe because she's an immigrant." Holly Grace perched one hip on the back of the couch and looked at him thoughtfully. "You, on the other hand, don't care much about fancy stuff, and you lean so far to the right on the political spectrum that you're just about ready to fall off. Looking at the surface, two people couldn't be any more different."

"I guess that's pretty much an understatement." The Springsteen tape had reached "Darlington County" again, and Dallie tapped out the rhythm with the toe of his shoe while he waited for Holly Grace to get to the point.

"Except you're alike in the most peculiar ways. The first

344

thing she said when she saw this apartment was that it reminded her of a doctor's office. And, Dallie, that girl just about has you beat when it comes to picking up strays. First it was cats. Then she branched off into dogs, which was interesting because she's scared to death of them. Finally, she began picking up people—teenage girls, fourteen, fifteen years old, who'd run away from home and were selling their wares on the street."

"No kidding," Dallie said, his interest finally caught. "What does she do with them once she—" But then he stopped as Holly Grace pulled off her coat and he caught sight of the bruise on her neck. "Hey, what's that? It looks like a sucker bite."

"I don't want to talk about it." She hunched up her shoulders to cover the mark and escaped into the kitchen.

He followed her. "Damn, I haven't seen one of those things in years. I remember when I put a few of those on you myself." He propped himself in the doorway. "You feel like telling me about it?"

"You'll only start yelling."

Dallie gave a snort of displeasure. "Gerry Jaffe. You saw your old commie lover again."

"He's not a commie." Holly Grace yanked a Miller Lite from the refrigerator. "Just because you don't happen to agree with somebody's politics doesn't mean you should go around calling him a commie. Besides, you're not half as conservative as you try to make people believe."

"My politics don't have anything to do with it. I just don't want to see you get hurt again, honey."

Holly Grace deflected the conversation by curving her mouth into a syrupy sweet smile. "Speaking of old lovers, how's Bambi? Has she learned to read those movie magazines yet without moving her lips?"

"Aw, come on, Holly Grace . . ."

She looked at him with disgust. "I swear to God I would never have divorced you if I'd known you were going to start dating women with names that end in *i.*"

"Are you finished yet?" It aggravated him when she teased him about Bambi, even though he pretty much admitted the girl had been a low point in his amorous career. Still, Holly Grace didn't have to rub it in. "For your information,

Bambi's getting married in a few weeks and moving to Oklahoma, so I'm currently looking for a replacement."

"Are you interviewing applicants yet?"

"Just keeping my eyes open."

They heard a key turn in the door and then a child's voice, shrill and breathless, rang out from the foyer. "Hey, Holly Grace, I did it! I climbed every step!"

"Good for you," she called out absentmindedly. And then she sucked in her breath. "Damn, Francie will kill me. That's Teddy, her little boy. Ever since she moved to New York, she's made me promise I wouldn't let the two of you get together."

Dallie was offended. "I'm not exactly a child molester. What does she think I'm going to do? Kidnap him?"

"She's embarrassed is all."

Holly Grace's response told Dallie exactly nothing, but before he could question her, the boy burst into the kitchen, his auburn hair standing up at the cowlick, a small hole in the shoulder seam of his Rambo T-shirt.

"Guess what I found on the stairs? A really cool bolt. Can we go to the Seaport Museum again sometime? It's really neat and—" He broke off as he spotted Dallie standing to the side, one hand resting on the countertop, the other lightly balanced on his hip. "Gee . . ." His mouth opened and closed like a goldfish's.

"Teddy, this is the one and only Dallas Beaudine," Holly Grace said. "Looks like you finally got your chance to meet him."

Dallie smiled at the boy and held out his hand. "Hey, Teddy. I've heard a lot about you."

"Gee," Teddy repeated, his eyes widening with awe. "Oh, gee . . ." And then he rushed forward to return Dallie's handshake, but before he got there, he forgot which hand he was supposed to put out, and he stopped.

Dallie rescued him by reaching down and grabbing the right hand for a shake. "Holly Grace tells me you two are buddies."

"We watched you play on television about a million times," Teddy said enthusiastically. "Holly Grace has been telling me all about golf and stuff."

"Well, that's real good." The boy certainly wasn't anything to look at, Dallie thought, amused by Teddy's awe-struck expression—as if he'd just landed in the presence of God. Since his mama was drop-dead beautiful, old Nicky must have been three-quarters ugly.

Too excited to stand still, Teddy shifted his weight from one foot to the other, his eyes never leaving Dallie's face. His glasses slid down on his nose and he reached up to push them back, but he was too distracted by Dallie's presence to pay any attention to what he was doing, and he knocked the frames askew with his thumb. The glasses tilted toward one ear and then went flying.

"Hey, there . . ." Dallie said, reaching down to pick them up.

Teddy reached, too, so that they both crouched down. Their heads drew close together, the small auburn one and the larger blond one. Dallie got to the glasses first and held them out toward Teddy. Their faces were so close, less than a foot apart. Dallie felt Teddy's breath on his cheek.

On the stereo in the living room, the Boss was singing about being on fire and a knife that was cutting a six-inch valley through his soul. And for that small space of time while the Boss sang about knives and valleys, everything was still all right in Dallie Beaudine's world. And then, in the next space of time, with Teddy's breath falling like a whisper on his cheek, the fire reached out and grabbed him.

"Christ."

Teddy looked at Dallie with puzzled eyes and then lifted his glasses back toward his face.

Dallie's hand slashed out and grabbed Teddy's wrist, making the child wince.

Holly Grace realized something was wrong and stiffened at the sight of Dallie staring so chillingly into Teddy's face. "Dallie?"

But he didn't hear her. Time had stopped moving forward for him. He had tumbled back through the years until he was a kid again, a kid gazing into the angry face of Jaycee Beaudine.

Except the face wasn't large and overpowering, with unshaven cheeks and clenched teeth.

The face was small. As small as a child's.

* * *

Prince Stefan Marko Brancuzi had bought his yacht, *Star of the Aegean,* from a Saudi oil sheik. As Francesca stepped aboard and greeted the *Star's* captain, she had the uneasy sensation that time had slipped away and she was nine years old again, coming aboard Onassis's yacht, the *Christina,* with bowls of caviar lying in wait along with vacuous people who had too much time on their hands and nothing worthwhile to do with it.

She shivered, but it might very well have been a reaction to the damp December night. The sable definitely would have been more appropriate for the weather than her fuchsia shawl. A steward led her across the afterdeck toward the welcoming lights of the lounge. As she stepped inside the opulent room, His Royal Highness, Prince Stefan Marko Brancuzi, came forward and kissed her lightly on the cheek.

Stefan had the thoroughbred look shared by so much of European royalty—thin, elongated features, a sharp nose, a chiseled mouth. His face would have been forbidding had he not been blessed with so ready a smile. Despite his image as a playboy prince, Stefan had an old-fashioned manner about him that Francesca found endearing. He was also a hard worker who had spent the last twenty years turning his tiny backward country into a modern resort that rivaled Monaco in its opulent pleasures. Now he needed only his own Grace Kelly to cap off his achievements, and he made no secret of the fact that he had selected Francesca for the role.

His clothes were stylish and expensive—an unstructured taupe blazer subtly windowpaned in peach, dark pleated trousers, a silk shirt, open at the throat. He took her hand and drew her toward the mahogany bar where two tulip-shaped Baccarat goblets waited. "Forgive me for not coming to get you myself. My schedule today has been beastly."

"Mine, too," she said, shrugging off her shawl. "I can't tell you how much I'm looking forward to taking Teddy to Mexico. Two weeks with nothing to do but brush the sand off my feet." She took the champagne glass and perched on one of the bar stools. Inadvertently, she let her hand stray over the soft leather, and once again her mind drifted back to the *Christina* and another set of bar stools.

"Why not bring Teddy over here instead? Wouldn't you rather sail through the Greek Islands for a few weeks?"

The offer was tempting, but Stefan was pushing her too fast. Besides, something inside her rejected the idea of watching Teddy roam the decks of the *Star of the Aegean*. "Sorry, but I'm afraid my plans are set. Maybe another time."

Stefan frowned but didn't press her. He gestured toward a cut-glass bowl mounded with tiny golden-brown eggs. "Caviar? If you don't like osetra, I'll call for some beluga."

"No!" The exclamation was so sharp that Stefan stared at her in surprise. She gave him a shaky smile. "I'm sorry. I—I'm not fond of caviar."

"Gracious, darling, you seem on edge tonight. Is anything wrong?"

"Just a bit tired." She smiled and made a joke. Before long they were engaged in the sort of lighthearted exchange they did so well. They dined on slivers of artichoke heart drizzled with a peppery sauce of black olives and capers, followed by slices of chicken that had been marinated in lime, coriander, and juniper. By the time the raspberry charlotte arrived in a puddle of ginger *crème anglaise,* she was too full to eat more than a few bites. As she sat bathed in candlelight and Stefan's affection, she thought how much she was enjoying herself. Why didn't she just tell Stefan she would marry him? What woman in her right mind could resist the idea of being a princess? For all her valued independence, she was working too hard and spending too much time away from her son. She loved her career, but she was beginning to realize that she wanted more out of life than spectacular Nielsens. Still, was this marriage what she really wanted?

"Are you listening, darling? This isn't the most encouraging response I've ever received to a marriage proposal."

"Oh, dear, I'm sorry. I'm afraid I was woolgathering." She smiled apologetically. "I need a bit more time, Stefan. To be honest, I'm not all that certain how good you are for my character."

He looked at her, puzzled. "What a curious thing to say. Whatever do you mean?"

She couldn't explain to him how afraid she was that after a few years in his company, she might be right back where she had started from—staring into mirrors and throwing a temper tantrum if her nail polish chipped. Leaning forward, she kissed him, taking a nip at his lip with her small, sharp teeth and distracting him from his question. The wine had warmed her blood, and his solicitude chipped away at the barriers she'd built around herself. Her body was young and healthy. Why was she letting it shrivel up like an old leaf? She brushed his lips with her own again. "Instead of a proposal, how about a proposition?"

A combination of amusement and desire sparked in his eyes. "I suppose that would depend on the kind of proposition."

She gave him a saucy grin. "Take me to your bedroom, and I'll show you."

Picking up her hand, he kissed the tips of her fingers, his gesture so courtly and elegant he might have been leading her onto the ballroom floor. As they walked through the hallway, she found herself enveloped in a haze of wine and laughter so pleasurable that, by the time they actually entered his opulent stateroom, she might have believed she was really in love if she hadn't known herself better. Still, it had been so long since a man had held her in his arms that she let herself pretend.

He kissed her, gently at first and then more passionately, muttering foreign words in her ear that excited her. His hands moved to the fastenings on her clothing. "If only you knew how long I have wanted to see you naked," he murmured. Drawing down the bodice of her gown, he nuzzled at the tops of her breasts as they rose over the lacy border of her slip. "Like warm peaches," he murmured. "Full and rich and scented. I'm going to suck out every sweet drop of their juice."

Francesca found his line a little corny, but her body wasn't as discriminating as her mind and she could feel her skin growing deliciously warm. She cupped her hand around the back of his head and arched her neck. His lips dipped lower, burrowed beneath the lace of her slip for her nipple. "Here," he said, closing around her. "Oh, yes . . ."

Yes, indeed. Francesca gasped as she felt the suction of his mouth and then the delicious scrape of his teeth.

"My darling, Francesca . . ." He sucked deeper, and her knees began to feel as if they would buckle.

And then the telephone rang.

"Those imbeciles!" He cursed in a language she didn't understand. "They know I am never to be disturbed here."

But the mood had been broken, and she stiffened. She suddenly felt embarrassed to be getting ready to have sex with a man she only loved a little bit. What was wrong with her that she couldn't fall in love with him? Why did she still have to make such a big *thing* out of sex?

The phone continued to ring. He snatched it and barked into the receiver, listened a moment, then held it out to her, obviously irritated. "It's for you. An emergency."

She let out an oath that was purely Anglo-Saxon, determined to have Nathan Hurd's scalp for this. No matter what his current crisis, her producer had no right to interrupt her tonight. "Nathan, I'm going to—" Stefan banged a heavy crystal brandy decanter down on a tray, and she pushed her finger into her exposed ear to shut him out. "What? I can't hear."

"It's Holly Grace, Francie."

Francesca was immediately alarmed. "Holly Grace, are you all right?"

"Not really. If you're not sitting down, you'd better do it."

Francesca sank down on the side of the bed, apprehension growing inside her at the strangely subdued sound of Holly Grace's voice. "What's wrong?" she demanded. "Are you sick? Did something happen with Gerry?" Stefan's tirade quieted as he heard the worried tone in her voice, and he came over to stand next to her.

"No, Francie, nothing like that." Holly Grace paused for a moment. "It's Teddy."

"Teddy?" A surge of primal fear shot through Francesca, and her heart began to race.

Holly Grace's words came out in a rush. "He disappeared. Tonight, not long after I took him home."

Raw terror swept through Francesca's body with such intensity that all her senses seemed to short-circuit. An instant array of ugly pictures flashed into her mind from programs she had done, and she felt herself skimming over the edge of consciousness.

"Francie," Holly Grace went on, "I think Dallie's kidnapped him."

Her first feeling was a numbing surge of relief. The dark visions of a shallow grave and a small, mutilated body receded; but then other visions began to appear and she could barely breathe.

"Oh, God, Francie, I'm sorry." Holly Grace's words tumbled over each other. "I don't know exactly what happened. They accidentally met at my apartment today, and then Dallie showed up at your place about an hour after I'd dropped Teddy off and told Consuelo I'd sent him back to pick up Teddy so he could spend the night with me. She knew who he was, of course, so she didn't think anything of it. He had Teddy pack a suitcase, and nobody has seen either of them since. I've called everywhere. Dallie's checked out of his hotel, and Skeet doesn't know a thing. The two of them were supposed to go to Florida this week for a tournament."

Francesca felt a sickness growing in the pit of her stomach. Why would Dallie take Teddy? She could only think of one reason, but that was impossible. No one knew the truth; she had never told a soul. Still, she couldn't come up with any other reason. A bitter rage mounted inside her. How could he do something so barbaric?

"Francie, are you still there?"

"Yes," Francesca whispered.

"I've got to ask you something." There was another long pause, and Francesca braced herself for what she knew had to be coming. "Francie, I've got to ask you why Dallie would do this. Something funny happened when he saw Teddy. What's going on?"

"I—I don't know."

"Francie . . ."

"I don't know, Holly Grace!" she exclaimed. "I don't know." Her voice softened. "You understand him better than anyone. Is there any possibility Dallie would hurt Teddy?"

"Of course not." And then she hesitated. "Not physically anyway. I can't say what he might do to him psychologically, since you won't tell me what this is all about."

"I'm going to hang up now and try to get a plane to New York tonight." Francesca tried to sound brisk and efficient, but her voice was quivering. "Would you call everybody you can think of who might know where Dallie is? But be careful what you say. And whatever you do, don't let the newspapers find out. Please, Holly Grace, I don't want Teddy turned into a sideshow freak. I'll be there as soon as I can."

"Francie, you've got to tell me what's going on."

"Holly Grace, I love you . . . I really do." And then she hung up.

As Francesca flew across the Atlantic that night, she stared vacantly into the impenetrable blackness outside the window. Fear and guilt ate away at her. This was all her fault. If she had been home, she could have prevented it from happening. What kind of mother was she to let other people raise her child? All the devils of working-mother guilt buried their pitchforks in her flesh.

What if something terrible happened? She tried to tell herself that no matter what Dallie might have discovered, he would never hurt Teddy—at least the Dallie she'd known ten years ago wouldn't have. But then she remembered the programs she'd done on ex-spouses kidnapping their own children and vanishing with them for years at a time. Surely someone with as public a career as Dallie's couldn't do that—could he? Once again, she attempted to unravel the puzzle of how Dallie had discovered that Teddy was his son—that was the only explanation she could find for the abduction—but the answer eluded her.

Where was Teddy right now? Was he frightened? What had Dallie told him? She had heard enough stories from Holly Grace to know that when Dallie was angry, he was unpredictable—even dangerous. But no matter how much he might have changed over the years, she couldn't believe he would hurt a little boy.

What he might do to her, however, was another matter.

Chapter
25

Teddy stared at Dallie's back as the two of them stood in line at the counter of a McDonald's off I-81. He wished he had a red and black plaid flannel shirt like that, along with a wide leather belt and jeans with a torn pocket. His mother threw out his jeans as soon as they got the tiniest little hole in the knee, just when they were starting to feel soft and comfortable. Teddy stared down at his leather play sneakers and then ahead at Dallie's scuffed brown cowboy boots. He decided to put cowboy boots on his Christmas list.

As Dallie picked up the tray and walked toward a table at the back of the restaurant, Teddy trotted along behind him, his small legs taking two quick skips, trying to keep up. At first when they'd been heading out of Manhattan into New Jersey, Teddy had tried asking Dallie a few questions about whether he had a cowboy hat or rode a horse, but Dallie hadn't said much. Teddy had finally fallen silent, even though he had a million things he wanted to know.

For as long as Teddy could remember, Holly Grace had told him stories about Dallie Beaudine and Skeet Cooper— how they'd met up on the road when Dallie was only fifteen after Dallie had escaped from the evil clutches of Jaycee Beaudine, and how they'd traveled the interstates hustling the rich boys at the country clubs. She'd told him about bar fights and playing a round of golf left-handed and miraculous eighteenth-hole victories snatched from the jaws of defeat. In his mind, Holly Grace's stories had gotten mixed up with his Spiderman comic books and *Star Wars* and the legends he read in school about the wild West. Ever since they'd moved to New York, Teddy had begged his mom to let him meet Dallie when he came to visit Holly Grace, but she always had one excuse or another. And now that it had finally happened, Teddy knew this should be just about the most exciting day of his life.

Except that he wanted to go home now because it wasn't turning out anything like he'd imagined.

Teddy unwrapped the hamburger and lifted the top off the bun. It had ketchup on it. He wrapped it back up. Suddenly Dallie turned in his seat and looked right across the table into Teddy's face. He stared at him, just stared without saying a word. Teddy began to feel nervous, like he'd done something wrong. In his imagination, Dallie would have done things like reach over and slap him ten, the way Gerry Jaffe did. Dallie would say, "Hey, pardner, you look like the kind of man me and Skeet might like to have on the road with us when things get tough." In his imagination, Dallie would have liked him a whole lot more.

Teddy reached for his Coke and then pretended to study a sign over on the side of the room about eating breakfast at McDonald's. It seemed funny to him that Dallie was taking him so far away to meet his mother—he hadn't even known that Dallie and his mom knew each other. But if Holly Grace had told Dallie it was all right, he guessed it was. Still, he wished his mom was with them right now.

Dallie spoke so abruptly that Teddy jumped. "Do you always wear those glasses?"

"Not always." Teddy slipped them off, carefully folded in the stems, and put them on the table. The sign about eating breakfast at McDonald's blurred. "My mom says it's important what's inside a person, not what's outside—like if they wear glasses or not."

Dallie made some kind of noise that didn't sound very nice, and then nodded his head toward the hamburger. "Why aren't you eating?"

Teddy pushed at the package with the end of his finger. "I said I wanted a plain hamburger," he muttered. "It's got ketchup."

Dallie's face got a funny, tight look. "So what? A little bit of ketchup never hurt anybody."

"I'm allergic," Teddy replied.

Dallie snorted, and Teddy realized that he didn't like people who didn't like ketchup or people who had allergies. He thought about eating the hamburger anyway, just to show Dallie he could do it, but his stomach was already feeling funny, and ketchup made him think about blood and guts and eating eyeballs. Besides, he would end up with an itchy rash all over his body.

Teddy tried to think of something to say that would make Dallie like him. He wasn't used to having to think about making grown-ups like him. With kids his own age, sometimes they thought he was a jerk or he thought they were jerks, but not with grown-ups. He chewed on his bottom lip for a minute, and then he said, "I've got an I.Q. of one hundred sixty-eight. I go to gifted class."

Dallie snorted again, and Teddy knew he'd made another mistake. It had sounded like he was bragging, but he'd just thought Dallie might be interested.

"Where did you get that name—Teddy?" Dallie asked. He said the name funny, like he was trying to get rid of it fast.

"When I was born, my mom was reading a story about some kid named Teddy by this famous writer—J. R. Salinger. It's short for Theodore."

Dallie's expression grew even more sour. "J. *D.* Salinger. Doesn't anybody call you Ted?"

"Oh, yeah," Teddy lied. "About everybody. All the kids and everything. I mean, just about everybody except Holly Grace and Mom. You can call me Ted if you want to."

Dallie reached into his pocket and pulled out his wallet. Teddy saw something frozen and hard in his face. "Go on up and get yourself another hamburger fixed the way you want it."

Teddy looked at the dollar bill Dallie was holding out and then back down at his hamburger. "I guess this'll be all right." He slowly pushed back the wrapper.

Dallie's hand slammed down over the hamburger. "I said go get another one, dammit."

Teddy felt sick. Sometimes his mom yelled at him if he made a fresh remark or didn't do his chores, but it never made his stomach feel all wiggly like this, because he knew his mom loved him and didn't want him to grow up to be a jerk. But he could tell that Dallie didn't love him. Dallie didn't even like him. Teddy's jaw set in a small, rebellious line. "I'm not hungry, and I want to go home."

"Well, that's just too damned bad. We're going to be on the road for a while, just like I told you."

Teddy glared at him. "I want to go home. I have to go to school on Monday."

Dallie got up from the table and jerked his head toward the door. "Come on. If you're going to act like a spoiled brat, you can do it while we're on the road."

Teddy lagged behind on the way out the door. He didn't care anymore about all Holly Grace's dumb old stories. As far as he was concerned, Dallie was a big old butt-wipe. Slipping his glasses back on, Teddy tucked his hand in his pocket. The switch comb felt warm and reassuring as it settled against his palm. He wished it was real. If Lasher the Great was here, he could take care of old Dallie Butt-Wipe Beaudine.

As soon as the car moved onto the interstate, Dallie punched the accelerator and shot into the left lane. He knew he was acting like a real son of a bitch. He knew, but he couldn't stop himself. The rage wouldn't leave him, and he wanted to hit something about as badly as he'd ever wanted anything in his life. His anger kept eating away at him, growing bigger and stronger until he could hardly contain it. He felt as if some of his manhood had been stripped away. He was thirty-seven years old and he didn't have a goddamn thing to show for it. He was a second-rate pro golfer. He'd been a failure as a husband, a goddamn criminal as a father. And now this.

That bitch. That goddamn selfish, spoiled little rich-girl bitch. She'd given birth to his child and never said a word. All those stories she'd told Holly Grace—those lies. He'd believed them. Christ, she'd gotten back at him all right, just like she'd said she would the night they'd had that fight in the Roustabout parking lot. With a snap of her fingers, she'd given him the most contemptuous fuck-you a woman could give a man. She'd taken away his right to know his own son.

Dallie glanced over at the boy sitting in the passenger seat next to him, the son who was the flesh of his body just as surely as Danny had been. Francesca must have discovered by now that he had disappeared. The thought gave him a moment's bitter satisfaction. He hoped she was hurting real bad.

Wynette looked very much as Francesca remembered it, although some of the stores had changed. As she studied the town through the windshield of her rental car, she realized that life had carried her in a huge circle right back to the point where everything had really begun for her.

She hunched her shoulders in a futile attempt to relieve some of the tension in her neck. She still didn't know if she'd done the right thing by leaving Manhattan to fly to Texas, but after three unbearable days of waiting for the phone to ring and dodging reporters who wanted to interview her about her relationship with Stefan, she had reached the point where she had to do something.

Holly Grace had suggested she fly to Wynette. "That's where Dallie always heads when he's hurting," she had said, "and I guess he's hurting pretty bad right now."

Francesca had tried to ignore the accusation in Holly Grace's voice, but it was difficult. After ten years of friendship, their relationship was seriously strained. The day Francesca had returned from London, Holly Grace had announced, "I'll stick by you, Francesca, because that's the way I'm made, but it's going to be a while before I trust you again."

Francesca had tried to make her understand. "I couldn't tell you the truth. Not as close as you are to Dallie."

"So you lied to me? You fed me that stupid story about Teddy's father in England, and I believed it all these years." Holly Grace's face had darkened with anger. "Don't you understand that family means something to Dallie? With other men it might not matter, but Dallie isn't like other men. He's spent all his life trying to create a family around him—Skeet, Miss Sybil, me, all those strays he's picked up over the years. This is going to just about kill him. His first son died, and you stole his second one."

A wave of anger had shot through Francesca, all the sharper because she had felt a prick of guilt. "Don't you judge me, Holly Grace Beaudine! You and Dallie both have some awfully freewheeling ideas of morality, and I won't have either of you shaking your finger at me. You don't know what it's like to hate who you are—to have to remake yourself. I did what I needed to do at the time. And if I had to go through it again, I'd do exactly the same thing."

Holly Grace had been unmoved. "Then you'd be a bitch twice over, wouldn't you?"

Francesca blinked her eyes against tears as she turned onto the street that held Dallie's Easter egg house. She was heartsick over Holly Grace's inability to understand that Dallie's long-ago affair with her hadn't been anything more than a small sexual diversion in his life—certainly nothing to justify the kidnapping of a nine-year-old child. Why was Holly Grace taking sides against her? Francesca wondered if she was doing the right thing by not involving the police, but she couldn't bear the idea of seeing Teddy's name smeared all over the tabloids. "Love Child of Television Personality Kidnapped by Golf Pro Father." She could see it now—photographs of all of them. Her relationship with Stefan would become even more public, and they would dig up all the old stories about Dallie and Holly Grace.

Francesca remembered all too well what had happened after "China Colt" had made Holly Grace famous. Every detail of her unusual marriage to one of professional golf's most colorful players had suddenly become fodder for the media, and as one wild story followed another, neither of them could go anywhere without being dogged by paparazzi. Holly Grace handled it better than Dallie, who was accustomed to sports reporters but not the sensationalistic press. It hadn't taken him long to start throwing his fists, which had eventually attracted the attention of the PGA commissioner. Following a particularly nasty altercation in Albuquerque, Dallie had been suspended from tournament play for several months. Holly Grace had divorced him soon after to try to make both their lives more peaceful.

The house still bore its lavender trim and chain of leaping jackrabbits, although the tangerine paint had been touched up by a less skillful hand than Miss Sybil's. The old schoolteacher met Francesca at the door. It had been ten years since they'd seen each other. Miss Sybil had shrunk in size and her shoulders were more stooped, but her voice hadn't lost its authority.

"Come in, my dear, come in and get out of the cold. My, my, you'd think this was Boston instead of Texas, the way the temperature's dropped. My dear, I've been at sixes and sevens ever since you called."

Francesca gave her a gentle hug. "Thank you for letting me come. After everything I told you on the phone, I wasn't sure you'd want to see me."

"Not want to see you? My gracious, I've been counting the hours." Miss Sybil led the way toward the kitchen and asked Francesca to pour them both coffee. "I don't like to complain, but life hasn't been very interesting lately. I can't get around the way I used to, and Dallas was keeping company with such a dreadful young woman. I couldn't even interest her in Danielle Steel, let alone the classics." She gestured Francesca into a seat across from her at the kitchen table. "My, my, I can't tell you how proud I am of you. When I think of how far you've come . . ." She suddenly drilled Francesca with her schoolteacher's gaze. "Now tell me all about this dreadful situation."

Francesca told her, sparing nothing. To her relief, Miss Sybil wasn't nearly as condemnatory as Holly Grace had been. She seemed to understand Francesca's need to establish her independence; however, she was clearly worried about Dallie's reaction to discovering that he had a child. "I believe Holly Grace is correct," she finally said. "Dallas must be on his way back to Wynette, and we can be quite certain he won't take this well. You'll stay in the guest room, Francesca, until he gets here."

Francesca had planned to stay at the hotel, but she gratefully accepted the invitation. As long as she remained in the house, she would feel that she'd somehow gotten closer to Teddy. Half an hour later, Francesca found herself curled up beneath an old patchwork quilt while the winter sunlight trickled in through the lace curtains and the old radiator hissed out a comforting flow of heat. She fell asleep almost instantly.

By noon of the next day, Dallie still hadn't appeared and she was nearly frantic with anxiety. Maybe she should have stayed in New York? What if he wasn't coming to Wynette?

And then Holly Grace called and told her that Skeet had disappeared.

"What do you mean, disappeared?" Francesca exclaimed. "He said he'd contact you if he heard anything."

"Dallie probably called him and told him to keep his mouth shut. I expect Skeet's gone to meet him."

Francesca felt angry and impotent. If Dallie had told Skeet to put a gun to his head, he would probably have done that, too. By midafternoon, when Miss Sybil left to go to her pottery class, Francesca was ready to jump out of her skin. What was taking Dallie so long? Afraid to leave the house for fear Dallie would appear, she tried to study the American history material for her citizenship exam, but she couldn't concentrate. She began pacing through the house and ended up in Dallie's bedroom, where a collection of his golf trophies sat in the front window catching the thin wintry light. She picked up a copy of a golf magazine with his picture on the cover. "Dallas Beaudine—Always a Bridesmaid, Never a Bride." She noticed that the laugh lines at the corners of his eyes were deeper and his features had a sharper cast, but maturity hadn't robbed him of one morsel of his good looks. He was even more gorgeous than she remembered.

She searched his face for some small sign of Teddy, but saw nothing. Once again, she wondered how he had known that Teddy was his son. Putting down the magazine, she looked over at the bed and a shower of memories drifted over her. Was that where Teddy had been conceived, or had it happened earlier, in a Louisiana swamp when Dallie had stretched her out over the trunk of that Buick Riviera?

The phone next to the bed rang. She banged her foot on the bed frame as she raced over to it and snatched up the receiver. "Hello! Hello?"

Silence greeted her.

"Dallie?" The name came out like a sob. "Dallie, is that you?"

There was no answer. She felt a prickling along the back of her neck, and her heart began to race. She was certain someone was there; her ears strained to catch a sound. "Teddy?" she whispered. "Teddy . . . it's Mommy."

"It's me, Miss Fancy Pants." Dallie's voice was low and bitter, making her old nickname sound like an obscenity. "We've got some talking to do. Meet me at the quarry north of town in half an hour."

She heard the finality in his voice and she cried out, "Wait! Is Teddy there? I want to talk to him!"

But the line had gone dead.

She raced downstairs, snatched her suede jacket from the hall closet, and pulled it on over her sweater and jeans. That morning, she had tied her hair at the nape of her neck with a scarf, and now, in her haste, she got the thin silk tangled in the jacket collar. Her hands trembled as she pulled the scarf free. Why was he doing this? Why didn't he bring Teddy to the house? What if Teddy was sick? What if something had happened?

Her breathing was quick and shallow as she started the car and backed it out onto the street. Ignoring the speed limit, she drove to the first service station she could find and asked for directions. The instructions were complex, and she missed a route marker north of town, going miles out of her way before she found the flat dirt road that led to the quarry. Her hands ached from their tight grip on the steering wheel. Over an hour had passed since his call. Would he wait for her? She told herself that Teddy was safe—Dallie might hurt her, but he would never hurt a child. The thought brought her only a small measure of comfort.

The quarry sat back from the road like a giant wound, bleak and forbidding in the fading gray winter light, overwhelming in its size. The last shift of workers had apparently left for the day because the vast, flat yard that fronted the quarry was deserted. Pyramids of reddish stone stood near the idle trucks. Miles of silent conveyer belts led to green-painted hoppers sitting like giant funnels above the ground. Francesca drove across the yard toward a corrugated metal building, but she saw no sign of life, no vehicles other than the idle quarry trucks. She was too late, she thought. Dallie had already left. Her mouth dry with anxiety, she drove her car out of the yard and along the road to the maw of the quarry.

It looked to Francesca, in her agitated state of mind, as if a giant knife had sliced open the earth, gouging its way straight down to hell. Desolate, eerie, raw, the canyon of the quarry dwarfed everything on the horizon. A scattering of bare winter trees above the rim on the opposite side looked like toothpick twigs, the hills in the distance like baby sandpiles. Even the darkening sky no longer loomed so large; it seemed more like a lid that had been dropped down over an enormous empty cauldron. She shuddered as she forced herself to drive to the edge, where two hundred feet of red granite had been sliced open layer by layer, the process of desecration paradoxically revealing the secrets of its creation.

In the last of the light, she could dimly make out one of Teddy's toy cars sitting at the bottom.

For a fraction of a moment she felt disoriented, and then she realized the car was real, not a toy at all. It was just as real as the Lilliputian man who leaned against the hood. She pressed her eyes shut for a moment, and her chin quivered. He had chosen this awful place purposely because he wanted her to feel dwarfed and powerless. Struggling for control, she backed the car away from the rim and then drove along it, almost missing a steep gravel road that led into the quarry's depths. Slowly, she began her descent.

As the dark quarry walls rose above her, she mentally steadied herself. For years, she'd been charging at seemingly impenetrable barriers, battering herself against them until they gave way. Dallie was merely another barrier she had to move. And she had an advantage he couldn't anticipate. No matter what he might have told himself, he was expecting to confront the girl he remembered, his twenty-one-year-old Fancy Pants.

Even as she had gazed down at him from the lip of the quarry, she had sensed that he was alone. As she drove nearer, she saw nothing that made her think differently. Teddy wasn't there. Dallie wanted to extract his full pound of flesh before he gave her back her child. She parked her car at an angle to the front of his, but nearly forty feet away. If this was to be a showdown, she would play her own war of nerves. The light was almost gone and she left her headlights on. Opening the door, she got out deliberately—no haste, no wasted motion, no glances spared for those looming granite walls. She came toward him slowly, walking in the path of the headlights with her arms at her sides and her spine straight. A chill blast of wind tore at her scarf and spanked the end against her cheek. She locked her eyes with his.

He stood facing her with his back to the car, hips leaning at an angle against the front of the hood, ankles crossed, arms crossed—all of him locked tight and closed away. His head was bare, and he wore only a sleeveless down vest over his flannel shirt. His boots were dusty with the red grit from the quarry, as if he had been there for some time.

She drew near him, her chin high, her gaze steady. Only when she was close enough could she see how terrible he looked, not at all like the magazine-cover photograph. In the glare from the headlights, she noted that his skin had a drawn, gray cast, and his jaw was covered with stubble. Only those Newman-blue eyes were familiar, except that they had turned as cold and hard as the rock beneath her feet. She stopped in front of him. "Where's Teddy?"

A blade of night wind cut through the quarry, lifting the hair away from his forehead. He stepped away from the car and straightened to his full height. For a moment he didn't say anything. He just stood there looking down at her as if she were a particularly loathsome piece of human refuse.

"I only hit two women in my life," he finally said, "and you didn't count because it was more a reflex action since you hit me first. But I've got to tell you that ever since I found out what you did to me, I've been thinking about getting hold of you and doing the job right."

She needed the full force of her will to speak calmly. "Let's go someplace where we can sit down and have a cup of coffee so we can discuss all this."

His mouth twisted into an ugly sneer. "Don't you think the time to be sitting down and drinking coffee was ten years ago, after you found out you were going to have my kid?"

"Dallie—"

He raised his voice. "Don't you think that might have been the time to call me up on the telephone and say, 'Hey, Dallie, we've got a little problem here I think we should maybe sit down and talk about'?"

She buried her fists in the pockets of her jacket and hunched her shoulders against the chill, trying not to let him see how much he was frightening her. Where was the man who had once been her lover—a man quick to laugh, a man amused by human foibles, a man as slow and easy as warm molasses? "I want to see Teddy, Dallie. What have you done with him?"

"He looks just like my old man," Dallie declared angrily. "A pint-sized replica of that old bastard Jaycee Beaudine. Jaycee beat up women, too. He was real good at it."

So that's how he had known. She gestured toward her car, unwilling to stay any longer in this dark quarry and listen to him talk about beating up women. "Dallie, let's go—"

"You didn't figure on Teddy looking like Jaycee, did you? You didn't count on my recognizing him when you planned this dirty little private war."

"I didn't plan anything. And it's not a war. People do what they have to. You remember what I was like back then. I couldn't go running back to you and ever have a shot at growing up."

"It wasn't just your decision," he said, his eyes sparking with anger. "And I don't want to hear any of that feminist horseshit about how I don't have any rights because I'm a man and you're a woman, and it was your body. It was my body, too. I'd damn well like to have seen you have that boy without me."

She went on the attack. "What would you have done if I'd come to you ten years ago and told you I was pregnant? You were married then, remember?"

"Married or not, I'd have seen you were taken care of, that's for damn sure."

"But that's the point! I didn't want you to take care of me. I didn't have anything, Dallie. I was a silly little girl who thought the world had been invented to be her personal toy. I had to learn how to work. I had to scrub toilets and live on scavenged food and lose whatever pride I had left before I could gain any self-respect. I couldn't give that up and go running back to you for a handout. Having that baby by myself was something I had to do. It was the only way I could redeem myself." The closed, settled expression on his face didn't ease, and she was angry with herself for trying to make him understand. "I want Teddy back tonight, Dallie, or I'm going to the police."

"If you were going to the police, you'd have done it by now."

"The only reason I've waited is because I didn't want the publicity for him. Believe me, I won't put it off any longer." She stepped closer to him, determined to let him see that she wasn't powerless. "Don't underestimate me, Dallie. Don't get me mixed up in your mind with the girl you knew ten years ago."

Dallie didn't say anything for a moment. He turned his head and stared off into the night. "The other woman I hit was Holly Grace."

"Dallie, I don't want to hear—"

His hand whipped out and caught her arm. "You're going to listen, because I want you to understand exactly what kind of a son of a bitch you're dealing with. I slapped the shit out of Holly Grace after Danny died—that's the kind of man I am. And you know why?"

"Don't—" She tried to pull away, but he only gripped her tighter.

"Because she cried! That's why I slapped her. I slapped that woman because she cried after her baby died." Harsh shadows cast by the headlights slashed his face. He dropped her arm, but his expression remained fierce. "Does that give you any idea what I might do to you?"

He was bluffing. She knew it. She felt it. In some way, he had cut himself open so she could see inside him. She had hurt him badly and he had made up his mind to punish her. He probably did want to hit her—only he didn't have the stomach to do it. She could see that, too.

With more clarity than she wished for, she finally understood the depth of his pain. She felt it through every one of her senses because it mirrored her own so closely. Everything inside her rejected the idea of living things being hurt.

Dallie had her son, but he knew he wouldn't be able to keep him for long. He wanted to hit her, but it went against his nature, so he was looking for another way to punish her, another way to make her suffer. She felt a creeping chill. Dallie was smart, and if he thought long enough he just might find his revenge. Before that happened, she had to stop him. For both their sakes, and for Teddy's sake, she couldn't let this go any further.

"I learned a long time ago that people who have lots of possessions spend so much energy trying to protect what they have that they lose sight of what's important in life." She stepped forward, not touching him, just making certain she could look him directly in the eye. "I have a successful career, Dallie—a seven-figure bank account, a blue-chip portfolio. I've got a house and beautiful clothes. I have four-carat diamond studs in my ears. But I never forget what's important." Her hands went to her ears. She pulled the backs off the studs and then slipped the diamonds from her earlobes. They nestled in the center of her palm, cool as chips of ice. She held them out to him.

For the first time he looked uncertain. "What are you doing? I don't want those. I'm not holding him for ransom, for chrissake!"

"I know that." She rolled the diamonds in her palm, letting them catch the glare from the headlights. "I'm not your Fancy Pants anymore, Dallie. I just want to make certain you understand exactly what my priorities are— how far I'll go to get him back. I want *you* to know what you're up against." Her hand closed around the diamonds. "The most important thing in my life is my son. As far as I'm concerned, everything else is just spit."

And then while Dallie watched, Black Jack Day's daughter did it again. With one strong movement of her arm, she threw her flawless four-carat pear-shaped diamond studs far out into the darkest reaches of the quarry.

Dallie didn't say anything for a moment. He lifted his foot and rested his boot on the bumper of the car, staring out in the direction she had thrown the stones and finally looking back at her. "You've changed, Francie. You know that?"

She nodded.

"Teddy's not an ordinary boy."

The way he said it, she knew he wasn't issuing a compliment. "Teddy's the best kid in the world," she answered sharply.

"He needs a father. A man's influence to get him toughened up. The boy's too soft. The first thing you have to do is tell him about me."

She wanted to scream at him, tell him she would do no such thing, but she saw with painful clarity that too many people knew the truth for her to keep it a secret from her son any longer. She nodded reluctantly.

"You've got a lot of lost years to make up for," he said.

"I don't have anything to make up for."

"I'm not going to disappear from his life." Once again his face grew hard. "We can either work something out ourselves, or I can hire one of those bloodsucking lawyers to stick it to you."

"I won't have Teddy hurt."

"Then we'd better work it out ourselves." He took his foot off the bumper, walked around to the driver's door, and climbed in. "Go on back to the house. I'll bring him to you tomorrow."

"Tomorrow? I want him now! Tonight!"

"Well, now, that's too bad, isn't it?" he said with a sneer. And then he slammed the car door.

"Dallie!" She ran toward him, but he was already heading out of the quarry, his tires spitting gravel. She yelled after him until she realized how futile that was, and then she raced to her own car.

The engine wouldn't start for her at first, and she was afraid she had run the battery down by leaving her lights on. When it finally turned over, Dallie had already disappeared. She raced the car up the steep road after him, ignoring the way the rear end fishtailed. At the top, she caught sight of two dim red taillights in the distance. Her tires spun as she accelerated. If only it wasn't so dark! He turned out onto the highway and she raced after him.

For several miles, she stayed with him, ignoring the squeal of her tires as she accelerated around wild curves, pushing the car to reckless speeds when the pavement straightened. He knew the narrow back roads and she didn't, but she refused to fall back. He wasn't going to do this to her! She knew she'd hurt him, but that didn't give him the right to terrorize her. She pushed the speedometer to sixty-five and then to seventy. . . .

If he hadn't finally turned off his lights, she might have had him.

Chapter
26

Francesca felt numb by the time she returned to Dallie's house. As she climbed wearily out of the car, she found herself replaying bits and pieces of the encounter in the quarry. Most men would be glad to have been spared the burden of an unwanted child. Why couldn't she have picked one of them?

"Uh . . . Miss Day?"

Francesca's heart sank as she heard the young female voice coming to her from the vicinity of the pecan trees at the side of the drive. Not tonight, she thought. Not now, when she felt as if she were already carrying a thousand pounds on her shoulders. How did they always manage to find her?

Even before she turned in the direction of the voice, she knew what she would see—the desperately young face, tough and sad, the cheap clothes undoubtedly topped by gaudy earrings. She even knew the story she would hear. But tonight she wouldn't listen. Tonight she had too much trouble clouding her own life to take on anyone else's.

A girl dressed in jeans and a dirty pink jacket stepped just to the edge of a puddle of light that shone dimly on the drive from the kitchen window. She wore too much makeup, and her center-parted hair fell like a double door over her face.

"I . . . uh . . . I saw you earlier at the gas station. At first I didn't believe it was you. I . . . uh . . . I heard from this girl I met a long time ago that . . . you know . . . you might, uh . . ."

The runaways' grapevine. It had followed her from Dallas to St. Louis, then on to Los Angeles and New York. Now it seemed her reputation as the world's biggest sucker had even spread to small towns like Wynette. Francesca willed herself to turn her back and walk away. She willed it, but her feet wouldn't move.

"How did you find me?" she asked.

"I—uh—I asked around. Somebody said you were staying here."

"Tell me your name."

"Dora—Doralee." The girl lifted the cigarette that was shoved between her fingers and took a drag.

"Would you step into the light so I can see you?"

Doralee did as she was asked, moving reluctantly, as if lifting her red canvas high-top sneakers required superhuman effort. She couldn't be more than fifteen, Francesca thought, although she would insist that she was eighteen. Walking closer, she studied the girl's face. Her pupils weren't dilated; her speech had been hesitant, but not slurred. In New York, if she suspected that a girl was strung out on drugs, she took her to an old brownstone in Brooklyn run by nuns who specialized in helping addicted teenagers.

"How long since you've had anything decent to eat?" Francesca asked.

"I eat," the girl said defiantly.

Candy bars, Francesca guessed. And Styrofoam cupcakes stuffed with chemical frosting. Sometimes the street kids pooled their money and treated themselves to fast-food french fries. "Would you like to come inside and talk?"

"I guess." The girl shrugged her shoulders and flipped her cigarette down onto the drive.

As Francesca led her toward the kitchen door, she thought she could hear Holly Grace's scornful voice mocking her: "You and your teenage hookers! Let the government take care of these kids like it's supposed to. I swear to God, you don't have the sense you were born with." But Francesca knew the government didn't have enough shelters to take care of all these kids. They simply shipped them back to their parents where, all too frequently, the problems started all over again.

The first time Francesca had become involved with a runaway was in Dallas after she'd done one of her early television shows. The subject had been teenage prostitution, and Francesca had been horrified at the power the pimps exerted over the girls, who were, after all, still children. Without quite knowing how it had happened, she'd found herself bringing two of them home and then badgering the social welfare system until they found foster homes for them.

The word had slowly spread, and every few months since then she'd found herself with a runaway on her hands. First in Dallas, then in Los Angeles, then in New York, she would leave work at night to find someone standing outside the building, having heard through the grapevine of the streets that Francesca Day helped girls who were in trouble. Frequently they just wanted food, other times a place to hide from their pimps. Seldom did they say much; they had suffered too many rejections. They just slouched in front of her like this girl, smoking a cigarette or biting their fingernails and hoping that Francesca Day would somehow understand that she was their last hope.

"I have to call your family," Francesca announced as she warmed a plate of leftovers in the microwave and then set it out, along with an apple and a glass of milk.

"My mom don't give a shit what happens to me," Doralee said, her shoulders slumped so far forward that the ends of her hair nearly touched the table.

"I still have to call her," Francesca replied firmly. While Doralee tucked into the leftovers on her plate, Francesca called the number in New Mexico that the girl grudgingly gave her. It was just as she'd said. Her mother didn't give a shit.

After Doralee had finished eating, she began to respond to Francesca's questions. She had been hitchhiking when she saw Francesca pull into the service station and ask for directions to the gravel quarry. She'd lived on the streets of

Houston for a while and spent some time in Austin. Her pimp beat her up because she wasn't turning enough tricks. She was starting to worry about AIDS.

Francesca had heard it all so many times before—these poor, sad children cast out too young into the world. An hour later, she tucked the girl into the small hideaway bed in the sewing room and then gently awakened Miss Sybil to tell her what had happened at the quarry.

Miss Sybil stayed up with her for several hours until Francesca insisted she go back to bed. Francesca knew she could never fall asleep herself, and she returned to the kitchen where she rinsed the dirty dishes from Doralee's dinner and loaded them into the dishwasher. Then she lined the kitchen drawers with fresh shelf paper she found in the cupboard. At two o'clock in the morning, she began to bake. Anything to make the long hours of the night pass faster.

"What's that over there, Skeet?" Teddy jumped up and down in the back seat and pointed out the side window of the car. "Over there! Those animals by the hills!"

"I thought I told you to put your seat belt on," Dallie snapped from behind the wheel. "Dammit, Teddy, I don't want you jumping around like that when I'm driving. You put that seat belt on right now or I'm going to pull this car right off the road."

Skeet frowned at Dallie and then looked over his shoulder at Teddy, who was scowling at the back of Dallie's neck in exactly the same way Skeet had seen Dallie scowl at people he didn't like. "Those are angora goats, Teddy. People around here raise 'em for mohair to make fancy sweaters."

But Teddy had lost interest in the goats. He was scratching his neck and toying with one end of the open seat belt.

"Did you fasten it?" Dallie snapped.

"Uh-huh." Teddy secured the belt as slowly as he dared.

"Yes, *sir*," Dallie reprimanded. "When you're talkin' to grown-ups, you say 'sir' and 'ma'am.' Just because you live in the North doesn't mean you can't have some manners. You understand?"

"Uh-huh."

Dallie spun around toward the back seat.

"Yes, *sir,*" Teddy mumbled sullenly. And then he looked toward Skeet. "How much longer till I get to see my mom?"

"Not too long now," Skeet replied. "Why don't you dig in that cooler there and see if you can find yourself a can of Dr Pepper?" As Teddy busied himself with the cooler, Skeet reached for the radio and flipped the sound to the rear speakers so he couldn't be overheard from the back seat. Sliding a few inches closer to Dallie, he remarked, "You're acting pretty much like a sumbitch, you know that?"

"Stay out of this," Dallie retorted. "I don't even know why I called you and told you to meet me." He fell silent for a moment, and his knuckles tightened on the wheel. "You see what she's done to him? He goes around talking about his I.Q. scores and his allergies. And look what happened at the motel when I tried to throw the football around with him a little bit. He's the clumsiest kid I ever saw in my life. If he can't handle something the size of a football, you can just imagine what he'd do with a golf ball."

Skeet thought about that for a minute. "Sports isn't everything."

Dallie lowered his voice. "I know that. But the kid acts funny. You can't tell what he's thinking behind those glasses, and he pulls his pants up to his armpits. What kind of kid wears his pants high like that?"

"He's probably afraid they'll fall down. His hips aren't much bigger than your thigh."

"Yeah? Well, that's another thing. He's puny. You remember how big Danny was, right from the beginning."

"Danny's mama was a lot taller than Teddy's."

Dallie's jaw set in a hard, straight line, and Skeet didn't say any more.

In the back seat, Teddy closed one eye and peered down into the depths of his Dr Pepper can with the other. He scratched the rash on his stomach underneath his T-shirt. Although he couldn't hear what they were saying in the front, he knew they were talking about him. And he didn't care, either. Skeet was neat, but Dallie was a big jerk. A great big butt-hole.

The depths of the Dr Pepper can clouded in his vision, and he felt like he had a big green slimy frog caught in his throat. Yesterday he'd finally stopped pretending to himself that everything was all right, because he knew it wasn't. He didn't believe his mom had told Dallie to take him away from New York like this, no matter what Dallie said. He thought maybe Dallie had kidnapped him, and he tried not to be scared. But he knew something was wrong, and he wanted his mom.

The frog swelled up in his throat. It made him mad to be crying like some jerky baby, so he glanced toward the front seat. When he was satisfied that Dallie's attention was on his driving, his fingers crept to his seat-belt buckle. Soundlessly, he slipped it open. No butt-hole was going to tell Lasher the Great what to do.

Francesca dreamed about Teddy's science project. She was caught in a glass cage with insects crawling all over her, and someone was using a giant pin, trying to spear the bugs to mount them. She was next. And then she saw Teddy's face on the other side of the glass, calling out to her. She tried to get to him, to reach him. . . .

"Mom! Mom!"

She jerked awake. With her mind still foggy from sleep, she felt something small and solid fly across the bed at her, tangling itself in the covers and the sash from her robe. "Mom!"

For a few seconds, she was caught between her dream and reality, and then she felt only a piercing sense of joy. "Teddy? Oh, Teddy!" She caught his small body and pulled him to her, laughing and crying. "Oh, baby . . ." His hair felt chilly against her cheek, as if he'd just come in from outside. She pulled him up in the bed and caught his face between her hands, kissing him again and again. She rejoiced in the familiar feeling of his small arms around her neck, his body pressed against hers, that fine hair, his little-boy smell. She wanted to lick his cheeks, just like a mother cat.

She was vaguely aware of Dallie leaning just inside the door of the bedroom watching them, but she was too caught up in the exquisite joy of having her son back to care. One of Teddy's hands was in her hair. He'd buried his face in her neck, and she could feel him trembling. "It's all right, baby," she whispered, tears sliding down her own cheeks. "It's all right."

When she lifted her head, her eyes inadvertently met Dallie's. He looked so sad and so alone that, for a second, she had a crazy urge to hold out her hand and beckon him to join the two of them on the bed. He spun around to walk away, and she was disgusted with herself. But then she forgot about Dallie as Teddy claimed all of her attention. It was some time before either of them could calm down enough to talk. She noticed that Teddy was covered with dull red blotches, and he kept scratching himself with stubby fingernails. "You ate ketchup," she scolded gently, reaching under his T-shirt to stroke his back. "Why did you eat ketchup, baby?"

"Mom," he murmured, "I want to go home."

She dropped her legs over the side of the bed, still holding on to his hand. How was she going to tell Teddy about Dallie? Last night while she'd been lining drawers and baking cakes, she had decided it would be best to wait until they were back in New York and events had returned to normal. But now, looking at his small, wary face, she knew postponement wasn't possible.

As she'd raised Teddy, she had never permitted herself to utter those convenient little lies most mothers told their children to buy themselves peace. She hadn't even been able to manage the Santa Claus story with any degree of conviction. But now she had been caught out in the one lie she had told him, and it was a whopper.

"Teddy," she said, clasping both his hands between hers, "we've talked a lot about how important it is to tell the truth. Sometimes, though, it's hard for a mother to always do that, especially when her child is too young to understand."

Without warning, Teddy snatched his hands away and jumped up from the bed. "I have to go see Skeet," he said. "I told him I'd be right back down. I have to go now."

"Teddy!" Francesca jumped up and caught his arm before he could reach the door. "Teddy, I need to talk to you."

"I don't want to," he mumbled.

He knows, Francesca thought. On some subliminal level, he knows I'm going to tell him something he doesn't want to hear. She wrapped her arms around his shoulders. "Teddy, it's about Dallie."

"I don't want to hear."

She held him tighter, whispering into his hair. "A long time ago, Dallie and I knew each other, sweetheart. We—we loved each other." She grimaced at this additional face-saving lie, but decided it was better than confusing her son with details he wouldn't understand. "Things didn't work out between us, honey, and we had to separate." She knelt down in front of him so she could look into his face, her hands sliding down his arms to catch his small wrists as he still tried to pull away from her. "Teddy, what I told you about your father—about how I'd known him in England, and he died—"

Teddy shook his head, his small, blotched face contorted with misery. "I have to go! I mean it, Mom! I have to go! Dallie's a jerk! I hate him!"

"Teddy—"

"No!" Using all his strength, he twisted out of her hands and before she could catch him, he'd raced from the room. She heard his feet making fast, angry thumps down the stairs.

She sagged back on her heels. Her son, who liked every adult male he'd ever met in his life, didn't like Dallie Beaudine. For a moment she felt a petty rush of satisfaction, but then, in a sickening flash of insight, she realized that no matter how much she might hate it, Dallie was bound to become a factor in Teddy's life. What effect would it have on her son to dislike the man who, sooner or later, he must realize was his father?

Shoving her hands through her hair, she got up and pushed the door shut so she could get dressed. As she pulled on slacks and a sweater, she saw a vision of Dallie's face as he had looked when he was watching them. There had been something familiar about his expression, something that reminded her of the lost teenage girls who waited for her outside the studio at night.

She scowled at herself in the mirror. She was too fanciful.

Dallie Beaudine wasn't a teenage runaway, and she refused to waste a moment's sympathy on a man who was little better than a common criminal.

After peeking into the sewing room to reassure herself that Doralee was still asleep, she took a few minutes to collect herself by making a phone call to set up an appointment with one of the county social workers. Afterward, she went in search of Teddy. She found him slumped on a stool next to a workbench in the basement where Skeet was sanding the bare wooden head of a golf club. Neither of them was talking, but the silence seemed to be companionable rather than hostile. She saw some suspicious streaks on her son's cheeks and slid her arm around his shoulders, her heart aching for him. She hadn't seen Skeet in ten years, but he nodded at her as casually as if it had been ten minutes. She nodded back. The heating duct above her head clattered.

"Teddy here's gonna be my assistant while I regrip those irons over there," Skeet announced. "Most times I wouldn't even think about letting a little kid help me regrip clubs, but Teddy's about the most responsible boy I ever met. He knows when to talk, and he knows when to keep his mouth shut. I like that in a man."

Francesca could have kissed Skeet, but since she couldn't do that, she pressed her lips to the top of Teddy's head instead. "I want to go home," Teddy said abruptly. "When can we go?" And then Francesca felt him stiffen.

She sensed that Dallie had come into the workroom behind them even before she heard his voice. "Skeet, how 'bout you take Teddy upstairs for some of that chocolate cake in the kitchen?"

Teddy jumped up from the stool with a rapidity that she suspected spoke more of his desire to get away from Dallie than of his craving for his chocolate cake. What had gone on between the two of them to make Teddy this miserable? He had always loved Holly Grace's stories. What had Dallie done to alienate him so completely? "Come on, Mom," he said, grabbing her hand. "Let's go get some cake. Come on, Skeet. Let's go."

Dallie touched Teddy's arm. "You and Skeet go on up. I want to talk to your mother for a minute."

Teddy tightened his grip on Francesca's hand and turned to Skeet. "We got to regrip those clubs, don't we? You said we had to do those clubs. Let's get started right now. Mom can help us."

"You can do it later," Dallie said more sharply. "I want to talk to your mother."

Skeet put down the wooden club head he was holding. "Come on, boy. I got some golf trophies I want to show you anyway."

As much as Francesca would have liked to put it off, she knew she couldn't postpone the confrontation. Gently disengaging herself from Teddy's grasp, she nodded toward the door. "Go on now, sweetheart. I'll be up in a minute."

Teddy's jaw set stubbornly. He looked at her and then at Dallie. He began walking away, his footsteps dragging, but before he got to the door, he spun back around and angrily turned on Dallie. "You better not hurt her!" he shouted. "If you hurt her, I'll kill you!"

Francesca was shocked, but Dallie didn't say a word. He just stood looking at Teddy.

"Dallie's not going to hurt me," she interjected quickly, distressed by Teddy's outburst. "He and I are old friends." The words nearly stuck in her throat, but she managed a halfhearted smile. Skeet caught Teddy's arm and steered him toward the stairs, but not before her son had shot a threatening look over his shoulder.

"What have you done to him?" Francesca demanded the moment Teddy was out of earshot. "I've never seen him act like that with anybody."

"I'm not trying to win any popularity contests with him," Dallie said coldly. "I want to be his father, not his best friend."

His answer infuriated her almost as much as it scared her. "You can't just pop into his life after nine years and expect to take over as his father. In the first place, he doesn't want you. And in the second place, I won't allow it."

A muscle jumped in his jaw. "Like I told you at the quarry, Francesca—we can work this out for ourselves, or we can let the bloodsuckers do it. Fathers have rights now, or don't you read the papers? And it'd probably be smart to forget any ideas you might have about flying back east for the next few days. We need some time to sort all this out."

At some point in her subconscious she had reached the same conclusion, but now she looked at him incredulously. "I have no intention of staying here. I have to get Teddy back in school. We're leaving Wynette this afternoon."

"I don't think that's a good idea, Francie. You had your nine years. Now you owe me a few days."

"You kidnapped him!" she exclaimed. "I don't owe you a bloody—"

He stabbed the air with his finger like an angry recruitment poster. "If you can't even manage a couple of days to work this thing through, then I guess all the stuff you told me at the quarry about knowing what's important in life is pretty much bullshit, isn't it?"

His belligerence made her furious. "Why are you doing this? You don't care anything about Teddy. You're just using a little boy to pay me back for stabbing your male ego."

"Don't you practice any pop psychology on me, Miss Fancy Pants," he said coldly. "You don't have the slightest idea what I care about."

She tilted up her chin and glared at him. "All I know is that you've managed to alienate a child who likes absolutely everybody in the world—especially if they're male."

"Yeah?" Dallie sneered. "Well, that's no surprise, because I never saw a kid in so much need of a man's influence in my life. Were you so busy with your damn career that you couldn't find a few hours to put him on a Little League team or something?"

Icy rage filled Francesca. "You son of a bitch," she hissed. Pushing past him, she walked quickly to the stairs.

"Francie!" She ignored the call behind her. Her heart thudding in her chest, she told herself she was every kind of fool for having wasted even a moment's sympathy on him. She raced upstairs and pushed open the door that led into the back hallway. He could throw all the bloodsucking lawyers in the world at her, she promised herself, but he would never get near her son again.

"Francie!" She heard his footsteps on the stairs, but she merely walked faster. And then he caught up with her, grabbing her arm to pull her to a stop. "Listen, Francie, I didn't mean—"

"Don't you touch me!" She tried to shake him off, but he held on, determined to have it out with her. She was vaguely aware that he was trying to apologize, but she was too upset to listen.

"Francie!" He caught her more firmly by the shoulders and looked down at her. "I'm sorry."

She pushed against him. "Let me go! We don't have anything more to talk about."

But he wouldn't let her go. "I'm going to talk to you if I have to hog-tie—"

He broke off abruptly as, out of nowhere, a small tornado threw himself at one of his legs. *"I told you not to touch my mother!"* Teddy screamed, kicking and punching with all his might. "You butt-hole! You're a butt-hole!"

"Teddy!" Francesca cried, whirling toward him as Dallie instinctively released her.

"I hate you!" Teddy screamed at Dallie, his face florid with rage, tears running down his cheeks as he escalated his attack. "I'll kill you if you hurt her!"

"I'm not going to hurt her," Dallie said, trying to step back from Teddy's flying fists. "Teddy! I'm not going to hurt her."

"Stop it, Teddy!" Francesca cried. But her voice was so shrill she only made things worse. For an instant, her eyes caught Dallie's. He looked exactly as helpless as she felt.

"I hate you! I hate you!"

"Well, now, doesn't this just about beat all?" a female voice drawled from the other end of the hallway.

"Holly Grace!" Teddy thrust himself away from Dallie and ran for one of the few safe harbors he knew he could count on in a world that was growing increasingly bewildering.

"Hey, Teddy." Holly Grace caught him against her and cupped his small head gently to her chest. Then she gave him a comforting rub across his narrow shoulders. "You did real good there, honey. Dallie's big, but you held your own just fine."

Francesca and Dallie exploded in unison.

"What the hell's wrong with you, tellin' him something like that?"

"Really, Holly Grace!"

Holly Grace gazed at them over the top of Teddy's head, taking in their rumpled clothes and flushed, stricken faces. Then she shook her head. "Damn. It looks to me like I just missed the best reunion since Sherman got together with Atlanta."

Chapter
27

Francesca pulled Teddy away from Holly Grace. With her son clasped to her side, she led him out of the hallway and toward the front of the house, intent on taking him upstairs, packing her things, and getting out of Wynette forever. But as she walked through the archway into the living room, she came to a dead stop.

The entire world seemed to have gathered to watch her life fall apart. Skeet Cooper stood by the window eating a piece of chocolate cake. Miss Sybil sat next to Doralee on the couch. The cleaning lady hired to help Miss Sybil had just come in through the front door. And Gerry Jaffe paced back and forth across the carpet.

Francesca turned to confront Holly Grace with Gerry's presence only to see that her best friend was preoccupied with wrapping her arm around Dallie's waist. If there had ever been any question in her mind about where Holly Grace's loyalties lay, her protective attitude toward Dallie had just answered it. "Did you have to bring the entire world down here with you?" Francesca snapped.

Holly Grace looked past Francesca and, spotting Gerry for the first time, uttered an oath that Francesca would just as soon Teddy had not overheard.

Gerry looked like a man who could use a good night's

sleep, and he immediately walked toward Holly Grace. "Couldn't you have called me and told me what was going on?"

"Called you?" Holly Grace shouted. "Why should I have called you, and what in the hell are you doing here?"

The cleaning lady took her time hanging up her coat while she regarded them all with ill-concealed curiosity. Dallie studied Gerry with a combination of hostility and interest. This was the only man besides himself who had been able to send the beauteous Holly Grace Beaudine into a tailspin.

Francesca felt a nagging ache start up at her temples.

"What do you mean, what the hell am I doing here?" Gerry said. "I called Naomi from Washington and found out that Teddy had been kidnapped and that you were all upset. What did you expect me to do? Stay in Washington and pretend nothing was wrong?"

The argument between Holly Grace and Gerry accelerated and then the telephone rang. Everyone, including the cleaning woman, ignored it. Francesca felt as if she was suffocating. All she could think about was that she had to get Teddy out of here. The telephone continued to ring and the cleaning lady finally began to move toward the kitchen to answer it. Holly Grace and Gerry abruptly lapsed into angry silence.

At that moment, Dallie looked over at Doralee. "Who's that?" he asked, his tone displaying little more than mild curiosity.

Skeet shook his head and shrugged.

Miss Sybil rummaged through her needlepoint bag for her canvas.

Holly Grace shot Francesca a disgusted glare.

Following the direction of his ex-wife's gaze, Dallie turned his head toward Francesca for an explanation.

"Her name is Doralee," Francesca informed him stiffly. "She needs a place to stay temporarily."

Dallie thought for a moment, and then nodded pleasantly. "Howdy, Doralee."

Sparks flashed in Holly Grace's eyes and her lips pursed ominously. "I don't believe the two of you! Haven't you got enough trouble without looking for more?"

The cleaning lady stuck her head back in the living room from the kitchen. "There's a phone call for Miss Day."

Francesca ignored her. Although her head had begun to pound in earnest, she decided she'd taken enough abuse from Holly Grace. "You just be quiet, Holly Grace Beaudine. I want to know what you're doing here. All of this is awful enough without you showing up to flap your wings around Dallie like some sort of mother hen. He's a grown man! He doesn't need you to fight his battles. And he certainly doesn't need you to protect him from me."

"Maybe I didn't just come here for him, did you ever think of that?" Holly Grace retorted. "Maybe I didn't trust either one of you to have enough common sense to handle this situation."

"I've heard enough about your common sense," Francesca answered just as angrily. "I'm sick of hearing about—"

"What should I do about this telephone call?" the cleaning lady asked. "The man says he's a prince."

"Mom!" Teddy wailed, scratching the rash on his stomach and glaring daggers at Dallie.

Holly Grace thrust her pointed finger toward Doralee. "There's a perfect example of what I'm talking about! You never think. You just—"

Doralee jumped up. "I don't have to listen to this shit!"

"This is really none of your business, Holly Grace," Gerry interrupted.

"Mom!" Teddy wailed again. "Mom, my rash itches! I want to go home!"

"Are you going to talk to this prince fellow or not?" the cleaning lady demanded.

A jackhammer went off inside Francesca's skull. She wanted to scream at all of them to leave her alone. Her friendship with Holly Grace was crumbling before her eyes; Doralee looked as if she was going to attack; Teddy was ready to cry. "Please . . ." she said. But no one heard her.

No one except Dallie.

He leaned toward Skeet and said quietly, "How about holding on to Teddy for me?" Skeet nodded and moved closer to the boy. The angry voices grew louder. Dallie stepped forward and, before anyone could stop him, hoisted

Francesca over his shoulder. She gasped as she found herself upended.

"Sorry, folks," Dallie said. "But y'all are gonna have to wait your turn." And then, before any of them could stop him, he carried her out the door.

"Mom!" Teddy shrieked.

Skeet caught hold of Teddy before he could run after Francesca. "Now, don't get yourself riled, boy. This is the way your mama and Dallie always carry on when they're together. You might as well get used to it."

Francesca shut her eyes and leaned her head against the window of Dallie's car. The glass felt cool against her temple. She knew she should be filled with righteous outrage, lambasting Dallie for his high-handed macho theatrics, but she was too glad to be away from all those demanding, censorious voices. Abandoning Teddy upset her, but she knew Holly Grace would settle him down.

A Barry Manilow tune began to play softly on the radio. Dallie reached forward to punch the button, and then, glancing over at her, stopped himself and left it alone. Several miles slipped by, and she began to feel calmer. Dallie didn't say anything to her, but considering what they'd been through, the silence was relatively restful. She'd forgotten how quiet Dallie could be when he wasn't talking.

She shut her eyes and let herself drift until the car turned into a narrow lane that ended in front of a two-story stone house. The rustic little house was set in a grove of chinaberry trees with a line of old cedars forming a windbreak along the side and a row of low blue hills in the distance. She looked over at Dallie as they pulled up to the front walk. "Where are we?"

He turned off the ignition and got out without answering her. She watched warily as he walked around the front of the car and opened her door. Resting one hand on the roof of the car and the other on the top of the door frame, he leaned in toward her. As she gazed into those cool blue eyes, something strange happened in the vicinity of her middle. She suddenly felt like a hungry woman who had just been presented with a tempting dessert. Her moment of sensory weakness embarrassed her, and she frowned.

"Damn, you're pretty," Dallie said softly.

"Not half as pretty as you," she snapped, determined to squash whatever strangeness was lurking in the air between them. "Where are we? Whose house is this?"

"It's mine."

"Yours? We can't be more than twenty miles from Wynette. Why do you have two houses so close together?"

"After what happened back there, I'm surprised you can even ask that question." He stood aside to let her out.

She stepped from the car and gazed thoughtfully toward the front porch. "This is a hideaway, isn't it?"

"I guess you might call it that. And I'd appreciate it if you didn't tell anybody that I brought you here. They all know about this place, but so far they've kept their distance. If they find out you've been here, though, it'll be open season and they'll be lining up with sleeping bags and knitting needles and coolers full of Dr Pepper."

She walked toward the front step, curious to see the inside, but before she could get there he touched her arm. "Francie? The thing of it is, it's my house, and we can't fight in it."

His expression was as serious as she had ever seen it. "What makes you think I want to fight?" she inquired.

"I guess it's pretty much in your nature."

"My nature! First you kidnap my son, then you kidnap me, and now you have the nerve to say that *I* want to fight!"

"Call me a pessimist." He sat down on the top step.

Francesca clutched her arms, uncomfortably aware that he'd gotten the best of her on that exchange. And then she shivered. He'd carried her out of the house without her jacket, and it couldn't be much more than forty degrees. "What are you doing? Why are you sitting down?"

"If we're going to have it out, let's do it right here, because once we go inside that house, we have to be real polite to each other. I mean it, Francie, that house is my retreat, and I'm not going to have it spoiled by the two of us going after each other."

"That's ridiculous." Her teeth began to chatter. "We have things to talk about, and I don't think we're going to be able to do it without getting upset."

He patted the step next to him.

"I'm freezing," she said, thumping down at his side, but even as she complained, she found herself secretly pleased by the idea of a house where no arguments were allowed. What would happen to human relationships if there were more houses like this one? Only Dallie could have thought of something so interesting. Surreptitiously, she moved closer to his warmth. She'd forgotten how good he always smelled—like soap and clean clothes. "Why don't we sit in the car?" she suggested. "You only have on a flannel shirt. You can't be all that warm yourself."

"If we stay here, we'll get done quicker." He cleared his throat. "First of all, I apologize for making that smarmy remark about your career being more important to you than Teddy. I never said I was perfect, but still, that was a low blow and I'm ashamed of myself."

She pulled her knees closer to her chest and hunched into them. "Do you have any idea what it does to a working mother to hear something like that?"

"I wasn't thinking," he mumbled. Then he added defensively, "But damn, Francie, I wish you wouldn't fly off the handle every time I say the slightest little thing wrong. You get too emotional."

She dug her fingers into her arms in frustration. Why did men always do this? What made them think they could say the most outrageous—the most painful—things to a woman, and then expect her to keep silent? She thought of a number of pointed comments she wanted to make, but bit them back in the interest of getting into the house. "Teddy marches to the beat of his own drummer," she said firmly. "He's not like me and he's not like you. He's completely himself."

"I can see that." His knees were spread. He propped his forearms on them and stared down at the step for a few moments. "It's just that he's not like a regular kid."

All her maternal insecurities jangled like bad music. Because Teddy wasn't athletic, Dallie didn't approve of him. "What do you want him to do?" she countered angrily. "Go out and beat up some women?" He stiffened beside her, and she wished she'd kept her mouth shut.

"How are we going to work this out?" he asked quietly. "We fight like cats and dogs the minute we get within sniffing distance of each other. Maybe we'd be better off if we turned this over to the bloodsuckers."

"Is that really what you want to do?"

"All I know is that I'm getting tired of fighting with you, and we haven't even been together for a whole day."

Her teeth had begun to chatter in earnest. "Teddy doesn't like you, Dallie. I'm not going to force him to spend time with you."

"Teddy and I just rub each other the wrong way is all. We'll have to work it out."

"It won't be that easy."

"Lots of things aren't easy."

She looked hopefully toward the front door. "Let's stop talking about Teddy and go inside for a few minutes. Then after we get warmed up we can come back out and finish."

Dallie nodded his head, then stood and offered his hand. She accepted it, but the contact felt much too good, so she let go as quickly as she could, determined to keep the pressing of flesh between them to a minimum. For a moment he looked as if he'd read her thoughts, and then he turned to unlock the door. "You got a real challenge for yourself with that Doralee," he remarked. Stepping aside, he gestured her into a terra-cotta hallway lit by an arched window. "How many strays you figure you picked up in the last ten years?"

"Animal or human?"

He chuckled, and as she walked into the living room, she remembered what a wonderful sense of humor Dallie had. The living room held a faded Oriental rug, a collection of brass lamps, and some overstuffed chairs. Everything was comfortable and nondescript—everything except the wonderful paintings on the walls. "Dallie, where did you get these?" she asked, walking over to an original oil depicting stark mountains and bleached bones.

"Here and there," he said, as if he wasn't quite sure.

"They're wonderful!" She moved on to study a large canvas splashed with exotic abstract flowers. "I didn't know you collected art."

"I don't collect it so much as just nail up a few things I like."

She lifted an eyebrow at him so he'd know his country-bumpkin act wasn't fooling her for a minute. Hayseeds didn't buy paintings like these. "Dallas, is it remotely possible for you to carry on a conversation that's not loaded down with manure?"

"Probably not." He grinned and then gestured toward the dining room. "There's an acrylic in there you might like. I bought it at this little gallery in Carmel after I double-bogeyed the seventeenth at Pebble Beach two days in a row. I got so depressed I either had to get drunk or buy me a painting. I got another one by the same artist hanging in my house in North Carolina."

"I didn't know you had a house in North Carolina."

"It's one of those contemporaries that sort of looks like a bank vault. Actually, I'm not too crazy about it, but it's got a pretty view. Most of the houses I been buying lately are more traditional."

"There are more?"

He shrugged. "It got so I could hardly stand staying in motels anymore, and since I started finishing in the money at a few tournaments and picking up some decent endorsements, I needed something to do with my cash. So I bought a couple of houses in different parts of the country. You want something to drink?"

She realized that she'd had nothing to eat since the night before. "What I'd really like is food. And then I think I'd better get back to Teddy." And call Stefan, she thought to herself. And meet with the social worker to discuss Doralee. And talk to Holly Grace, who used to be her best friend.

"You coddle Teddy too much," Dallie commented, leading her toward the kitchen.

She stopped in her tracks. The fragile truce between them was broken. It took him a moment to realize she wasn't following him, and then he turned to see what was holding her up. When he spotted the expression on her face, he sighed and reached for her arm to lead her to the front porch. She tried to pull away, but he held her fast.

A chilly blast hit her as he pushed her outside. She spun around to confront him. "Don't make judgments about my mothering, Dallie. You've spent less than a week with Teddy, so don't start imagining you're an authority on raising him. You don't even know him!"

"I know what I see. Damn, Francie, I'm not trying to hurt your feelings, but he's a disappointment to me is all."

She felt a sharp stab of pain. Teddy—her pride and joy, blood of her blood, heart of her heart—how could he be a disappointment to anyone? "I don't really care," she said coldly. "The only thing that bothers me is what a disappointment you apparently are to him."

Dallie stuffed one of his hands in the pocket of his jeans and looked out toward the cedar trees, not saying anything. The wind caught a lock of his hair, blowing it back from his forehead. Finally he spoke quietly. "Maybe we'd better get back to Wynette. I guess this wasn't such a good idea."

She looked out at the cedars herself for a few moments before she nodded slowly and walked toward the car.

The house was empty except for Teddy and Skeet. Dallie went back out without saying where he was going, and Francesca took Teddy for a walk. Twice she tried to introduce Dallie's name, but he resisted her efforts and she didn't push him. He couldn't say enough, however, about the virtues of Skeet Cooper.

When they returned to the house, Teddy ran off to get a snack and she went down to the basement where she found Skeet putting a coat of varnish on the club head he'd been sanding earlier. He didn't look up as she came into the workroom, and she watched him for a few minutes before she spoke. "Skeet, I want to thank you for being so nice to Teddy. He needs a friend right now."

"You don't have to thank me," Skeet replied gruffly. "He's a good boy."

She propped her elbow on top of the vise, taking pleasure in watching Skeet work. The slow, careful movements soothed her so that she could think more clearly. Twenty-four hours before, all she had wanted to do was to get Teddy away from Dallie, but now she toyed with the idea of trying to bring them together. Sooner or later, Teddy was going to have to acknowledge his relationship to Dallie. She couldn't bear the idea of her son growing up with emotional scars because he hated his father, and if freeing him of those scars meant she would have to spend a few more days in Wynette, she would simply do so.

Her mind made up, she looked over at Skeet. "You really like Teddy, don't you?"

"'Course I like him. He's the kind of kid you don't mind spending time with."

"It's too bad everybody doesn't feel that way," she said bitterly.

Skeet cleared his throat. "You give Dallie time, Francie. I know you're the impatient type, always wanting to rush things, but some things just can't be rushed."

"They hate each other, Skeet."

He turned the club head to inspect it and then dipped his brush in the varnish can. "When two people are so much alike, it's sometimes hard for them to get along."

"Alike?" She stared at him. "Dallie and Teddy aren't anything alike."

He looked at her as if she were the stupidest person he'd ever met, and then he shook his head and went back to varnishing the club head.

"Dallie's graceful," she argued. "He's athletic. He's gorgeous—"

Skeet chuckled. "Teddy sure is a homely little cuss. Hard to figure how two people as pretty as you and Dallie managed to produce him."

"Maybe he's a little homely on the outside," she replied defensively, "but he's a knockout on the inside."

Skeet chuckled again, dipped his brush, and then looked over at her. "I don't like to give advice, Francie, but if I were you I'd concentrate more on nagging Dallie about his golf than on nagging him about Teddy."

She looked at him in astonishment. "Why ever should I nag him about his golf?"

"You're not going to get rid of him. You realize that, don't you? Now that he knows Teddy's his boy, he's going to keep popping up whether you like it or not."

She'd already come to the same conclusion, and she nodded reluctantly.

He stroked the brush along the smooth curve of the wood. "My best piece of advice, Francie, is that you use those brains of yours to figure out how to get him to play better golf."

She was completely mystified. "What are you trying to tell me?"

"Just exactly what I said, is all."

"But I don't know anything about golf, and I don't see what Dallie's game has to do with Teddy."

"The thing about advice is—you can either take it or leave it."

She gave him a searching look. "You know why he's being so critical of Teddy, don't you?"

"I got a few ideas."

"Is it because Teddy looks like Jaycee? Is that it?"

He snorted. "Give Dallie credit for having more sense than that."

"Then what?"

He propped the club head on a rod to dry and put the brush in a jar of mineral spirits. "You just concentrate on his golf is all. Maybe you'll have better luck than I've had."

And he wouldn't say anything more than that.

When Francesca went upstairs, she spotted Teddy playing with one of Dallie's dogs in the yard. An envelope lay on the kitchen table with her name scrawled across it in Gerry's handwriting. Opening it, she read the message inside.

Baby, Sweetie, Lamb Chop, Love of My Life,

How's about you and me tie one on tonight? Pick you up for dinner and debauchery at 7:00. Your best friend is the queen of the morons, and I'm the world's biggest chump. I promise not to cry on your shoulder for more than most of the evening. When are you going to stop being so lily-livered and put me on your television show?

Sincerely,
Zorro the Great

P.S. Bring a birth control device.

Francesca laughed. Despite their rocky beginning on that Texas road ten years ago, she and Gerry had formed a comfortable friendship in the two years since she'd moved to Manhattan. He had spent the first few months of their acquaintance apologizing for having abandoned her, even though Francesca told him he'd done her a favor that day. To her astonishment, he had produced an old yellowed envelope containing her passport and the four hundred dollars that had been in her case. She had long ago given Holly Grace the money to repay Dallie what she owed him, so Francesca had treated the three of them to a night on the town.

When Gerry came to pick her up that evening, he was wearing his leather bomber jacket with dark brown trousers and a cream-colored sweater. Sweeping her into his arms, he gave her a friendly smack on the lips, his dark eyes sparkling with wickedness. "Hey, gorgeous. Why couldn't I have fallen in love with you instead of Holly Grace?"

"Because you're too smart to put up with me," she said, laughing.

"Where's Teddy?"

"He conned Doralee and Miss Sybil into taking him to see some horrid movie about killer grasshoppers."

Gerry smiled and then sobered, looking at her with concern. "How're you really doing? This has been rough on you, hasn't it?"

"I've had better weeks," she conceded. So far, only her problem with Doralee was any closer to solution. That afternoon Miss Sybil had insisted on taking the teenager to the county offices herself, telling Francesca in no uncertain terms that she intended to keep Doralee until a foster family could be found.

"I spent some time with Dallie this afternoon," Gerry said."

"You did?" Francesca was surprised. It was difficult to imagine the two of them together.

Gerry held the front door open for her. "I gave him some not-so-friendly legal advice and told him if he ever tried anything like this with Teddy again, I would personally bring the entire American legal system down on his head."

"I can just imagine how he reacted to that," she replied dryly.

"I'll do you a favor and spare you the details." They walked toward Gerry's rented Toyota. "You know, it's strange. Once we stopped trading insults, I almost found myself liking the son of a bitch. I mean, I hate the fact that he and Holly Grace used to be married, and I especially hate the fact that they still care so much about each other, but once we started talking, I had this weird feeling that Dallie and I had known each other a long time. It was crazy."

"Don't be fooled," Francesca said, as he opened the car door for her. "The only reason you felt comfortable with him is because being with him is a lot like being with Holly Grace. If you like one of them, it's pretty hard not to like the other one."

They ate at a cozy restaurant that served wonderful veal. Before they had finished the main course, they were once again embroiled in their standard argument about why Francesca wouldn't put Gerry on her television show.

"Just put me on once, gorgeous, that's all I ask."

"Forget it. I know you. You'd show up with fake radiation burns all over your body or you'd announce on the air that Russian missiles are on their way to blow up Nebraska."

"So what? You have millions of complacent androids watching your show who don't understand that we're living on the eve of destruction. It's my job to shake up people like that."

"Not on my program," she said firmly. "I don't manipulate my viewers."

"Francesca, these days we're not talking about a little thirteen-kiloton firecracker like the one we dropped on Nagasaki. We're talking megatons. If twenty thousand megatons hits New York City, it's going to do more than ruin one of Donald Trump's dinner parties. It'll send fallout over a thousand square miles, and eight million fried bodies will be left rotting in the gutters."

"I'm trying to eat, Gerry," she protested, setting down her fork.

Gerry had been talking about the horrors of nuclear war for so long that he could demolish a five-course meal while he described a terminal case of radiation poisoning, and he dug into his baked potato. "Do you know the only thing that has any chance of surviving? The cockroaches. They'll be blind, but they'll still be able to reproduce."

"Gerry, I love you like a brother, but I won't let you turn

my show into a circus." Before he could launch his next round of arguments, she changed the subject. "Did you talk to Holly Grace this afternoon?"

He put down his fork and shook his head. "I went over to her mother's house, but she ducked out the back door when she saw me coming." Pushing away his plate, he took a sip of water.

He looked so miserable that Francesca was torn between the desire to comfort him and the urge to smack some sense into him. Gerry and Holly Grace obviously loved each other, and she wished they would stop camouflaging their problems. Although Holly Grace hardly ever talked about it, Francesca knew how badly she wanted a child, but Gerry wouldn't even discuss the matter with her.

"Why don't the two of you try to come up with some sort of compromise?" she offered tentatively.

"She doesn't understand the word," Gerry replied. "She's got it in her head that I've been using her name, and—"

Francesca groaned. "Not this again. Holly Grace wants a *baby*, Gerry. Why won't either of you admit what the real problem is? I know it's none of my business, but I think you'd make a wonderful father, and—"

"Christ, have you and Naomi been taking nagging lessons together or what?" He abruptly pushed his plate away. "Let's go on over to the Roustabout, okay?"

The Roustabout was the last place she wanted to go. "I don't really—"

"The high school sweethearts are sure to be there. We'll walk in, pretend we don't see them, and then have sex on top of the bar. What do you say?"

"I say no."

"Come on, gorgeous. The two of them have been tossing a ton of shit our way. Let's toss a little back."

True to form, Gerry ignored every one of her protests and hustled her from the restaurant. Fifteen minutes later, they were walking through the door of the honky-tonk. The place looked much as Francesca remembered, although most of the neon Lone Star beer signs had been replaced with signs for Miller Lite, and video games now occupied one corner. The people were the same, however.

"Well, look who just walked through the door," a throaty female voice drawled from a table twenty feet to their right. "If it isn't the queen of England herself with the king of the Bolsheviks walking right next to her." Holly Grace sat with a beer bottle in front of her, while at her side Dallie sipped a glass of club soda. Francesca felt another of those queer little jumps in her middle at the sight of those cool blue eyes studying her over the rim of the glass.

"No, I'm wrong," Holly Grace went on as she took in the black and ivory print Galanos dress Francesca was wearing with an oversize cinnabar red jacket. "She's not the queen of England. She's that lady mud wrestler we saw down in Medina County."

Francesca grabbed Gerry's arm. "Let's go."

Gerry's full lips were growing thinner by the minute, but he refused to move. Holly Grace tilted back the brim of her Stetson, studiously ignoring him while she scrutinized Francesca's outfit. "Galanos in the Roustabout. Shit. You're liable to get us all kicked out. Don't you get tired always being the center of attention?"

Francesca forgot about Gerry and Dallie and looked at Holly Grace with genuine concern. She really was acting bitchy. Letting go of Gerry's arm, she walked over to her and slipped into the chair at her side. "Are you all right?" she asked.

Holly Grace scowled into her beer glass, but otherwise remained silent.

"Let's go to the bathroom so we can talk," Francesca whispered, and when Holly Grace didn't respond, she added more forcefully, "Right now."

Holly Grace gave her a rebellious look that resembled Teddy at his worst. "I'm not going anywhere with you. I'm still mad at you for not telling me the truth about Teddy." She turned to Dallie. "Dance with me, baby."

Dallie had been regarding them both with interest. Now he unwound himself from his chair and looped his arm over Holly Grace's shoulders as she stood up. "Sure, honey."

The two of them began to walk away, but Gerry took a step forward, blocking their path. "Isn't it interesting the way they grab on to each other?" he said to Francesca. "It's

397

the most fascinating case of arrested development I've ever seen."

"You go ahead and dance, Holly Grace," Francesca said quietly, "but while you're doing it, think about the fact that I might need you right now just as much as Dallie does."

For a moment Holly Grace hesitated, but then she turned into Dallie's arms and together they moved out onto the dance floor.

At that moment, one of the patrons of the Roustabout came up to ask Francesca for her autograph, and before long she was surrounded by fans. She chatted with them while inwardly she was filled with frustration. Out of the corner of her eye, she saw Gerry talking to a buxom young thing at the bar. Holly Grace danced past with Dallie, the two of them moving together like one single, graceful body, their casual intimacy so absolute they seemed to shut out the rest of the world. Her cheeks began to ache from smiling. She signed more autographs and acknowledged more compliments, but the patrons of the Roustabout refused to let her go. They were accustomed to having the star of "China Colt" in their midst, but seeing the glamorous Francesca Day was something else entirely. It wasn't long before she spotted Holly Grace slipping out the back door by herself. A hand touched her from behind.

"Sorry, folks, but Francie promised me this dance. You still remember the two-step, honey?"

Francesca turned toward Dallie and, after a moment's hesitation, went into his arms. He caught her against him, and she had the unsettling feeling that she'd been pitched back ten years to the time when this man had formed the center of her world.

"Damn, it feels funny to be dancing with somebody who's wearing a dress," he said. "You got shoulder pads in that jacket?"

His tone was soft, gentle with amusement. It felt so good to be close to him. Much too good.

"Don't you let Holly Grace hurt your feelings," he said quietly. "She just needs some time."

Dallie's sympathy, under the circumstances, surprised her. She managed to reply, "Her friendship means a lot to me."

"If you ask me, the way that old commie lover has taken advantage of her is bothering her more than anything."

Francesca realized that Dallie didn't understand the true nature of the trouble between Holly Grace and Gerry, and she decided it wasn't her place to enlighten him.

"Sooner or later, she'll come around," he went on. "And I know she'd appreciate it if you'd be there waiting for her. Now, how 'bout you stop worrying about Holly Grace and concentrate on the music so we can get down to some serious dancing?"

Francesca tried to oblige, but she was so aware of him that serious dancing was beyond her. The music slowed into a romantic country ballad. His jaw brushed the top of her head.

"You look awful pretty tonight, Francie."

His voice held a trace of huskiness that unnerved her. He drew her infinitesimally closer. "You're such a tiny little thing. I forgot how little you are."

Don't charm me, she wanted to plead as she felt the warmth of his body seep through into her own. *Don't be sweet and sexy and make me forget everything that's standing between us.* She had the disconcerting sense that the sounds around them were fading, the music growing still, the other voices disappearing so that it seemed as if the two of them were alone on the dance floor.

He pulled her closer and their rhythm subtly changed, no longer quite a dance but something closer to an embrace. His body felt hard and solid against hers, and she tried to summon the energy to fight her attraction to him. "Let's— let's sit down now."

"All right."

But instead of letting her go, he tucked their clasped hands between their bodies. His other hand slipped under her jacket so that only the thin silk of her dress separated her skin from his touch. Somehow her cheek seemed to find his shoulder. She leaned into it as if she had come home. Drawing in her breath, she shut her eyes and drifted with him.

"Francie," he whispered into her hair, "we're going to have to do something about this."

She thought about pretending that she didn't understand

what he meant, but at that moment coquetry was beyond her. "It's—it's just a simple chemical attraction. If we ignore it, it'll go away."

He pulled her closer. "You sure about that?"

"Absolutely." She hoped he didn't hear the slight quaver in her voice. She was suddenly frightened, and she found herself saying, "Gracious, Dallie, this has happened to me hundreds of times before. Thousands. I'm sure it's happened to you, too."

"Yeah," he said flatly. "Thousands of times." Abruptly he stopped moving and dropped his arms. "Listen, Francie, if it's all the same to you, I don't feel too much like dancing anymore."

"Fine." She gave him her best cocktail party smile and busied her hands by straightening the front of her jacket. "That's fine with me."

"See you later." He turned to walk away.

"Yes, later," she said to his back.

Their parting was cordial. No angry words had been spoken. No warnings had been issued. But as she watched him disappear into the crowd, she had the vague feeling that a new set of battle lines had been drawn between them.

Chapter
28

Although Dallie made several halfhearted attempts to smooth his relationship with Teddy, the two of them were like oil and water. When his father was around, Teddy bumped into furniture, broke dishes, and sulked. Dallie was quick to criticize the child, and the two of them grew increasingly miserable in each other's company. Francesca tried to act as a conciliator, but so much tension had built up between herself and Dallie since the evening they had danced at the Roustabout that she only succeeded in losing her own temper.

The afternoon of her third and final day in Wynette, she confronted Dallie in the basement after Teddy had run upstairs and kicked a chair across the kitchen. "Couldn't you sit down and do a puzzle with him or read a book together?" she demanded. "What in God's name made you think he could learn to shoot pool with you yelling at him the entire time?"

Dallie glared at the jagged tear in the green felt that covered his pool table. "I wasn't yelling, and you stay out of this. You're leaving tomorrow, and that doesn't give me much time to make up for nine years of too much female influence."

"Only partial female influence," she retorted. "Don't forget that Holly Grace spent a lot of time with him, too."

His eyes narrowed. "And just what do you mean by that remark?"

"It means she was one hell of a better father than you'll ever be."

Dallie stalked away from her, every muscle in his body taut with belligerence, only to reappear at her side moments later. "And another thing. I thought you were going to talk to him—explain about how I'm his father."

"Teddy's not in the mood for any explanations. He's a smart kid. He'll catch on when he's ready."

His eyes raked her body with deliberate insolence. "You know what I think's wrong with you? I think you're still an immature child who can't stand not getting her own way!"

Her eyes raked him right back. "And I think you're a brainless jock who's not worth a damn without a bloody golf club in his hand!"

They threw angry words at each other like guided missiles, but even as the hostilities between them mounted, Francesca had the vague sensation that nothing either of them said was hitting its target. Their words were merely an ineffective smoke screen that did little to hide the fact that the air between them was smoldering with lust.

"It's no wonder you never got married. You're about the coldest woman I ever met in my life."

"There are a number of men who'd disagree. *Real* men, not glamour boys who wear their jeans so tight you have to wonder what they're trying to prove."

"It just shows where you've been putting your eyes."

"It just shows how bored I've been." The words flew around their heads like bullets, leaving both of them seething with frustration and putting everyone else in the household on edge.

Finally Skeet Cooper had had enough. "I've got a surprise for the two of you," he said, sticking his head through the basement door. "Come on up here."

Not looking at each other, Dallie and Francesca climbed the steps to the kitchen. Skeet was waiting by the back door holding their jackets. "Miss Sybil and Doralee are gonna take Teddy to the library. You two are coming with me."

"Where are we going?" Francesca asked.

"I'm not in the mood," Dallie snapped.

Skeet threw a red windbreaker at Dallie's chest. "I don't give a good goddamn whether you're in the mood or not, because I guaran-damn-tee you that you're gonna be shy one caddy if you don't hustle yourself into my car in about the next thirty seconds."

Grumbling under his breath, Dallie followed Francesca out to Skeet's Ford. "You ride in the back," Skeet told him. "Francie's riding up here with me." Dallie grumbled some more, but did as he was told.

Francesca did her best to drive Dallie even crazier during the ride by indulging in a pleasant conversation with Skeet and pointedly leaving him out. Skeet ignored Dallie's questions about where they were going, saying only that he had the solution to at least some of their problems. They were nearly twenty miles outside of Wynette on a road that looked vaguely familiar to Francesca, when Skeet pulled the car over to the side.

"I've got something real interesting in the trunk of my car that I want both of you to see." Sliding up on one hip, he pulled a spare key from his pocket and tossed it back to Dallie. "You go look, too, Francie. I think this'll make the two of you feel a whole lot better."

Dallie regarded him suspiciously, but opened the door and climbed out. Francesca zipped up her jacket and did the same. They walked along opposite sides of the car to the back, and Dallie reached toward the trunk lock with the key. Before he could touch it, however, Skeet hit the accelerator and peeled away, leaving the two of them standing at the side of the road.

Francesca stared at the rapidly vanishing car in bewilderment. "What—"

"You son of a bitch!" Dallie yelled, shaking his fist at the back end of the Ford. "I'm going to kill him! When I get my hands on him, he's gonna regret the day he was born. I should have known— That rotten no-good—"

"I don't understand," Francesca cut in. "What's he doing? Why is he leaving us?"

"Because he can't stand listening to you argue anymore, that's why!"

"Me!"

There was a short pause before he grabbed her upper arm. "Come on."

"Where are we going?"

"My house. It's about a mile or so down the next road."

"How convenient," she said dryly. "Are you sure the two of you didn't plot this together?"

"Believe me," he snarled, starting to walk again, "the last thing in the world I want is to be stuck in that house with you. There's not even a telephone."

"Look on the bright side," she replied sarcastically. "With those Goody Two-shoes rules you've laid down, we won't be able to fight once we get in the house."

"Yeah, well you'd better stick to those rules or you'll find yourself spending the night on the front porch."

"Spending the night?"

"You don't really think he's going to come back and get us before morning, do you?"

"You're kidding."

"Do I look like it?"

They walked for a little bit, and then, just to aggravate him, she started humming Willie Nelson's "On the Road Again." He stopped and glared at her.

"Oh, don't be such a sourpuss," she chided. "You have to admit this is at least a little amusing."

"Amusing!" Once again his hands slammed down on his hips. "I'd like to know what's so damned amusing about it! You know just as well as I do what's going to happen between the two of us in that house tonight."

A truck whipped by them, tossing Francesca's hair against her cheek. She felt her pulse jump in her throat. "I don't know any such thing," she replied haughtily. He gave her a scornful look, telling her without words that he thought she was the world's biggest hypocrite. She glared at him and then decided the best course lay in advance rather than retreat. "Even if you're right—which you're not—you don't have to act as if you're heading for a root canal operation."

"That'd probably be a hell of a lot less painful."

One of his barbs had finally pricked, and now she was the one who stopped walking. "Do you really mean that?" she asked, genuinely hurt.

He shoved one hand in the pocket of his parka and kicked a stone with his foot. "Of course I mean it."

"You do not."

"I absolutely do."

She must have looked as upset as she felt, because his expression softened and then he took a step toward her. "Aw, Francie . . ."

Before either of them quite knew what was happening, she was in his arms and he was gently lowering his mouth to hers. The kiss began soft and sweet, but they were so hungry for each other that it changed almost immediately. His fingers plowed into her hair, sweeping it back from her temples to fall over his hands. She wrapped her arms around his neck and, standing on tiptoe, parted her lips to welcome his tongue.

The kiss shattered them. It was like a great typhoon sweeping away all their differences with its strength. One of his hands reached beneath her hips, lifting her just off the ground. His kiss moved from her mouth to her neck and then back to her mouth. His hand found the bare skin where her jacket and sweater had risen above her slacks, and he stroked upward along her spine. Within seconds, the two of them were hot and wet, full of juice, ready to eat each other up.

A car sped past, horn blasting, catcalls sounding out the window. Francesca released her grasp around his neck. "Stop," she moaned. "We can't . . . Oh, God . . ." He lowered her slowly to the ground. Her skin was hot.

Slowly, Dallie withdrew his hand from beneath her sweater and let her go. "The thing of it is," he said, his voice slightly breathless, "when this sort of thing happens between people—this kind of sexual chemistry—they lose their common sense."

"Does this sort of thing happen to you often?" she snapped, suddenly as nervous as a cat with its fur being stroked the wrong way.

"The last time was when I was seventeen, and I promised myself I'd learn a lesson from it. Damn, Francie, I'm thirty-seven years old, and you're—what—thirty?"

"Thirty-one."

"Both of us are old enough to know better, and here we

are, acting like a couple of horny teenagers." He shook his blond head in self-disgust. "It'll be a miracle if you don't end up with a sucker bite on your neck."

"Don't blame me for what happened," she retorted. "I've been on the wagon for so long that anything looks good to me right now—even you."

"I thought you and that Prince Stefan—"

"We're going to. We just haven't gotten around to it yet."

"Something like that you probably shouldn't put off much longer."

They started walking again. Before long, Dallie took her hand and gave her fingers a gentle squeeze. His gesture should have been friendly and comforting, but it sent threads of heat traveling up Francesca's arm. She decided that the best way to dissipate the electricity between them was to use the cold voice of logic. "Everything is already so complicated for us. This—this—sexual attraction is going to make it impossible."

"You could kiss good ten years ago, honey, but you've moved into the major leagues since then."

"I don't do that with everybody," she replied irritably.

"No offense, Francie, but I remember back all those years ago that once the serious business got started, you still had a few things to learn—not that you weren't a real good student. Tell me why I get the feeling that you've pretty much put yourself on the honor roll since then?"

"I haven't! I'm terrible at sex. It—it messes up my hair."

He chuckled. "I don't think you care too much about your hair anymore—not that it doesn't look real good—and your makeup, too, by the way."

"Oh, God," she moaned. And then, "Maybe we should pretend none of this happened, just go back to the way things were."

He tucked his hand, along with hers, into the pocket of his parka. "Honey, you and I have been circling each other ever since the second we got back together—sniffing and snarling like a couple of mongrel dogs. If we don't let things take their natural course pretty soon, we're both going to end up half crazy." He paused for a moment. "Or blind."

Instead of disagreeing with him, as she should have,

Francesca found herself saying, "Assuming we decide to go ahead with this, how long do you think it will take for us to—to burn out?"

"I don't know. We're entirely different people. My guess is if we do it two or three times, the mystery'll be gone, and that'll pretty much be the end of it."

Was he right? She chastised herself. Of course he was right. This kind of sexual chemistry was just like a brushfire —it burned hot and quickly, but had no real staying power. Once again she was making too big a deal out of sex. Dallie was acting completely casual about the whole thing and so should she. This was a perfect opportunity to get him out of her blood without losing her dignity.

They walked the rest of the way to the farmhouse in silence. When they got inside, he performed all the rituals of a host—hanging up their jackets, adjusting the thermostat so the house would be comfortable, pouring her a glass of wine from a bottle he'd brought in from the kitchen. The silence between them had begun to feel oppressive, and she took refuge in sarcasm. "If that bottle has a screw top, I don't want any."

"I took the cork out with my very own teeth."

She repressed a smile and sat down on the couch, only to discover that she was too nervous to sit still. She got back up. "I'm going to use the bathroom. And, Dallie . . . I didn't—bring anything with me. I know it's my body and I consider myself responsible for it, but I didn't plan to end up in your bed—not that I've actually made up my mind about that yet—but if I do—if we do—if you're not better prepared than I am, you'd better tell me right now."

He smiled. "I'll take care of it."

"You'd better." She gave him her most ferocious scowl, because everything was moving too quickly for her. She knew she was getting ready to do something she would regret, but she didn't seem to have the willpower to stop herself. It was because she'd been celibate for a year, she reasoned. That was the only explanation.

When she returned from the bathroom, he was sitting on the sofa, with one boot crossed over his knee, drinking a glass of tomato juice. She sat at the opposite end of the couch, not pressed up against the arm exactly, but not cuddled next to him, either. He looked over at her. "Jeez, Francie, I wish you'd loosen up a little bit. You're starting to make *me* nervous."

"Don't give me that," she retorted. "You're as nervous as I am. You just hide it better."

He didn't deny it. "You want to take a shower together to warm up?"

She shook her head. "I don't want to take off my clothes."

"It's going to be pretty difficult—"

"That's not what I mean. I'll probably take off my clothes—eventually—maybe—if I decide to—it's just that I plan to be already warmed up before I do it."

Dallie grinned. "You know what, Francie? This is sort of fun, just sitting here talking about it. I almost hate to start kissing you."

So she started kissing him instead, because she absolutely couldn't stand to talk anymore.

This kiss was even better than the one by the side of the road. Their verbal foreplay had put them both on edge and there was a roughness about their caresses that seemed exactly right for an encounter that was absurdly foolish for both of them. As their mouths pressed together and their tongues touched, Francesca once again had the sensation that the rest of the world had drifted away.

She pushed her hands beneath his shirt. Within seconds, her sweater was off and the buttons on the front of her silk blouse opened. Her lingerie was beautiful—lace shells of oyster silk cupping her breasts. He peeled back one of the shells to find her creamy nipple and suckle it.

When she couldn't stand it anymore, she pulled his head up and began a relentless attack on his bottom lip, tracing the curve with her tongue, gently teasing it with her teeth. Finally she slipped her fingers along his spine and pushed them inside the waistband of his jeans. He groaned and pulled her to her feet, then stripped down her slacks and slipped off her shoes and stockings. "I want to see you," he said huskily, freeing the silk blouse from her shoulders. The fabric felt like a caress as it slid down over her arms.

Dallie caught his breath. "Does all your underwear look like it belongs in a high-class strip show?"

"Every bit of it." She rose up on tiptoe to take a nip at his ear. His fingers toyed with the two little strings on her hip that held the tiny silk triangle of her panties in place, leaving the curve of her thigh bare. Goose bumps slithered over her skin. "Carry me upstairs," she whispered.

He slipped his arm under her knees, lifted her, and held her close to his chest. "You don't weigh as much as a full bag of clubs, honey."

His bedroom was large and comfortable, with a fireplace at one end and a bed tucked beneath a sloping ceiling. He laid her gently down on the spread and then reached toward the delicate ties at her hips. "No, no." She pushed his hand away and pointed toward the center of the room. "Take it off first, soldier."

He looked at her suspiciously. "Take what off?"

"Your clothes. Entertain the troops."

"My clothes?" He frowned. "I was sort of thinking you might want to do that for me."

She shook her head and leaned back on one elbow, giving him her witchiest, bitchiest smile. "Strip."

"Now, listen here, Francie—"

Lifting a languid hand, she once again pointed toward the center of the room. "Do it real slow, good-looking," she purred. "I want to enjoy every minute."

"Aw, Francie . . ." He looked longingly toward the twin shells over her breasts and then lower to the small silk triangle. She moved her legs slightly apart to inspire him.

"I feel stupid making a big show out of taking off my clothes," he grumbled as he moved toward the center of the room.

She let her fingers trail delicately over the triangle of silk. "That's just too bad. As far as I'm concerned, men like you were put on this world to entertain women like me."

His eyes followed her fingers. "Now, is that so?"

She toyed with the little string. "All brawn, no brain, what else are you good for?"

Lifting his gaze, he gave her a lazy grin and slowly began unbuttoning his cuffs. "Well, now, I guess you're about to find out."

Francesca felt a surge of heat flow through her blood. The simple act of unfastening a shirt cuff suddenly struck her as the most erotic thing she had ever seen. Dallie must have noticed her breath quicken, because a smile flickered at the corner of his mouth and then disappeared as he began to play her in earnest. He took his time unfastening the rest of his shirt buttons and then let the garment hang open for a moment before he took it off. Her lips parted slightly. She studied the play of muscles in his chest as he reached down to pull off his boots and his socks. Dressed only in jeans and a wide leather belt, he straightened up and linked one thumb in his waistband.

"Slip down that bra," he said. "Nothing more comes off here until I see something good."

She pretended to think it over and then slowly reached behind her back to open the small clasp. The straps drifted down along her shoulders, but she held the shells in place over her breasts. "Take off your belt first," she said, her voice deep and throaty. "And then unzip."

He pulled the belt from the denim loops. For a moment, he let it hang at his side, the buckle curling from his fist. Then he surprised her by tossing it over to the bed, where it fell across her ankles. "In case I need to use it on you," he said, his voice full of sexy menace.

She swallowed hard. He pulled open the top snap on his jeans and pushed the zipper down a scant few inches, revealing his flat abdomen. And then he rested his hand lightly on the slide, waiting for her. She eased the silky shells off her breasts, delicately arching her back so he could look his fill. Now he was the one who swallowed hard.

"The jeans, soldier boy," she whispered.

He pulled the zipper down the rest of the way, then tucked both his thumbs inside the waistband, snagging the jeans and his briefs together, and slid them off. He finally stood naked before her.

Without any pretense of shyness, she looked her fill. He was hard and proud, sleek and shiny and beautiful. She let her head drift back on the pillows, her hair spilling out in a corona around her, and watched him as he walked to the side of the bed. Reaching down with his index finger, he stroked a long line from her throat to the top of the triangle of her panties. "Open the ties," he ordered.

"You do it," she replied.

He sat down on the edge of the bed and reached toward one of the satin ribbons. She stilled his hand. "With your mouth."

He chuckled, then leaned over and did as she had ordered. As he pulled the silky triangle from between her legs, he kissed her and then began stroking the insides of her thighs. She took off on an exploratory mission of her own, her hand greedy to touch him. After a few minutes, he groaned and broke away to reach into the drawer of the bedside table. When he turned his back to her, she laughed and lifted herself up on her knees to nuzzle his neck. "Never send a man to do a woman's job," she whispered. Reaching around him, she took over his task, dallying and teasing until his skin was damp with perspiration.

"Damn, Francie," he said huskily, "you keep on like that and you're not going to get anything out of this encounter but a boring memory."

She smiled and slipped back onto the pillows, parting her legs for him. "Somehow I doubt that."

He took advantage of what she was offering him, tormenting her with expert caresses until she begged him to stop, and then kissing her breathless. When he finally entered her, she dug her hands into his hips and cried out. He reared up, driving himself deeper. They began talking in breathless little words.

"Please . . ."

"So good . . ."

"Yes . . . hard . . ."

"Sweet . . ."

Each was accustomed to being a cool lover—considerate, giving, but always in control. Now they were hot and wet, strung out on passion, oblivious to everything but the mad cry of one beautiful body reaching out for the other. They came, seconds apart, spilling open in gushing, noisy abandonment, filling the air with cries, moans, and breathless obscenities.

Afterward, neither could have said who was the more embarrassed.

Chapter
29

They ate a tense meal, with both of them cracking jokes that weren't all that funny. Then they went back to bed and made love again. With their mouths glued together and their bodies joined, they couldn't talk, but talking was something neither of them wanted to do much of. They slept restlessly, waking in the wee hours to find that they still hadn't gotten enough of each other.

"How many times was that?" Dallie groaned after they were finished.

She nuzzled closer under his chin. "Uh—four, I think."

He kissed the top of her head and muttered, "Francie, I don't think this fire burning between us is going to be as easy to put out as we figured."

It was past eight the next morning before either of them stirred. Francesca stretched lazily and Dallie pulled her close for a cuddle. They were just beginning to fool around a little when they heard footsteps coming up the stairs. Dallie cussed under his breath. Francesca jerked her head toward the door and then watched in alarm as the knob began to turn. An ugly vision flashed through her mind of an army of Dallie's old girlfriends stalking in, each with a house key dangling from her fingers. "Oh, God . . ." She couldn't help it. She slid down beneath the covers and pulled the sheet over her head. At that exact moment, she heard the door open.

Dallie sounded mildly exasperated. "For Pete's sake, couldn't you even knock?"

"I was afraid I'd spill my coffee. I hope that's Francie under there or I'm going to be embarrassed."

"As a matter of fact, it's not Francie," Dallie said. "And you should be embarrassed."

The mattress sagged as Holly Grace settled down on the side of the bed, her hips brushing against Francesca's calves. The faint fragrance of coffee penetrated the sheet.

"The least you could do was bring me a cup, too," Dallie complained.

Holly Grace apologized. "I wasn't thinking; I've got a lot on my mind. You *were* kidding, weren't you, about that not being Francie under there?"

Dallie patted Francesca's hip through the covers. "You stay right there, Rosalita honey. This crazy person'll be gone in a few minutes."

Holly Grace tugged on the top of the sheet. "Francie, I need to talk to both of you."

Francesca clutched the sheet tighter and muttered something in Spanish about turning left at the corner to get to the post office. Dallie chuckled.

"Come on, Francie, I know it's you," Holly Grace said. "Your underwear's all over the floor—what there is of it."

Francesca saw no graceful way out. With as much dignity as possible, she lowered the sheet to her chin and glared at Holly Grace, who sat on the edge of the bed wearing old jeans and a Cowboys sweat shirt. "What do you want?" she demanded. "For three days you've refused to talk to me. Why did you have to pick this morning to get chatty?"

"I needed some time to think."

"Couldn't you have chosen a more appropriate place to meet?" Francesca asked. Next to her, Dallie leaned up against the headboard, sipping Holly Grace's coffee and looking as relaxed as ever. As the only person lying down, Francesca suddenly realized she had put herself at a disadvantage. Anchoring the sheet under her arms, she swallowed her embarrassment and pushed herself up until she was sitting, too.

"Want a sip?" Dallie asked, holding out the coffee mug.

She pushed her hair out of her face and thanked him with exaggerated politeness, determined to out-casual them both. As she took the mug, Holly Grace stood and walked toward the window, her hands jumping from her front pockets to her rear pockets. Watching the gesture, Francesca realized that her friend was a lot more nervous than she pretended. As she looked more closely, she saw telltale signs of tension in the set of Holly Grace's shoulders.

Holly Grace played with the edge of the drapery. "See, the thing of it is—this situation that's happened between the two of you has sort of gotten in the way of some plans I made."

"What situation?" Francesca inquired defensively.

"What plans?" Dallie asked.

Holly Grace turned. "Francie, you've got to understand that none of this has anything to do with disapproval. I've been telling you for years that you missed out on one of life's great opportunities by not spending more time in bed with Dallas Beaudine."

"Holly Grace!" Francesca protested.

"Thanks, honey," Dallie said.

Francesca realized they were starting to get the best of her again, and she took a slow, calming sip of coffee. Holly Grace wandered to the foot of the bed and gazed at her ex-husband. "Dallie, my biological clock is about to hit midnight. I kept thinking that sooner or later I'd find somebody I wanted to marry. For a while I even hoped Gerry and I— Anyway, I planned to settle down and let the 'China Colt' producers shoot me from the chest up every few seasons while I had a couple of babies. But lately I've realized that's a fantasy and the thing of it is . . . I've got an ache inside me." She walked around to Francesca's side of the bed, hugging herself as if she were cold.

Francesca saw the sadness in her friend's beautiful, proud features, and she could guess what it had cost Holly Grace to be so open about her need for a child. She passed the coffee mug off to Dallie and patted the bed beside her. "Sit down, Holly Grace, and tell me what's wrong."

Holly Grace sat, her blue eyes locking with Francesca's green ones. "You know how much I want to have a baby,

Francie, and I guess everything that's happened with Teddy has made me think about it even more. I'm tired of only being able to love other people's kids; I want my own. Dallie's been telling me for years not to wrap all my happiness up in a dollar bill, and I guess I've finally realized that he's right."

Francesca reached out and touched her arm sympathetically. She wished Gerry hadn't flown home yesterday, although after three days of trying unsuccessfully to get Holly Grace to talk to him, she didn't blame him. "When you get back to New York, you and Gerry need to get together. I know you love him, and he loves you, and—"

"Forget about Gerry!" she retorted. "He's Peter Pan. He won't ever grow up. Gerry's made it perfectly clear that he wants to marry me. But he's also made it clear that he won't give me any children."

"You never told me anything about that," Dallie said, obviously surprised at this revelation.

"You and Gerry have to start being open with each other," Francesca insisted.

"I won't beg." Holly Grace straightened, trying to keep her dignity. "I'm financially independent, I'm at least semi-mature, and I don't see any reason in the world why I have to shackle myself in marriage just to have a child. Only I need your help."

"I'll do anything I can, you know that. After the way you helped me when—"

"Will you lend me Dallie?" Holly Grace asked abruptly.

Dallie shot up in bed. "Now, wait a minute here!"

"Dallie's not mine to lend," Francesca replied slowly.

Holly Grace ignored Dallie's indignation. Without taking her eyes off Francesca, she said, "I know there are dozens of men I could ask, but it's not in my nature to have just anybody's baby. I love Dallie, and we still have Danny between us. Right now he's the only man I trust." She looked at Francesca with gentle reprimand. "He knows I wouldn't try to cut him out like you did. I understand how important family is to him, and the baby would be his just as much as mine."

"This is between the two of you," Francesca said firmly.

Holly Grace looked back and forth between Francesca

and Dallie. "I don't think so." She turned her attention to Dallie. "I realize it would be a little creepy getting back into bed with you after all this time—sort of like sleeping with my brother. But I figure if I had a few drinks and made up a fantasy about me and Tom Cruise . . ."

Her weak attempt at humor fell flat. Dallie looked as if she'd just punched him in the stomach. "That does it!" He reached down and snatched up a towel that was lying on the carpet next to the bed.

Holly Grace looked pleadingly at him. "I know you have something to say about all this, but just for a few minutes, do you think you could let Francie and me talk?"

"No, I do not," he replied coldly. "I can't believe the two of you. This is a perfect example of how entirely out of hand the women in this country have gotten. You act like men aren't anything more than extraneous amusements, little toys to keep you entertained." Under the covers, he wrapped the towel around himself. "And no matter what anybody says, I don't believe all this trouble started when women got the vote. As far as I'm concerned, it goddamn well got started when you taught each other how to *read.*" He rose up out of bed, pulling the towel tighter at his waist. "And another thing—I'm getting a little tired of the two of you treating me like a walking sperm bank!" With that, he stalked into the bathroom and slammed the door.

Unimpressed with Dallie's anger, Holly Grace looked back at Francesca. "Assuming I could bring Dallie around to my way of thinking, what would you have to say about that?"

The idea gave Francesca a lot more discomfort than she liked to admit. "Holly Grace, just because Dallie and I succumbed to a night of temporary insanity doesn't mean I have any decision to make in this. Whatever happens is between the two of you."

Holly Grace looked at Francesca's underwear scattered over the floor. "Hypothetically speaking, if you really were in love with Dallie, how would you feel about it?"

There was such naked need in Holly Grace's face that Francesca decided she had to answer honestly. She thought for a few moments. "As much as I love you, Holly Grace—

as much as I sympathize with your desire to have a child—if I really loved Dallie, I wouldn't let you touch him."

Holly Grace didn't reply for a moment, and then she gave a sad sort of smile. "That's exactly what I'd say, too. For all your flightiness, Francie, it's moments like this that make me remember why we're best friends."

Holly Grace squeezed her hand, and Francesca was glad to see that she had finally been forgiven for lying about Teddy. But as she looked at her friend's face, she frowned. "Holly Grace, there's something about this that doesn't ring true to me. You know very well that Dallie won't agree. I'm not convinced you even want him to."

"He might," Holly Grace said defensively. "Dallie's full of surprises."

But not this kind of surprise. Francesca didn't believe for a minute that he would go along with Holly Grace's idea, and she doubted if Holly Grace believed it either. "Do you know what you remind me of?" Francesca said thoughtfully. "You remind me of someone with a bad toothache who's hitting herself in the head with a hammer to distract herself from the pain in her mouth."

"That's ridiculous," Holly Grace snapped, her reply coming so quickly that Francesca knew she had struck a nerve. It occurred to her that Holly Grace was frightened. She had begun to grab at straws, hoping to find some distraction to ease the ache in her heart from losing Gerry. There wasn't anything Francesca could do to help her friend except lean forward and give her a sympathetic hug.

"Now, isn't this a sight to warm a man's heart?" Dallie drawled as he came out of the bathroom buttoning his shirt. He looked like a man who'd been doing a slow burn for the past few minutes, and it was immediately apparent that his anger had shifted from righteous indignation into a serious, full-fledged forest fire. "Did the two of you decide what you're going to do with me, yet?"

"Francie says I can't have you," Holly Grace replied.

Alarmed, Francesca cried out, "Holly Grace, that's not what I—"

"Oh, does she?" Dallie shoved his shirttail inside his jeans. "Goddamn, I hate women." He pointed his finger toward Francesca angrily. "Just because we set off a few million fireworks last night doesn't mean you have any right to make personal decisions for me."

Francesca was outraged. "I didn't make any personal—"

He turned on Holly Grace. "And if you want to have yourself a baby, you go look in somebody else's pants, because, by damn, I am *not* providing you with stud service."

Francesca felt an anger toward him that she understood wasn't totally reasonable. But couldn't he see that Holly Grace was in real pain and that she wasn't thinking very clearly? "Aren't you being just a little insensitive?" she inquired quietly.

"Insensitive?" His face grew pale with anger. His hands balled into fists, and he looked very much like a man who wanted to destroy one of the higher life-forms.

As he came toward them, Francesca instinctively shrank down into the sheet, and even Holly Grace seemed to move back. His hand slashed out toward the bottom of the bed. Francesca let out a small hiss of alarm only to see that he had grabbed Holly Grace's purse from the place where she'd tossed it. Pulling it open, he dumped out the contents and snatched up her car keys.

When he spoke, his voice was bleak. "As far as I'm concerned, the two of you can go straight to hell." With that, he stalked from the room.

As Francesca heard the distant sound of a car driving away a few moments later, she felt a stab of regret for the loss of a house where no angry words had ever been spoken.

Chapter
30

Six weeks later, Teddy got off the elevator and walked down the hallway to his apartment, dragging his backpack the whole way. He hated school. All his life he'd loved it, but now he hated it. Today Miss Pearson had told the class that they would have to do a social studies project at the end of the year, and Teddy already knew he would probably flunk it. Miss Pearson didn't like him. She said she was going to kick him out of gifted class if his attitude didn't improve.

It was just— Ever since he'd gone to Wynette, nothing seemed to be fun anymore. He felt confused all the time, like there was a monster hiding in his closet ready to jump out at him. And now he might get kicked out of gifted class.

Teddy knew he somehow had to think up a really great social studies project, especially since he'd messed up so bad on his science bug project. This project had to be better than everybody else's—even dorky old Milton Grossman who was going to write Mayor Ed Koch and ask if he could spend part of the day with him. Miss Pearson had loved that idea. She said Milton's initiative should be an inspiration to the entire class. Teddy didn't see how anybody who picked his nose and smelled like mothballs could be an inspiration.

As he walked in the door, Consuelo came out from the kitchen and told him, "A package came for you today. It's in your bedroom."

"A package?" Teddy peeled off his jacket as he walked down the hallway. Christmas had come and gone, his birthday wasn't until July, and Valentine's Day was still two weeks away. Why was he getting a package?

As he entered his bedroom, he spotted an enormous cardboard carton with the return address of Wynette, Texas, sitting in the middle of the floor. He dropped his jacket, pushed his glasses back up on the bridge of his nose, and chewed on his thumbnail. Part of him wanted the box to be from Dallie, but the other part of him didn't even like to think about Dallie. Whenever he did, he felt like the monster in the closet was standing right behind him.

Slitting open the packing tape with his sharpest scissors, he pulled apart the box flaps and looked around for a note. All he saw was a pile of smaller boxes, and one by one, he began to open them. When he was done, he sat dazed, looking at the bounty that surrounded him, an array of presents so admirably suited to a nine-year-old boy that it was as if someone had read his mind.

On one side of him rested a small stack of wonderfully gross stuff, like a whoopee cushion, hot pepper gum, and a phony plastic ice cube with a dead fly in the middle. Some of the presents appealed to his intellect—a programmable calculator and the complete set of *The Chronicles of Narnia*. Another box held objects representing a whole world of masculinity: a real Swiss Army knife, a flashlight with a black rubber handle, a set of grown-up Black & Decker screwdrivers. But his favorite present was at the bottom of the box. Unwrapping the tissue paper, he let out a cry of pleasure as he took in the best, the neatest, the most awesome sweat shirt he had ever seen.

Gracing the navy blue front was a cartoon of a bearded, leering motorcycle rider with popping eyeballs and drool coming from his mouth. Beneath the biker was Teddy's name in Day-Glo orange letters and the inscription "Born to Raise Hell." Teddy hugged the sweat shirt to his chest. For a fraction of a moment he let himself believe that Dallie had sent him all this, but then he understood that these weren't the kinds of things you sent to a kid you thought was a wimp, and since he knew how Dallie felt about him, he also knew the gifts had to have come from Skeet. He squeezed the sweat shirt tighter and told himself he was lucky to have a friend like Skeet Cooper, somebody who could see past his glasses and stuff all the way to the real kid.

Theodore Day—Born to Raise Hell! He loved the sound of those words, the feel of them, the grit and spit of them, the whole idea that an undersize kid like himself, who was a jerk at sports and might even get kicked out of gifted class, was Born to Raise Hell!

While Teddy was admiring his sweat shirt, Francesca was winding up the taping of her show. As the red light went off on the camera, Nathan Hurd came over to congratulate her. Her producer was balding and chubby, physically unimpressive but mentally a dynamo. In some ways he reminded her of Clare Padgett, who was currently driving the news department at a Houston television station to contemplate suicide. Both were maddening perfectionists, and both of them knew exactly what worked for her.

"I love it when they walk off the show like that," Nathan said, his double chin quivering with pleasure. "We'll run the program as is—the ratings will go right through the ceiling."

She had just finished doing a program on electronic evangelism in which the guest of honor, the Reverend Johnny T. Platt, had walked off in a huff after she'd charmed him into revealing more than he wished to about several failed marriages and his Neanderthal attitude toward women.

"Thank goodness I only had a few minutes left to fill or we would have had to retape," she said as she unclipped her microphone from the paisley scarf draped around the neck of her dress.

Nathan fell into step beside her and they walked from the studio together. Now that the taping was finished and Francesca didn't have to focus all of her concentration on what she was doing, the familiar heaviness settled over her. Six weeks had passed since she'd returned from Wynette. She hadn't seen Dallie since he stormed out of his house. So much for all her worries about how she was going to accommodate having him back in Teddy's life. She felt as confused as one of her teenage runaways. Why had something that was so wrong for her felt so very right? And then she realized that Nathan was talking to her.

". . . so the press release went out today about the Statue of Liberty ceremony. We'll schedule a show on immigration for May—the rich and the poor, that sort of thing. What do you think?"

She nodded her agreement. She had passed her citizenship exam early in January, and not long afterward, she had received a letter from the White House inviting her to participate in a special ceremony to be held that May at the Statue of Liberty. A number of well-known public figures, all of whom had recently applied for American citizenship, would be sworn in together. In addition to Francesca, the group included several Hispanic athletes, a Korean fashion designer, a Russian ballet dancer, and two widely respected scientists. Inspired by the success of the 1986 rededication of the Statue of Liberty, the White House planned for the President to make a welcoming speech, generating a little patriotic fervor as well as strengthening his position with ethnic voters.

Nathan stopped walking as they reached his office. "I've got some great plans for next season, Francesca. More political stuff. You have the damnedest way of cutting through—"

"Nathan." She hesitated for a moment and then, knowing she'd already put it off too long, made up her mind. "We need to talk."

He gave her a wary look before he gestured her inside. She greeted his secretary and then walked into his private office. He closed the door and perched one chubby hip on the corner of his desk, straining the already overtaxed seams of his chinos.

Francesca took a deep breath and told him of the decision she'd reached after months of deliberation. "I know you're going to be less than delighted about this, Nathan, but when my contract with the network comes up for renewal in the spring, I've told my agent to renegotiate."

"Of course you'll renegotiate," Nathan said cautiously. "I'm sure the network will come up with a few extra dollars to sweeten the pot. Not too many, mind you."

Money wasn't the problem and she shook her head. "I'm not going to do a weekly show any longer, Nathan. I want to cut back to twelve specials a year—one show a month." A feeling of relief came over her as she finally spoke the words aloud.

Nathan shot up from the corner of the desk. "I don't believe you. The network will never go along with it. You'll be committing professional suicide."

"I'm going to take that chance. I won't live like this anymore, Nathan. I'm tired of being tired all the time. I'm tired of watching other people raise my child."

Nathan, who saw his own daughters only on weekends and left the business of child rearing to his wife, didn't seem to have the vaguest idea what she was talking about. "Women look at you as a role model," he said, apparently deciding to attack her political conscience. "Some of them will say you sold out."

"Maybe . . . I'm not sure." She pushed aside a stack of magazines and sat down on his couch. "I think women are realizing that they want to be more than burned-out carbon copies of men. For nine years I've done everything the male way. I've turned the raising of my child over to other people, I've scheduled myself so tightly that when I wake up in a hotel room I have to pull a piece of stationery out of the drawer to remember what city I'm in, I go to bed with a knot in my stomach thinking about everything I have to do the next day. I'm tired of it, Nathan. I love my job, but I'm tired of loving it twenty-four hours a day, seven days a week. I love Teddy, and I've only got nine years left before he'll be off to college. I want to be with him more. This is the only life I've been given, and to tell you the truth, I haven't been all that happy with the way I'm living it."

He frowned. "Assuming the network goes along with this, which I seriously doubt, you'll lose a lot of money."

"Right," Francesca scoffed. "I'll have to cut my yearly clothing budget down from twenty thousand dollars to ten thousand. I can just see a million burned-out working mothers losing sleep over that while they try to figure out how to buy their kids new shoes for school." How much money did a woman need? she wondered. How much power? Was she the only woman in the world who was tired of buying into all those male yardsticks of success?

"What do you really want, Francesca?" Nathan asked, switching his tactics from confrontation to pacification. "Maybe we can work out some sort of compromise."

"I want time," Francesca replied wearily. "I want to be able to read a book just because I want to read it, not because the author is going to be on my show the next day. I want to be able to go through an entire week without anyone sticking a single hot roller in my hair. I want to chaperon one of Teddy's class trips, for God's sake." And then she gave voice to an idea that had been gradually growing inside her. "I want to take some of the energy that's gone into my job and give serious thought to doing something significant for all those fourteen-year-old girls who are selling their bodies on the streets of this country because they don't have anyplace to go."

"We'll do more shows on runaways," he said quickly. "I'll work something out so you can take a little more vacation time. I know we've been working you hard, but—"

"No sale, Nathan," she said, getting up from the couch. "This merry-go-round is slowing down for a while."

"But, Francesca—"

She gave him a quick kiss on the cheek and then left his office before he could say any more. She knew her popularity wasn't any guarantee that the network wouldn't fire her if they felt she was being unreasonable, but she had to take that chance. The events of the past six weeks had shown her where her priorities lay, and they had also taught her something important about herself—she no longer had anything to prove.

Once she arrived at her own office, Francesca found a pile of telephone messages waiting for her. She picked up the first one, then set it aside without looking at it. Her gaze drifted to the file on her desk, which held a detailed summary of the professional golfing career of Dallas Beaudine. At the same time she had been trying to put Dallie out of her mind, she had been gathering the material. Although she toyed thoughtfully with the pages, she didn't bother to reread what she'd already studied so thoroughly. Every article, every phone call she'd made, every piece of information she had been able to gather pointed in the same direction. Dallas Beaudine had all the talent it took to be a champion; he just didn't seem to want it badly enough. She thought about what Skeet had said and wondered what all this had to do with Teddy, but the answer continued to elude her.

Stefan was in town and she had promised to go with him to a private party at La Côte Basque that night. For the rest of the afternoon, she considered canceling, but she knew that would be the coward's way out. Stefan wanted something from her that she now understood she couldn't give, and it wasn't fair to postpone talking to him about it any longer.

Stefan had been in New York twice since she'd gotten back from Wynette, and she had seen him both times. He had known about Teddy's kidnapping, of course, so she had been forced to tell him something about what had happened in Wynette, although she had omitted giving him any details about Dallie.

She studied the photograph of Teddy on her desk. It showed him floating in a Flintstones inner tube, his small, skinny legs glistening with water. If Dallie hadn't wanted to contact her again, he should at least have made some attempt to get in touch with Teddy. She felt sad and disillusioned. She had thought that Dallie was a better person than he had turned out to be. As she headed home that evening, she told herself she had to accept the fact that she had made a gigantic mistake and then forget about it.

Before she got dressed for her date with Stefan, she sat with Teddy while he ate his dinner and thought about how carefree she had been only two months before. Now she felt as if she were carrying the troubles of the world on her shoulders. She should never have had that ridiculous one-night stand with Dallie, she was getting ready to hurt Stefan, and the network might very well fire her. She was too miserable to cheer up Holly Grace, and she was terribly worried about Teddy. He was so withdrawn and so obviously unhappy. He wouldn't talk about what had happened in Wynette, and he resisted all of her efforts to draw him out about the trouble he was having in school.

"How did things go with you and Miss Pearson today?"

she asked casually, as she watched him sneak a forkful of peas underneath his baked potato.

"Okay, I guess."

"Just okay?"

He pushed his chair back from the table and cleared his plate. "I've got some homework to do. I'm not too hungry."

She frowned as he left the kitchen. She wished Teddy's teacher weren't so rigid and punitive. Unlike Teddy's former teachers, Miss Pearson seemed more concerned with grades than with learning, a quality that Francesca believed was disastrous when working with gifted children. Teddy had never worried about his marks until this year, but now that seemed to be all he thought about. As Francesca slipped into a beaded Armani gown for her evening with Stefan, she decided to schedule another appointment with the school administrator.

The party at La Côte Basque was lively, with wonderful food and a satisfying number of famous faces in the crowd, but Francesca was too distracted to enjoy herself. A group of paparazzi was waiting as she and Stefan emerged from the restaurant shortly after midnight. She pulled the fur collar of her coat high around her chin and looked away from the flashing strobes. "Sable sucks," she muttered.

"That's not exactly a popularly held opinion, darling," Stefan replied, leading her toward his limousine.

"That media circus happened because of this coat," she complained after the limo had slipped out into the traffic on East Fifty-fifth Street. "The press hardly ever bothers you. It's me. If I'd worn my old raincoat . . ." She chattered on about the sable, stalling for time while she tried to find the courage to hurt him. Finally she fell silent and let the old memories that had been nagging at her all evening take hold—thinking about her childhood, about Chloe, about Dallie. Stefan kept gazing over at her, apparently lost in thoughts of his own. As the limousine swept past Cartier, she decided she couldn't put it off any longer, and she touched his arm. "Do you mind if we walk for a bit?"

It was past midnight, the February night was chill, and Stefan looked at her uneasily—as if he might suspect what was coming—but he ordered the driver to stop anyway. As they stepped out onto the sidewalk, a hansom cab passed, the hooves of the horse clomping rhythmically on the pavement. They began walking down Fifth Avenue together, their breath clouding the air.

"Stefan," she said, resting her cheek for a brief moment against the fine woolen sleeve of his overcoat. "I know you're looking for a woman to share your life, but I'm afraid I'm not the one."

She heard him take a deep breath, then expel it. "You're tired tonight, darling. Perhaps this discussion should wait."

"I think it's waited long enough," she said gently.

She talked for some time, and in the end she could see that she had hurt him, but perhaps not as much as she had feared. She suspected that someplace inside him, he had known all along that she was not the right woman to be his princess.

Dallie called Francesca the following day at the office. He began the conversation without preamble, as if he'd just talked to her the day before instead of six weeks ago and there were no bad feelings between them.

"Hey, Francie, you've got half of Wynette ready to lynch you."

She had a sudden vision of all those glorious temper tantrums she used to throw in her youth, but she kept her voice calm and casual, even though her spine was rigid with tension. "Any particular reason?" she asked.

"The way you ran all over that TV minister last week was a real shame. People down here take their evangelists seriously, and Johnny Platt is a real favorite."

"He's a charlatan," she replied, as calmly as she could manage. Her fingernails dug into her palms. Why couldn't Dallie just once say what was on his mind? Why did he have to go through all these elaborate camouflaging rituals?

"Maybe, but they've got him scheduled opposite 'Gilligan's Island' reruns, so when people consider the alternative, nobody's too anxious to see his program get canceled." There was a short, thoughtful pause. "Tell me something, Francie—and this should be right up your alley—with Gilligan and his buddies shipwrecked on that island so long, how's come those women never ran out of eye makeup? And toilet paper? You think the captain and Gilligan used banana leaves all that time?"

She wanted to scream at him, but she refused to give him the satisfaction. "I have a meeting, Dallie. Did you call for any particular reason?"

"As a matter of fact, I'm flying to New York next week to meet with the boys at the network again, and I thought I might stop by around seven on Tuesday night to say hello to Teddy and maybe take you out to dinner."

"I can't make it," she said coldly, resentment leaking from every one of her pores.

"Just for dinner, Francie. You don't have to make a big deal out of it."

If he wouldn't say what was on his mind, she would. "I won't see you, Dallie. You had your chance, and you blew it."

There was a long silence. She willed herself to hang up, but she couldn't quite coordinate the motion. When Dallie finally spoke, his easy tone was gone. He sounded tired and troubled. "I'm sorry for not calling you earlier, Francie. I needed some time."

"And now I need some."

"All right," he said slowly. "Just let me stop by and see Teddy, then."

"I don't think so."

"I have to start fixing things with him, Francie. I'll take it easy. Just a couple of minutes."

She had grown tough over the years; she'd had to. But now when she needed that toughness the most, all she could do was visualize a little boy shoving peas under his baked potato. "Just for a few minutes," she conceded. "That's all."

"Great!" He sounded as exuberant as a teenager. "That's just great, Francie." And then, quickly, "After I see Teddy, I'll take you out for a bite of dinner." Before she could open her mouth to protest, he had hung up.

She put her head down on the desk and groaned. She didn't have a spine; she had a strand of limp spaghetti.

By the time the doorman buzzed her on Tuesday evening to announce Dallie's arrival, Francesca was a nervous wreck. She had tried on three of her most conservative outfits before she'd rebelliously settled on one of her wildest—a mint green satin *bustier* set off by an emerald velvet miniskirt. The colors deepened the green of her eyes and, in her imagination at least, made her look more dangerous. The fact that she was probably overdressed for an evening with Dallie didn't deter her. Even though she suspected they would end up in some seedy dive with plastic-covered menus, this was still her city and Dallie would have to be the one to fit in.

After fluffing her hair into casual disarray, she draped a pair of Tina Chow's crystal pendants around her neck. Although she had more faith in her own powers than in the mystical ones of Tina Chow's fashionable necklaces, she decided that she shouldn't overlook anything that would help her get through what could only be a difficult evening. She knew she didn't have to go to dinner with Dallie—she didn't even have to be here when he arrived—but she wanted to see him again. It was that simple.

She heard Consuelo opening the front door, and she nearly jumped out of her skin. She forced herself to wait in her room for a few minutes until she felt calmer, but only ended up making herself more nervous, so she walked out to the living room to greet him.

He was carrying a wrapped parcel and standing by the fireplace admiring the red dinosaur that hung above it. He turned at the sound of her approach and gazed at her. She noted his well-cut gray suit, dress shirt with French cuffs, and deep blue tie. She had never seen him in a suit, and unconsciously she found herself waiting for him to start pulling at the collar and unknotting his tie. He did neither.

His eyes took in the little velvet miniskirt, the green satin *bustier,* and he shook his head in admiration. "Damn, Francie, you look better in hooker clothes than any woman I know."

She wanted to laugh, but it seemed more prudent to fall back on sarcasm. "If any of my old problems with personal vanity ever crop back up, remind me to spend five minutes in your company."

He grinned, then walked over to her and brushed her lips with a light kiss that tasted vaguely of bubble gum. The skin on the side of her neck prickled with goose bumps. Looking squarely into her eyes, he said, "You're just about the prettiest woman in the world, and you know it."

She moved quickly away from him. He began looking around the living room, his gaze drifting from Teddy's orange vinyl beanbag chair to a Louis XVI mirror. "I like this place. It's real comfortable."

"Thank you," she replied a little stiffly, still trying to take in the fact that they were face to face again and that he seemed a lot more at ease than she. What were they going to say to each other tonight? They had absolutely nothing to talk about that wasn't either controversial, embarrassing, or emotionally explosive.

"Is Teddy around?" He passed the wrapped parcel from his left hand to his right.

"He's in his room." She saw no sense in explaining that Teddy had thrown a fit when she'd told him that Dallie was coming over.

"Do you think you could ask him to come out here for a minute?"

"I—I doubt that it'll be that easy."

A shadow fell over his face. "Then just show me which room is his."

She hesitated for a moment, then nodded and led him down the hallway. Teddy was sitting at his desk idly pushing a G.I. Joe jeep back and forth.

"What do *you* want?" he asked, as he looked up and saw Dallie standing behind Francesca.

"I brought you a little something," Dallie said. "Sort of a late Christmas present."

"I don't want it," Teddy retorted sullenly. "My mom buys me everything I need." He pushed the jeep over the edge of the desk and let it crash to the carpet. Francesca shot him a warning look, but Teddy pretended not to notice.

"In that case, why don't you just give these to one of your friends?" Dallie walked over and laid the box on Teddy's bed.

Teddy eyed it suspiciously. "What's in there?"

"It might be a pair of cowboy boots."

Something flickered in Teddy's eyes. "Cowboy boots? Did Skeet send them?"

Dallie shook his head.

"Skeet sent me some other stuff," Teddy announced.

"What stuff?" Francesca asked.

Teddy shrugged his shoulders. "Just a whoopee cushion and stuff."

"That was nice of him," she replied, wondering why Teddy hadn't mentioned it to her.

"Did the sweat shirt fit?" Dallie asked.

Teddy straightened up in his chair and stared at Dallie, his eyes alert behind his glasses. Francesca looked at them both curiously, wondering what they were talking about.

"It fit," Teddy said, his voice so soft it was barely audible.

Dallie nodded, lightly touched Teddy's hair, then turned and left the room.

The cab ride was relatively quiet, with Francesca nestled into the velvet collar of a beaded jacket and Dallie glaring at the driver. Dallie had brushed off her question when she'd asked him about the incident with Teddy and, even though it went against her nature, she didn't press.

The cab pulled up in front of Lutèce. She was surprised and then illogically disappointed. Although Lutèce was probably the best restaurant in New York, she couldn't help but think less of Dallie for trying so obvious a ploy to impress her. Why didn't he just take her someplace where he'd be comfortable, instead of a restaurant so obviously foreign to his nature? He held the door for her as they walked inside and then took her jacket and passed it over to be checked in the *vestiaire*. Francesca envisioned an uncomfortable evening ahead, as she tried to interpret both the menu and the wine list without damaging his male ego.

Lutèce's hostess saw Francesca and gave her a welcoming smile. "Mademoiselle Day, it is always a pleasure to have you with us." And then she turned to Dallie. "Monsieur Beaudine, it's been almost two months. We've missed you. I've held your old table."

Old table! Francesca stared at Dallie while he and *madame* exchanged pleasantries. She'd done it again. Once more she'd let herself buy into the image Dallie had created for himself and forgotten that this was a man who had spent the best part of the last fifteen years hanging out in the most exclusive country clubs in America.

"The scallops are especially good tonight," *madame* announced, as she led them down Lutèce's narrow brick hallway to the antegarden.

"Just about everything's good here," Dallie confided after they were settled in the wicker chairs. "Except I make sure to get an English translation of anything that looks suspicious before I eat it. Last time they almost stuck me with liver."

Francesca laughed. "You're a wonder, Dallie, you really are."

"Now, why's that?"

"It's hard to imagine too many people who are just as comfortable at Lutèce as they are in a Texas honky-tonk."

He looked at her thoughtfully. "It seems to me you're pretty comfortable both places."

His comment knocked Francesca slightly off balance. She had grown so accustomed to musing over their differences that it was hard to adjust to the suggestion that they had any similarities. They chatted about the menu for a while, with Dallie making irreverent observations about any item of food that struck him as overly complex. All the time he talked, his eyes seemed to be drinking her up. She began to feel beautiful in a way she had never felt before—a visceral kind of beauty that came from deep within. The softness of her mood alarmed her, and she was glad of the distraction when the waiter appeared to take their order.

After the waiter left, Dallie swept his eyes over her again, his smile slow and intimate. "I had a good time with you that night."

Oh, no, you don't, she thought. He wasn't going to win her over that easily. She had played games with the best of them, and this was one fish who would have to wiggle on the hook for a while. She widened her eyes innocently, opening her mouth to ask him what night he was talking about, only to find herself smiling at him instead. "I had a good time, too."

He reached across the table and squeezed her hand, but then let go of it almost as quickly as he had touched it. "I'm sorry about yelling at you like that. Holly Grace got me pretty upset. She shouldn't have busted in on us. What happened wasn't your fault, and I shouldn't have taken it out on you."

Francesca nodded, not actually accepting his apology, but not quite throwing it back in his face, either. The conversation drifted in safer directions until the waiter appeared with their first course. After they were served, Francesca asked Dallie about his meeting with the network. He was guarded in his reply, a fact that interested her enough to make her probe a little deeper.

"I understand that if you sign with the network, you'll have to stop playing in most of the bigger tournaments." She extracted a snail from a small ceramic pot where it lay bathed in a buttery sauce rich with herbs.

He shrugged. "It won't be long before I'm too old to be competitive. I might as well sign the deal while the money's good."

The facts and figures of Dallie's career flashed through her head. She sketched a circle on the tablecloth and then, like an inexperienced traveler cautiously setting foot in a strange country, commented, "Holly Grace told me you probably won't play in the U.S. Classic this year."

"Probably not."

"I wouldn't think you'd let yourself retire until you'd won a major tournament."

"I've done all right for myself." His knuckles tightened ever so slightly around the glass of club soda he'd picked up. And then he began telling her how well Miss Sybil and Doralee were getting along. Since Francesca had just spoken with both women on the telephone, she was far more interested in the way he had changed the subject than in what he was saying.

The waiter arrived with their entrées. Dallie had selected scallops served in a rich dark sauce of tomatoes and garlic, while she had chosen a flaky pastry stuffed with an aromatic mixture of crabmeat and wild mushrooms. She picked up her fork and tried again. "The U.S. Classic is becoming almost as important as the Masters, isn't it?"

"Yeah, I guess." Dallie captured one of the scallops with his fork and dredged it through the thick sauce. "You know what Skeet told me the other day? He said as far as he's concerned you're the most interesting stray we ever picked up. That's quite a compliment, especially since he didn't used to be able to stand you."

"I'm flattered."

"For a long time he was holding out for this one-armed drifter who could burp 'Tom Dooley,' but I think you changed his mind during your recent memorable visit. Of course, there's always a chance he'll reconsider."

He rattled on and on. She smiled and nodded and waited for him to run down, disarming him with the easiness of her manner and the attentive tilt of her head, lulling him so completely that he forgot he was sitting across the table from a woman who had spent the last ten years of her life prying out secrets most people wanted to keep hidden, a woman who could go in for the kill so skillfully, so guilelessly, that the victim frequently died with a smile on his face. Gently she decapitated a stalk of white asparagus. "Why don't you wait until after the U.S. Classic before you go into the announcers' booth? Whatever are you afraid of?"

He bristled like a cornered porcupine. *"Afraid* of? Since when did you get to be such an expert on golf that you know what a professional player might be afraid of?"

"When you host a television show like mine, you get to know a little bit about everything," she replied evasively.

"If I'd known this was going to be a damned interview, I'd have stayed home."

"But then we would have missed a lovely evening together, wouldn't we?"

Without anything more than the evidence presented by the dark scowl on his face, Francesca became absolutely, totally convinced that Skeet Cooper had told her the truth, and that not only did her son's happiness depend upon the game of golf, but quite possibly her own did as well. What she didn't know was how to make use of that newfound understanding. Thoughtfully, she picked up her wine goblet, took a sip, and changed the subject.

Francesca didn't plan on ending up in bed with Dallie that night, but as the dinner progressed her senses seemed to go on overload. Their conversation grew more infrequent, the looks between them more lingering. It was as if she'd taken a powerful drug and she couldn't break the spell. By the time their coffee arrived, they couldn't take their eyes off each other and before she knew it, they were in Dallie's bed at the Essex House.

"Um, you taste so good," he murmured.

She arched her back, a groan of pure pleasure coming from deep in her throat, as he loved her with his mouth and tongue, giving her all the time she needed, sweeping her up the mountains of her own passion, but never quite letting her cross the peak.

"Oh . . . please," she begged.

"Not yet," he replied.

"I—I can't stand any more."

"I'm afraid you're going to have to, honey."

"No . . . please . . ." She reached for herself, but he caught her wrists and pinioned them at her sides.

"You shouldn't have done that, darlin'. Now I'm going to have to start all over again."

Her skin was damp, her fingers rigid in his hair, when he finally gave her the release she was desperate for. "That was a dreadful thing to do," she sighed after she had tumbled back to earth. "You're going to pay for that torture."

"Did you ever notice that the clitoris is the only sexual organ that doesn't have a dirty-word nickname." He nuzzled at her breasts, still taking his time with her even though he hadn't been satisfied himself. "It has an abbreviation, but not a real scummy nickname like everything else. Think about it. You got your—"

"Probably because men have only recently discovered the clitoris," she said wickedly. "There hasn't been time."

"I don't think so," he replied, seeking out the object under discussion. "I think it's because it's pretty much an insignificant organ."

"An insignificant organ!" She caught her breath as he began working his magic again.

"Sure," he whispered huskily. "More like one of those puny little electronic keyboards than the mighty ol' Wurlitzer."

"Of all the male, egotistical—" With a deep, throaty laugh, she rolled on top of him. "Watch out, mister! This little keyboard's about to make your mighty ol' Wurlitzer play the symphony of its life."

During the next few months, Dallie found a number of excuses to come to New York. First he had to meet with some advertising executives about a promotion he was doing for a line of golf clubs. Then he was "on his way" from Houston to Phoenix. Later he had a wild craving to sit in gridlocked traffic and breathe exhaust fumes. Francesca could never remember having laughed so much or felt so absolutely sassy and full of herself. When Dallie put his mind to it he was irresistible, and since she'd long ago gotten out of the habit of telling herself lies, she stopped trying to cheapen her feelings for him by hiding them under the convenient label of lust. No matter how potentially heartbreaking—she realized that she was falling in love with him. She loved his look, his laughter, the easygoing nature of his manliness.

Still, the obstacles between them loomed like skyscrapers, and her love had a bittersweet edge. She wasn't an idealistic twenty-one-year-old anymore, and she couldn't envision any fairy-tale future. Although she knew Dallie cared for her, his feelings seemed much more casual than her own.

And Teddy continued to be a problem. She sensed how much Dallie wanted to win him over, yet he remained stiff and formal with her son—as if he was afraid to be himself. Their outings too frequently ended in disaster as Teddy misbehaved and Dallie reprimanded him. Although she hated admitting it, she sometimes found herself feeling relieved when Teddy had other plans and she and Dallie could spend their time alone together.

On a Sunday late in April, Francesca invited Holly Grace to come over and watch the final round of one of the year's more important golf tournaments. To their delight, Dallie was only two shots off the lead. Holly Grace was convinced that if he made a strong finish, he'd play out the season instead of going into the announcers' booth in two weeks to do color commentary for the U.S. Classic.

"He'll blow it," Teddy said as he came into the room and plopped himself on the floor in front of the television. "He always does."

"Not this time," Francesca told him, irritated with his know-it-all attitude. "This time he's going to do it." He'd better do it, she thought. The night before on the phone, she'd promised him a variety of erotic rewards if he came through today.

"When did you get to be such a golf fan?" he had asked.

She had no intention of telling him about the hours she had spent reviewing every detail of his professional career, or the weeks she had spent looking at videotapes of his old tournaments as she tried to find the key to unlock Dallie Beaudine's secrets.

"I became a fan after I developed this incredible crush on Seve Ballesteros," she had replied breezily, as she settled back into the satin pillows on her bed and propped the receiver on her shoulder. "He is *so* gorgeous. Do you think you could fix me up with him?"

Dallie had snorted at her reference to the darkly handsome Spaniard who was one of the best professional golfers in the world. "Keep talking like that and I'll fix you up, all right. You just forget about old Seve tomorrow and keep your eye on the All-American Kid."

Now as she watched the All-American Kid, she definitely liked what she saw. He parred the fourteenth and fifteenth holes and then birdied sixteen. The leader board shifted and he was one stroke out of first place. The camera picked up Dallie and Skeet walking toward the seventeenth hole and then cut for a Merrill Lynch commercial.

Teddy got up from his spot in front of the television and disappeared into his bedroom. Francesca put out a plate of cheese and crackers, but both she and Holly Grace were too nervous to eat. "He's going to do it," Holly Grace said for the fifth time. "When I talked to him last night, he said he was feeling real good."

"I'm glad the two of you are speaking to each other again," Francesca remarked.

"Oh, you know Dallie and me. We can't stay mad at each other for long."

Teddy returned from the bedroom wearing his cowboy boots and a navy blue sweat shirt that fell past his hips. "Where on earth did you get that hideous thing?" She eyed the drooling motorcyclist and the Day-Glo inscription with distaste.

"It was a present," Teddy muttered, plopping himself back down on the carpet.

So this was the sweat shirt she'd heard about. She looked thoughtfully at the television screen, which showed Dallie teeing up his ball on the seventeenth hole, and then back at Teddy. "I like it," she said.

Teddy pushed his glasses back up on his nose, all his attention on the tournament. "He's going to clutch."

"Don't say that," Francesca snapped.

Holly Grace stared intently at the screen. "He's got to put it just beyond the bunker, over toward the left side of the fairway. That'll give him a real good look at the flag."

Pat Summerall, the CBS commentator, spoke over the picture to his partner Ken Venturi. "What do you think, Ken? Is Beaudine going to be able to hold it together for two more holes?"

"I don't know, Pat. Dallie's looked real good today, but he's got to be feeling the pressure right now, and he never plays his best during these big tournaments."

Francesca held her breath as Dallie hit his drive, and then Pat Summerall said ominously, "It doesn't look as if he's caught it flush."

"He's coming down awfully close to that left fairway bunker," Venturi observed.

"Oh, no," Francesca cried, her fingers tightly crossed as she stared at the ball flying across the small screen.

"Dammit, Dallie!" Holly Grace shrieked at the television.

The ball dropped from the sky and buried itself in the left fairway bunker.

"I told you he'd blow it," Teddy said.

Chapter
31

Dallie had an excellent view of Central Park from his hotel room, but he impatiently turned away from the window and began pacing the floor. He had tried to read on the plane flying into JFK, but had found that nothing held his attention, and now that he had reached his hotel he felt claustrophobic. Once again he had let a tournament victory get away from him. The thought of Francesca and Teddy sitting in front of the television and watching him lose was just about more than he could stand.

But the loss of the tournament wasn't all that was bothering him. No matter how hard he tried to distract himself, he couldn't stop thinking about Holly Grace. They'd made up since their fight at the farmhouse and she hadn't mentioned anything about using him for stud service again, but some of the spunk had gone out of her, and he didn't like that one bit. The more he thought about what had happened to her, the more he wanted to put his fist through Gerry Jaffe's face.

He tried to forget about Holly Grace's troubles, but an idea had been nagging at the back of his mind ever since he'd gotten on the plane, and now he found himself picking up the piece of paper that held Jaffe's address. He'd gotten it from Naomi Perlman less than an hour ago, and since then he had been trying to make up his mind whether or not to use it. Glancing at his watch, he saw that it was already seven-thirty. He was going to meet Francie at nine for dinner. He was tired and jagged, in no mood to be reasonable, and certainly in no condition to try to straighten out Holly Grace's troubles. Still, he found himself tucking Jaffe's address into the pocket of his navy blue sport coat and heading down to the lobby to get a cab.

Jaffe lived in an apartment building not far from the United Nations. Dallie paid the driver and began walking toward the entrance, only to see Gerry coming out through the front door.

Gerry spotted him immediately, and Dallie could tell by the expression on his face that he'd received better surprises in his life. Still, he managed a polite nod. "Hello, Beaudine."

"Well, if it isn't Russia's best friend," Dallie replied.

Gerry lowered the hand he had been extending for a shake. "That line's starting to wear thin."

"You're a real bastard, you know that, Jaffe?" Dallie said slowly, not seeing any need for preliminaries.

Gerry had a hot temper of his own, but he managed to turn his back on Dallie and begin walking off down the street. Dallie, however, had no intention of letting him get away so easily, not when Holly Grace's happiness was at stake. For some reason she wanted this guy, and he just might be able to give her a shot at having him.

He began to move forward and soon fell in step next to Gerry. It was dark and there were few people on the street. Garbage cans lined the curb. They passed the grate-covered windows of a bakery and a jeweler.

Gerry picked up his pace. "Why don't you go play with your golf balls?" he said.

"As a matter of fact, I was just stopping by to have a little talk with you before I went to see Holly Grace." It was a lie. Dallie had no intention of seeing Holly Grace that night. "Do you want me to give her your regards?"

Gerry stopped walking. The glow from a streetlight fell on his face. "I want you to stay away from Holly Grace."

Dallie still had yesterday's defeat on his mind, and he wasn't in the mood for subtlety, so he went in for a swift, merciful kill. "Now, that would be kind of hard for me to do. It's just about impossible to get a woman good and pregnant if you're not right there on top of the job."

Gerry's eyes turned black. His hand shot out and he grabbed the front of Dallie's sport coat. "You tell me right now what you're talking about."

"She's determined to have a baby, is all," Dallie said, not making any attempt to get away, "and only one of us seems to be man enough to do the job."

Gerry's olive skin paled as he released Dallie's jacket. "You fucking son of a bitch."

Dallie's answering drawl was soft and menacing. "Fucking is something I'm real good at, Jaffe."

Gerry ended two decades of dedicated nonviolence by drawing back his fist and slamming it into Dallie's chest. Gerry wasn't much of a fighter and Dallie saw the blow coming, but he decided to let Jaffe have his one shot because he knew damn well he wasn't going to give him another. Righting himself, Dallie started back toward Gerry. Holly Grace could have this son of a bitch if she wanted him, but first he was going to rearrange his face.

Gerry stood with his arms at his sides, his chest heaving, and watched Dallie coming at him. When Dallie's fist caught him in the jaw, he flew across the sidewalk and banged into the garbage cans, sending them clattering out into the street. A man and woman coming down the sidewalk saw the fight and rapidly turned back. Gerry got up slowly, lifting the back of his hand to wipe the blood that was flowing from his lip.

Then he turned and began to walk away.

"Fight me, you son of a bitch," Dallie called after him.

"I won't fight," Gerry called back.

"Well, now, aren't you a prime example of American manhood? Come on and fight. I'll give you another free punch."

Gerry kept walking. "I shouldn't have hit you in the first place, and I won't do it again."

Dallie rapidly closed the distance between them, jerking Gerry around by his shoulder. "For Christ's sake, I just told you I was getting ready to knock up Holly Grace!"

Gerry's fists clenched at his side, but he didn't move.

Dallie grabbed the front of Gerry's bomber jacket and

pushed him against a light post. "What the hell's wrong with you? I'd have fought an army for that woman. Can't you even fight one person?"

Gerry looked at him contemptuously. "Is that the only way you know how to solve a problem? With your fists?"

"At least I try to solve my problems. All you've done is make her miserable."

"You don't know jackshit, Beaudine. I've been trying for weeks to talk to her, but she won't see me. The last time I managed to get past the guards at the studio, she called the cops on me."

"Did she, now?" Dallie smiled unpleasantly and slowly let go of Gerry's jacket. "You know something? I don't like you, Jaffe. I don't like people who act like they have all the answers. Most of all, I don't like smug do-gooders who make all kinds of noble noises about saving the world but screw over the people who care about them."

Gerry was breathing harder than Dallie, and he had trouble getting out his words. "This doesn't have anything to do with you."

"Anybody who gets tangled up in Holly Grace's life sooner or later runs into me. She wants a baby, and for some reason that I sure as hell can't figure out, she wants you, too."

Gerry leaned back against the light post. For a moment his head dropped, and then he lifted it again, his eyes dark with misery. "Tell me why it's such a goddamn crime not to want to bring a kid into this world. Why does she have to be so stubborn? Why can't it just be the two of us?"

Gerry's obvious pain touched Dallie, but he did his best to ignore it. "She wants a baby, is all."

"I'd be the worst father in the world. I don't know anything about being a father."

Dallie's laugh was soft and bitter. "You think any of us do?"

"Listen, Beaudine. I've had enough of people nagging me about this. First Holly Grace, then my sister, and then Francesca. Now you're on my case, too. Well, it's none of your goddamn business, do you understand me? This is between Holly Grace and me."

"Answer a question for me, Jaffe," Dallie said slowly.

"How are you going to go about living the rest of your life knowing that you let the best thing that ever happened to you get away?"

"Don't you think I'm trying to get through to her?" Jaffe cried out. "She won't even *talk* to me, you crazy son of a bitch! I can't even get into the same room with her."

"Maybe you're not trying hard enough."

Gerry's eyes narrowed and his jaw clenched. "Just leave me the hell alone. And stay away from Holly Grace. The two of you are old worn-out history, and if you even think about touching her, I'll come after you, do you understand me?"

"I'm trembling in my boots," Dallie replied with deliberate insolence.

Gerry looked him straight in the eye and there was such menace on the man's face that Dallie actually experienced a moment of grudging respect.

"Don't underestimate me, Beaudine," Gerry said, his tone flat and hard. He held Dallie's gaze for several long moments without flinching, and then he walked away.

Dallie stood watching him for a while; then he headed back down the sidewalk. As he stepped off the curb to hail a cab, a faint, satisfied smile tugged at the corners of his mouth.

Francesca had agreed to meet Dallie at nine o'clock at a neighborhood restaurant they both liked that served southwestern food. She slipped into a black cashmere T-shirt and zebra-patterned slacks. Impulsively, she fastened a pair of wildly asymmetrical silver earrings to her earlobes, taking devilish pleasure in wearing something outrageous to tease him. It had been a week since she had seen him, and she was in the mood to celebrate. Her agent had concluded nearly three months of difficult negotiations and the network had finally given in. Beginning in June, "Francesca Today" would be a monthly special instead of a weekly series.

When she arrived at the restaurant, she saw Dallie sitting in a high-backed booth at the rear away from the crowd. Spotting her, he stood and for a fraction of a moment, a puppy dog grin flashed over his face, an expression more appropriate to a teenage boy than a grown man. Her heart gave a queer thump in response.

"Hey, honey."

"Hey, Dallie."

She had attracted a great deal of attention as she walked through the restaurant, so he gave her only the briefest of kisses when she reached him. As soon as she sat, however, he leaned across the table and did the job right. "Damn, Francie, it's good to see you."

"You, too." She kissed him again, closing her eyes and enjoying the heady sensation of being near him.

"Where'd you get those earrings? Ace Hardware?"

"They're not earrings," she retorted loftily, settling back into the booth. "According to the artist who made them, they're free-form abstractions of conceptualized angst."

"No kidding. Well, I sure hope you had them exorcised before you put them on."

She smiled, and his eyes seemed to drink in her face, her hair, the shape of her breasts underneath her cashmere T-shirt. Her skin began to feel warm. Embarrassed, she pushed her hair back from her face. Her earrings jangled. He gave her a crooked grin, as if he could see every one of the erotic images that flashed through her head. Then he settled back in his chair, his navy sport coat falling open over his shirt. Despite his smile, she thought he looked tired and troubled. She decided to postpone telling him the good news about her contract until she found out what was bothering him.

"Did Teddy watch the tournament yesterday?" he asked.

"Yes."

"What'd he say?"

"Not too much. He wore the cowboy boots you gave him, though, and this unbelievably hideous sweat shirt that I can't believe you bought."

Dallie laughed. "I'll bet he loves that sweat shirt."

"When I tucked him in that night, he was wearing it with his pajama bottoms."

He smiled again. The waiter approached, and they turned their attention to the blackboard that listed the day's specials. Dallie opted for chili-spiced chicken with a side helping of barbecued beans. Francesca hadn't been hungry when she arrived, but the delicious smells of the restaurant had piqued her appetite and she decided on grilled shrimp and a small salad.

He fiddled with the saltshaker, looking a little less relaxed. "They had the pin placement all screwed up yesterday or I would have done better. It threw me off. And there was a hell of a lot more crowd noise than there should have been. One son of a bitch clicked his camera just when I got to the top of my backswing. Damn, I hate that."

She was surprised that he felt the need to explain himself to her, but by now she was also too familiar with the patterns of his professional career to believe any of his excuses. They chatted for a while about Teddy, and then he asked her to save some time for him that week. "I'm going to be in the city for a while. They want to give me some lessons on how to find the red light on the camera."

She gazed at him sharply, her good mood evaporating. "You're going to take the announcing job they offered you?"

He didn't quite look at her. "My bloodsucker's bringing me the contracts to sign tomorrow."

Their food arrived, but Francesca had lost her appetite. What he was about to do was wrong—more wrong than he seemed to realize. There was an air of defeat about him, and she hated the way he wouldn't look at her. She probed at a shrimp with her fork and then, unable to contain herself, confronted him. "Dallie, you should at least finish the season. I don't like the idea of your quitting like this with the Classic only another week away."

She could see his tension as his jaw set and he stared at a point just above the top of her head. "I have to hang up my clubs sooner or later. Now is as good a time as any."

"Television announcing will be a wonderful career for you someday, but you're only thirty-seven. Lots of golfers still win major tournaments at your age or older. Look what Jack Nicklaus did at the Masters last year."

His eyes narrowed and he finally looked at her. "You know something, Francie. I liked you a hell of a lot more before you turned into such a damned golf expert. Did it ever occur to you that I've got enough people telling me how to play, and I goddamn well don't need another one?"

Caution told her the moment had come to back off, but

she couldn't do it, not when she felt that she had something important at stake. She toyed with the stem of her wineglass and then met his hostile gaze head on. "If I were you, I'd win the Classic before I quit playing."

"Oh, you would, would you?" A small muscle ticked in his jaw.

"I would." She dropped her voice until it was a barely audible whisper and looked him straight in the eye. "I'd win that tournament just so I knew I could do it."

His nostrils flared. "Since you barely know the difference between a driver and a one-iron, I'd be mighty interested in watching you try."

"We're not talking about me. We're talking about you."

"Sometimes, Francesca, you are the most ignorant woman I've ever known in my entire life." Banging down his fork, he looked at her and thin, hard lines formed brackets around his mouth. "For your information, the Classic is one of the toughest tournaments of the year. The course is a killer. If you don't hit the greens in just the right spot, you can go from a birdie to a bogey without even seeing it coming. Do you have any idea who's playing in the Classic this year? The best damned golfers in the world. Greg Norman will be there. They call him the Great White Shark, and it's not just because of his white hair—it's because he loves the taste of blood. Ben Crenshaw's playing—he putts better than anybody on the tour. Then there's Fuzzy Zoeller. Ol' Fuzzy cracks jokes and acts like he's taking a Sunday walk in the woods, but all the time he's figuring out how deep he can dig your damned grave. And your buddy Seve Ballesteros is going to show up, muttering in Spanish under his breath and plowing right through everybody who gets in his way. Then we come to Jack Nicklaus. Even though he's forty-seven, he's still capable of blowing every one of us right out of the running. Nicklaus isn't even human, Francie."

"And then there's Dallas Beaudine," she said quietly. "Dallas Beaudine who has played some of the best opening rounds in tournament golf, but always falls apart at the end. Why is that, Dallie? Don't you want it badly enough?"

Something seemed to snap inside him. He pulled his

napkin from his lap and wadded it on the table. "Let's get out of here. I'm not hungry anymore."

She didn't budge. Instead, she hugged her arms over her chest, lifted her chin, and silently dared him to try to move her. She was going to have it out with him once and for all—even if it meant losing him. "I'm not going anywhere."

At that exact moment Dallie Beaudine finally seemed to comprehend what he had only dimly perceived as he'd watched a pair of incomparable four-carat diamond studs sail out into the depths of a gravel quarry. He finally understood her strength of will. For months now, he had chosen to ignore the deep intelligence that lay behind her green cat's eyes, the steely determination hidden beneath that sassy smile, the indomitable strength at the heart of the woman who sat across from him so absurdly packaged as a frivolous ball of fluff. He had let himself forget that she had come to this country with nothing—not even much strength of character—and that she had been able to look every one of her weaknesses straight in the eye and overcome them. He had let himself forget that she had turned herself into a champion, while he was still only a contender.

He saw that she had no intention of leaving the restaurant, and the sheer force of her will staggered him. He felt a moment of panic, as if he were a child again and Jaycee's fist was headed right for his face. He felt the Bear breathing down his neck. *Watch it, Beaudine. She's got you now.*

And so he did the only thing he could—the only thing he could think of that might distract this bullheaded, bossy little woman before she sliced him apart.

"I swear, Francie, you've put me in such a bad mood, I'm thinking about changing my plans for tonight." Surreptitiously, he slid his napkin back into his lap.

"Oh? What plans did you have?"

"Well, all this nagging has almost made me change my mind, but—what the hell—I guess I'll ask you to marry me anyway."

"Marry you?" Francesca's lips parted in astonishment.

"I don't see why not. At least I didn't until a few minutes ago when you turned into such a damn nag."

Francesca leaned back into the booth, possessed by an

awful feeling that something inside her was breaking apart. "You don't just blurt out a marriage proposal like that," she said shakily. "And with the exception of a nine-year-old boy, we don't have a single thing in common."

"Yeah, well I'm not so sure about that anymore." Reaching into the pocket of his suit coat, he drew out a small jeweler's box. Extending it toward her, he flipped open the lid with his thumb, revealing an exquisite diamond solitaire. "I bought this from a guy I went to high school with, but I think it's only fair to tell you he spent some time as an unwilling guest of the state of Texas after he walked into a Piggly Wiggly with a Saturday night special in his hand. Still, he told me he found Jesus in prison, so I don't think the ring's hot. But I suppose you can't be too sure about that sort of thing."

Francesca, who had already taken note of Tiffany's distinctive robin's-egg blue packaging, was paying only the vaguest attention to what he was saying. Why hadn't he mentioned anything about love? Why was he doing it like this? "Dallie, I can't take that ring. I—I can't believe you're even suggesting it." Because she didn't know how to say what was really on her mind, she threw out all the logical impediments between them. "Where would we live? My job is in New York; yours is everywhere. And what would we talk about once we got out of the bedroom? Just because there's this—this cloud of *lust* hanging between us doesn't mean we're qualified to set up housekeeping together."

"Jeez, Francie, you make everything so complicated. Holly Grace and I were married for fifteen years, and we only set up housekeeping in the beginning."

Anger began to form a haze inside her head. "Is that what you want? Another marriage like the one you had with Holly Grace? You go your way and I go mine, but every few months we get together so we can watch a few ball games and have a spitting contest. I won't be your *buddy*, Dallas Beaudine."

"Francie, Holly Grace and I never had a spitting contest in our lives, and it can't have escaped your notice that boy of ours is technically a bastard."

"So is his father," she hissed.

Without losing a beat, he shut the Tiffany box and slipped it back in his pocket. "All right. We don't have to get married. It was just a suggestion."

She stared at him. Seconds ticked by. He lifted a forkful of chicken to his mouth and slowly began to chew.

"Is that it?" she asked.

"I can't exactly force you."

Anger and hurt rose up so far inside her she thought she would choke. "That's all, then? I say no, and you pick up your toys and go home?"

He took a sip of his club soda, the expression in his eyes as abstract as the silver earrings at her lobes. "What do you want me to do? The waiters would throw me out if I got down on my knees."

His sarcasm in the face of something so important to her was like a knife through her ribs. "Don't you know how to fight for anything you want?" she whispered fiercely.

The silence that came over him was so complete that she knew she had hit a raw nerve. Suddenly she felt as if the scales had dropped from her eyes. That was it. That was what Skeet had been trying to tell her.

"Who said I wanted you? You take everything too seriously, Francie."

He was lying to her, lying to himself. She felt his need as much as she felt her own. He wanted her, but he didn't know how to get her and, more important, he wasn't even going to try. What did she expect, she asked herself bitterly, from a man who had played some of the best opening rounds in tournament golf, but who always fell apart at the end?

"Are you going to have room for dessert, Francie? They got this chocolate thing. If you ask me, it could use a couple dabs of Cool Whip on the top, but it's still pretty good."

She felt a scorn for him that bordered on real dislike. Her love now seemed to be an oppressively heavy weight, too much for her to carry. Reaching over the table, she grabbed his wrist and squeezed it until her fingernails had dug into his skin and she was sure he knew for certain that he needed to listen to every word she had to say. Her words were low and condemning, the words of a fighter. "Are you so afraid of failing that you can't go after one single thing you want? A tournament? Your son? Me? Is that what's been holding you back all this time? You're so afraid of failing that you won't even try?"

"I don't know what you're talking about." He attempted to pull his hand away, but her grip was so tight he couldn't do it without drawing attention to them.

"You haven't even gotten out of the starting blocks, have you, Dallie? You just hang out on the sidelines. You're willing to play the game as long as you don't have to sweat too much and as long as you can make enough wisecracks so everybody understands you don't really care."

"That's the stupidest—"

"But you do care, don't you? You want to win so much you can bloody well taste it. You want your son, too, but you're holding yourself back from him just in case Teddy won't have you—my wonderful little boy who wears his heart on his sleeve and would give anything in the world for a father who respected him."

Dallie's face had paled, and his skin beneath her fingers was clammy. "I respect him," he said sharply. "As long as I live, I'll never forget that day he came after me because he thought I was hurting you—"

"You're a whiner, Dallie—but you do it with so much style that everybody lets you get away with it." She released her grip, but she didn't let up on him. "Well, the act's wearing thin. You're getting too old to keep slipping by on your good looks and charm."

"What the hell do you know about it?" His voice was quiet, slightly hoarse.

"I know everything about it because I started out with some of those same handicaps. But I grew up, and I kicked my bloody life in the tail until it did what I wanted."

"Maybe it was easier for you," he retorted. "Maybe you had a few breaks thrown your way. I was on my own when I was fifteen. While you were taking walks in Hyde Park with your nanny, I was dodging my old man's fists. When I was real little, you know what he used to do to me when he got drunk? He used to turn me upside down and hold my head underwater in the toilet."

Her face didn't soften with even a moment's sympathy. "Tough shit."

She saw that her coldness had infuriated him, but she didn't let up. Her pity wasn't going to help him. At some point people either had to throw off the wounds of their childhood or go through life permanently crippled. "If you want to play games with yourself, that's your choice, but don't play them with me, because I'll bloody well call your bluff." She rose from the booth and then stared down at him, her voice frigid with scorn. "I've decided to marry you."

"Forget it," he said, cold with fury. "I don't want you. I wouldn't take you if you were gift wrapped."

"Oh, you want me all right. And it's not just because of Teddy. You want me so badly it scares you. But you're afraid to fight. You're afraid to put anything on the line for fear your head's going to get dunked in that toilet again." She leaned forward slightly, resting one hand on the table. "I've decided to marry you, Dallie." She gave him a long, cool look of appraisal. "I'll marry you the day you win the United States Classic."

"That's the stupidest—"

"But you have to *win it,* you bastard," she hissed. "Not third place, not second place—*first place.*"

He gave her a scornful, shaky laugh. "You're crazy."

"I want to know what you're made of," she said contemptuously. "I want to know if you're good enough for me—good enough for Teddy. I haven't settled for second rate in a long time, and I'm not going to start now."

"You've got a mighty high opinion of what you're worth."

She threw her napkin straight at his chest. "You bet I do. If you want me, you'll have to earn me. And, mister, I don't come cheap."

"Francie—"

"You lay that first-place trophy at my feet, you bloody son of a bitch, or don't bother to come near me again!"

Grabbing her purse, she swept past the startled diners at the front tables and dashed out the door. The night had grown cold, but her anger burned so hot that she didn't feel the chill. Stalking down the sidewalk, she was propelled by fury, by hurt, and by fear. Her eyes stung and she couldn't blink them rapidly enough to hold off the tears. Two glistening drops beaded on the waterproof mascara that coated her bottom lashes. How could she have fallen in love with him? How could she have let such an absurd thing happen? Her teeth began to chatter. For almost eleven years, she had felt nothing more than strong affection for a handful of men, shadows of love that faded nearly as quickly as they appeared. But now, just when her life was coming together, she had once again let a second-rate golf pro break her heart.

Francesca passed through the next week with the feeling that something bright and wonderful had slipped from her life forever. What had she done? Why had she challenged him so cruelly? Wasn't half a pie better than none? But she knew she couldn't live with half of anything, and she didn't want Teddy to live that way either. Dallie had to start taking risks, or he would be useless to them both—a will-o'-the-wisp neither of them could ever count on. With every breath she took, she mourned the loss of her lover, the loss of love itself.

The following Monday as she poured Teddy a glass of orange juice before he left for school, she tried to find consolation in the thought that Dallie was as miserable as she. But she had trouble believing that anyone who kept his emotions so carefully protected could have feelings that ran all that deep.

Teddy drank his juice and then stuffed his spelling book into his backpack. "I forgot to tell you. Holly Grace called last night and told me to tell you that Dallie's playing in the U.S. Classic tomorrow."

Francesca's head shot up from the glass of juice she had started to pour for herself. "Are you sure?"

"That's what she said. I don't see what the big deal is, though. He'll only blow it. And, Mom, if you get a letter from Miss Pearson, don't pay any attention."

The pitcher of orange juice remained suspended in midair over Francesca's glass. She shut her eyes for a moment, willing her mind away from Dallie Beaudine so she could concentrate on what Teddy was trying to tell her. "What kind of letter?"

Teddy fastened the zipper on his backpack, working with single-minded concentration so he wouldn't have to look up at her. "You might get a letter saying I'm not working up to my potential—"

"Teddy!"

"—but don't worry about it. My social studies project is due next week, and I've got something so awesome planned that Miss Pearson's going to give me about a million A-pluses and beg me to stay in the class. Gerry said—"

"Oh, Teddy. We have to talk about this."

He grabbed his backpack. "I've got to go or I'll be late."

Before she could stop him, he had raced out of the kitchen and she heard the slam of the front door. She wanted to climb back into bed and pull the covers over her head so she could think, but she had a meeting scheduled in an hour. She couldn't do anything about Teddy at the moment, but if she hurried she would have time for a quick stop at the studio where "China Colt" was being shot to make certain Teddy had understood Holly Grace's message correctly. Was Dallie really playing in the Classic? Had her words actually touched him?

Holly Grace had already filmed the first scene of the day when Francesca got there. In addition to a carefully positioned rip on the front of her dress that revealed the top of her left breast, she had a fake bruise on her forehead. "Rough day?" Francesca said, coming toward her.

Holly Grace looked up from the script she was studying. "I got attacked by this demented hooker who turns out to be a transvestite psychopath. They're doing this great *Bonnie and Clyde* slow-motion shot at the end where I plug this guy with two bullets right through his silicone implants."

Francesca barely heard her. "Holly Grace, is it true that Dallie's playing in the Classic?"

"He told me he was, and I'm not too happy with you right now." She tossed her script down on the chair. "Dallie didn't give me any details, but I gather that you handed him his walking papers."

"You might say that," Francesca replied cautiously.

A look of disapproval crossed Holly Grace's face. "Your timing stinks, you know that? Would it have been too much for you to wait until after the Classic before you did your number on him? If you'd set your mind to it, I don't think you could have found a better way to screw him up."

Francesca began to explain, but then, with a sense of shock, she realized that she understood Dallie better than

Holly Grace did. The idea was so startling, so new to her, that she could barely take it in. She made a few noncommittal comments, knowing that if she tried to explain herself, Holly Grace would never understand. Then she made a production out of looking at her watch and rushing off.

As she left the studio, her thoughts were in a turmoil. Holly Grace was Dallie's best friend, his first love, his soul mate, but the two of them were so much alike that they had become blind to each other's faults. Whenever Dallie lost a tournament, Holly Grace made excuses for him, sympathized with him, and in general treated him like a child. As well as Holly Grace knew him, she didn't understand how his fear of failure was screwing up his golf. And if she didn't understand that, she would never understand how that same fear was ruining his life.

Chapter

32

Since it was first played in 1935, the United States Classic had grown in prestige until it was now considered the "fifth major"—right along with the Masters, the British Open, the PGA, and the U.S. Open. The course where the Classic was held had become legendary, a place to be mentioned in the same breath as Augusta, Cypress Point, and Merion. Golfers called it the Old Testament and for good reason. The course was one of the most beautiful in the South, lush with pines and ancient magnolias. Beards of Spanish moss draped the oaks that served as a backdrop to the small, perfectly manicured greens, and oyster-white sand, soft as powder, filled the bunkers. When the day was still and the sun warm, the fairways glistened with light so pure it seemed heavenly. But the natural beauty of the course was part of its treachery. While it warmed the heart, it could also lull the senses, so that the bedazzled player didn't realize until a fraction of a second too late that the Old Testament forgave no sins.

Golfers snarled at it and cursed it and swore they would never play it again, but the best of them always came back, because those heroic eighteen holes provided something that life itself could never deliver. They provided perfect justice. The good shot was always rewarded, the bad met with swift, terrible punishment. Those eighteen holes provided no second chance, no time for jury-rigging, no opportunity to plea-bargain. The Old Testament vanquished the weak, while on the strong it bestowed glory and honor forever. Or at least until the next day.

Dallie hated the Classic. Before he'd given up drinking and his game had improved, he hadn't always qualified for it. The last few years, however, he'd played well enough to find himself on the roster. Most of the time he wished he'd stayed home. The Old Testament was a golf course that demanded perfection, and Dallie damned well knew he was too imperfect to live up to that kind of expectation. He told himself that the Classic was a tournament like any other, but when this course defeated him, it seemed to shrink his very soul.

Every part of him wished that Francesca had chosen another tournament when she'd issued her challenge. Not that he was taking her seriously. No way. As far as he was concerned, she had kissed him good-bye when she'd thrown that little tantrum. Still, someone else was in the announcers' booth when Dallie teed up at the first hole, taking a few seconds to shoot a grin at a pretty little blonde who was smiling at him from the front row of the gallery. He'd told the network honchos they were going to have to wait a little bit longer for him and handed back their contract unsigned. He just hadn't been able to sit this one out. Not this year. Not after what Francesca had said to him.

The grip on his driver felt good in his hand as he addressed the ball, solid and comforting. He felt loose. He felt fine. And he was damned well going to show Francesca that she didn't know what she was talking about. He hit a big booming drive that shot out into the sky—rocket-driven, a NASA special. The gallery applauded. The ball sped through space on its way to eternity. And then, at the very last instant before it descended, it drifted ever so slightly . . . just enough so that it missed the edge of the fairway and landed in a clump of magnolias.

Francesca bypassed her secretary and dialed her contact in the sports department directly, making her fourth call to him that afternoon. "How's he doing now?" she asked when the male voice answered.

"Sorry, Francesca, but he lost another shot on the seventeenth hole, which puts him at three over par. It's only the first round, so—assuming he survives the cut—he has three more rounds to go, but this isn't the best way to start a tournament." She pressed her eyes shut as he continued. "Of course, this isn't his kind of tournament anyway, you know that. The Classic is high pressure, high voltage. I remember when Jack Nicklaus owned the place." She barely listened as he went on, reminiscing about his favorite game. "Nicklaus is the only golfer in history who could regularly bring the Old Testament to its knees. Year after year, all through the seventies and even into the early eighties, he'd come into the Classic and blow everybody away, walking those fairways like he owned them, making those tiny little greens beg for mercy with those superhuman putts of his. . . ."

By the end of the day, Dallie was four over par. Francesca felt heartsick. Why had she done this to him? Why had she issued such a ridiculous challenge? At home that night, she tried to read, but nothing held her attention. She started to clean out the hall closet, but she couldn't concentrate. At ten o'clock that night, she began phoning the airlines trying to find a late flight. Then she gently awakened Teddy and told him the two of them were taking a trip.

Holly Grace banged on the door of Francesca's motel room early the next morning. Teddy had just gotten up, but since dawn Francesca had been pacing the perimeters of the shabby little room that was the best accommodation she could find in a town bursting at the seams with golfers and their fans. She nearly threw herself into Holly Grace's arms. "Thank God you're here! I was afraid something had happened."

Holly Grace deposited her suitcase just inside the door and sagged wearily into the nearest chair. "I don't know why I let you talk me into this. We didn't finish shooting until nearly midnight, and I had to take a six A.M. flight. I barely got an hour's sleep on the plane coming down here."

"I'm sorry, Holly Grace. I know this is an absolutely miserable thing to do to you. If I didn't think it was so important, I'd never have asked." She hoisted Holly Grace's suitcase to the foot of the bed and opened the latches.

"While you're taking a shower, I'll get some fresh clothes out and Teddy can pick up some breakfast for you at the coffee shop. I know it's dreadful of me to rush you like this, but Dallie tees off in an hour. I've got the passes ready. Just make sure he sees both of you right away."

"I don't understand why *you* can't take Teddy to watch him play," Holly Grace complained. "It's ridiculous to drag me all the way down here just to escort your son to a golf tournament."

Francesca pulled Holly Grace to her feet and then pushed her toward the bathroom. "I need some blind faith from you right now. Please!"

Forty-five minutes later, Francesca stood well back from the door as she let Holly Grace and Teddy out, making certain none of the people milling around in the parking lot could see her clearly enough to recognize her. She knew how fast news traveled, and unless it became absolutely necessary, she had no intention of letting Dallie know she was anywhere near. As soon as the two of them had disappeared, she rushed to the television so she could be ready and waiting for the tournament coverage to begin.

Seve Ballesteros was leading the tournament after the first round, so Dallie wasn't in the best of moods as he came off the practice green. Dallie used to like Seve, until Francesca had started making cracks about how good looking he was. Now just the sight of that dark-haired Spaniard made him feel out of sorts. He looked over toward the leader board and confirmed what he already knew, that Jack Nicklaus had ended up at five strokes over par the day before, shooting a round even worse than Dallie's own. Dallie felt a mean-spirited satisfaction. Nicklaus was getting old; the years were finally doing what human beings couldn't—putting an end to the incomparable reign of the Golden Bear from Columbus, Ohio.

Skeet walked ahead of Dallie to the first tee. "There's a little surprise for you over there," he said, gesturing toward his left. Dallie followed the direction of his gaze and then grinned as he spotted Holly Grace standing just behind the ropes. He began to walk over to her, only to freeze in mid-stride as he recognized Teddy standing at her side.

Anger rushed through him. How could one small woman be so vindictive? He knew Francesca had sent Teddy and he knew why. She had sent the boy to taunt him, to remind him of every nasty word she had hurled at him. Normally he would have liked having Teddy watch him play, but not at the Classic—not at a tournament where he had never done well. It occurred to him that Francesca wanted Teddy to see him get beaten, and the thought made him so furious he could barely contain himself. Something of his feelings must have shown because Teddy looked down at his feet and then back up again with that mulishly stubborn expression that Dallie had grown to recognize all too well.

Dallie reminded himself that it wasn't Teddy's fault, but it still took all of his self-control to walk over and greet them. His fans in the gallery immediately began asking him questions and calling out encouragement. He joked with them a little bit, glad of the distraction because he didn't know what to say to Teddy. *I'm sorry I screwed everything up for us*—that's what he should say. *I'm sorry I haven't been able to talk to you, to tell you what you mean to me, to tell you how proud I was when you protected your mama that day in Wynette.*

Skeet was holding out his driver as Dallie turned away from the gallery. "This is the first time ol' Teddy's going to see you play, isn't it?" Skeet said, handing him the club. "Be a shame if he didn't see your best game."

Dallie shot him a black look, and then walked over to tee up. The muscles in his back and shoulders felt as tight as steel bands. Normally he joked with the crowd before he hit, but today he couldn't manage it. The club felt foreign in his hand. He looked over at Teddy and saw the tight little frown in his forehead, a frown of total concentration. Dallie forced himself to focus his attention on what he had to do—on what he *could* do. He took a deep breath, eye on the ball, knees slightly bent, drew back the club and then whipped it through, using all the strength of his powerful left side. *Airborne.*

The crowd applauded. The ball fired out over the lush green fairway, a white dot speeding against a cloudless sky. It began to descend, heading directly toward the clump of magnolias that had done Dallie in the day before. And then, at the end, the ball faded to the right so that it landed on the fairway in perfect position. Dallie heard a wild Texas cheer from behind him and turned to grin at Holly Grace. Skeet gave him a thumbs-up, and even Teddy had a half-smile on his face.

That night, Dallie went to bed knowing he'd finally brought the Old Testament to its knees. While the tournament leaders had fallen victim to a strong wind, Dallie had shot three under par, enough to make up for the disaster of the first day and push him way up on the leader board, enough to show his son just a little bit about how the old game of golf was played. Seve was still in there, along with Fuzzy Zoeller and Greg Norman. Watson and Crenshaw were out. Nicklaus had shot another mediocre round, but the Golden Bear never gave up easily, and he had scored just well enough to survive the cut.

As Dallie tried to fall asleep that night, he told himself to concentrate on Seve and the others, not to worry about Nicklaus. Jack was eight over par, too far behind to be in contention and too old to pull off any of his miraculous last-minute charges. But as Dallie punched his pillow into shape, he heard the Bear's voice whispering to him as if he were standing right there in the room. *Don't ever count me out, Beaudine. I'm not like you. I never quit.*

Dallie couldn't seem to hold his concentration on the third day. Despite the presence of Holly Grace and Teddy, his play was mediocre and he ended at three over par. It was enough to put him in a three-way tie for second place, but he was two shots out of the lead.

By the end of the third day's play, Francesca's head ached from watching the small motel television screen so intently. On CBS, Pat Summerall began to summarize the day's action.

"Dallie Beaudine has never played well under pressure, and it seemed to me he looked tight out there."

"The noise from the crowd obviously bothered him," Ken Venturi observed. "You've got to remember that Jack Nicklaus was playing in the group right behind Dallie, and when Jack is hot, like he was today, the gallery goes wild. Every time those cheers went up, you'd better believe the other players could hear, and they all knew Jack had made another spectacular shot. That can't help but shake up the tournament leaders."

"It'll be interesting to see if Dallie can change his pattern of final-round defeats and come back tomorrow," Summerall said. "He's a big hitter, he has one of the best swings on the tour, and he's always been popular with the fans. You know they'd like nothing better than to see him finally pull one out."

"But the real story here today is Jack Nicklaus," Ken Venturi concluded. "At 47 years of age, the Golden Bear from Columbus, Ohio, has shot an unbelievable sixty-seven—five under par—putting him in a three-way tie for second place, right along with Seve Ballesteros and Dallas Beaudine. . . ."

Francesca flipped off the set. She should have been happy that Dallie was one of the tournament leaders, but the final round was always his weakest. From what had happened in today's round, she had to conclude that Teddy's presence alone wouldn't be enough to spur him on. She knew stronger measures were called for, and she bit down on her bottom lip, refusing to let herself consider how easily the only strong measure she had been able to think of could backfire.

"Just stay away from me," Holly Grace said the next morning as Francesca hurried after her and Teddy across the country club lawn toward the crowd that surrounded the first tee.

"I know what I'm doing," Francesca called out. "At least I think I do."

Holly Grace spun around as Francesca caught up with her. "When Dallie sees you, it's going to ruin his concentration for good. You couldn't have come up with a better way to blow this final round for him."

"He'll blow it for himself if I'm not there," Francesca insisted. "Look, you've coddled him for years and it hasn't worked. Do it my way for a change."

Holly Grace whipped off her sunglasses and glared at Francesca. "Coddled him! I never coddled him in my life."

"Yes, you have. You coddle him all the time." Francesca grabbed Holly Grace's arm and began pushing her toward the first tee. "Just do what I asked you. I know a lot more about golf than I used to, but I still don't understand the subtleties. You've got to stick right by me and translate every shot he makes."

"You're crazy, do you know that—"

Teddy cocked his head to one side as he observed the argument taking place between his mother and Holly Grace. He didn't often see grown-ups argue, and it was interesting to watch. Teddy's nose was sunburned and his legs were tired from having walked so much the past two days. But he was looking forward to today's final round, even though he got a little bored standing around waiting for the players to hit. Still, it was worth the wait because sometimes Dallie walked over to the ropes and told him what was going on, and then everybody smiled at him and knew that he was a pretty special kid, since he was getting so much of Dallie's attention. Even after Dallie had made some bad shots the day before, he'd walked over and talked to Teddy, explaining what had happened.

The day was sunny and mild, the temperature too warm for his Born-to-Raise-Hell sweat shirt, but Teddy had decided to wear it anyway.

"There's going to be hell to pay over this," Holly Grace said, shaking her head. "And why couldn't you put on slacks or shorts like a normal person wears to a golf tournament? You're attracting all kinds of attention."

Francesca didn't bother to tell Holly Grace that was exactly what she'd intended when she'd pulled on this tomato red slip of a dress. The simple cotton jersey tube dipped low at the neck, gently cupped her hips, and ended well above her knees in a saucy little polka-dot flounce. If she'd calculated right, the dress, along with her unmatched silver "angst" earrings, should just about drive Dallas Beaudine crazy.

In all his years of tournament golf, Dallie had seldom played in the same group as Jack Nicklaus. The few times he had, the round had been a disaster. He had played in front of him and behind him; he'd eaten dinner with him, shared a podium with him, exchanged a few golf stories with him. But he'd seldom *played* with him, and now Dallie's hands were shaking. He told himself not to make the mistake of confusing the real Jack Nicklaus with the Bear in his head. He reminded himself that the real Nicklaus was a flesh and blood human being, vulnerable like everybody else, but it didn't make any difference. Their faces were the same and that was all that counted.

"How you doin' today, Dallie?" Jack Nicklaus smiled pleasantly as he walked onto the first tee, his son Steve behind him acting as his caddy. *I'm going to eat you alive,* the Bear in Dallie's head said.

He's forty-seven years old, Dallie reminded himself as he shook Jack's hand. A man of forty-seven can't compete with a thirty-seven-year-old at the top of his form.

I won't even bother spitting out your bones, the Bear replied.

Seve Ballesteros was back by the ropes talking to someone in the crowd, his dark skin and chiseled cheekbones catching the attention of many of the women who made up Dallie's gallery. Dallie knew he should be more worried about Seve than about Jack. Seve was an international champion, considered by many to be the best golfer in the world. His driving was as powerful as any on the tour, and he had an almost superhuman touch around the greens. Dallie forced his attention away from Nicklaus and walked over to shake Seve's hand—only to stop cold in his tracks when he saw who Ballesteros was talking to.

At first he couldn't believe it. Even *she* couldn't be this evil. Standing there in a bright red dress that looked like underwear, and smiling at Seve like he was some sort of Spanish god, was Miss Fancy Pants herself. Holly Grace stood on one side of her looking miserable, and Teddy was on the other. Francesca finally tore her attention away from Seve and looked toward Dallie. She gave him a smile that was as cool as the inside of a frosted beer mug, a smile so lofty and superior that Dallie wanted to go right over and shake her. She tipped her head slightly, and her silver earrings caught the sun. Lifting her hand, she pushed chestnut tendrils away from her ears, tilting her head so that her neck formed a perfect curve and preening for him— *preening,* for God's sake! He couldn't believe it.

Dallie began to stalk toward her to choke her to death, but

he had to stop because Seve was coming toward him, hand extended, all flashing eyes and Latin charm. Dallie hid behind a phony Texas grin and gave Seve's hand a couple of pumps.

Jack was up first. Dallie was so aggravated he was barely aware that Nicklaus had hit until he heard the crowd applaud. It was a good drive—not quite as long as the behemoth drives of his youth, but in perfect position. Dallie thought he saw Seve sneak a look at Francesca before he teed up. His hair glinted blue-black in the morning light, a Spanish pirate come to plunder American shores, and maybe walk off with a few of their women while he was at it. Seve's lean body wound tightly as he drew back the club and hit a long drive out to the center of the fairway, where it rolled ten yards past Nicklaus and came to a stop.

Dallie sneaked a glance at the gallery, only to wish he hadn't. Francesca was applauding Seve's drive enthusiastically, bouncing up on tiptoes in a pair of tiny red sandals that didn't look as if they would make it through three holes of walking, much less eighteen. He snatched his driver from Skeet's hand, his face dark as a thundercloud, his emotions even darker. Taking his stance, he was hardly even thinking about what he was doing. His body went on automatic pilot as he stared down at the ball and visualized Francesca's beautiful little face imprinted right on the top of the Titleist trademark. And then he swung.

He didn't even know what he'd done until he heard Holly Grace's cheer and his vision cleared enough to see the ball fly out two hundred ninety-five yards and roll to a stop well beyond Seve's drive. It was a great shot, and Skeet slapped him jubilantly on the back. Seve and Jack nodded in polite acknowledgment. Dallie turned toward the gallery and nearly choked at what he saw. Francesca had her snooty little nose tilted up in the air, as if she were ready to *expire* from boredom, as if she were saying in that exaggerated way of hers, "Is *that* the absolute best you can do?"

"Get rid of her," Dallie snarled under his breath at Skeet.

Skeet was wiping the driver with a towel and didn't seem to hear. Dallie marched over to the ropes, his voice full of venom but pitched low enough so that he couldn't be overheard by anyone except Holly Grace. "I want you to get off this course right *now*," he told Francesca. "What the hell do you think you're doing here?"

Once again she gave him that lofty, superior smile. "I'm just reminding you what the stakes are, darling."

"You're crazy!" he exploded. "In case you're too ignorant to have figured it out, I'm in a three-way tie for second place in one of the biggest tournaments of the year, and I don't need this kind of distraction."

Francesca straightened, leaned forward, and whispered in his ear, "Second place isn't good enough."

Afterward Dallie figured that no jury in the world would have convicted him if he'd strangled the life out of her right there on the spot, but his playing partners were moving off the tee, he had another shot coming up, and he couldn't spare the time.

For the next nine holes he made that ball beg for mercy, ordered it to follow his wishes, punished it with every ounce of his strength and every morsel of his determination. He *willed* his putts into the cup on one sure stroke. *One* stroke—not two, not three! Each shot was more awesome than the last, and every time he turned to the gallery, he saw Holly Grace talking furiously to Francesca, translating the magic of what he was doing, telling Miss Fancy Pants that she was seeing golf history being made. But no matter what he did, no matter how astounding his shot, how breathtaking his putts, how *heroically* he was playing—every goddamn time he looked at her, Francesca seemed to be saying, "Is *that* the best you can do?"

He was so caught up in his anger, so immersed in her scorn, that he couldn't quite comprehend the consequences of the rapidly changing leader board. Oh, he understood what it said, all right. He saw the numbers. He knew that the tournament leaders playing behind him had fallen back; he knew Seve had dropped off. He could read the numbers, all right, but it wasn't until he'd birdied the fourteenth hole that he could actually comprehend in his gut the fact that he had pulled ahead, that his angry, vicious attack on the course had put him at two under par for the tournament. With four holes left to play, he was tied for first place in the United States Classic.

Tied with Jack Nicklaus.

Dallie shook his head, trying to clear it as he walked toward the fifteenth tee. How could this have happened to him? How had it happened that Dallas Beaudine from Wynette, Texas, was going one-on-one with Jack Nicklaus? He couldn't think about it. If he thought about it, the Bear would start talking to him in his head.

You're going to fail, Beaudine. You're going to prove everything Jaycee used to say about you. Everything I've been saying for years. You're not man enough to pull this off. Not against me.

He turned back toward the gallery and saw that she was watching him. As he glared at her, she placed one sandaled foot in front of the other and bent her knee slightly so that ridiculous little polka-dot flounce at the bottom of her dress rode up higher on her legs. She pressed her shoulders back, making the soft cotton jersey cling to her breasts, outlining them in memorable detail. *Here's your trophy*, that little body told him quite plainly. *Don't forget what you're playing for.*

He slammed the ball down the fifteenth fairway, promising himself that when this was all over he would never again let himself near a woman with a bitch's heart. As soon as the tournament was finished, he was going to teach Francesca Day the lesson of her life by marrying the first sweet-voiced country girl who came along.

He scrambled for par on the fifteenth and the sixteenth holes. So did Nicklaus. Jack's son was with him the whole way, handing him clubs, helping read the greens. Dallie's own son stood by the ropes wearing a Born-to-Raise-Hell T-shirt and a look of furious determination on his face. Dallie's heart swelled every time he looked at him. Damn, he was a feisty little kid.

The seventeenth hole was short and nasty. Jack talked a little bit to the crowd as he walked toward the green. He had cut his teeth on pressure shots, and there was nothing he loved more than a tight spot. Dallie had sweat through his golf shirt and through two gloves. He was famous for joking with the crowd, but now he maintained an ominous silence. Nicklaus was playing some of the best golf of his life, chomping up the fairways, burning up the greens. Forty-seven was too old to play like that, but somebody had forgotten to tell Jack. And now only Dallie Beaudine stood between the greatest player in the history of the sport and one more title.

Somehow Dallie pulled off another par, but Jack did, too. They were still tied going into the final hole.

Cameramen balancing portable video units on their shoulders followed every movement as the two players headed for the eighteenth tee. The network announcers heaped one superlative after another on them while word of the blood contest taking place on the Old Testament spread throughout the world of sports, sending dials flicking and the network's Sunday afternoon ratings soaring into the stratosphere. The crowd around the players had grown to the thousands, their excitement feverish because they knew that whatever happened, they couldn't lose. This crowd had been charmed by Dallie when he was still a rookie, and they had been waiting for years for him to win a major title. But the thought of being on the spot when Jack won again was irresistible, too. It was the 1986 Masters all over again, with Jack charging like a bull toward the finish, as unstoppable as the force of nature.

Dallie and Jack both hit solid drives off the eighteenth tee. The hole was a long par five with a lake placed diabolically in front of all but the left corner of the green. They called it Hogan's Lake, because it had cost the great Ben Hogan the U.S. Classic championship in 1951 when he'd tried to hit over it instead of around it. They could just as easily have called it Arnie's Lake or Watson's Lake or Snead's Lake because at one time or other all of them had fallen victim to its treachery.

Jack didn't mind gambling, but he hadn't won every important championship in the world by taking foolhardy chances, and he had no intention of going directly for the flag by making a suicide shot over that lake. He lined up his second shot safely to the left of Hogan's Lake and hit a beautiful fade that landed just short of the green. The crowd let out a roar and then held its collective breath as the ball bounced up in the air and came to a stop on the edge of the green, sixty feet from the pin. The noise was deafening.

Nicklaus had made a spectacular shot, a magic shot, a shot for a possible birdie on the hole—a shot that even gave him an outside chance at an eagle.

Dallie felt panic, as insidious as poison, creeping through his veins. In order to keep up with Nicklaus he had to make that same shot—hit to the left of the lake and then bounce the ball up on the green. It was a difficult shot in the best of circumstances, but with thousands of people watching from the gallery, millions more watching at home on their televisions, with a tournament title at stake and hands that wouldn't stop shaking, he knew he couldn't pull it off.

Seve hit to the left of the lake on his second shot, but the ball fell well short of the green. Panic rose up in Dallie's throat until it seemed to be choking him. He couldn't do this—he just couldn't! He spun around, instinctively searching out Francesca. Sure enough, her chin shot up in the air, her snooty little nose lifted higher—daring him, challenging him—

And then, as he watched, it all fell apart for her. She couldn't pull it off any longer. Her chin dropped, her expression softened, and she gazed at him with eyes that saw straight through into his soul, eyes that understood his panic and begged him to set it aside. For her. For Teddy. For all of them.

You're going to disappoint her, Beaudine, the Bear taunted. *You've disappointed everybody you've ever loved in your life, and you're getting ready to do it again.*

Francesca's lips moved, forming a single word. *Please.*

Dallie looked down at the grass, thinking about everything Francie had said to him, and then he walked over to Skeet. "I'm going straight for the flag," he said. "I'm going to hit across the lake."

He waited for Skeet to yell at him, to tell him he was all kinds of a fool. But Skeet merely looked thoughtful. "You're going to have to carry that ball two hundred and sixty yards and make it stop on a nickel."

"I know that," Dallie replied quietly.

"If you make the safe shot—go around the lake—you've got a good chance at tying Nicklaus."

"I'm tired of safe shots," Dallie said. "I'm going for the flag." Jaycee had been dead for years, and Dallie didn't have a damned thing left to prove to that bastard. Francie was right. Not trying at all was a bigger sin than failing. He took a last look over toward Francesca, wanting her respect more than he'd ever wanted anything. She and Holly Grace were clutching each other's hands as if they were getting ready to fall off the edge of the world. Teddy's legs had gotten tired and he was sitting on the grass, but the look of determination hadn't faded from his face.

Dallie focused all his attention on what he had to do, trying to control the rush of adrenaline that would harm him more than it would help.

Hogan couldn't carry the lake, the Bear whispered. *What makes you think you can?*

Because I want it more than Hogan ever did, Dallie answered back. *I just plain want it more.*

When he lined up for the ball and the spectators realized what he was going to do, they emitted a murmur of disbelief. Nicklaus's face was as expressionless as ever. If he thought Dallie was making a mistake, he kept it to himself.

You'll never do it, the Bear whispered.

You just watch me, Dallie replied.

His club lashed through the ball. It shot into the sky on a high, strong trajectory and then faded to the right so that it hung over the water—over the center of the lake that had claimed Ben Hogan and Arnold Palmer and so many other legends. It sailed through the sky for an eternity, but it still hadn't cleared the lake when it began to come down. The spectators held their breath, their bodies frozen into position like extras in an old science-fiction movie. Dallie stood like a statue watching the slow, ominous descent. In the background, a flag with the number 18 printed on it caught a puff of breeze and lifted ever so slightly, so that in all the universe only that flag and the ball were moving.

Screams went up from the crowd, and then an ear-splitting wall of sound struck Dallie as his ball cleared the edge of the lake and hit the green, bouncing slightly before it came to a dead stop ten feet from the flag.

Seve put his ball on the green and two-putted, then shook his head dejectedly as he walked off onto the fringe. Jack's heroic sixty-foot putt lipped the cup, but didn't drop. Dallie stood alone. He only had a ten-foot putt, but he was mentally and physically exhausted. He knew that if he made the putt he would win the tournament, but if he missed it he would be tied with Jack.

He turned to Francesca, and once again her pretty lips formed that one word: *please*.

As tired as he was, Dallie didn't have the heart to disappoint her.

Chapter
33

Dallie's arms shot up in the air, one fist holding his putter aloft like a medieval standard of victory. Skeet was crying like a baby, so overcome with joy that he couldn't move. As a result, the first person who reached Dallie was Jack Nicklaus.

"Great game, Dallie," Nicklaus said, putting his arm over Dallie's shoulders. "You're a real champion."

Then Skeet was hugging him and pounding him on the back, and Dallie was hugging back, except his eyes were moving the whole time, searching the crowd until he found what he was looking for.

Holly Grace broke through first; then Francesca, with Teddy in tow. Holly Grace rushed toward Dallie on her long-stemmed legs—legs that had first won fame as they ran the bases at Wynette High, legs that had been American-designed for both speed and beauty. Holly Grace ran toward the man she had loved just about all her life, and then she stopped cold as she saw those blue eyes of his slip right past her and come to rest on Francesca. A spasm of pain went through her chest, a moment of heartbreak, and then the pain eased as she felt herself let him go.

Teddy nudged up next to her, not quite ready to join in such extravagant emotion. Holly Grace slipped her arm around his shoulders, and they both watched as Dallie lifted

Francesca high off the ground, hoisting her by the waist so that her head was higher than his. For a fraction of a moment, she hung there, tilting her face into the sun and laughing at the sky. And then she kissed him, brushing his face with her hair, battering his cheeks with the joyous swaying of her silly silver earrings. Her little red sandals slid from her toes, one of them balancing itself on top of his golf shoe.

Francesca turned away first, searching for Holly Grace in the crowd, holding out her arm. Dallie set Francesca down without letting go of her and held out his arm, too, so that Holly Grace could join them. He hugged them both—these two women who meant everything to him—one the love of his boyhood, the other the love of his manhood; one tall and strong, the other tiny and frivolous, with a marshmallow heart and a spine of tempered steel. Dallie's eyes sought out Teddy, but even in his moment of victory, he saw the boy wasn't ready and he didn't press him. For now it was enough that they could exchange smiles.

A UPI photographer caught the picture that was to grace the front pages of the nation's sports sections the next day—a jubilant Dallie Beaudine lifting Francesca Day up off the ground while Holly Grace Beaudine stood to one side.

Francesca had to be back in New York the next morning, and Dallie needed to perform all the duties that fell to the winner immediately following a major championship. As a result, their time together after the tournament was much too short and all too public. "I'll call you," he mouthed as he was swept away.

She smiled in answer, and then the press engulfed him.

Francesca and Holly Grace traveled back to New York together, but their flight was delayed and they didn't reach the city until late. It was past midnight by the time Francesca had tucked Teddy into bed, too late to expect a call from Dallie. The following day, she attended a briefing on the upcoming Statue of Liberty citizenship ceremony, a luncheon for women in broadcasting, and two meetings. She left a series of phone numbers with her secretary, making certain that she wasn't out of contact anywhere she went, but Dallie didn't call.

By the time she left the studio, she had worked herself into a froth of righteous indignation. She knew he was busy, but he certainly could have spared a few minutes to call her. Unless he'd changed his mind, a little voice whispered. Unless he'd had second thoughts. Unless she'd misread his feelings.

Consuelo and Teddy were gone when she got home. She set down her purse and briefcase, then slipped wearily out of her jacket and headed down the hallway to her bedroom, only to come to a halt in the doorway. A crystal and silver trophy nearly three feet long lay in the exact center of her bed.

"Dallie!" she screeched.

He came out of her bathroom, hair still wet from the shower, one of her fluffy pink towels wrapped around his hips. Grinning at her, he hoisted the trophy off the bed, walked over to her, and deposited it at her feet. "Was this pretty much what you had in mind?" he asked.

"You wretch!" She threw herself into his arms, almost knocking over both him and the trophy in the process. "You darling, impossible, wonderful wretch!"

And then he was kissing her, and she was kissing him, and they were holding each other so tightly it seemed as if the life force from one body had poured into the other. "Damn, I love you," Dallie murmured. "My sweet little Fancy Pants, driving me half crazy, nagging me to death." He kissed her again, long and slow. "You're almost the best thing that ever happened to me."

"Almost?" she murmured against his lips. "What's the best?"

"Being born good-looking." And then he kissed her again.

Their lovemaking was full of laughter and tenderness, with nothing forbidden, nothing withheld. Afterward, they lay face to face, their naked bodies pressed together so they could whisper secrets to each other.

"I thought I was going to die," he told her, "when you said you wouldn't marry me."

"I thought I was going to die," she told him, "when you didn't say you loved me."

"I've been afraid so much. You sure were right about that."

"I had to have the best from you. I'm a miserable, selfish person."

"You're the best woman in the world."

He began telling her about Danny and Jaycee Beaudine and the feeling he'd gotten early in life that he wasn't going to amount to much. It was easier not to try too hard, he had discovered, than to have all his shortcomings proven to him.

Francesca said that Jaycee Beaudine sounded like a perfectly odious person and Dallie should have had enough sense early on to realize that the opinions of unsavory people like that were completely unreliable.

Dallie laughed and then kissed her again before he asked when they were getting married. "I won you fair and square," he said. "Now it's time for you to pay up."

They were dressed and sitting in the living room when Consuelo and Teddy returned several hours later. The two of them had spent a wonderful evening at Madison Square Garden, where Dallie had sent them earlier with a pair of ringside tickets to see the Greatest Show on Earth. Consuelo took in Francesca's and Dallie's flushed faces and wasn't fooled for a minute about what had been going on while she and Teddy were watching Gunther Gebel-Williams tame tigers. Teddy and Dallie eyed each other politely but warily. Teddy was still pretty sure Dallie was only pretending to like him because of his mom, while Dallie was trying to figure out how to undo all the damage he'd inflicted.

"Teddy, how about taking me to the top of the Empire State Building tomorrow after school?" he said. "I'd sure like to see it."

For a moment Dallie thought Teddy was going to refuse. Teddy picked up his circus program, rolled it into a tube, and blew through it with elaborate casualness. "I guess it'd be okay." He turned the tube into a telescope and looked through it. "As long as I get back in time to watch *The Goonies* on cable TV."

The next day the two of them went up to the observation platform. Teddy stopped well back from the protective metal grating at the edge because heights made him dizzy. Dallie stopped right at his side because he wasn't all that crazy about heights himself. "It's not clear enough today to see the Statue of Liberty," Teddy said, pointing toward the harbor. "Sometimes you can see it over there."

"Did you want me to get you one of those rubber King Kongs they're selling at the concession stand?" Dallie asked.

Teddy liked King Kong a lot, but he shook his head. A guy wearing an Iowa State windbreaker recognized Dallie and asked for his autograph. Teddy was an old hand at waiting patiently while grown-ups gave autographs, but the interruption irritated Dallie. When the fan finally walked away, Teddy looked at Dallie and said wisely, "It goes with the territory."

"How's that again?"

"When you're a famous person, people feel like they know you, even though they don't. You have a certain obligation."

"That sounds like your mama talking."

"We get interrupted a lot."

Dallie looked at him for a moment. "You know these interruptions are only going to get worse, don't you, Teddy? Your mama'll be upset if I don't win a few more golf tournaments for her, and whenever the three of us go out, there'll be that many more people looking at us."

"Are you and my mom getting married?"

Dallie nodded his head. "I love your mama a lot. She's about the best lady in the world." He took a deep breath, charging in just as Francesca would have. "I love you, too, Teddy. I know that might be hard for you to believe after the way I've been acting, but it's true."

Teddy pulled off his glasses and submitted the lenses to an elaborate cleaning on the hem of his T-shirt. "What about Holly Grace?" he said, holding the lenses up to the light. "Does this mean we won't see Holly Grace anymore, because of how you and her used to be married?"

Dallie smiled. Teddy might not want to acknowledge what he'd just heard, but at least he hadn't walked away. "We couldn't get rid of Holly Grace even if we tried to. Your mama and I both love her; she'll always be part of our family. Skeet, too, and Miss Sybil. Along with whatever runaways your mom manages to pick up."

"Gerry, too?" Teddy asked.

Dallie hesitated. "I guess that's up to Gerry."

Teddy wasn't feeling so dizzy now, and he took a few steps closer to the protective grating at the edge. Dallie wasn't quite as eager to move forward, but he did, too. "You and I still have some things to talk about, you know," Dallie said.

"I want one of those King Kongs," Teddy declared abruptly.

Dallie saw that Teddy still wasn't ready for any father-son revelations, and he swallowed his disappointment. "I have something to ask you."

"I don't want to talk about it." Teddy mutinously laced his fingers through the metal grating.

Dallie laced his fingers through, too, hoping he could get this next part right. "Did you ever go to play with a friend, and when you got there you found out that he had built something special when you weren't around? A fort, maybe, or a castle?"

Teddy nodded warily.

"Maybe he made a swing when you weren't around, or built a racetrack for his cars?"

"Or maybe he built this neat planetarium out of garbage bags and a flashlight," Teddy interjected.

"Or a planetarium out of garbage bags," Dallie quickly amended. "Anyway, maybe you looked at this planetarium, and you thought it was so terrific that you felt a little jealous you hadn't made it yourself." Dallie let go of the fence, keeping his eyes on Teddy to make sure the boy was following him. "So, because you were jealous, instead of telling your friend what a great planetarium he'd made, you sort of stuck your nose up in the air and told him you didn't think what he'd made was all that terrific, even though it was about the best planetarium you'd ever seen."

Teddy nodded slowly, interested that a grown-up would know about something like that. Dallie rested his arm on top of a telescope that was pointing toward New Jersey. "That's pretty much what happened when I saw you."

"It is?" Teddy declared in astonishment.

"Here's this kid, and he's a real great kid—smart and brave—but I didn't have anything to do with making him that way, and I was jealous. So instead of saying to his mom, 'Hey, you raised yourself a pretty neat kid,' I acted like I didn't think the kid was all that great, and that he would

have been a lot better if I'd been around to help raise him."
He searched Teddy's face, trying to read by his expression
whether he was following, but the boy wasn't giving anything away. "Could you understand something like that?"
he asked finally.

Another child might have nodded, but a child with an I.Q.
of one hundred sixty-eight needed some time to sort things
out. "Could we go look at those rubber King Kongs now?"
he asked politely.

The Statue of Liberty ceremony took place on a poet's day
in May, complete with a soft, balmy breeze, a cornflower
blue sky, and the lazy swoop of sea gulls. Three launches
decorated with red, white, and blue bunting had crossed
New York Harbor toward Liberty Island that morning and
had landed at the dock where the Circle Line ferry normally
disgorged tourists. But for the next few hours, there would
be no tourists, and only a few hundred people populated the
island.

Lady Liberty towered over a platform that had been
specially built on the lawn at the south side of the island
next to the statue's base. Normally, public ceremonies were
held in a fenced-in area behind the statue, but the White
House advance team thought this location, beneath the face
of the statue and with an unblocked view of the harbor, was
more photogenic for the press. Francesca, in a pale pistachio
dress with an ivory silk-shantung jacket, sat in a row with
the other honorees, various government dignitaries, and a
Supreme Court Justice. At the lectern, the President of the
United States talked about the promise of America, his
words echoing from the loudspeakers set up in the trees.

"We celebrate here today—old and young, black and
white, some from humble roots, others born into prosperity.
We have different religions and different political beliefs.
But as we rest in the shadow of the great Lady Liberty, we
are all equals, all inheritors of the flame. . . ."

Francesca's heart was so full of joy she thought she would
burst. Each participant had been permitted to invite twenty
guests, and as she gazed out over her diverse group, she
realized that these people she had come to love represented
a microcosm of the country itself.

Dallie, wearing an American flag pin on the lapel of his navy suit coat, sat with Miss Sybil on one side of him, Teddy and Holly Grace on the other. Behind them, Naomi leaned to one side to whisper something in her husband's ear. She looked healthy after having given birth, but she seemed nervous, undoubtedly worried about leaving her four-week-old baby girl even for half a day. Both Naomi and her husband wore black armbands to protest apartheid. Nathan Hurd sat with Skeet Cooper, an interesting combination of personalities in Francesca's opinion. From Skeet to the end of the row stretched a group of young female faces—black and white, some with too much makeup, but all of them possessing a spark of hope in their own futures. They were Francesca's runaways, and she had been touched when so many of them wanted to be with her today. Even Stefan had called her from Europe this morning to congratulate her, and she had pried out the welcome news that he was currently enjoying the affection of the beautiful young widow of an Italian industrialist. Only Gerry hadn't acknowledged her invitation, and Francesca missed him. She wondered if he was still angry with her because she had turned down his latest demand to appear on her program.

Dallie caught her looking at him and gave her a private smile that told her as clearly as if he'd spoken the words how much he loved her. Despite their superficial differences, they had discovered that their souls were a matched set.

Teddy had snuggled over close to Holly Grace instead of to his father, but Francesca thought that situation would soon resolve itself and she didn't permit it to disturb her pleasure in the day. In a week she and Dallie would be married, and she was happier than she had ever been in her life.

The President was revving up for a big finish. "And so America is still the land of opportunity, still the home of individual initiative, as witnessed by the success of those we honor this day. We are the greatest country in the world. . . ."

Francesca had done programs on the homeless in America, on poverty and injustice, racism and sexism. She knew all the country's flaws, but for now she could only agree with the President. America wasn't a perfect country; it was too often self-serving, violent, and greedy. But it was a country that frequently had its heart in the right place, even if it couldn't always get all the details worked out correctly.

The President finished to a rousing ovation, captured by the network cameras for airing on the news that night. Then the Supreme Court Justice stepped forward. Although she couldn't see Ellis Island behind her, Francesca felt its presence like a blessing, and she thought of all those throngs of immigrants who had come to this land with only the clothes on their backs and the determination to make a new life for themselves. Of all the millions who had passed through these golden gates, surely she had been the most worthless.

Francesca stood along with the others, a smile tugging at the corners of her lips as she remembered a twenty-one-year-old girl in a pink antebellum gown trudging down a Louisiana road carrying a Louis Vuitton suitcase. She lifted her hand and began to repeat the words being spoken by the Supreme Court Justice.

"I hereby declare, on oath, that I absolutely and entirely renounce and abjure all allegiance and fidelity to any foreign prince, potentate, state or sovereignty. . . ."

Good-bye, England, she thought. It wasn't your fault that I made such a muddle of things. You're a good old country, but I needed a rough, young scrapper of a place to teach me how to stand on my own.

". . . that I will support and defend the Constitution and laws of the United States of America against all enemies, foreign and domestic . . ."

She would try her best, even though the responsibilities of citizenship awed her. If a society was to remain free, how could it take those duties lightly?

". . . that I will bear arms on behalf of the United States . . ."

Gracious, she certainly hoped not!

". . . that I will perform work of national importance under civilian direction when required by law . . ."

Next month, she was to testify before a congressional committee on the problem of runaways, and she had already started forming an organization to raise funds to build shelters. With "Francesca Today" broadcasting only once a month, she would finally have a chance to give something back to the country that had already given her so much.

". . . that I take this obligation freely without any mental reservation or purpose of evasion; so help me God."

As the ceremony ended, a series of Texas cheers went up from the audience. With tears in her eyes, Francesca watched her guests making spectacles of themselves. Then the President greeted the new citizens, followed by the Supreme Court Justice and the other government dignitaries. A band struck up the first bars of "Stars and Stripes Forever," and the White House staff member who was in charge of the ceremony began moving the participants toward bunting-draped tables set up under the trees and laden with punch and tea sandwiches, just like a Fourth of July picnic.

Dallie got through the crowd to her first, a Texas-size grin spread all over his face. "The last thing this country needs is another voting liberal, but I'm real proud of you anyway, honey."

Francesca laughed and hugged him. On the east side of the island there was a noisy roar from the lawn as the presidential helicopter took off, bearing away the Chief Executive and some of the ceremony's other dignitaries. With the President gone, the mood of the occasion relaxed. As the helicopter disappeared, an announcement was made that the statue had been opened for private viewing by those who wished to enter.

"I'm proud of you, Mom," Teddy said. She gave him a squeeze.

"You looked almost as good up there as that Korean dress designer," Holly Grace told her. "Did you know he had on pink socks with rhinestone butterflies?" Francesca appreciated Holly Grace's attempt at good humor, especially since she knew it was mostly pretense. Too much of Holly Grace's sparkle had faded over the past few months.

"Over here, Miss Day," one of the photographers called out.

She smiled into the camera and talked to everyone who

came up to greet her. Her former runaways lined up to meet Dallie. They flirted with him outrageously, and he flirted right back until he had them all giggling. The photographers wanted pictures of Holly Grace, and each of the networks asked to film a brief interview with Francesca. After she had finished the last one, Dallie pressed a cup of punch into her hands. "Have you seen Teddy?"

Francesca glanced around. "Not for a while." She turned to Holly Grace who had just come up next to them. "Have you seen Teddy?"

Holly Grace shook her head. Dallie looked worried and Francesca smiled at him. "We're on an island," she said. "He can't get into too much trouble."

Dallie didn't seem convinced. "Francie, he's your son, too. With a gene pool like that to draw from, it seems to me he could manage to get into trouble just about anywhere."

"Let's go look for him." She offered the suggestion more from a desire to be alone with Dallie than from any concern about Teddy. The island was closed to tourists for another hour. What harm could come to him?

As she set down her punch cup, she noticed that Naomi was clutching Ben Perlman's hand and looking up into the sky. Shielding her eyes, Francesca looked up, too, but all she saw was a small plane circling overhead. And then she noticed that something seemed to have dropped from the plane. As she watched, a square-canopy parachute opened. One by one, the people around her gazed up into the sky and observed the descent of the parachutist toward Liberty Island.

As he fell, a long white banner gradually unfurled behind him. It had letters printed on it in black, but they were impossible to read as the wind whipped the banner in one direction and then the other, threatening to tangle in the parachutist's rig. Suddenly the banner straightened.

Francesca felt a set of sharp fingernails digging into the sleeve of her silk shantung jacket. "Oh, my God," Holly Grace whispered.

The eyes of every onlooker—as well as those of the network television cameras—were glued to the banner and the message it carried:

MARRY ME, HOLLY GRACE

Although he was concealed inside a helmet and a white jumpsuit, the parachutist could only be Gerry Jaffe.

"I'm going to kill him," Holly Grace said, venom dripping from every syllable. "This time he's gone too far." And then the wind shifted and the banner's other side was visible.

It held a drawing of a barbell.

Naomi came up next to Holly Grace. "I'm sorry," she said. "I tried to talk him out of it, but he loves you so much, and he refuses to do anything the easy way."

Holly Grace didn't reply. She kept her eyes glued on the descent. The parachutist dropped closer to the island and then began to drift. Naomi let out a small squeak of alarm, and Holly Grace's fingers dug deeper into Francesca's arm. "He's going into the water," Holly Grace cried. "Oh, God, he'll drown. He'll get tangled in his parachute or that stupid banner—" She broke away from Francesca and began running toward the seawall, shrieking for all she was worth. "You stupid commie! You dumb, stupid—"

Dallie draped his arm over Francesca's shoulder. "You got any idea why he has a picture of two doorknobs on that banner?"

"It's a barbell," she replied, holding her breath as Gerry just cleared the seawall and landed on the lawn about fifty yards away.

"Holly Grace is really going to give him hell for this," he commented, thoroughly enjoying himself. "Damn, she's mad."

"Mad" wasn't the word for it. Holly Grace was furious. She was so enraged she could barely contain herself. While Gerry struggled to gather up the parachute, she screamed every foul word at him that she could think of.

He balled the parachute and the banner together and threw them down on the grass so that he finally had two hands free to deal with her. When he saw her flushed face and felt the heat of her fury, he realized he was going to need both of them.

"I'll never forgive you for this," she cried, taking a punch at his arm, to the delight of the network cameramen. "You don't have enough experience to make a jump like that. You could have been killed. I wish you had been!"

He pulled off his helmet, and his curly hair was as disheveled as a dark angel's. "I've been trying to talk to you for weeks, but you wouldn't see me. Besides, I thought you'd like it."

"Like it!" She nearly spit at him. "I've never been so humiliated in my life! You've made a spectacle out of me. You don't have an ounce of common sense. Not one single ounce."

"Gerry!" He heard Naomi call out and from the corner of his eye, he saw the statue's security people running toward him.

He knew he didn't have much time. What he had done was definitely illegal, and he didn't doubt for a moment that they were going to arrest him. "I just publicly committed myself to you, Holly Grace. What more do you want from me?"

"You publicly made a fool of yourself. Jumping out of an airplane and almost drowning with that stupid banner. And why did you put a dog bone on it? Do you mind telling me what you meant by that?"

"Dog bone?" Gerry threw up his arms in frustration. No matter what he did, he couldn't seem to please this woman, and if he lost her this time, he would never get her back. Just the thought of losing her gave him a cold chill. Holly Grace Beaudine was the one woman he'd never been able to bring to heel, the one woman who made him feel that he could conquer the world, and he needed her the same way he needed oxygen.

The security people had almost reached him. "Are you blind, Holly Grace? That wasn't a dog bone. Jesus, I just made the most terrifying commitment of my entire life, and you missed the whole point."

"What are you talking about?"

"It was a baby rattle!"

The first two security men grabbed him.

"A baby rattle?" Her fierce expression melted in surprise and her voice softened. "That was a baby rattle?"

A third security officer pushed Holly Grace aside. Apparently deciding Gerry wasn't going to give them any real trouble, the officer cuffed Gerry's hands in front of his body.

"Marry me, Holly Grace," Gerry said, ignoring the fact that his rights were being read to him. "Marry me and have my baby—have a dozen of them! Just don't ever leave me."

"Oh, Gerry . . ." She stood looking at him with her heart in her eyes, and the love he felt for her swelled in his chest until he ached. The security people didn't want to look like bad guys in front of the press, so they let him lift his cuffed wrists and slip his arms over her head. He kissed her so intently that he forgot to make sure they were turned to face the network television cameras.

Luckily, Gerry had a partner who wasn't as easily distracted by females.

Far overhead, from a small window in the crown of the Statue of Liberty, another banner began to unfurl, this one a bright canary yellow. It was made from a synthetic material that had been developed for the space program—a material that was lightweight and could be compacted for portability into a package not much bigger than a wallet, and then would generously expand once it was released. The canary yellow banner slipped down over Lady Liberty's forehead, unrolled along the length of her nose, and gradually opened as it came to a stop at the base of her chin. Its message was clearly legible from the ground, simply printed in seven thick black letters.

NO NUKES

Francesca saw it first. And then Dallie. Gerry, who had reluctantly ended his embrace with Holly Grace, smiled when he spotted it and gave her a quick kiss on the nose. Then he lifted his handcuffed wrists to the sky, tilted back his head, and balled his hands into fists. "Way to go, Teddy!" he cried.

Teddy!

Francesca and Dallie looked at each other in alarm and then began running across the lawn toward the entrance to the statue.

Holly Grace shook her head at Gerry, not sure whether she should laugh or cry, knowing only that she had an interesting life ahead of her.

"It was too good an opportunity to pass up," he began to explain. "All these cameras—"

"Be quiet, Gerry, and tell me how I go about getting you out of jail." It was a skill that Holly Grace suspected she would be making good use of in the years to come.

"I love you, babe," he said.

"I love you, too," she replied.

Political actions weren't unknown at the Statue of Liberty. In the sixties, Cuban exiles chained themselves to Liberty's feet; in the seventies, anti-war veterans hung an upside-down flag from the crown; and in the eighties, two mountain climbers scaled the surface of the statue to protest the continued imprisonment of one of the Black Panthers. Political actions weren't unknown, but none of them had ever involved a kid.

Teddy sat by himself in the hallway outside the statue's security office. From behind the closed door, he could hear his mom's voice and occasionally Dallie's. One of the park rangers had brought him a can of 7-Up, but he couldn't drink it.

The week before, when Gerry had taken Teddy over to Naomi's to see her new baby, Teddy overheard Gerry and Naomi arguing, and that was how he learned about Gerry's plan to parachute onto the island. When Gerry had taken him home, Teddy questioned him. He felt like a hotshot when Gerry finally confided in him, even though he thought it might have been just because Gerry was feeling sad about losing Holly Grace.

They had talked about the No Nukes banner, and Teddy begged Gerry to let him help, but Gerry said he was too young. Teddy hadn't given up. For two months he had been trying to think of a social studies project spectacular enough to impress Miss Pearson, and he realized this was it. When he tried to explain that, Gerry had given him a long lecture about how political dissent shouldn't be undertaken for selfish reasons. Teddy had listened closely and pretended to agree, but he really wanted an A on his social studies project. Dorky old Milton Grossman had only visited Mayor Koch's office, and Miss Pearson had given him an A.

It defied Teddy's imagination to think what she might do to a kid who helped disarm the world!

Now that he had to face the consequences, however, Teddy knew that breaking the window in the crown had been stupid. But what else could he have done? Gerry had explained to him that the windows in the crown opened with a special key some of the maintenance people carried. One of those people was a friend of Gerry's, and this guy had promised to slip up into the crown as soon as the President's security people left and unlock the middle window. But when Teddy got to the crown, all sweaty and out of breath from having climbed the stairs as fast as he could to get there ahead of everybody else, something had gone wrong because the window was still locked.

Gerry had told Teddy that if there was a problem with the window he was supposed to climb right back down and forget about the No Nukes banner, but Teddy had too much at stake. Quickly, before he had time to think about what he was doing, he had snatched the metal lid from a trash can and banged it against the small center window a few times. After four tries, he finally broke the glass. It had probably only been an echo in the crown, but when the glass broke, he thought he could hear the statue cry out.

The office door opened and the man who was in charge of security came out. He didn't even look at Teddy; he just went right on down the corridor without saying anything. Then his mom was standing in the doorway, and Teddy could see she was really mad. His mom didn't get mad too often, unless she was really scared about something, but when it did happen, he got a sick feeling in his stomach. He swallowed hard and slid his eyes down, because he was scared to look her in the face.

"Come in here, young man," she said, sounding like she'd just eaten icicles. *"Now!"*

His stomach did a somersault. He was really in trouble. He'd expected to get into a little trouble, but not this much. He'd never heard his mom sound so mad. His stomach seemed to be turning upside down, and he thought he might have to throw up. He tried to stall for time by dragging his good shoes as he walked toward the door, but his mom caught his arm and pulled him into the office. The door shut hard behind him.

None of the statue people were there. Just Teddy, his mom, and Dallie. Dallie was standing over by the window with his arms crossed over his chest. Because of the sunlight, Teddy couldn't see his face too well and he was glad about that. On top of the Empire State Building, Dallie had said he loved Teddy and Teddy had wanted to believe it so bad, except he was afraid that Dallie had said it just because his mom had made him.

"Teddy, I'm so ashamed of you," his mother began. "What in the world made you get involved in something like this? You vandalized the statue. How could you do that?" His mom's voice was quivering a little bit, like she was really, really upset, and her accent had gotten thicker than normal. He wished he wasn't too big to be spanked, because he knew a spanking wouldn't hurt as much as this did. "It's a miracle they're not going to press charges against you. I've always trusted you, Teddy, but it will be a long time before I'll be able to trust you again. What you did was illegal. . . ."

The more she talked, the lower Teddy's head dropped. He didn't know which was worse—hurting the statue or upsetting his mom so much. He could feel his throat start to close up and he realized he was going to cry. Right there in front of Dallie Beaudine, he was going to cry like a jerk. He kept his eyes glued to the floor and felt like somebody was shoving rocks into his chest. He took a deep, shaky breath. He couldn't cry in front of Dallie. He'd stab himself in the eyes before he'd do that.

A tear dropped and made a big splat on the top of one of his good shoes. He slid the other shoe over it so Dallie wouldn't see. His mom kept talking about how she couldn't trust him anymore, how disappointed she was, and another tear splatted on his other shoe. His stomach hurt, his throat was closing up on him, and he just wanted to sit down on the floor and hug one of his old teddy bears and cry real hard.

"That's enough, Francie." Dallie's voice wasn't very loud, but it was serious, and his mom stopped talking. Teddy took a swipe at his nose with his sleeve. "You go on outside for a minute, honey," Dallie said to her.

"No, Dallie, I—"

"Go on, now, honey. We'll be out in a minute."

Don't go! Teddy wanted to scream. *Don't leave me alone with him.* But it was too late. After a few seconds, his mother's feet began to move and then he heard the door shut. Another tear dropped off his chin and he made a soft little hiccup as he tried to breathe.

Dallie came over next to him. Through his tears, Teddy could see the cuffs on Dallie's trousers. And then Teddy felt an arm slip around his shoulders and pull him close.

"You go ahead and cry all you want, son," Dallie said softly. "It's sometimes hard to cry real good with a woman around, and you've had a rough day."

Something hard and painful that Teddy had been holding rigidly inside him far too long seemed to break apart.

Dallie knelt down and pulled Teddy against him. Teddy wrapped his arms around Dallie's neck and held on to him as tight as he could and cried so hard he couldn't catch his breath. Dallie rubbed Teddy's back underneath his shirt and called him son and told him that sooner or later everything would be all right.

"I didn't mean to hurt the statue." Teddy sobbed into Dallie's neck. "I love the statue. Mom said she wouldn't ever trust me again."

"Women aren't always reliable when they're as upset as your mom is right now."

"I love my mom." Teddy hiccuped again. "I didn't mean to get her so mad."

"I know that, son."

"It makes me feel scared inside to have her so mad at me."

"I'll bet it makes her feel scared inside, too."

Teddy finally got the nerve to look up. Dallie's face seemed all blurry through his tears. "She'll take away my allowance for a million years."

Dallie nodded. "You're probably right about that." And then Dallie cupped Teddy's head, pulled it against his chest, and kissed Teddy right next to his ear.

Teddy held on, not saying anything for a few seconds, just accustoming himself to the feel of a scratchy cheek against his own instead of a smooth one. "Dallie?"

"Uh-huh."

Teddy buried his mouth in Dallie's shirt collar so the

words came out muffled. "I think—I think you're my real dad, aren't you?"

Dallie was quiet for a moment, and when he finally spoke he sounded like his throat was closing up, too. "You bet I am, son. You bet I am."

Later, Dallie and Teddy went out into the hallway to face his mom together. Except this time, when she saw the way Teddy was holding on to Dallie, she was the one who started to cry, and before he knew it, his mom was hugging him and Dallie was hugging her, and the three of them were standing right there in the middle of the hallway at the Statue of Liberty security office hugging each other and crying like a dumb old bunch of babies.

Epilogue

Dallie sat in the passenger seat of his big Chrysler New Yorker, the brim of his cap tilted over his eyes to block the morning sun, while Miss Fancy Pants passed two semis and a Greyhound bus in less time than it took most people to say amen. Damn, he liked the way she drove a car. A man could relax with a woman like her behind the wheel because he knew he had half a chance at arriving at his destination before his arteries hardened from old age.

"Are you going to tell me yet where you're taking me?" he asked. When she'd shanghaied him away from his morning coffee, he hadn't protested too much because three months of married life had taught him that it was more fun to go along with his pretty little wife than to spend half his time arguing with her.

"Out by that old landfill," she replied. "If I can find the road."

"The landfill? That place has been closed for the last three years. There's nothing out there."

Francesca made a sharp right turn onto an old asphalt road. "That's what Miss Sybil said."

"Miss Sybil? What's she got to do with all this?"

"She's a woman," Francesca replied mysteriously. "And she understands a woman's needs."

Dallie decided the best course of action in a situation like this was not to ask any more questions, just to let events take their natural course. He grinned and tilted the brim of his cap down a little farther. Who would have ever thought that being married to Miss Fancy Pants would turn out to be so much fun? Their life was working out even better than he'd expected. Francie had hauled him over to the French Riviera for a honeymoon that had been just about the greatest time of his life, and then they'd come to Wynette for the summer. During the school year, they had decided to make New York City their base because it was the best place for Teddy and Francie. Since Dallie would be playing in the bigger tournaments this fall, he could hang his clothes just about anywhere. And whenever they got bored, they could go stay in one of those houses that he owned scattered all around the country.

"We have to be back in Wynette in exactly forty-five minutes," she said. "You have an interview with that reporter from *Sports Illustrated,* and I have a conference call scheduled with Nathan and my production people."

She didn't look old enough to know anything about conference calls, let alone to have production people. Her hair was pulled into a cute ponytail that made her seem like she was about fourteen, and she had on this stretchy white top with a little denim skirt he'd bought for her because he knew it wouldn't do much more than cover her backside.

"I thought we were going to the driving range," he said. "No offense, Francie, but your golf swing could use some work." Which was a polite way of putting it. She had the worst golf swing he had ever seen on any person, male or female, but he enjoyed messing around with her so much at the range that he acted like she was improving.

"I don't see how my swing is ever going to get better if you keep telling me so many different things to do," she grumbled. "Keep your head down, Francie. Pull with your left side, Francie. Lead with your knees, Francie. Honestly, no one in her right mind could remember all of that. It's no wonder you can't teach Teddy to hit a baseball. You make everything so complicated."

"Now, don't you worry about that boy playing baseball. You should know by now that sports isn't everything, especially when my son has more brain power in that head of his than all of Wynette's Little Leaguers put together." As far as Dallie was concerned, Teddy was the best boy in the world, and he wouldn't trade him for all the jock kids in America.

"Speaking of the driving range," she began. "With the PGA Championship coming up—"

"Uh-oh."

"Sweetheart, I'm not saying that you had a *problem* with your long irons last week. Gracious, you *won* the tournament, so it couldn't have been much of a problem. Still, I thought you might want to spend a few hours at the range after your interview to see if you can't improve them just a little bit." She glanced over, giving him one of those soft, innocent looks that didn't fool him one bit. "I certainly don't expect you to *win* the PGA," she went on. "You've already won two titles this summer, and you don't have to win *every* tournament, but . . ." Her voice faded, as if she realized she'd already said enough. More than enough. One thing that he had discovered about Francie was that she was just about insatiable when it came to golf titles.

She swung the New Yorker off the narrow asphalt road and onto a dirt lane that probably hadn't been used by anybody since the Apaches. The old Wynette landfill was about a half-mile in the opposite direction, but he didn't mention that. Half the fun of being with Francie was watching her improvise.

She caught her bottom lip between her teeth and frowned. "The landfill should be around here someplace, although I don't actually suppose it matters."

He crossed his arms over his chest and pretended he was falling asleep.

She giggled. "I couldn't believe Holly Grace showed up at the Roustabout last night in a maternity dress—she's barely three months pregnant. And Gerry has absolutely no idea how to behave in a honky-tonk. He spent the entire evening drinking white wine and talking to Skeet about the wonders of natural childbirth." Francesca turned onto an even bumpier road. "I'm also not absolutely certain Holly Grace did the right thing by bringing Gerry to Wynette. She wanted him to get to know her parents better, but poor Winona is absolutely terrified of him."

Francesca looked over at Dallie and saw that he was pretending to sleep. She smiled to herself. It was probably just as well. Dallie still wasn't absolutely rational on the subject of Gerry Jaffe. Of course, she hadn't been all that rational herself for a while. Gerry should never have involved Teddy in his scheme, no matter how much her son had begged to be part of it. Since the incident at the Statue of Liberty, she, Dallie, and Holly Grace had made certain that Teddy and Gerry were never left alone together for more than five minutes.

She gently pressed the brake and steered the New Yorker onto a rutted path that ended in a clump of straggly cedars. Satisfied that the area was completely deserted, she pushed the buttons that lowered the front windows and turned off the ignition. The morning air that blew in was warm and pleasantly dusty.

Dallie still pretended to be asleep, his arms folded over his faded gray T-shirt and one of a series of caps sporting an American flag pulled low over his eyes. She postponed the moment when she would actually touch him, enjoying the anticipation. For all the laughter and teasing that went on between them, she and Dallie had found a serenity together, a sense of perfect homecoming that could only happen after having known the darkest side of another person and then having walked together out into the sunshine.

Reaching over, she pulled off his cap and dropped it into the back seat. Then she kissed his closed eyelids, working her fingers into his hair. "Wake up, sweetheart, you have some work to do."

He nibbled at her bottom lip. "Do you have anything specific in mind?"

"Uh-huh."

He reached beneath her stretchy white top and traced the

small bumps of her spine with his fingertips. "Francie, we have a perfectly good bed back in Wynette and another one twenty-five miles to the west of here."

"The second one is too far away and the first one is too crowded."

He chuckled. Teddy had banged on their bedroom door early that morning and then climbed into bed with them to ask their opinion about whether he should be a detective or a scientist when he grew up.

"Married people aren't supposed to have to make love in a car," he said, closing his eyes again as she settled into his lap and began kissing his ear.

"Most married people don't have a meeting of the Friends of Wynette Public Library going on in one room and an army of teenage girls camped out in the other," she replied.

"You've got a point there." He lifted her skirt a little so that she could straddle his legs with her thighs. Then he began to caress one of those thighs, gradually working upward. His eyes shot open.

"Francie Day Beaudine, you don't have any underpants on."

"Don't I?" she murmured in that bored-little-rich-girl voice of hers. "How naughty of me."

She was rubbing her breasts against him, kissing his ear, deliberately driving him crazy. He decided it was long past time he showed Miss Fancy Pants who was the boss of the family. Pushing open the car door, he climbed out, taking her with him.

"Dallie . . ." she protested.

He wrapped his arm around her waist and hoisted her up off the ground. As he carried her toward the trunk of his New Yorker, she delighted him by starting to struggle, although he did think she could have put a little more effort into it if she'd concentrated harder.

"I'm *not* the kind of woman you make love to on the back of a car," she said in a voice so haughty she sounded like the queen of England. Except Dallie didn't imagine the queen of England would be moving her hand up and down the front of his jeans in quite the same way.

"You can't fool me with that accent of yours, ma'am," he drawled. "I know exactly how you red-blooded American girls like to make love."

As she opened her mouth to reply, he took advantage of her parted lips to give her the kind of kiss that guaranteed him a few minutes of silence. Eventually she began to work at the zipper on the front of his jeans, which didn't take her long at all—Francie was magic with anything that had to do with clothes.

Their lovemaking started out raunchy, with a little bit of dirty talk and a lot of shifting around, but then everything turned tender and sweet, exactly like their feelings for each other. Before long, they were sprawled across the trunk of the New Yorker, lying right on top of the pink satin Porthault sheet that Francesca kept stored in the car for just such an emergency.

Afterward, they looked into each other's eyes, not saying a word, just looking, and then they exchanged a kiss so full of love and understanding that it was hard to remember that any barriers had ever existed between them.

Dallie took the wheel to drive back to Wynette. When he turned out onto the main highway, Francesca was cuddled up against him and he was feeling lazy and contented, pleased with himself for having had the good sense to marry Miss Fancy Pants. Just then the Bear made one of his increasingly rare appearances.

Looks like you're in real danger of making a fool of yourself over this woman.

You've got that right, Dallie replied, brushing the top of her head with a kiss.

And then the Bear chuckled. *Good work, Beaudine.*

On the opposite side of Wynette, Teddy and Skeet sat next to each other on a slatted wooden bench, the mulberry trees overhead shielding them from the summer sun. They sat quietly, neither of them having any need to talk. Skeet gazed off down the gently rolling slope of grass, and Teddy sipped at the dregs of his Coke. He was wearing his favorite pair of camouflage pants belted low on his hips, along with a baseball hat sporting an American flag. A No Nukes button occupied a place of honor in the exact center of his Aggies T-shirt.

Teddy thought that this summer in Wynette had been about the best time in his life. He had a bike here, which he couldn't have in New York, and him and his dad had built this neat solar collector in the back yard. Still, he missed some of his friends and he didn't absolutely hate the idea of going back to New York in a few weeks. Miss Pearson had given him an A on the social studies project he'd done on immigration. She said the story he'd written about how his mom had come to this country and everything that had happened to her once she got here was the most interesting student report she had ever read. And his gifted teacher next year was the nicest one in the whole school. Also, there were lots of museums and stuff in New York that he wanted to show his dad.

"You about ready?" Skeet said, getting up from the bench where they had been sitting.

"I guess." Teddy noisily drained the last of his Coke and then got up to toss the empty cup into the trash can. "I don't see why we have to make such a secret out of this," he grumbled. "If this wasn't such a big secret, we could come here more often."

"Never you mind," Skeet replied, shielding his eyes to look down the grassy slope toward the first green. "We'll tell your dad about this when *I* decide we're going to tell him and not before."

Teddy loved coming out on the golf course with Skeet, so he didn't argue. He took the three-wood from a bag of old clubs that Skeet had cut down for him. After drying the palms of his hands on the legs of his pants, he set up the ball, enjoying its perfect balance on the red wooden tee. As he took his stance, he gazed down the grassy slope toward the distant green. It looked so pretty sitting there, all sparkly with sunlight. Maybe it was because he was a city kid, but he loved golf courses. He took a little sniff of clean air, balanced himself, and swung.

The club head hit the ball with a satisfying thwack.

"How was it?" Teddy asked, peering down the fairway.

"About a hundred and eighty yards," Skeet said, chuckling. "I never saw a little kid hit a ball so far."

Teddy was aggravated. "It's not a big deal, Skeet. I don't know why you always make such a big deal out of it. Hitting a golf ball is easy. It's not like trying to catch a football or hit a baseball or something really hard like that. *Anybody* can hit a golf ball."

Skeet didn't say anything. He was carrying Teddy's clubs down the fairway and he was laughing too hard to talk.